Barefoot

with a

BODYGUARD

Barefoot Bay Undercover #1

roxanne st. claire

Barefoot with a Bodyguard
Copyright © 2015 South Street Publishing

COVER ART: The Killion Group, Inc.
INTERIOR FORMATTING: Author E.M.S.
Seashell graphic used with permission under Creative Commons CC0 public domain.

ISBN-13: 978-0-9908607-3-0

Published in the United States of America.

Critical Reviews of
Roxanne St. Claire Novels

"St. Claire, as always, brings a scorching tear-up-the-sheets romance combined with a great story: dealing with real issues starring memorable characters in vivid scenes."
— *Romantic Times Magazine*

"Non-stop action, sweet and sexy romance, lively characters, and a celebration of family and forgiveness."
— *Publishers Weekly*

"Plenty of heat, humor, and heart!"
— *USA Today's Happy Ever After blog*

"It's safe to say I will try any novel with St. Claire's name on it."
— *www.smartbitchestrashybooks.com*

"The writing was perfectly on point as always and the pace of the story was flawless. But be forewarned that you will laugh, cry, and sigh with happiness. I sure did."
— *www.harlequinjunkies.com*

"The Barefoot Bay series is an all-around knockout, soul-satisfying read. Roxanne St. Claire writes with warmth and heart and the community she's built at Barefoot Bay is one I want to visit again and again."
— *Mariah Stewart, New York Times bestselling author*

"This book stayed with me long after I put it down."
— *All About Romance*

Dear Reader,

Welcome to a whole new twist on the love stories of Barefoot Bay! In this new series, readers can expect a light splash of suspense and a dash of danger on the gorgeous sun-baked shores of this tiny island off the Gulf Coast of Florida. Like every book set in Barefoot Bay, this novel stands entirely alone, but why stop at just one?

The Barefoot Bay Billionaires
Secrets on the Sand
Seduction on the Sand
Scandal on the Sand

The Barefoot Bay Brides
Barefoot in White
Barefoot in Lace
Barefoot in Pearls

Barefoot Bay Undercover
Barefoot Bound (prequel)
Barefoot with a Bodyguard
Barefoot with a Stranger
Barefoot with a Bad Boy (Gabe's book!)

Want to know the day the next Barefoot Bay book is released? Sign up for the newsletter! You'll get brief monthly e-mails about new releases and book sales.

http://www.roxannestclaire.com/newsletter.html

Acknowledgments

As is the case with every novel I write, I'm surrounded by a team of amazing people who help bring my imagination to life for you. In particular, I am deeply grateful for one of the best editors in the business, Kristi Yanta, along with copyeditor and proofreader Joyce Lamb, who is ruthless on her hunt for any errors in the work. Also, Amy Atwell and the formatters at Author E.M.S. and incredibly talented cover designer Kim Killion make sure my stories are delivered in the prettiest possible package.

In *Barefoot with a Bodyguard*, I also called on some experts and want to thank Tatiana Lammers, Russian translator, and attorney Gregg MacGregor, for the research assistance. And a huge shout-out to my awesome assistant, Maria Connor, and my always supportive Street Team (the fabulous Rocki Roadies!) who help spread the word about my books. And, of course, my little family, the best humans and dogs on earth.

Barefoot

with a

BODYGUARD

roxanne st. claire

Dedication

For the WriterChicks…
a brain trust without equal,
a circle of friends who never let go,
and women I love with my whole heart.

Chapter One

Blood trickled from Alec's shredded knuckles, red trails sliding over the purple Cyrillic letters that marked him. The cuts stung like a mother under a dribble of water, the best he could get from a sink that barely hung on the wall with a pipe and a prayer. His head throbbed from the last few hits, and his chest heaved from the run for his life. He leaned against the rusty metal door of the gas station bathroom and finally looked in the dingy, cracked mirror at his face.

And wished he hadn't. Oh, he was used to seeing a fighter's mug in the glass, but now blood crusted around his broken nose, and one eye had already swollen shut. Somehow he'd managed to keep his teeth, but…he winced on the next breath. One rib, at least, was broken.

Bastards.

That was the third time this month he'd been ambushed, and things were getting worse.

He'd taken out one of them with well-placed elbow strikes and got another guy in a leg lock that probably wrecked the son of a bitch's knee for life, but Alec had no finesse with that last moron. He just slammed that fucker's head on the concrete and grounded-and-pounded with all he had. Might have killed him.

Wouldn't be the first man he'd killed, but it would have been the first time he'd actually done it with his bare hands using the mixed martial arts he taught. Firing at an insurgent who'd just buried an IED in a Baghdad schoolyard didn't count as murder—it was war.

But now he was in another war, for his life, not his country. The enemy wasn't a ruthless terrorist, but filthy, murderous *Mafiya* enforcers who loved nothing more than following Dmitri Vlitnik's orders.

Alec stared at his hands, raw and swollen from the fight. He didn't think it was possible for his hands to get any uglier, but they had tonight. Too bad. They were all he had, all he needed. And his knees, feet, elbows, and head—all his weapons of choice. Could they keep him alive during the next attack? And the one after that?

In his pocket, his phone vibrated. He blew out a breath when he saw Grigori Nyekovic's name on the screen. Of course. The former KGB agent turned Russian millionaire who had a soft spot for Brighton Beach kids and a determination to bring down the notorious "brotherhood" had always been there when Alec needed him the most.

After that dark night when Vlitnik "tested" a thirteen-year-old Alec, Gregg showed up and led Alec to martial arts to channel his anger and frustration. When Alec needed that financial boost to pay for college, Gregg wrote the check. And when Vlitnik came calling again only a year after that, determined to have his due, Gregg pulled strings to get Alec into the Marines. And when Alec could no longer fight for his country, Gregg had helped him heal and found him a home in Philly so he could open an MMA training facility.

And now, here was Gregg again, when he was needed the most.

"Yeah?" Alec answered, copping the attitude that had

gotten him through the shittiest of shitty times. Even though he owed Gregg his life several times over, Alec wasn't about to go all gooey on him now.

"Two hundred thousand dollars." The man's voice was still tinged with a Russian accent, despite the fact that he'd traveled the world and lived most of the past decade in New York City.

"You want it? You have it? Or I need it?" Alec asked.

"That's the price Dmitri Vlitnik has put on your fucking head. After tonight, it might be more."

His head? Alec's gaze slipped to his hands again—the price should be on those things, not his head, which, after that last patrol in Iraq, was good for only one thing: butting an opponent. Dropping onto the edge of the yellowed toilet seat, he ignored a cockroach that scurried under the door, letting it escape. Alec had kicked enough ass for one night.

"I figured I had some value," he finally said. "Considering what they sent after me tonight."

"You have to get out of Philadelphia now." Gregg spoke with complete authority.

Damn it. He'd finally made the place a home and had his training business in the black. "There's no other way?" Like someone take that bastard out for good? "Isn't he ever going to back off?"

"You know he won't," Gregg said. "It's like he's obsessed with the idea of getting what was promised to him."

And *Alec* had been promised to him.

"I don't belong to anyone," he ground out.

"That's not how Vlitnik sees it." True enough, in the rules of the *Mafiya*, Alec did, technically, "belong" to the mob leader. Alec's father had forged the deal in blood, from his cancer-ridden deathbed, bartering for *krysha*, protection that normally cost thousands. Sergei Petrov didn't have thousands, but he had something that the Brighton Beach mob boss wanted—a big lug nut of a teenage son who would grow into a fine enforcer someday.

Protect my wife, and you can have Alec when he's ready and trained.

So, Alec had been essentially sold into slavery, sealing his fate as a man whose only value was his ability to kill. Yes, Vlitnik's monsters had left the family butcher shop alone; Mama had never been beaten, raped, or robbed. But when Alec was nineteen and his mother died, Dmitri Vlitnik came to collect what was his.

Alec had been running from the mob boss ever since, and he was so damn sick of it. "He's never going to give up." Alec could hear the resignation in his voice, and he hated it.

"Unless we get him on something. And we are close." In his role as a protector of the Brighton Beach kids, Gregg might be on the side of the angels in this war, but he had spies in Vlitnik's mob. That was how he quietly, secretly, and carefully fed information to the authorities to assist in the effort to stop one of the worst gangs of Russian mobsters in the US.

"I can wait him out," Alec said. "I can fight him off."

"Not forever, and not now. It's better if you hide."

"Fuck that. I'd rather face him down and choke the life out of him with my bare hands."

"I'm sure you would," Gregg said. "And then you couldn't testify when we do get him, because you'd either be dead or in jail."

"Okay, look, I'm in an Exxon bathroom in the middle of north Philly. My car is—"

"Probably wired to blow the minute you stick a key in the ignition." Gregg nearly growled the words. "You're done,

Alexander. You have to hide or die before the sun comes up."

That was a great choice.

"Alec, I want you to go somewhere they can't find you."

"Like where, the moon? Vlitnik has eyes and ears everywhere."

"Not quite everywhere, not where I'm sending you. You know my wife's boss owns one of the best security firms in the world."

"I don't need a fucking bodyguard, Gregg." He held a black belt in Brazilian jiu-jitsu and trained MMA fighters for a living.

"You're not getting a bodyguard. You're going to *be* a bodyguard. And that's going to take you as far off Vlitnik's radar as we can get you."

Alec opened his mouth to respond, then shut it again. *We.* Gregg was more than a friend—he was like a father. And too smart, good, and connected to deserve Alec's argument.

"Raquel's boss knows a guy who has just started a covert operation that is essentially the equivalent of a privatized wit-sec deal down in Florida."

Witness security? The government wouldn't give him protection, since he had nothing concrete to put Vlitnik away. "How?"

"That's what this guy does. He'll get you a new identity and find you a place to go. In the meantime, you hide on an island in the Gulf of Mexico."

"Bet the price is steep." How many times could Gregg throw his money at Alec's problems? How many times could Alec let him?

"It is, and I would pay it, but he wants you to work instead."

"Okaaay." He dragged the word out, more in response to the way Gregg said *work*—like it was something he wouldn't like. "As a bodyguard."

"Yeah, but you'll be undercover, too. On your honeymoon."

"*What?*"

"This guy's got another client who also needs to hide out for a while, since she's been the target of some threats. You'll be there as newlyweds, staying at a resort on a secluded island, and you will be with her twenty-four seven to be sure she's safe. Both of you will have assumed names—the same last one—and no one, not a single soul except this guy who runs the operation and his top people, will know you are anything but head over heels in love with your new bride."

Alec blinked into the shadows of the foul bathroom, not even able to wrap his head around this plan. "Look, I know I'm not firing on all cylinders right now, but there's no way in hell you said what I think you said."

Gregg laughed softly. "I thought you'd like the idea."

"I didn't say I—" The scuff of a footstep outside shut him up. "Shit. They found me," he whispered.

"No, I'm using an advanced satellite tracking system on this call. That's my man outside your door. Go with him."

Alec closed his eyes, a cocktail of mixed feelings rising up. "Guess I'm running again, huh, Gregg?"

"Running to stay alive long enough to testify if the feds can shut down Vlitnik's mob."

"And if they can't?"

"Then you get yourself a new name and move your ass to a new country. There's nothing cowardly about keeping yourself alive."

Alec let the advice sink in, pinching his throbbing nose as

he tried to think. "Okay, what do I have to know about this chick?"

"That she's not a chick. She's the daughter of a high-profile judge who wants his precious girl protected. You have to act like her husband in public and treat her like daddy's little princess in private. Hands off."

He looked down at his raw, bruised knuckles and his ugly, blistered fingers. Hands that could do nothing but hurt and maim and fight and...kill. Hands that wouldn't know how to touch a bride if he'd even deserved one.

"No problem," he promised.

"But in public, the two of you are madly in love."

Alec looked in the mirror and saw his bruised and battered face, shadowed with the pain he was either receiving or inflicting. "Hope she has low standards," he muttered, but Gregg had already hung up.

Kate Kingston leaned back into the leather sedan seat and exhaled with the exhaustion of travel, pulling the elastic from her ponytail and shaking out her hair as an act of pure relief. As she rubbed her head and gave in to a satisfied smile, her driver, Mr. Rossi, a little old man with a slight accent she guessed to be Italian, occasionally glanced into his rearview mirror to make sure she had everything she needed.

Or to evaluate her. Despite his efficiency and kindness, she couldn't help but feel the man was examining her.

She shrugged it off, determined to wallow in what she craved: silence, sunshine, salt air, and solitude. And, staying with her mental alliteration, a chance to study. Don't forget safety and security, a voice in her head whispered. A voice that sounded an awful lot like Dad. Okay, if it made him happy to think she'd be safer outside of Boston, so be it.

For the first time since she signed her married name for the last time—on divorce papers—five months ago, Kate actually let go of her personal mantra: *No man, no husband, no*body *takes care of Kate Kingston except Kate Kingston.*

She unclenched her hands as if she could physically remind herself that independence should be clung to with both hands. And this journey along a mile-long causeway over the Gulf of Mexico on her way to a place with the precious name of Barefoot Bay was not *exactly* an infringement on her independence.

Yes, she'd compromised her principles and mantra when she let her father make these arrangements, but, as he noted over and over again, it was his fault that some weirdo kept leaving him untraceable messages and notes that threatened Kate. In thirty years on the bench, Judge Kingston had never had anything like this happen, and he'd certainly dismissed plenty of cases due to lack of evidence, which seemed to be what launched the threat campaign.

That was enough to get her to agree to what was essentially a vacation that gave her time to study for the Massachusetts Bar Exam. She'd stay under the watchful eye of Mr. Rossi, who Dad claimed was some kind of legendary former spy and security specialist.

She fought a smile, doubting the little old man could fend off any attackers in his ill-fitting jacket and crooked, red bow tie. If he'd been a spy, it was probably in World War II. But she didn't think there would be any attackers fifteen hundred miles from Boston, so she didn't question the age or capabilities of the nice man who'd met her at the regional airport in southwest Florida.

He certainly took his job seriously, expertly guiding her through baggage claim, rolling her luggage to a neatly appointed black sedan with the words "Casa Blanca Resort & Spa" printed in tiny letters on the driver's door. He kept conversation to a minimum, which Kate appreciated. She didn't come here to talk or make friends or even to hide from some nut job in Boston. She just wanted to study for the test she should have taken five years ago. She was finally going in the direction she should have gone before Steven Douglas Jessup III derailed everything by persuading her to marry him and give up her dream to practice law.

It didn't matter, she reminded herself, enjoying the deep-blue waters of the gulf below instead of wallowing in past mistakes. The future was bright with possibilities, especially once she passed the bar and started practicing. She would never, ever again let a man make decisions for her, run her life, control her actions, or trample all over her independence. And she sure as hell would never be anyone's *wife*.

Live and learn, Katie. Live and learn.

She watched a formation of sea gulls take flight over the sun-sparkled water, a few pleasure craft leaving long, white wakes in the cobalt waves. All beautiful, peaceful, and calm. By the time they arrived at the resort, she was practically humming with happiness over this lovely turn of events, secretly thanking the anonymous note-leaver, especially since he seemed to pose no threat to her father.

It had all worked in her favor.

Mr. Rossi parked in a far corner of a large lot, a good distance from Casa Blanca's main hotel building. With effortless competence that belied his age, he unloaded Kate's bags and ushered her onto a waiting golf cart.

"One more little leg of this trip and you'll be all tucked

into your villa," he said with a kind, but yellowed, smile.

"I just need to check in," she said, fluffing the collar of a cashmere sweater that was already way too hot.

"No checking in," he said. "I'll take you directly to Caralluma." When she frowned, he nodded as though he anticipated a question. "It's a plant from North Africa. All the villas are named after them, and yours is one of the brand new ones. Just finished a few weeks ago."

She glanced back at the creamy archways of the main hotel building, a new resentment growing. She didn't want Dad paying for everything on this trip. "I need to go to the registration desk and give them my credit card."

"Are you kidding?" The older man's eyes grew wide as if she'd suggested running naked down the beach. "You'll get into that villa without talking to a soul, young lady, or being seen by anyone."

Katie opened her mouth to reply and got a single finger of warning. "It's for your safety, Mrs. Carlson."

"Kingston," she corrected, already thinking of how she'd go see the spa later, after she ditched this guy. "It's *Ms*. Kingston."

He shot her a look, shaking his head. "It's Carlson. *Mrs*. Carlson."

She tamped down the argument that welled up. One of her best friends had recently warned that her bitter divorce had left her sounding like a man-hater, and she didn't want to. *You don't have to pick a fight with every guy who crosses your path*, Laurie had told her.

Of course, her friend was right. She didn't have to hate them all just because Steven was a Dick With a Capital D, especially this dear little man who was probably a retired cop desperately searching for a purpose in his life.

"You can just call me Kate," she said, adding a warm smile to take away any edge in her voice.

10

"No, that's not your name," he said, reaching into the inside of his jacket. "Not while you're on this property, which, by the way, you can't leave."

Any thought of warmth or not fighting or lying back and being nice evaporated instantly. "Excuse me?"

From a pocket, he produced an envelope. "Here's your identity package. You'll have to give me your license and passport, plus anything else that might have your name on it. You can keep your phone, but we'll have to erase all record of your name on it and block all incoming calls, with a few exceptions, like those from your father. Any letters or prescription bottles, also. Nothing on your person can have your real name. That's very important."

Was she actually hearing him correctly?

"I'll have everything in a lockbox during your stay," he added, taking in the look on her face. "Of course we'll give you new bottles with your new name if you have medicines and, oh"—he glanced at her bags in the back of the golf cart—"tags for your luggage. Do you wear an ID bracelet or anything with your name or initials on it?"

Kate's jaw dropped wide open. "You're serious."

"As a stroke." He frowned. "Or is it a heart attack? I don't know, but you bet your backside I'm serious. Being undercover is serious business. And that's why you're here, right?"

Wrong. "I'm here to study."

"Then study that packet," he said, indicating the envelope. "Learn your name and use it. Don't answer to your given name even if someone calls it out. It could be a test or…" He gave her a harsh look of warning. "It could blow your cover."

Her *cover.* Good God, he was serious. "Are you going to tell me I have to dye my hair next?"

He gave a two-shouldered shrug, his mouth turned down. "Not a bad idea. But that's just me. Redheads are trouble."

"So I've heard." Steven had hated redheads, too. Which was exactly why she'd added the auburn to her brown hair after the divorce.

"I hope you like the name," Mr. Rossi said. "I picked it myself."

She opened the envelope and found an Illinois driver's license in the name of Mathilda Carlson.

"Mathilda?" She couldn't help choking a laugh. "You've got to be kidding me."

"It was my Monica's mother's name. She was German, but…" He waved a gnarled, oversized hand. "We overlook some things for love, you know?"

She blinked at him, really not sure if she should laugh or slap that hand with her *identity packet*.

"Not everything," she said dryly. "And while I appreciate the thorough security measures, Kate is common enough. I'll just use Kate Carlson, if I must."

"You *must* use the name you've been given."

The command prickled her skin, summing up everything she hated most in the whole world. "No, I *mustn't*. And I will thank you, Mr. Rossi, not to ever tell me what I must or must not do, is that clear?"

Mr. Rossi stuck his lower lip out and glowered, a slight flush growing under his crepe-paper complexion. She braced for his next comment, probably something about how her father had warned him she was spirited or maybe how everything everyone did was for her safety. If he did, she'd bound out of this damn cart and get her own ass back to the airport and go right back to Boston with her middle finger raised.

"Let's compromise, miss." His soft voice completely

disarmed her. "How about you go by Tilly? It's young and pretty like you."

"It also rhymes with *silly*, which is what I think of this whole overkill scheme to keep me safe while I'm on vacation."

"Not safe. *Alive*."

Irritation pirouetted up her spine, but she really had no beef with this man. "Mr. Rossi, honestly, I know there were some random suggestions to my father that I might be on someone's hate list, but I plan to spend the entire time I'm here completely alone, studying for a big test I have to take, and avoiding contact with everyone. I really don't care what you or the housekeeper call me."

"Poppy."

"Pardon me?" Was that yet another ridiculous name suggestion?

"The housekeeper is Poppy. A Jamaican lady, and she was specially selected because she can be trusted. Although"—he lifted a shoulder—"she can't be trusted with *everything*, I'm learning."

At the obtuse comment, she frowned. "But she knows my secret identity?" she asked, only half-joking.

"She knows you are a client." There was no humor in the reply. "She does not know your real name. That's only for the inner circle."

Oh, for God's sake. Next he'd be giving her dark glasses with secret cameras embedded in them.

She stifled a smart-aleck response, using the vista of cobalt-blue water frothing up on a wide stretch of white sand as a distraction. Sunny yellow umbrellas dotted the horizon, with chaises and hammocks and a few gauze-draped private cabanas for the well-heeled guests of Casa Blanca.

So the circumstances were a little weird. Who cared? The

place rocked, and she would not let an octogenarian 007 ruin her satisfaction.

In a few minutes, he slowed the cart in front of a sand-colored villa that backed up to the beach, the column, arches, and golden, barrel-tile roof looking both brand new and Old World. Any trace of a bad mood vanished.

"Put me up here, and you can call me anything you want," she said with a sigh of pure pleasure.

Straightening a little uncomfortably, Mr. Rossi climbed out and reached for one bag, while Kate grabbed the smaller one, knowing it was heavy with legal books and files for studying.

At the door, he slipped the card key into the lock, getting a green light. But when he turned the handle, the door didn't budge. He tried again, grunting a little with the effort.

"I swear those electronic keys never work," she said, putting the suitcase down, ready to help him.

"No, it's not that. It's locked from the inside."

"How can that be?"

"For your protection."

"How is that protective? I'm out here, locked out and"—she glanced over her shoulder, getting a glimpse of sun-dappled palm fronds and not a stray guest in sight—"trapped in this hotbed of criminal activity."

He didn't even smile at the tease. Instead, he scooped up both suitcases without giving her the chance to get the smaller one. "I assure you that no one else can do this, but there is a back entrance through the gate. Come with me."

She followed him around the side of the villa, stealing glances inside the windows, eager to see her new temporary home. They walked along a hedged path to a large metal gate, ornate but clearly not for decoration, locked with a digital keypad.

"This villa is going to be exclusively for our clients," he said, gesturing to the security device. "I'm one of the only souls who knows the code."

She fought a smile at how solemn he was, her heart softening toward the elderly gentleman who obviously just wanted to be relevant. Where did Dad find this guy? No matter, she was in the mood to humor him, if only to get into the place, strip down to a bathing suit, and soak up some rays. Hopefully, the wet bar was equipped with margarita mix and plenty of tequila.

For *after* studying, of course.

He tapped in a few numbers on the keypad, and the latch released. As she stepped forward, she caught a glimpse of the edge of a natural pool surrounded by stone and a small waterfall tucked behind palm trees. Delighted, she couldn't help but dart forward, leaving Mr. Rossi behind in her excitement to see her little slice of paradise.

"Mrs. Carlson!" he called.

She waved him off and stepped around the side of the house…and froze in shock.

Who the holy hell was that?

A man whirred and kicked and sliced his hands through the air. He stood in the shadows under a pergola, the streaks of sunlight and shade bathing him in a constant movement of light and dark, his eyes closed, his fists taut, his legs flying and turning and kicking so hard she could hear them cut through the air.

He grunted and turned so she could see his face, and she almost stumbled, gasping softly.

Instantly he stopped, every muscle—and, God, there were a lot of those—suddenly as still as if he'd been carved in stone and put on display to…admire.

All she could do was take in a mighty male chest inching

through the opening of a snow-white kimono-type of jacket tied with a knotted black belt, and hold her breath as ice-cold blue eyes sliced right through her.

"We used the gate," Mr. Rossi said, coming up behind her, and not a bit fazed by the man's presence. "I meant to call and tell you we were on the property, but I got distracted."

The man breathed, once and slowly, not a bit winded by that...that fighting dance he'd been doing. Then he nodded once, so slight it was almost imperceptible.

He came closer then, like an animal approaching its prey, each slow step silent in his loose-fitting karate pants. She tried to take him in, guess who he was, and examine his features all at the same time, but it was impossible to even have a coherent thought in the face of such...such a *man.*

Everything was too much. Too many muscles, too many angles, too many tattoos peeking through that top. His nose was too big, his neck too dense, his cheeks too hollow and shadowed, his mouth much too...much.

"You must be Mathilda." His voice was low, a rumble in his chest, somehow as terrifying as it was compelling.

"I'm..." Speechless. Helpless. Breathless. She glanced at Mr. Rossi, who'd suddenly morphed from hapless escort into her lifeline to sanity.

"She goes by Tilly," he said smoothly. "And this is Benjamin."

Who the hell was Benjamin? Other than a brute who looked like he crawled out of hell and would be more comfortable going back there.

"Benjamin Carlson," Mr. Rossi finished. "Your bodyguard."

"*Bodyguard?*" Few words conjured the hated image of a

helpless female as much as that one. The only other possessive, soul-sucking title that made her want to gag more was—

"And your husband."

That one.

Chapter Two

Alec hadn't been prepared for beauty. Not on this level. For some reason, he'd expected someone ordinary. Plain. Maybe even unattractive. Otherwise, how could this ruse even work?

His body still burning from a drill warm-up, sweat rolling down his torso and soaking his gi, Alec ventured one step closer. And he managed not to react to the blow when her spring-green gaze landed on him with the expression of someone who'd just opened a prison door to discover an unwanted cellmate.

"My husband?" Blood drained from her cheeks, leaving her creamy skin as pale as the sand he'd run on at dawn today. "Is this some kind of joke?"

Nino Rossi cleared his throat. Twice.

Alec had come to know the man well in the past few weeks of hiding and waiting for his cover to arrive. Throat clearing was a sign the old guy was dying of discomfort, despite his best efforts to seem like he knew his way around the job.

"Your father knew we were arranging this operation," Nino said to her.

She cut him in half with a harsh look. "No one ever told

18

me about an *operation* or an *arrangement* or, for God's sake, a *husband*." She flipped a thick lock of auburn hair over her shoulder, looking past Alec at the villa, then around the patio, as if searching for an escape route that wasn't there.

Realizing that, she stayed planted, her gaze darting this way and that, to his face, then away again. "Can I get another villa, please?" she asked, tapping her foot exactly like a fallen fighter using the universal signal of submission. "Or a hotel room? Hell, I'll take a cabana on the beach, but I have to be alone."

Alec gave himself a swift mental hammerfist for agreeing to this stupid plan. He had enough shit on his brain and didn't need some green-eyed goddess looking down her perfect nose at him.

"And you are *not* my husband," she added with a bite in her voice. "Real, pretend, or otherwise. No husband. Let's just get that clear right now."

Alec crossed his arms, hiding his hands, hearing her revulsion at the idea of being married to him.

Nino put a hand on the woman's back. "Mathilda."

She gave the old man a withering look.

"*Tilly*," Nino corrected, not that the nickname seemed to make her any happier. "A tremendous amount of time, money, and thought has gone into this arrangement, and I assure you we only have your best interests at heart."

She closed her eyes for a second, like she needed to scoop up some inner peace and came up empty-handed. "My father." She shook her head. "He means well."

Nino jumped on the opportunity, flicking his hand toward the villa. "Please, why don't you go inside?"

She looked from one to the other, the tornado in her eyes fading. After a slight nudge from Nino, she headed inside, disappearing through French doors.

Alec stayed back for a few seconds, centering himself. "That went well."

Nino smile was shaky. "You know what they say? Happy wife, happy life."

Alec almost laughed. "So now what?"

Nino lifted his shoulder. "I'll go talk to Gabriel. And you make nice." He turned and left the way he came, through the side yard, the gate clanging behind him.

Taking one more breath, Alec braced for this new opponent, who, despite her slender size, was obviously going to give him the fight of his life. He suddenly wished he were anywhere other than in a one-bedroom honeymoon villa with a woman who would probably choose solitary in an outhouse over being stuck here with him. He'd rather be anywhere...

Except on the receiving end of Vlitnik's knife or pistol. How bad could one beautiful woman be? All he had to do was pretend to be a professional bodyguard, pretend to be her husband, and pretend it didn't bother him that she seemed to draw back in displeasure every time she accidentally looked at him.

Damn lot of pretending, so he'd better start practicing.

Taking her suitcases, he stepped through into the living area, where his new responsibility sat perched on the edge of a sofa, madly tapping at her phone.

"My name isn't really Mathilda," she said.

"I know. Mine isn't Benjamin."

That got her attention. "What is it?"

"For security purposes, we're only going to use our cover names. They didn't even tell me your real name. I'll call you Mathilda."

"My name is Kate Kingston." She stared at him, the longest she'd looked at him yet, eyes sparking like crushed emeralds. "I see no intelligent reason to call me anything else."

He set the suitcases on the floor with a soft thud. "Except that I've been instructed not to. *Mathilda.*"

She merely pointed at the suitcases. "Don't take them too far." Then, into the phone, "Hello, Jennifer? It's Kate. Is my father available?"

Kate Kingston. The name suited her. A classy, clean, pretty name that matched her flawless skin and hair the color of a wild sorrel pony. The name of a woman who was attractive and sophisticated and smart and, when she wasn't mad as a cat, probably very nice.

But she was pissed now.

She fidgeted for a second, fluttering her hair, then rubbing her fingers together in silent, impatient snaps. She stood and turned away from him, the sun through the French doors giving her a halo of gold and him a view of a long, lean but surprisingly curved frame in fuzzy pink sweater and tight jeans.

"Is there any way you can pull him out of that meeting?" she asked, almost looking over her shoulder at him as if she half-expected him to pounce on her. "I have an emergency."

So that's what he was. An emergency.

"A *serious* emergency."

Alec almost smiled, staying right where he was, locking his hands in front of his body like he would while helping a trainee go through the motions of a practice. Oh, she'd be fun to train.

Find your balance, Kate. Breathe in rhythm. Move like liquid. Dig for power. Now, let's get on the mat, Kate.

He shook off the last one, actually jerking his head from side to side as if he could shake the thought from his brain and body. There'd be none of that.

"Oh, for crying out loud," she exclaimed, exasperation blowing off her like steam from a whistling kettle. "Put a note in front of him and tell him to call a recess." At her side, her hand flexed and opened nervously as she tossed him a warning look over her shoulder, even though he hadn't moved.

Jeez, she was wound tight. "Oh, yes, Jennifer, you can give him a really simple message. We need to change this *arrangement*. Immediately." After a pause, she mumbled, "Thanks," and hung up.

With a low grunt at her failure, she dropped her phone into the bag that hung on her narrow shoulder.

"He's calling me back," she said, finally turning to face him.

"I got that."

"We'll…have to do something else."

He let a long pause pass, then leveled his gaze on her despite the fact that she still refused extended eye contact. He was used to that, double takes from people he scared just by being there. But for some reason, he didn't want her to make it so obvious she wanted to run hard, fast, and far. Well, no mysterious reason. They were stuck together, playing house.

She crossed her arms, and there it was, that tiny step backward, as if she were afraid of him. *Make nice*, Nino had said. Okay then.

"I'm not sure you understand exactly how personal protection works," he said. "I'm not going to hurt you."

Her eyes widened a little, then her pretty features relaxed into the first real emotion, other than ticked off, he'd seen since she'd arrived. "I don't think you're going to hurt me. I just want to be alone while I'm here. I have things to do. A test to…pass."

"You're going to pass a test every time you walk out that door and pretend to be Mrs. Benjamin Carlson."

Her eyes flashed. "I am *nobody's* Mrs. I signed all the papers to make sure of it."

"You're my Mrs. At least for the time we're here. That's the deal. In exchange, I'll break anyone who comes near you into small pieces and crush them." He added a smile, wishing it could get one in return. "But not you. I promise I won't crush you."

He saw her work to swallow and wondered what she was thinking. "I'm pretty certain you won't have to do any heavy breaking or crushing. This place seems pretty secure."

"The resort is, but you're defenseless, and I'm—"

She iced him with a glare and pointed one slender finger at him. "I am *not* defenseless."

He moved one inch closer. He could have her on the ground, under him, screaming for mercy and completely *defenseless*, in less than a second.

"What are your stats?" he asked.

She almost smiled. Almost. "Stats?"

"You know, your numbers."

"My numbers?" She lifted her chin. "The ones that matter are twenty-nine, which is my age; sixteen, which was my Yale Law graduation ranking; and one, which is how I roll: alone at all times, without assistance from any man, anywhere."

"Except you called Daddy within fifteen seconds of arrival."

She bristled. "Extenuating circumstances."

"The numbers I meant are your height and weight. Five-five and about a hundred and twenty?" he guessed.

A frown pulled. "One thirty."

"Yoga, I'm guessing?"

"Occasionally. What difference does it make?"

"Some light weights and a jog now and then?"

23

"What is your *point*?"

"My point is that you might be very smart and in decent shape, but when push comes to shove—literally—you're defenseless."

Her eyes narrowed, and she sucked in a seething breath. "Then your point would be wrong."

"Don't make me prove it to you."

"Great," she muttered, turning away. "Just great. Another jerk trying to run my life."

"I'm not trying to be a jerk or run your life." When she looked back at him, he continued, "I'm trying to do a job, and one hit to a soft target, and you'd be down." He released his arms and stepped back. A natural move in the face of any threat, especially hands like his.

He locked them behind him and angled his head to show her he was no threat. "I'm thinking you should stop fighting this plan and get comfortable with the idea of a bodyguard."

"A bodyguard." She looked toward the ceiling like she couldn't even believe she had to say the word. "Look, I'm more than a thousand miles from some yahoo trying to upset my father by mentioning my name in a few anonymous notes. Yes, if I were walking around the streets of Boston, clueless to my surroundings, then I can see him hiring a...a...*man* to watch me."

She struggled with the word *man*. Did she hate them all in general, or just the one who appeared in her villa today?

"So, I'm fine here, and I don't need a bodyguard, and for God's sake, I don't want a husband, real or otherwise. One was plenty." She added a tight smile to underscore the point she'd made every possible way since she'd arrived.

"It's not about what you want, Miss..." Kate. God, he wanted to call her Kate so bad. "*Mathilda.*"

"Excuse me." Her back straightened as she jutted her jaw.

"It's *all* about what I want, Mr. *Benjamin*. This was all done behind my back, and it can be undone by—" The phone in her bag hummed and dinged, and she grabbed it, giving a satisfied smirk. "By this phone call." She whirled around, putting the phone to her ear. "This is preposterous, Dad!"

Preposterous. Not stupid, silly, or pointless. Because why use two syllables when four would do for Miss Extenuating Circumstances?

Shit. His head already hurt.

"No, I won't—" She snapped her mouth closed, and in the silence, Alec could hear a man's voice on the phone, but not the words. The tone was serious, though, and strong.

"No, you listen to me," she replied, "a bodyguard is excessive, and one who is supposed to be my husband is patently ridiculous. Who ever heard of such a thing?"

Patently? Oh, that's right. *Yale* Law School. Maybe she thought she could beat an attacker with her diploma.

She stepped toward the French doors, then opened one, going out to the patio for privacy. "I am *not* going to back down, Dad."

The door slammed, and the rest was lost to Alec.

He stayed rooted to his spot, not having to dig too hard for the natural state of peace that kept him sane and alive in situations far worse than this. He honestly could see her point, but he wasn't going anywhere. He'd made a promise to Gregg that he'd do whatever he had to do, and the deal was to babysit the beauty. In turn, she was his cover, too.

He watched her through the glass, counting the sighs as her shoulders rose and fell. She ran a hand through her hair and clenched her fist again. And again. Finally, her head dropped in resignation.

25

Fighter taps out, and the win goes to Judge Daddy.

Alec picked up Kate's two bags and walked into the bedroom—the only one in the villa.

Oh, she was going to *love* that.

Chapter Three

Kate listened to her father with an age-old burn in her belly. Always, *always*, a man in charge. When would she ever have control of her own life?

Never if she gave up as easily as she had with Steven for all those years. Barely listening to her father, she straightened up, squared her shoulders, and renewed her fight.

"No, Dad. No. This isn't how it's going to be. I'll stay away from people. I'll get room service and lock myself up. All I want to do is study. I don't need a...a..." She glanced over her shoulder, but the sun's reflection on the glass blinded her to the room inside. But she knew he was there. A big, hulking kind of scary-looking man who looked like he might eat her. And made her feel...tense.

Wasn't that why her throat was so damn dry? And her heart rate seemed to double when he sliced her with those piercing blue eyes.

"Katherine, this is not up for discussion. You need protection." Her father's voice was tight and focused, his judge's tone, which was not to be messed with.

Not that she messed with him very often, but sometimes, especially since her divorce, she'd been fighting back. And she would now. She didn't like this damn arrangement, or the fact that it was set up without her knowledge while she thought she was stealing some solitude and study time.

"Protection provided by some troglodyte pretending to be my husband?" She hissed the last word, that despicable word that represented entrapment and misery and indentured servitude.

"The honeymoon thing is a—"

"Cover," she said, hoping just the stupidity of that concept sank into the head of her generally very smart father.

"Yes. You're undercover, like a cop."

Nothing like a cop. More like a prisoner.

"You have to trust the people who are professionals," he continued. "And this is what they recommend."

"It's ludicrous, Dad!"

He was silent, and she could swear she heard him swallow. "I can't lose you, too."

And there it was. Fifteen years of fear all rolled into five words she'd heard ten thousand times from him.

"Please," she said, purposely taking the fight out of her tone. "Please don't play the guilt card. You promised me the day I divorced Steven that you wouldn't ever do that again. You promised me I could control my own life from now on."

"I know, and I want to keep that promise, honey, I really do. But..." His voice was laced with a desperation that seemed way out of proportion to the situation.

"But what?" she prodded.

He sighed. "Kate, listen to me." He went quiet for a moment, making her press the phone to her ear so she could do just that. "There was another note, left just outside my chambers." His voice was an ominous whisper.

"What did it say?"

"I won't tell you the exact words, but I made the right decision to get you far away from Boston."

Hadn't *she* actually made the decision? The question tweaked, but Dad continued, "Honey, you have to trust me on this. Even I have beefed-up security now, at the courthouse and at home. But it's you I'm worried about. We are dealing with someone who knows my most vulnerable spot."

She was his most vulnerable spot, a role Kate had alternately loved, hated, used, and refused her whole life. Well, since she was fifteen, and her mother had died. Her father's determination to protect—or smother, depending on your point of view—the only person he had left had started that day and had yet to end. Oh, he'd taken a break during her marriage because he'd thought the sun rose and set on Steven, but ultimately even Dad had to see his son-in-law for the control freak he was.

Even though he'd promised to let her have some breathing space, the divorce made Dad even more protective in some ways.

He felt guilty, too, for pushing that marriage.

"Did you turn the note over to the FBI like the others?"

"Of course. And Special Agent in Charge Colton Lang is handling it personally. And I'm using his wife's security company for my own protection, though it's you I'm worried about."

"But no one knows I'm here, and this absurd charade with a husband—"

"It's not absurd if it keeps you safe."

"I don't have to be locked in a guarded cell to stay safe," she countered, glancing at the cascade of water over stones in the pool and the breathtaking beach vista beyond that. She shoved away some remorse at calling paradise a prison, but no matter how beautiful it was, she was still trapped. By a man. *Men*, actually.

"Look, Katherine, I know you hate the feeling of not being in control of your destiny."

She snorted at the understatement.

"Please, for me." Dad's old pain was back in his voice, as clear as the day...the day she'd caused it. "Won't you just stick this out, Kate? Give the FBI some time to investigate?"

And, of course, she buckled with one more sigh of resignation. "Until we can figure out something else." Her words sounded as weak as her body felt. She was giving in only because of guilt and obligation and a daughter's love, right?

"I'm sure the FBI will nail this guy very soon, and then you can come home."

Suddenly, Kate was aware that the door behind her had opened. She was no longer alone on the sunny patio. She turned to face the man behind her, and once again she had to force herself to keep from taking in an audible breath at the sight of him. The martial arts jacket thing was open wider now, ink-decorated pecs on display.

"So you'll go along with it?" Dad's question sounded like it was coming from underwater, drowned out by the hammer of her pulse. "Please, I need to know you're safe. One week, two at the most."

Two weeks locked in a villa with a man who made her feel...off-balance? No. No way. Except...*Dad*. He was her weak spot, too.

"All right. We'll talk soon, Dad."

"Thank you, sweetheart. I'm sure you'll work things out with this...bodyguard."

Kate made the huge mistake of meeting the bodyguard's

cool, direct gaze. Three heartbeats of eye contact, and her chest felt like a fist had gone through it and her stomach flipped like she'd fallen off a cliff. The reaction made no sense, since she wasn't afraid of him. But he was just such a big...*presence.*

"I'll do my best." Ending the call, she gripped the phone, forcing herself not to turn away from the man a few feet away. She felt sweat prickling her skin, a result of the sun bearing down, of course. The splash of the waterfall and the distant cry of a gull from the nearby beach were the only sounds, other than her own strangled breathing.

He stood stone silent and still, a man who she imagined never wasted a word or made a move that wasn't absolutely necessary. She searched his face, lingering on protruding cheekbones and a strong jaw, a flattened, crooked nose, and lethal blue eyes.

"So, what is it?" she finally asked.

"What is what?"

"Your real name."

He gave his head a quick shake. "Not going to tell you."

"Don't dismiss me." She took a step closer, despite the fact that getting even an inch nearer to him made her pulse quicken and added to that frustrating sense of vulnerability she hated so much. Probably because he was just so damn big and strong. Anyone would feel a little...what was the word he used? *Defenseless.*

"You really don't need to know my name."

"I don't need a lot of things," she fired back, working for the composure that he somehow erased from her arsenal just by standing there and breathing. *Was* he breathing? She was damn near panting, while everything about him was still. "Starting with a bodyguard, a fake husband, a new name, an overprotective father, and an eighty-year-old man calling the

31

shots. But evidently, I have them all. So, humor me, and tell me your name."

He took a measured step closer. "My name is Benjamin Carlson."

She rolled her eyes. "Your *real* name."

"You don't—"

She lifted her hand to stop him, and in a flash, he enveloped her wrist, jerking it down with one lightning-fast move and a shocking amount of power but no pain.

At her gasp, he released her.

"I wasn't going to touch you," she said, her voice trapped in her constricted throat.

"Doesn't matter. I wouldn't have let you." He glanced at his hand, as if his reflexes surprised even him, then hid it behind him. "And I'm not going to tell you my name or anything else about me. Every single thing I say to you will be a lie, so you might as well know that now."

"Why?" His secrecy made no sense. She understood them using an alias for her because of the threats, but he was just a bodyguard.

"Because that's the arrangement. Just live a lie. Can you do that?"

She gave a soft laugh, thinking of Steven Jessup and how often she'd played a happy wife for the benefit of everyone but herself. "I was married for five years to a man I loathed and despised, so, yeah, I have mad lying skills. But I have a good reason, they say, for using a fake name. What's your reason?"

He shook his head, obviously not going to answer, which just sent a new wave of irritation over her.

"And by the way," he said, "the eighty-year-old man is *not* calling the shots."

"Who is?"

"*I* am."

They both turned to face another man standing in the French doors, his gaze just as blue, but not nearly as menacing.

"And if I can waltz into this fucking villa, so can some lunatic with a gun and bad intentions. That's twice today, cowboy." He turned those blue eyes on the bodyguard. "Next time someone walks into this place and isn't instantly on his ass and getting pummeled by your knee and fist, you'll be in training for a new job. In Moscow."

Benjamin—or whatever his name was—crossed his arms and seemed unfazed by the dressing down. "Glad you're here, Mr. Rossi. There seems to be a misunderstanding about my, uh, wife's role in the operation."

Kate felt like her head was going to explode. "Mr. Rossi? I thought that other man—"

"My grandfather," he said, adding a smile that somehow took the sting out of every word. "He's good, isn't he?"

"He's not in charge?"

"Nino? God help us. He'd be handing out cannoli instead of ID packets. I run things." He stepped forward and offered a hand to Kate. "Gabe Rossi, and welcome to life undercover. You are now officially off the grid, below the radar, and one hundred percent secure." He slid a vile look to the other man. "Assuming *you* aren't too busy arguing with her."

Benjamin lifted one eyebrow. "She's a lawyer."

"That explains it," Gabe said with a soft laugh.

"I'm sorry, but that explains nothing." Kate glared at one, then the other. "And I'm not ever going to be a lawyer if I don't have the solitude and serenity I need to study."

"And security," Gabe added. "You got this cover, right? You are his adoring bride who doesn't let anyone within five feet of him because you are incredibly jealous and clingy.

And make sure he keeps his hand covered when you're in public."

"His hand?" None of this made sense, but...his hand? "What are you talking about?"

"Show her," Gabe said.

He looked a little pained at the order, but he stuck his right fist forward so she could see the purplish-black writing tattooed on his fingers between his knuckles, exactly where he'd land a punch.

He didn't hold them long enough for her to make out the symbols. No, letters. The Cyrillic alphabet? So, Russian or Slavic, she presumed.

"It says *kill*," Gabe said in response to her frown. "And he will, if he has to."

"Why do I have to hold his hand?"

"Because that's not a tattoo he got while he was drunk with his friends. It's a tag that identifies him, and there are people who would love to separate that hand from his body, along with other choice parts, so do yourself a favor and help him cover it—casually—when you're out. Got it?"

So who was protecting whom, exactly? "I don't understand."

Gabe grinned, a playful, charismatic smile that probably set the hearts of hundreds of women into high gear. "Sorry, but one of the first rules of undercover work is that you don't know everything, because what you know can hurt you."

"I don't accept that," she said.

Gabe gave a soft snort and shared a look with the other man, a silent bonded-male communication that irked her even more.

"Let me ask you this," Gabe said. "Do you accept death?"

How did she answer a question that ridiculous? She didn't get a chance, because he got closer and continued,

"Because I just read the latest little love note your father received, and I hate to be the one to break it to you, sweet cheeks, but someone is getting off on the idea of locking you in a basement, raping the shit out of you, then cutting your body up into small pieces and, as he so poetically puts it, 'dismissing the evidence' in his kitchen disposal."

Blood drained from her head so fast she felt dizzy. "What?" She whispered the question, vaguely aware of a man's hand on her shoulder. A huge, strong, surprisingly warm hand that was exactly what she needed to stay standing.

She'd had no idea...

All joking evaporated from Gabe's expression. "You got yourself in the sights of one sick fuck, what can I say?"

She struggled to speak. Dad never told her that. If he had... "It really said that?"

"That's one of the more tender ones. Believe me, all you need to know to be safe is what you've been told. You have two contacts, other than me and Conan here. Nino Rossi, my grandfather, who I predict you will grow to love, because everyone does, is in on everything and able to take you two wherever you want to go, within reason. Poppy, your housekeeper, is also on my payroll. She knows you're undercover, but not your real identity. With the exception of the head of all security, Luke McBain, not another person at this resort—not the chef, owner, gardener, massage therapist, front-desk person, cabana boy, doorman, or the pretty blonde who flies the hot air balloons can or will know who you are."

"But what if—"

"Don't get friendly with guests, but don't act weird either. You're on your honeymoon, so no one will go out of their way to bother you, but you don't want to bring attention to yourselves by acting like you don't know or like each other. In fact, I prefer you drooling over each other in public. If you speak honestly to one person or let on to anyone that you are not who they think you are, I wash my hands of both of you. And, trust me, I have spies everywhere, and I will know if you so much as think about your real identity around another person anywhere on this island."

Kate stared at him, wanting so much to cling to her righteous indignation about being told what to do by *yet another man*. But all she could think was...*lock you in a basement, rape the shit out of you, and...a kitchen disposal?*

As if Benjamin could read her thoughts, his fingers tightened on her shoulder. And then, without thinking, Kate lifted her hand and put it over his. His tag that said *kill*.

Awesome, just awesome. What a fabulous vacation in paradise this turned out to be.

"Now that's what I'm talking about," Gabe said, his gaze noting the touch. "Oh, here, this is why I came over here in the first place." He reached into his pocket and pulled out a small black bag. "Don't go anywhere without these." He flipped the pouch to the bodyguard, who easily snagged it with one hand. "And I didn't make up a backstory about how you met and all that shit. You can dream one up together."

"We don't need that," Kate said.

"Yes, you do." Gabe headed toward the front door without looking back. "Follow the rules, kids, and everybody stays alive." Without waiting for an answer, he let himself out.

Benjamin opened the bag and poured out something that clinked in his hand. "Hardware," he said, holding up a small ring with a not-so-small diamond. "His and hers."

And they didn't need *that*, either. "I swore I would never, ever wear that handcuff again."

36

"It goes on your finger."

"Very funny. It does the same thing as a handcuff—traps you."

He handed one to her and took the much larger gold band for himself. "See if it fits."

It did, sliding easily over her knuckle and feeling as heavy as the one she'd finally ditched the day she moved out of the Beacon Hill apartment. Benjamin's wasn't going on so easily. He made a face as he tried to push it over a gnarled knuckle.

"Here, I'll help," she said.

He quickly turned away. "I got it."

Great, he was one of *those* kind of men. "Really? Because it doesn't look like you do."

"I got it." His voice was taut, telling her that for all his bravado, he hated this situation as much as she did. After a second, he turned back to her, his face dark with frustration. "Guess I'll need another one. This one won't fit."

She didn't answer, going into the kitchen and grabbing some dish soap she found on the sink. "Come here," she called as she poured some on her fingers. "Give me your hand."

He came around the counter reluctantly, still working the ring. "My fingers are...big."

Big and scarred and *big*. She glanced up at him, seeing nothing but shame in his rough features and riveting blue eyes. Something in her heart slipped, just like the ring as she eased it over his lubricated knuckle.

"There you go," she said.

He gave it a yank. "It may never come off."

"You can use a saw," she said dryly, walking by him.

"Kate."

She paused, turned, and looked at him, expecting a belated thank-you.

He swallowed, as if gathering his thoughts. His blue eyes lost all their sharpness for that moment, as he looked earnestly into hers. "I won't let anyone hurt you. I promise you're safe."

She waited for a retort to pop into her head, but she couldn't think how to answer, because she believed him, but yet she felt anything but safe right then. Maybe it was the news that the threats were far more terrifying than she'd been led to believe. Maybe it was this whole upside-down arrangement that stole her freedom and control. Or maybe it was this big man with blue eyes and scarred hands that embarrassed him.

She didn't know what she felt, but it sure as hell wasn't safe.

Chapter Four

Alec was in the kitchen, the room in the villa he'd come to like the best, when Kate came up to the counter and uttered the words he had been dreading the most: "I need to shower."

He'd never been a bodyguard before. Except for a few cursory meetings with Gabe Rossi and Luke McBain, who ran a personal-protection company based here at the resort called McBain Security, Alec was totally winging it.

Starting with what he was supposed to do to ensure her full security while his "wife" showered.

"There's a shower and a bathtub the size of a kid's pool in there." He pointed to the one and only bedroom, down a short hall next to the living area. "I put your bags by the door."

She crossed her arms, leaning against the kitchen counter, still obviously not comfortable with anything—the villa, the situation, the news of how much danger she clearly didn't know she was in. Before that, she'd been a firecracker, flinging fifty-dollar words like they were her best weapons.

But after she found out someone really wanted to hurt her? That spark definitely got drenched. So she probably needed a good hot shower and maybe a cry. Women liked to cry in the shower, right?

Only, she didn't seem like the weepy type.

"Where will you be?" she asked.

"Sitting on the bed or in the chair in the corner, staring at the locked bathroom door."

Her jaw unhinged. "That's just creepy."

"It's just common sense."

"You think I'm going to try to escape?"

"You're not in jail, Kate."

She started to turn, then froze, narrowing her eyes. "I thought that was against the rules."

He knew exactly what she was referring to. "You're right. I should call you Mathilda or Tilly or anything but your real name, but..." He let his eyes drift over her, lingering on that baby-pink sweater that draped over her body and her long, feminine thighs in jeans that were tight all the way to the ankle, where they grazed low black boots. "Kate suits you."

"Fine, break the rules. Call me Kate, and then I can call you..." Her voice rose in question.

"Benjamin."

She tipped her head, almost smiling. He watched her, waiting, a little surprised by how much he wanted to see her smile. How much he actually needed to see her face light up, just for the raw pleasure of it. But she didn't, and the disappointment was almost as unexpected as his thoughts.

"Come on, you know my name," she urged.

"Because you insisted on telling me. Your choice, not mine."

"But now that I know Benjamin isn't your real name, I'm going to obsess until I know what it is."

He gave a quick laugh, mostly to cover the slow burn that suddenly surged in him at the idea of her giving him that much thought. "You don't strike me as obsessive."

She scooped up the handbag she'd left on the counter, flipping it on her shoulder. "All women obsess, don't you know that?"

"I don't know much about women," he admitted as she started to walk toward the hall.

That stopped her. "But you know about being a bodyguard."

Why lie? "Not really. Never been one before."

"Then why are you one now?"

"Gabe explained it's a matter of convenience for both of us. I teach martial arts and have a black belt in Brazilian jiu-jitsu. Plus, I was a Marine for seven years. I'm perfectly qualified."

Her gaze dropped to his right hand. "But you're not entirely safe yourself, is that right?"

"I'm a marked man," he said simply. "That's why I'm here, and that's why I need a cover. You are in a similar situation. So it makes sense."

"No, nothing makes sense right now." She sighed as if she didn't want to think about it anymore. Then she glanced around the little house. "So this is it? The whole place? It seems small."

Actually, it was pretty spacious. But it probably seemed small for two people who weren't actually married, or even friends. "Want a tour?" he asked.

"Sure. How long have you been here?"

"A few weeks."

"All alone?"

He half-shrugged. "When I got here a while ago, I was…" *In pretty bad shape.* His broken rib had almost healed, and a doctor Gabe knew had set his busted nose. The bruises on his hands were gone now, and he was able to start slow workouts. Since he couldn't leave the villa, he'd improvised training on the back patio.

41

"You were what?" she prodded.

"Waiting for my cover."

"Which would be me." She sounded like a woman who'd finally accepted the truth.

"I couldn't go anywhere," he continued. "So I watched about six hundred movies on Netflix, read some books about how to be a bodyguard, and meditated a lot. And I cook." He gestured toward the gas stove next to him, an appliance he'd come to love.

"You meditate?"

"I do a lot of yoga."

"I thought you were making fun of yoga before."

He shook his head. "No, it's a big part of my training." He felt her intense gaze on him and tried to remember the last time anything that wasn't a fist in the face made him feel like squirming as much as right that minute. Maybe never. What the hell? She was just looking at him.

He cleared his throat and gestured toward the spread of sofas and chairs in the living room, a dining area off to the side. Wide planks of hardwood gleamed in the sunlight that came in from the patio doors, the overstuffed pale yellow sofas not the most practical things in the world, but the whole place looked like a model home to him.

"The living room," he said, gesturing toward it. "And over there is the master and a bathroom. It connects to the patio, too."

"There? Past that vestibule?"

"Vestibule?"

She stepped under the archway that led to an open space that served no purpose except to hold a huge vase full of fake flowers. "This is a vestibule."

"If you say so."

She opened the door to glance into the master that was

big enough to hold a king-size bed and plenty of furniture. She didn't go in, but nodded and came back to where he was standing in front of the counter that separated the kitchen from the rest of the main living area.

"A fully stocked kitchen," he said. "Oh, and there's a laundry room behind those doors."

"Mmm." She didn't seem too interested in the laundry facilities. "Where's the TV where you watched all those movies?" she asked.

"Back here." He led her to the other side of the kitchen to a media room with a wraparound sofa. "And there's this other bathroom."

"A powder room," she said, probably wondering where the hell he would shower as well as sleep.

He was wondering, too. *One shower problem at a time, Alec.*

"Now you've seen the whole place."

"This is where you'll sleep?" She pointed to the leather sofa in the media room, a cushy, sizable thing where he'd zoned out for days on mindless action flicks.

"I'll sleep where I can see you at all times."

She grunted softly, letting her head tip back to show how much she really didn't like that, but all the move did was reveal her feminine and slender neck. He tried not to stare at how...flawless it was.

"There's a sofa in the bedroom," he said. More like a two-person chair, but he'd already thought that through. "I'll be there."

"Watching me."

"Watching the entrances to the villa. I told you there are doors in your room that lead right to the patio."

She opened her eyes and stared up at the ceiling. "This is crazy."

"It's not crazy after you've seen the threats your father is receiving."

She lowered her head and tapered her gaze. "*You've* seen them? How?"

"I've been over to the security offices, and Gabe showed them to me. Well, copies. The FBI has the originals."

Her brows furrowed with a question, then her whole expression grew pained.

"What's the matter?" he asked.

She pushed out of the narrow doorjamb and away from him. "I don't even know where the security offices are, and you've been there and know my whole story and have seen these threats I'm not even allowed to lay eyes on. I don't even know your name. Does any of that seem fair to you?"

Actually, no. She was in a crappy place to be and probably felt like a POW. "The security offices are on the other side of the resort, by the farm that supplies most of the food to this resort. It's a full-service agency that handles the resort, but also provides personal protection to some Mimosa Key locals."

"People on this little island need bodyguards?"

"There are a few billionaires running around putting together a minor league baseball team. Nate Ivory is one."

She looked impressed. "I've heard of him."

"Plus, a shipwreck that apparently has gold was found recently off the coast, and that brings security issues with it."

Back in the living room, she paused at the patio doors to check out the pool area again. "For a guy living in hiding for a few weeks, you sure know the local gossip."

"Just what Nino tells me."

"The grandfather."

"He's been bringing me food and giving me some cooking tips. Also, Poppy."

"The housekeeper."

"That's it," he said. "The list of who I know in Barefoot Bay. Oh, and Luke, who's been training me." He realized how that must sound. "Not that I need much training."

She considered that, still studying the outdoors intently. "And do you have..." She finally turned to finish the question with a direct look. "A gun?"

He held up his hands, silencing her. "Deadly weapons."

She didn't turn away, but stared at his hands, no doubt trying not to recoil at the sight of his ugly, marked paws.

"Is it Russian?" she asked.

He glanced at the tattoo, then nodded. Gabe already told her what it said. What difference did the language make?

"Vladimir? Boris? Mikhail?"

He laughed again at the first names of some well-known Russian leaders, names he'd heard all his life. "None of those."

"I'll figure it out." She turned and headed toward the master bedroom, leaving him to wonder just how long it would take Miss Smarty-Pants to do just that.

Chapter Five

"You must be desperate to come here." Dmitri Vlitnik poured vodka into a glass and slowly twirled it, not looking up while he waited for an answer.

Desperate? Robyn Bickler was so far past desperate, it wasn't funny. Now the rent was late, she'd been fired from her job, and the boy she'd followed from Philadelphia to Brighton Beach because she thought he loved her had disappeared into thin air.

"You owe me money," she replied, trying to sound like some cool, street-smart con girl instead of a knocked-up eighteen-year-old runaway.

The fat Russian smiled, the glass he held distorting his skin and making his red, raw pockmarks even deeper. He reminded of her father, a drunk she hated with every bone in her body. Vodka mad her dad mean, too. Mean*er*.

"Can you please pay me the ten thousand dollars you owe me, Mr. Vlitnik?"

He sipped and made a noisy slurping sound with his tongue that turned her stomach. And spit the booze right in her face.

Jerking back, she swallowed the hot curse that rose up

and fought to still the hands that wanted to fly at him. Instead, she closed her eyes and wiped the droplets off her cheek.

He put the glass down and leaned his large frame forward. "I don't owe you shit, you little whore."

The two meatheads on either side of him moved closer, like trained dogs waiting for the signal to attack.

Robyn managed to swallow, her throat already closing up. *Come on, girl. Don't let him smell your fear.*

"We made a deal," she said.

"But I still don't have what I want," he said, slowly moving his girth back in the chair.

"The reward wasn't for bringing him to you," she fought back. "You said ten thousand if someone could tell you where he is. And I did."

"You didn't deliver him."

She choked with indignation. "The reward was for 'supplying the whereabouts' of the guy with that tattoo. And I did." She'd seen the flyer not long after her then-boyfriend got a job in Brooklyn and she moved with him from Philly. She'd been sitting in Cole's new gym, bored out of her mind, when her gaze landed on a picture of a hand she'd seen before.

$10,000 reward to anyone who can supply the whereabouts of a man with this tattoo.

There'd been no picture of the man, just that tattoo that she immediately had recognized. She had an eye for things like that, and she remembered the strange letters and could see them in her mind's eye right now—the big six, the backward N, the capital T and little b.

бить

And she'd known immediately that it belonged to that trainer Cole had worked with in Philadelphia. She'd ripped the phone number off the flyer at the time and forgotten about it, until she was broke, pregnant, and abandoned by her boyfriend.

So she'd called the number on that flyer. and some guy picked her up and brought her here, to this fancy house just outside of town, surrounded by high walls and plenty of trees. Right here in this room, she'd met Dmitri Vlitnik, big, ugly, and scary as hell.

"You promised to follow up on my information, and I'd get ten thousand dollars." Her voice rose in frustration. "You *promised*."

"Shut up." He gulped another drink of vodka, staring at her, thinking. And Robyn braced for another mouthful in the face.

Cole had taught her that: Don't let your opponent see you dance around. Look him right in the eye. Defy him.

A sudden clutching ache for the boy who'd left her high and dry threatened to bring on a rush of unwanted tears. Great. Some tough chick she was, crying and emotional and shit.

"I really need the money, Mr. Vlitnik." She wasn't above begging.

He narrowed cold, dark eyes. "I really need Alec Petrov, Miss Bickler."

She took a slow, stuttering breath. How did he know her last name? She'd never told him that.

"I already told you where he works in Philly."

"He's not there anymore. Find where he went, and I'll give you the money."

"How can I trust you?"

Vlitnik's fat mouth quivered. Then it pulled into a smile. "I like you," he said.

She flicked at a remaining drop of vodka on her cheek. "Really. You have a funny way of showing it."

"I like you a *lot*."

She felt her stomach clench, suddenly realizing how ridiculously defenseless she was in this room with three giant men who might not realize the baggy shirt she wore hid her pregnancy. Or might not care.

She tightened her grasp on the sofa cushions, steeling herself for what might come next.

"I'll give you a thousand dollars to find him," Vlitnik said.

Her exhale came out in a loud rush. A thousand would help. It might cover a clinic visit and some back rent. But it wasn't close to enough. "You promised ten. "

"One now." He inched closer. "And if you can *bring* me Alec Petrov, I will pay you the rest."

"Nine more?"

He nodded and raised his right hand as if his sausage-fingered oath meant anything. "You have my word," he said solemnly.

Without thinking, she put her hand on her stomach. Ten thousand dollars meant a doctor and a safe place to live while she was pregnant. Maybe she could call one of the girls she'd met at that studio and have them look around.

Vlitnik pushed himself up and reached into his back pocket and pulled out a wad of cash the size of her fist.

Before she knew what was happening, he was peeling off hundred-dollar bills until he had ten, and then he handed them to her. She was almost afraid to reach for the money.

Was this a trick? Would he snag her arm and throw her down so they could all gangbang her for laughs? But there was the money, held out like a real offering. She took it with a shaky hand, and nothing happened to her.

"Find him," he said. "You know what he looks like, what kind of places he hangs out."

She nodded, squeezing the bills so hard it was a wonder the edges didn't cut her palm.

"If you do, I'll pay the whole reward to you. If you don't, you'll be fucking sorry if you come sniffing around here again."

She nodded, wondering if she had to shake his hand or something. She stepped away from the sofa, and him.

If only she could find Cole. Maybe he'd have a cell phone number for his former trainer. And maybe…pigs would land at Newark. Her man had ditched her before she even had a chance to tell him she was pregnant.

"Thanks," she murmured, a little disgusted with herself for thanking him, but whatever.

Nobody moved, so she headed to the front of the house. Were they going to let her walk out of there with a thousand dollars? She waited for one of them to grab her from behind and take it away, but that didn't happen.

Instead, she walked toward the door. A hissing sound coming from a darkened corridor to her left made her glance there without slowing her step. She had a grand in her pocket, nothing was going to make her stop.

"Robyn!"

Except her name. She stopped and glanced over her shoulder, considering whether or not she should take a step backward and look down the hallway. But maybe it was a trick and someone was going to jump her for the money. She kept walking.

"Robyn!" The voice made her sway slightly and turn to see a blond head peek out from around the corner. Holy shit, it was him.

"Cole?"

"Shh!" He put his finger on his lips and looked left and right. "Meet me at the 7-Eleven down the street," he whispered, his breathy voice sounding urgent and even scared.

"Cole?" She put one hand on her stomach, another on her mouth, stifling a scream of joy. It was him!

"Miss Bickler?"

She spun all the way around to see Vlitnik standing ten feet behind her. "Yes?"

"We'll be watching you."

But...*Cole*. She almost opened her mouth to say something, but the look in Vlitnik's eyes stopped her. She couldn't risk that thousand dollars.

"'Kay." She kept walking, stealing one more glance back toward the hall, but Cole was gone. It didn't matter. She finally knew where Cole was, and he wanted to meet her. That's all that mattered.

She hustled out the door, doing exactly as she'd been told, practically running the two blocks to the 7-Eleven. She threw herself inside, looked around, got a strange look from the guy behind the counter.

She rushed up and down the aisles, but there was no sign of Cole.

She stood outside under the awning and waited. For half an hour. An hour. Two. Then she went back to her car, hid the money under the seat, drove past Vlitnik's house, rode around the neighborhood, and tried the 7-Eleven again.

But it was like she'd imagined him. Maybe she had. That's how bad she wanted to see Cole Morrow again.

Chapter Six

Kate finished a half-hour-long shower, stepped into denim cutoffs, pulled a T-shirt over her head, and shook out her damp hair. There was nothing she could do, at least not short-term.

She needed some lunch, a cold drink, and then she'd hit the books until well into the evening.

If Ivan the Terrible wanted to sit and stare at her, she'd turn the other way, put on her noise-canceling headphones, and ignore him.

She opened the door, fully expecting him to be on the love seat, staring at the door, ready to pounce. Instead, a large woman in a housekeeper's uniform was humming with earphones in, turning down the bed.

"Well, it's about time." The woman popped the buds out and tsked disapprovingly. "You could have bathed an entire orphanage in the time you've had that water running. Have you never thought of that?"

"Uh, no. I never have."

"What were you doing in there so long?"

Really? Now the maid had a say in how Kate lived her life? "You must be Poppy."

"I am. And you're Tilly." She angled her head and gave

Kate a long look of appraisal, up and down and back again. "I can see why Nino backed off the Mathilda business, though he was very excited when Mr. Gabriel agreed to the name. I told him it was the most foolish name I ever heard, but Mr. Gabriel can't seem to see straight when it comes to his grandfather."

Kate nodded, not at all sure how to respond to the company politics of this mysterious stealth firm that suddenly controlled her life. "And you'll be our housekeeper?"

A bushy black eyebrow rose. "That's my cover."

"Oh, dear God, isn't anyone around here who they say they are?"

Poppy put two hands on rather wide hips, her dark features fixed in a stern expression. "I'm going to give you a pass on that, under the circumstances. Plus, I don't usually count 'God' as a full-on curse, at least if it's not followed by the D-word."

Kate stared at her, frowning, feeling a little more like Alice in Wonderland than Kate in Paradise. "A pass. What are you talking about?"

"I may be working for Mr. Gabriel now, getting a little extra money on the side as one of his 'spies' and the only member of the entire housekeeping staff, including Miss Mandy, who owns the company that runs Casa Blanca housekeeping, who is being trusted with information about Mr. Gabriel's 'special guests,' but…"

She took a breath and paused, as if she couldn't remember where she'd actually started that sentence, since it might have gone on for a full minute. "But," she continued, nodding as she picked up her train of thought, "there is no swearing without a penalty, so bad words in my presence get tallied, and the funds go to the Jamaican Children's Fund so that I may bring my nephews home." Another breath, and a big smile of bright white teeth against dark coffee skin. "Rules are rules, and they cannot, will not, and may not be broken, ever."

Kate didn't know whether to laugh or cry. "Okay, I don't generally swear too much." Though she might be starting soon. "But I will tell you that I'm not here to follow or break rules. I'm going to study for the bar, soak up some sunshine, get my head cleared, and then fog it all up again at the end of the day with a good, stiff drink. So, let's not bog things down with rules, since there are already a number of people determined to get in the way of my plans."

"All righty, then, but I'll need your phone as well as anything that has your name on it, right now. I have a new one here for you that only your father can call." She reached into her pocket and held out a brand new iPhone. "We'll monitor your phone in case someone tries to get in touch with you. Mr. Gabriel has it all figured out."

"Oh, does he now?"

Both eyebrows went up now. "He said you were feisty."

"He…"

"Mr. Benjamin."

She closed her eyes, her blood pressure spiking with each new comment. *He* was passing judgment on her now? With the housekeeper/spy lady who charged for curses and scolded people for long showers?

"This was so not what I wanted," she muttered.

"You can't always get what you want," Poppy said.

Kate shook her head as she crossed the room. "So I've heard."

"But you do have a beautiful home to stay in on a tropical island, a kind man whose entire existence is to make sure you're safe, and the best housekeeper south of the Mason-Dixon Line and east of the Mississippi."

"That may be tr—"

"And you're alive and safe."

She couldn't argue with that.

"So be joyful!" Poppy practically shouted, and extended her sizable arms.

Then Kate did laugh. How could she not? "I'm going to try," she assured the other woman, heading to the door. "I'll give you my phone on your way out. In the meantime, I guess I'll go see what the warden suggests for lunch."

Poppy stopped her with a large hand held up in the air.

"Sorry, I mean Benjamin, my ever-faithful bodyguard." She winked at Poppy. "See? Joyous."

The hand became a single finger pointing up and down Kate's body. "That's not very many clothes, Miss Mathilda."

Okay, now she *was* going to swear, because it would hurt when she pulled out her own hair from the roots in abject frustration.

Instead, Kate lowered her voice and reached for the icy demeanor she hoped she'd exhibit in the courtroom...if she ever passed the damn bar exam.

"It's very hot outside," she managed to say through only a slightly clenched jaw. "And I realize that I'm here under bizarre and mitigating circumstances, which, I might add, continue to get stranger and more palliative with each passing moment, but I don't need your guidance on my wardrobe decisions."

The other woman crossed her arms and let her generous lower lip protrude a bit. "He's a man," she finally said.

"Yes, I noticed." Maybe more than she wanted to.

"And these are mighty tight quarters."

An old fire shot up her back and seared her brain, making Kate lean closer and stare down Poppy, because this conversation just went from amusing to annoying and was headed straight to a full-blown argument and dismissal.

"Are you suggesting I adjust the way I dress so as not to *tempt* him? Forget the fact that he is ostensibly here to protect me. What's most infuriating about that is...is..." Was it possible this woman was just out of touch with culture so much that she didn't know any better? She cleared her throat and tamped down her resentment. Instead of chastising Poppy, she should educate her. "There's an expression for what you're saying, Poppy, and I bet it won't pass your language standards."

Her frown deepened. "Well, based on the way you talk, I'm figuring that's a big, long expression with a whole lot of hard to understand words."

"Just two. Slut-shaming," Kate said softly. "And you're doing it when you blame a man's inappropriate behavior or thoughts on the way a woman dresses." She paused to let that sink in. "And it's wrong."

The other woman inched back, searching Kate's features as though trying to see behind the façade. "You'll make a good lawyer," she finally said.

"Thank you." Kate tipped her head in the general direction of her law books. "But I have to pass the bar first."

Poppy stepped aside and let her walk by with a look on her face that said Kate had won a round today, finally.

At midnight, after an evening of managing to stay out of her way to do his job, Alec put down the book he'd been reading and pushed up from the sofa, where, with the patio lights on, he could see the front entrance and the doors to her room. That wouldn't work for overnight, but he had to give Kate some privacy.

She'd gone to her room hours earlier—with a bottle of wine and one glass—but had not shut the door, and her light was still on.

He walked through the vestibule—he'd never forget that one—that led to the bedroom and cleared his throat loudly.

"You can come in, Leo."

He reached the open door to find her sitting in bed, under the covers, surrounded by books, wine in one hand, a pen in the other.

"Leo?" he asked.

"Tolstoy."

He couldn't help smiling. "Sorry, no."

She took a healthy sip of wine and set the glass on the nightstand next to her. "You're here for the sofa?"

"I can't think of any other way," he admitted. "If I'm outside, I have a clear view of your doors, but we'd have to leave the patio lights on all night, and I assume that would annoy you."

"So does someone sleeping in my room."

"This is the best arrangement. I'm close to you if anyone breaks in."

She made a face at that. "What if they want you and not me?"

Fair question. "Either way, I'll kill them."

He saw her tense at that. "Have you?" she asked. "Killed anyone?"

He ignored the question and lifted his chin toward her books. "How late are you going to study?"

"Forever," she said on a long sigh, but flipped one of the textbooks closed. "I have a lot to learn. You can come in."

He accepted the invitation, entering slowly. "I saw a

quote once that said the amount of time you spend focused on something is directly related to how important it is to you." He'd applied that quote to martial arts in general and jiu-jitsu in particular.

"This"—she swept her hand over two textbooks the size of dictionaries—"is my ticket to independence and security and self-reliance. It represents everything I want most in the world."

Sitting on the love seat tucked into the bay window near the French doors, he considered the sincerity of her confession. It took a lot to come right out and say what you wanted most, and he respected her for it.

"How many hours do you have to study to pass this test?"

"More like months, not hours." She stacked the books on top of each other, making him think she might be done for the night after all. "I've been out of law school for more than five years, so my legal brain is kind of rusty. I have to do considerably more work than the average *Juris Doctor* graduate."

"What took you so long to take the bar?" he asked. "Isn't that something you do right away when you finish law school?"

She didn't answer right away, instead letting the books hit the floor with a noisy clunk. "If I share personal information, then you have to...Nikolai."

"Nope."

"Rudolf? You know, like—"

"Nureyev. Got it, but no, not Rudolf." He smiled at her. "You're going to run out of famous Russians soon."

"With all that literature and history?" She reached over and got her glass, settling back into a mountain of pillows like royalty gazing on a subject. She was a little like royalty to him—a judge's daughter who went to Yale being watched over by the son of a butcher, an MMA trainer who didn't even finish a year of college.

"But your name *is* Russian, right?" she asked.

Don't tell her anything about yourself. He could still hear Gabe's warning, but it was fading. *And don't lay a hand on her except in public.*

"Come on," she said in a teasing voice, tapping the side of her wine glass impatiently. "Break the rules and tell me something."

He didn't answer, but could practically taste how much it mattered to her. Probably the lawyer in her who wanted to know everything. "No. It's not safe. It's best if you know nothing about me."

"You know I'll just guess. People's pasts aren't that hard to figure out. I was just studying a section on jury selection, and that's part of the process."

He barely reacted, keeping his face as expressionless as he did in a fight, never giving away his fear. Fear? He blinked as that word hit his brain. Was he afraid of her?

"How could we possibly be cooped up in this little house and stay silent or lie?" she asked, sounding more relaxed than since she'd arrived. Must be the wine.

"We have to."

She took a deep drink as if she needed to fortify herself. "Don't *have* to do a thing." She set the glass on the nightstand and fluffed her comforter a bit. "Would you like to know the reason I didn't take the bar?" Before he could tell her no, she leaned forward. "Because I wasn't *allowed* to." She drew out the word allowed, her dislike for the idea pretty obvious. "My husband believed a woman's place was on his arm, not in the courtroom."

"And you stood for that?" He found it impossible to

believe this spitfire would last with a guy like that for five minutes, let alone five years.

"I not only stood for it, I lay down and practically had 'welcome' stamped across my forehead I was such a doormat."

He frowned, utterly intrigued and wishing he weren't. "Why?"

She chewed on the inside of her lip, thinking before she answered. "He had a certain power over me," she admitted softly. "And, honestly, I spent most of my life under the thumb of a strong man, so it was like..." She stopped and gave a quick, dry laugh as if she caught herself. "Okay, that's enough from me. It's your turn, Dr. Zhivago." She squished up her pretty features in uncertainty. "I honestly don't know his first name."

He laughed at her game, taking a moment to appreciate how she looked in bed, her thick hair tumbling over her shoulders, her expression softened by the late hour and a few glasses of wine. Good, that's how she looked. Hot and sexy and soft and smart, all rolled into one green-eyed, auburn-haired beauty in bed.

"Yuri," he finally said. "Yuri Zhivago."

"Yuri? Oh, that's a good one. But not your name, I take it."

"No, but it could be. My dad loved that movie." He tensed at the admission, which had rolled out way too easily, with no wine for an excuse.

"Oh, let me guess." She sat up again, letting more hair fall over her face and revealing that she wore a thin tank top. He forced his gaze to stay on her face, but it wasn't easy. He wanted to look at her. He wanted to...do a lot of things he shouldn't even think about.

"He was born in Mother Russia," she said.

How the hell did she know that? "But I wasn't." For some reason, it was important that she know that. He was as American as she.

She narrowed her eyes at him. "Brighton Beach?"

Son of a bitch, she was smart.

At his expression of defeat, she gave a fist pump. "Got it."

"Kate, please." Though his childhood home wasn't that much personal information; it was a good guess. Most people knew about the huge Russian population in Brighton Beach—but how many knew about the mob activity? "So your dad kept you under his thumb?" he asked quickly, hoping to change the subject.

"Were you in trouble with the law? Dealing drugs? Do you owe someone a lot of money? Is it a woman?" She snapped her fingers. "You got involved with someone's wife and he wants to—"

"Stop it!"

She startled at the exclamation. "How bad can it be?"

"Don't," he said through ground teeth.

"Don't what? Be cavalier?"

"I don't even know what that means, but yeah. Don't treat this situation lightly."

She fell back on her pillows, sighing as she reached over and turned off the light, dousing the room in unexpected darkness. Neither of them spoke for a moment, but he heard her sheets rustle and imagined her sliding over the expensive cotton. Oh, fuck, it was going to be a long night.

"You didn't answer my other question," she said softly.

He frowned as he turned on the love seat and tried to get comfortable, but his legs hung off, and the armrest was hard. Damn it. "The witness is off the stand for the night. No more questions."

"Have you ever killed anyone?"

She wouldn't like the truth, but he really hated to lie. And, hell, she asked for it. Maybe she'd lay off if she didn't like the answers. "I have."

He heard her soft intake of breath, then the sound of her moving again. Turning over, fluffing the down pillow. Great. Now she thought he was a murderer. He'd mentioned he'd been in the Marines. Wouldn't she have expected him to kill the enemy on the field of battle?

No, she was probably thinking of real murder. And he had to let that go. It endangered her to know anything about him, and he'd already said too much.

The darkness pressed, but Alec kept his eyes open, determined to stay awake at least as long as she did. He'd never get into a deep sleep on this thing, which was good.

He heard her sigh one more time, not as deeply, maybe inching toward slumber. He looked into the darkness, but pictured her body in the bed he'd been sleeping in for weeks, her long legs, her narrow waist, her breasts rising and falling with each breath. He imagined that thin tank top and her hair spilling across the pillow, her eyes closed. What would it be like to kiss her?

He'd never been with a woman like her, that was for sure. He wasn't even close to worthy of a woman so…perfect. She was as flawless as he was flawed.

"Alex?"

"Yeah?"

She shot up and turned on the light, and immediately he realized his mistake. "That's it, isn't it?" Her eyes were bright with victory, her mouth open in a little O of happiness. "I had a Russian friend in college named Aleksandr, and he went by Alex." She even pronounced the Russian version exactly right. Aleksandr. "Am I right?"

So, so right. He didn't even bother to sit up. Why fight or lie or dig himself in any deeper?

"Good night, *Alex*."

Damn it. "Alec," he replied. "I go by Alec."

She beamed at him. "That's the perfect name for you."

He had to laugh. "You're going to be a helluva lawyer, Kate."

She dropped back on the bed. "You bet I am." Satisfied, she turned out the light again, and almost immediately, he could hear her breathe with the steadiness of sleep. Shit, that woman liked control.

He wanted to be furious, or worried, or make her promise to never use the name, but something about her knowing his real name felt good. Too good.

Chapter Seven

The next day, sitting poolside, Kate turned the page of the sample contract, her eyes glazing over. She'd spent the morning on evidence and torts and couldn't put off the contract section of the practice test any longer. It was a waste of time, of course. She'd no sooner be a contracts attorney than she'd be a farmer. That was how much she hated that aspect of the law.

She picked up the phone that Poppy had given her to check the time. And procrastinate. She knew she shouldn't log into any of her social media, but couldn't she find some kind of back door or open a fake account, so she could just check on her world? It took about fifteen seconds to create a Twitter account under the name TCarlson, and not much longer to use the account to see what was up with some of her friends.

Well, Laurie Geise was up to bar hopping, it would seem, based on the picture she'd posted with a cute guy on her arm. Who was that? He seemed vaguely familiar. Glancing inside, she didn't see Alec—whose name now settled on her brain as just right. She knew he'd be watching her, but he seemed to let her stay alone on the patio, though he certainly could see her from inside.

Surely she could make a phone call to her closest friend if she didn't tell her anything, right? She didn't have to ask permission to call a girlfriend. Anyway, Laurie already knew Kate had left town for a study vacation. No doubt she'd have called Kate a few times by now and it would just be weird if Kate didn't call her.

Rationalization firmly in place, she dialed Laurie's number from memory, and the phone was answered on the first ring. "This is Laurie Ann Giese!" Ever the PR professional, even her greeting was enthusiastic.

"Hey, girl."

"Katie! I've been trying to reach you!"

As she suspected. This was definitely the right thing to do. "Sorry, lost my phone."

"That explains this blocked number."

No, it didn't. But she wasn't about to tell Laurie any of what was going on. "Yep, it's me, checking in from paradise," Kate said, happily abandoning contract law to lean back and let the sun hit her face and her friend's voice hit her ears.

"Where did you end up going? I know you weren't exactly sure when you left, which, by the way, was so unlike you."

Swallowing a little guilt, Kate said, "I'm on an island."

"Narrows it right down." Laurie laughed. "Caribbean?"

"Florida," she replied. "Who's the hottie I saw you with on Twitter?"

"Oh my God, Kate, I've been dying to tell you about him." Fortunately, the subject change worked as she could practically hear Laurie settle in for a chat. "His name's Mike Wesley. He's a lawyer, totally hot."

Mike Wesley? "Oh, I know who he is," Kate said, flipping through mental files and remembering the guy

65

clearly. "He's one of the few attorneys to beat Steven in the courtroom." And Steven hated him, which was a point in Laurie's new boyfriend's favor. "How'd you meet him?"

"Starbucks. He was in front of me in line two days ago, and he paid for my coffee because they were having one of those 'buy the stranger behind you coffee' things going on. We just started talking, and then we had lunch, and last night we went out for a drink. That's when I snagged the picture."

"Whoa, moving fast."

"I know, right? Dinner date is next." Her voice rose with pent-up excitement. "I really like him. He's thirty-five and single."

"You hope."

Laurie grunted. "No shit. That is never going to happen to me again, Kate."

"It won't." Kate eyed the pool, the beating sun tempting her to at least slip her feet into the water. "I'm glad you're getting back into the saddle."

"Well, you know. Once burned, twice shy," she said, referring to her deepest, darkest secret—the fact that she'd inadvertently been involved with a married man. "I swear I held his hand up to the light to look for a tan line on his ring finger. I never want to make that mistake again."

Kate stood and walked to the side of the pool, dipping her toe in cool water. "So what's he like?"

"Funny, kind, and sweet. He has a place in North Carolina on the water, too, so maybe my own beach vacation is in the not-too-distant future."

"Nice. What kind of law does he practice?"

"Not exactly sure, but he's very close to making partner and he's very driven. Ugh, I guess that sounds too familiar to you."

Kate laughed, sitting on the brick pavers to get wet up to

her knees, the water heavenly. "Don't judge all attorneys and partners by my crappy experience. There are plenty of good ones, and it sounds like you found one."

"From your lips, baby. Where are you staying? A house or hotel or what?"

"With friends." She hated to lie, but...

He wants to rape the shit out of you.

She wasn't going to be stupid. What if Laurie slipped and told someone where she was? It would be like Laurie to befriend a stranger hanging around the apartment complex and suddenly spill. She was too friendly. "I'm in a villa," Kate added, feeling the need to elaborate. "But getting a ton of work done. Buried in contracts right now."

"You'll kill it, Kate. Nothing for you to worry about."

"Like you said, from your lips. It's a lot of work, but most of it is coming back to me." She splashed the water, feeling relaxed for the first time since she arrived. "What else are you up to while I'm killing myself under the palm trees in Florida?"

"Trying to put together a pitch for a new—"

"What the hell are you doing?"

Kate whipped around at the sound of the harsh, furious voice, half-expecting to see her ex-husband standing there. He was the last man to talk to her that way.

"I'm on the phone," she said icily as she met a cold, blue stare.

"Get off."

"Who are you talking to?" Laurie asked.

"One of the people I'm staying with," she said, making Alec's eyes spark with anger. "I need to go, Laurie."

"Kate, are you okay?"

"Yes, yes, of course. I'm fine." But she knew that Laurie was a good enough friend to sense the tension in Kate's voice. "Really, I just have to go now. Something came up."

"Something or someone?" Laurie asked. "Are you with a *guy* down there? Girl, no wonder you're being so evasive."

"No, no. I'm studying, I swear."

Laurie laughed softly, not buying it, but the sound was lost on Kate as Alec came closer, looking like he might yank the phone right out of her hand.

"I'll call you later," Kate said. "Have fun with your new guy."

"Have fun with yours." The implication was loud and clear and wrong. But there was no way to correct her now. Not with Godzilla bearing down on her.

Kate clicked off the call and crossed her arms, tucking the phone near her chest as if daring him to try to take it.

"What the hell are you doing, Kate?" he demanded.

"Talking on the phone with my trusted friend, and I didn't say where I was."

"You don't have to, and you're smart enough to know people can have tracking software to find you."

She let out a grunt. Tracking software? If her stalker was some kind of tech guru, why would he *write* notes? "Poppy gave me that phone and my name isn't even associated with it. Isn't the whole idea that it is *untrackable*?"

"You have to be careful."

The relaxation of the moment completely gone, and the sense of being totally and completely trapped nearly suffocating her again, Kate pushed up and shook off her wet feet.

"I have to get out of here." Where could she possibly go that he wouldn't follow her? "I'm going over to the spa to get a massage."

He looked at her like she said she was going to Mars, and the possibility was just as likely. "Fine, but I'll be in the room with you."

She looked to the sky. "Then I want to walk the beach or have lunch or see the resort. I'm going stir crazy."

"Fine. We'll go. Just remember the rules of the cover."

"Gah! Rules! I hate these stinkin' rules." She pushed past him, fury shooting through her. "The killer has rules," she muttered.

He stepped to the side and blocked her way, glaring down at her, so close she could count the navy flecks in his eyes even though they tapered in disgust.

Disgust? He had a lot of nerve.

"You don't have all the facts, counselor."

"I have enough." She wanted to turn away, wanted to do a nice pivot to a dramatic exit, but he held her with just the power of his look.

"I was in the Marines. In war. The men I killed were terrorists, insurgents, and jihadists. I killed them to save my comrades."

She stared at him. "I assumed…"

"The worst," he supplied.

For some reason, some indescribably bizarre reason, that nearly folded her heart in half. She *had* assumed he was some kind of hardened killer, not a hero. "I'm sorry," she said, hoping her voice conveyed that she really meant it.

"What you need to be sorry for is calling a friend."

"I didn't tell her where I was."

"Florida?" he challenged.

"It's a big state," she said.

"An island?"

"You were listening?"

"The door was partly open."

Huffing out a breath, she stepped away. "I'm taking a walk around the resort."

He put his hand on her shoulder, a huge, hot, masculine hand that tripled her pulse the moment he touched her.

"You're not going anywhere without your husband, Tilly."

She narrowed her eyes at him, ire rising at the all-too-familiar feeling of having lost a fight to a stronger man. "Then get some shoes on, because I'm leaving in thirty seconds, *Benjamin*."

Alec kept his left arm around Kate, his right hand in his pocket, scanning the resort grounds from under a ball cap and behind sunglasses, hoping he looked like a groom on his honeymoon and not a bodyguard on high alert.

Venturing out for the first time since he'd stepped foot on the resort was a strange sensation, but holding a woman possessively—a beautiful woman who seemed to shiver when he touched her—was beyond strange. Even though he suspected the physical was more because she would rather be anywhere, with anyone, than here with him, taking ownership of her felt...different. Good, even.

"So, where did you fight?"

He glanced down at her, not sure if she meant martial arts or the war. "No," he said quietly, leaning closer. "Tilly and Benjamin Carlson, remember?"

"Oh, yeah." She sighed, looking at the beach as they meandered down the path. "That's the main building?" She pointed to a three-story structure with wide columns and high archways and sharp-looking doormen all around.

"According to the pamphlet in the villa, that's the lobby and stores, plus a spa called Eucalyptus and a restaurant,

Junonia, which is apparently named after a rare seashell you can find here. Behind it is a pool and deck overlooking the beach."

She laughed softly. "You really did study that pamphlet."

"Out of sheer boredom."

"And you didn't come over here to see it all?"

He shook his head. "I couldn't be seen without you three weeks before we got here for our honeymoon. I did run a few times at dawn or after nightfall, but I haven't ventured into the hotel or restaurant. Nowhere in daylight."

"Like a good nocturnal animal."

"Like a rat," he agreed.

She glanced up at him. "Hey, I really am sorry about before. About the phone call and making assumptions about your past."

"S'okay." Then he smiled. "Is this your version of tapping out?"

"What is that?"

He patted her shoulder three times. "Tapping the mat or your opponent is how you signal that you've had enough and don't want to fight anymore. Though some bastards like to get one last yank on an elbow or knee in a direction nature didn't intend."

She curled her lip. "Has that happened to you?"

"Rarely," he said. "But that's because I'm a trainer, not a…" He closed his eyes, realizing how easily she got him to talk about things he didn't want to, and shouldn't. Not to mention they were supposed to be honeymooners. "You don't follow orders very well, do you?"

She let their footsteps fall into sync as they neared the end of the path and reached a little wooden bridge, one of several that crossed from the walkway over sea oats to the wide-open white sands of the bay.

"It's not that I can't," she finally said. "It's that I've followed orders for so long that I don't want to anymore."

He thought about that, pretending to take in the water view, but really thinking about why a strong and brilliant woman would let herself be pushed around.

"My dad is overbearing, as you might have guessed."

"And your mother?"

She sighed. "Lost her when I was fifteen."

He felt the tug of sympathy, knowing the pain so well. "I was thirteen when my dad died." The words were out before he even knew he said them.

She nodded, as if she understood, too.

"He had cancer," he added, hating that he couldn't seem to stop himself from confiding in her, which broke the first rule. Doing it outside of the villa broke the second rule. Not caring about breaking rules was probably the third of Gabe's rules he was smashing. "Your mom?"

"Car accident," she said, looking out to the water. "I was driving the car."

"Oh, man." It was the pain in her voice that twisted his gut, much more than the history she was sharing. "That sucks."

She sighed and feigned a smile. "Sure does. I was on my learner's permit and made the stupidest of rookie errors, a blind left turn and…" She closed her eyes and swallowed hard. "Long story short, I'll never forgive myself for making that turn that killed her, and turning my dad into the most overprotective parent on the planet. He practically threw me into the arms of one of the top criminal defense attorneys in Boston. He saw Steven as another man to ensure I don't make bad left turns in life."

No wonder she hated this situation. He squinted into the sunlight pouring over the creamy building, glinting off some bright blue square tiles.

"You want to know something interesting?" he asked.

She looked up at him, either studying his face or her own reflection in his sunglasses, but didn't answer, so he decided to tell her anyway.

"A couple built this resort."

As he'd hoped it would, that made her smile. "You really power-studied that brochure. I might need some tips for torts."

He laughed, guiding her toward the grand entrance of the hotel. "She owned all the property and grew up on this island, and lived in a little house right over there somewhere. About six years ago, a hurricane blew it down, and she spent the night in the bathtub with her teenage daughter."

"Get out!" She leaned back, her jaw loose. "That can't be true."

"No, it is." He felt a weird satisfaction that he'd taken her mind off her sadness. "After the storm, she decided to build a bed-and-breakfast-type place, but the architect she hired came up with this whole high-end resort idea. And then she married him."

"Really?"

"Some friends of hers invested in the place, and they all work here, and it's grown massive and successful, with corporate investors now. They named it Casa Blanca after their favorite movie."

She let out a sweet laugh. "That is a great story."

"Or they made the whole thing up to get more people to come here, I don't know."

"A made-up marriage?" she asked as he held a heavy glass door open for her. "Lots of that going around, I hear."

He shot her a warning look as they walked into the cool of the lobby, pausing to take in the long marble floor and Middle Eastern-looking rug hanging on one wall. But he no sooner saw the decoration, than he spotted a small crowd in the middle, and cameras flashing all around.

"What's going on?" Kate asked, trying to break free to get closer to the action.

He kept close to her as the small group of people approached, surrounding a tall man holding hands with a woman and a young boy.

"Let us through, please," the man said with an air of authority. "Please let my son through."

"Nate, are you staying here?" one asked.

"Let me get a picture," another called.

"Are you no longer naughty, Nate?" A woman held up her phone to get a shot over the crowd, the lens pointed directly at Alec. He tried to dodge the picture, but Kate's full attention was on the cause of the commotion.

"Oh, that's Nate Ivory," she said, moving closer. "You were right about him being on this island. That must be the woman he's marrying and her little boy he's adopting."

Alec tried to unobtrusively lead her away from the crowd and cameras, way more concerned about not getting his picture taken than some guy who was born with a silver spoon in his mouth fending off fans at a resort.

"Come on, Tilly."

"Wait, I have to get a picture. My friend Laurie is crazy about him." She searched for her phone just as the other woman got even closer with hers, forcing Alec to reach out and snag Kate to get her out of the picture, drawing some attention from the people standing next to them.

"You don't need to gawk at him, honey," he said, loud enough for them to hear. "Come on." She must have heard the determination in his voice, and maybe realized the situation they were in, because she instantly backed away and took his hand, as if she just remembered she was a cover, too. She tucked his tattooed fingers between her two hands and smiled up at him.

"You're right. You're the only man for me." She let him steer her away from the crowd as it dissipated when the celebrity family escaped out the front door to a waiting black SUV.

"Do you really need to look around anymore?" Alec asked when they were finally alone. "'Cause this place is crawling with people and cameras."

She shook her head, resignation and disappointment on her face. "No, let's just go back to the villa. I'm going to pass that contract practice test if it kills me."

"It won't." He leaned into her ear to whisper, "But if someone snags your picture"—or *his*—"it *could* kill you." Or him.

Thankfully, she didn't argue.

Chapter Eight

Taking the long commute of about fifty steps from the bungalow he called home to the one where he had an office, Gabriel Rossi was already a little itchy for progress. But he'd been restless since he'd arrived in this particular ass-end of space.

Restless for progress on something that he simply couldn't control.

Not his business, though. That was humming along, with two clients in the system. He still believed that the concept of his operation—helping people who didn't qualify for witness protection but needed to get off the grid either permanently or for a while—was brilliant, and would be lucrative.

And his guise that he worked as a freelance consultant to McBain Security, Inc. was perfect. He even liked that the resort had stashed all the outsourced functions like security, housekeeping, and excursions in a cul-de-sac of beachy bungalows that hugged the eastern edge of the Casa Blanca property.

Five of the cottages had been transformed into offices, save one, which was the comfy two-bedroom bachelor pad he was sharing with Nino. Those digs faced a sizable farmette that fed the resort, where Nino had already made friends with the head gardener and her three kids.

In fact, Nino had made friends with everyone, Gabe thought, as he unlocked his office door. He knew the change would be good for the old man, who got up every morning and put on a crisp white shirt and long pants, then went over to his cubicle at McBain Security, Inc. and did the administrative tasks Gabe gave him. He quit at noon, stopped by the break room so the ladies in the housekeeping department could coo over whatever he brought them to eat, then spent the afternoons digging in the dirt.

Shit, Nino had more to do than Gabe these days. But Gabe had to be patient...and continue his "project" behind the closed doors of the small private office Luke McBain had given him.

Which was exactly what he was doing today, taking out a non-traceable cell phone to make the call he'd scheduled a week ago. The bastard on the other end better answer, especially after making Gabe wait so long.

He did, with a gruff hello.

"How are you, Agent Drummand?" Gabe asked, purposely sucking up by using the formal title even though they'd once been acquaintances and colleagues. Never friends.

"Same as I was last time you came sniffin' around a year ago, Rossi. Nothing's changed."

Gabe swallowed a smartass retort, knowing this dicknose didn't even have enough of a sense of humor to appreciate a joke. "Everything's changed," Gabe said. "Cuba's open."

"Not as wide as your mama's legs, but yeah, Cuba's opening. Slowly. Not the US Embassy, though." A long pause and soft snort. "And not to you."

"What would happen if I showed up?" he asked.

"Well, let's see..." Drummand's voice sang with false playfulness. "Lots of things, Gabe Rossi. And I bet you can guess what they are."

He sure could.

But Drummand was on a roll now. "Let me help you out with some frequently asked questions by former intelligence consultants who didn't play by the rules," he said. "Will you get arrested the minute you step foot on one square inch of Cuba? Likely. Will they be able to find charges that would stick to you like superglue? No, but they will make up a few doozies that will keep you there longer than it takes Fidel Castro to get a hard-on. Will you be treated like a traitor and scumbag fuckwad and given some of that Gitmo juice that makes your ass hurt for the rest of your life? Quite possibly. Will you come out alive? Yes, but you might wish you hadn't."

Gabe closed his eyes, more pissed at himself for thinking it could be easy. The US and Cuba may be loosening their choke holds on each other, but the CIA wasn't letting up on any of its long list of enemies. And that list included Gabe.

"Take my advice and don't be booking the next flight to Havana, Mr. Rossi."

"No worries." He'd have to go about his business another way...his way.

"Listen, Gabe." Drummand lowered his voice. "No one has seen or heard from her for years. I'd bet my ass she managed to get out and is languishing on some Brazilian beach dreaming about those lazy nights in Cuba when you nailed her stupid and silly."

"Shut the fuck up, asswipe."

"Hey, is that any way to talk to the only person in the CIA with the clearance, authority, or remote desire to actually speak to you?"

"It's the only way I talk to you."

"It's always a pleasure to talk to a man who forgot where his bread was buttered. Where are you now? I see you're untraceable." He hacked a laugh. "Are you back in Boston or looking for work with ISIS? Heard they need hotshot former spooks."

Gabe gritted his teeth and didn't respond, as much as it killed him.

Fuck it. He needed this guy. "Any word on Mal?"

Drummand was quiet for a beat too long, then, "Mal's getting out real soon. But then, even you are smart enough to figure that out."

In other words, Drummand wasn't going to share anything of value. Still, Gabe inched forward, thinking of all the implications of Malcolm Harris being released from federal prison. "How soon?"

"Who knows? That mother must be giving blow jobs to sentencing commissioners, because they're letting him serve the rest of his time on house arrest. But don't worry. We'll get him again. One way or another, he'll spend life in prison. We'll be on him like flies on shit, which is what he is."

Gabe closed his eyes, hatred soaring.

"And we'll be on you," Drummand added, "if you so much as breathe on Cuban soil."

"Thanks for the tip."

"Anytime, Rossi. We haven't forgotten you. And we won't." And the connection died.

Gabe dropped the phone and thunked both elbows on his desk, looking up at a tap on the door.

"Gabriel, it's me. Unlock the door."

He stood to let Nino in, hoping the disappointment that grabbed his gut wasn't evident on his face. He could lie about almost anything to anyone...except Nino. He had a hard time lying to the grandfather who'd left his comfortable life and family in Boston to follow Gabe on this adventure.

But it was Nino who looked perturbed. His thin gray hair was mussed, and he plucked at the damp wrinkles of his usually crisp white shirt.

"Does it never cool off down here?" he demanded, walking to the only seat in the office, facing Gabe's desk. The room was sparse, and Gabe liked it that way. He didn't keep files. He shredded them. "Is it November or July?" Nino demanded.

"You don't have to dress up for work, Nino," Gabe said, returning to his own chair. "Shorts, commando, and T-shirt are all you need in this joint."

Nino scowled. "I told you I don't work in dungarees or those flipper-flopper things. When I'm here, I'm working." He adjusted his collar, which, thank God, didn't include a tie. "But I will be taking the afternoon off to help Tessa with the sweet potato harvest on the farm."

"That'll cool you down."

Nino shrugged. "I need to work off some frustrations."

Gabe scowled at him. "What are you frustrated about?"

Nino looked toward the open door and leaned forward to whisper, "I know she's a good woman and I don't really want to kill her, but..."

Gabe blinked, having lost track of what Nino said. "Who are you talking about?"

Nino's eyes widened. "The Jerk Chicken."

"Poppy?" He'd sensed from the beginning that the Jamaican housekeeper's overbearing and opinionated style might clash a little with his not-so-easygoing grandfather, but Gabe figured the two of them were smart enough to work it out. Apparently, no such luck.

"Now what?" Gabe asked.

"I'm just wondering what her exact job is, that's all."

Damn it, he didn't want to do this for a living, but here it was: adult day care.

He sucked in a breath, trying to put himself in Nino Rossi's ancient wing tips. "Look, I know she's a strong personality, but she's my eyes and ears at the resort, Nino. She talks to everyone, knows everything, and can keep me informed about the possibility of a blown cover. I need her out there," he said, thumbing over his shoulder in the general direction of the beach. "People tell her everything, and that's a spy's gift. And someone has to go in that villa where our clients are staying, so she's perfect." Nino's face grew progressively unhappier as Gabe talked. "What is the matter with that?"

Nino shifted in his seat and adjusted his collar again. "Nothing."

"Liar."

"No, no..." He waved a big, gnarled hand. "The last thing you need is bickering employees."

Thank you.

"And I don't want to be one, but that lady..."

"Thinks she knows everything," Gabe supplied.

"Exactly!" Nino slapped his legs loudly. "And after a while, I just want to say, 'Hey, Miss Mama, I got thirty years in the kitchen over you, and I don't give a flying...' Well, you can't say *that* to her, because she'll stick her greedy hand out and make you pay for using a bad—"

"Wait, this is about food?" Gabe shook his head a little, not sure he was following the story.

Nino stared at him. "Of course."

"What the hell are you two talking about food for?"

"Because...that's what I do," Nino said, a little note of disappointment in his voice. Was he disappointed Gabe didn't realize that's *what he did* or because he wasn't *doing* food as much as he used to? He didn't know, but he felt the sadness in Nino's words.

And he'd promised his family Nino would be happy here.

"It isn't all you do anymore," Gabe said. "You did that when you 'worked' for Vivi in Boston. Made lasagna for the staff and biscotti for the break room. But you were unhappy there, remember? Now you have a real job. And come to think of it, I have an assignment for you."

Nino nodded, but Gabe knew the old man well enough to recognize something bubbling under the surface like one of his tangy tomato sauces.

"When do you two talk about food?" Gabe asked.

Nino gave his signature shrug, hands out, Italian-style. "You know, over in the housekeeping bungalow, they have a pretty good kitchen. I pop in and chat with the ladies."

"I know." Nino talked about it every night.

"They love me." He smiled, baring aging teeth and deepening his creases. "Couple of them love you, too, but I'm thinking it's for a whole different reason."

Smiling, Gabe reached for a notepad. "It's impossible to keep you out of a kitchen, isn't it?"

"Why would you want to?" Nino fired back. "Anyway, I can do the work you ask of me and cook and help a little on that farm. I'm very happy here."

"Are you?" God, he wanted him to be happy. Needed him to be happy.

"Except for having to work with her." He stole another look at the door. "Who would even want to eat a piece of fish smothered in that mushy orange fruit?"

What the hell? "Mango?"

"Yeah. Who puts fruit with fish, Gabe? That's not how an Italian does it. And she says Jamaicans know more about fish than Italians."

Gabe tried to care, he really did. But he couldn't muster up a single fuck to give. Nino needed something to get his mind off this crap, and Gabe needed information. He wrote Cuba across the top page. "You know what's going on in Cuba, don't you?"

Nino crossed his arms across his once barrel-like chest. "Oh, I sure do. Now those bastards can cook. They do things with a pig that would bring you to your knees." Nino leaned back, a dreamy smile on his face. "I like a good piece of pork."

"Nino. *Cuba.*"

He straightened up. "Right. Communism and Castro." He frowned. "Isn't he dead yet?"

Gabe rolled his eyes. "No one really knows, but his brother runs the place now, and the restrictions are changing. Americans are going to be allowed to travel there again. I need you to dig around through any means you have and find out exactly what paperwork an American needs to get into that country, all the papers."

Nino nodded, finally focused on the task. "Are you thinking about that as a new home for your Russian boy?"

"Maybe." It could work as a way into the country. "Though I doubt he'd want to go there."

"Does he have a choice about where he goes?" Nino asked.

"I don't want to send him somewhere he'll hate, but—"

"Mr. Gabriel!" Poppy's wide face—and even wider body—filled the doorway.

Instantly, Nino stiffened and stifled a groan.

"Can I come in?" she asked. "I'm afraid we have a problem."

Nino pushed out of his seat, a little too fast. "I'm off to my cubicle to start this high-priority assignment." He waved the paper at Gabe and pointed to the in-box Nino had bought for him when they first moved in because he thought every office should have one. "That pile of crap right there needs—"

"That's a dollar for the Jamaican Children's Fund." Poppy pointed to a glass jar she'd placed on the empty bookshelf against the wall.

"Crap is not a swear word!" Nino and Gabe exclaimed in unison.

"Two more, one for each of you. It counts. It's a C-word, though not as bad as those other two."

Gabe dug into his pocket. "Jeez…"

She scowled at him, rocking her large frame in his direction. "Careful, Mr. Gabriel. My Lord and Savior—"

"Costs ten bucks. I know. I got you covered, Nino." He stuffed a few ones into the jar as his grandfather escaped. "How many nephews you have over there, Poppy?" Gabe asked.

"Three of them, Mr. Gabriel. Isaiah, Ezra, and baby Samuel."

"A veritable Old Testament of orphans," Gabe mused.

"And I mean to get them all over here and educated properly, Mr. Gabriel, since my po' sister went to be with the Almighty last year. Someday, they'll come here and live with me, and take care of me in my old age."

Gabe gave her a look. "If I just paid for all that right now, could I swear at will again?"

"Absolutely not. Then I'd start a fund for some other orphans. There are enough of them in Jamaica." She took the chair that Nino had vacated, spreading her pink housekeeper's skirt around her legs. "Do you want to make that payment now, Mr. Gabriel?"

"Not yet. But did you come in here because you need to tell me something?"

"Oh, yes," she said ominously.

Damn it, if this was another food fight, he might swear enough to cover those kids' tuition for a year. "What's the issue, Poppy?" he asked, congratulating himself on not asking about the *fucking* issue. That would have set him back another five bucks.

"That young couple in your villa."

That got his attention. He might not like the bickering of his only employees, but he did need to make a go of this business, and successfully hiding those two clients was a big part of that. "What about them?"

"People are talking about them."

"And by people, you mean..."

"The staff. And some guests."

It had been only a few days, so this could be either good news or bad news. "What are they saying?"

"Well, I heard one of the other maids saying she saw them walking back from the lobby yesterday and they were hardly speaking. So of course she started a rumor that they're fighting."

"Because every couple who walks through the lobby is engaged in animated conversation?"

She shook her head. "Not just that, but somebody said that while they were there, he got a little, I don't know, firm with her."

"Because there were cameras around, and they shouldn't have been there. I already know about this." Alec had texted him and told him within hours of the event.

"But maybe if they get out and play the happy couple, it would end those rumors," Poppy suggested.

He'd bet the thirty bucks that was already in the Swearing Jar that she wasn't wrong very often about anything, which was why he needed her on his team.

85

"Okay, I'll talk to them." He picked up his phone to send Alec a text. "Oh, and Poppy?" he asked as she stood.

"Yes, Mr. Gabriel?"

"You should steer clear of food discussions with my grandfather. It gets him, you know, riled up."

She narrowed her big brown eyes at him. "He's obstinate."

"In other news, birds fly."

"And thinks he's the only person who ever knew how to cook."

"Because, in my family, that was true."

"He's closed-minded, and I don't cotton to that."

He looked up from the text he was sending. "He's in his eighties, Popcorn. Don't try to change him."

She lifted a brow. "That a challenge, Mr. Gabriel?"

"That's an order."

But she sashayed out of the office like a woman who'd just been double-dog dared and was on her way out to think of every possible way she could make Nino Rossi's life hell until he changed. Obviously, the woman never met a stubborn Italian man before. Or else she wouldn't even bother to try.

Chapter Nine

Kate came out of a deep sleep with a sudden jolt, her eyes popping open with the sensation that she was being watched. But his little love seat was empty already.

She should be used to that by now. Alec generally had gone to sleep after she did and gotten up before she did during these four days in prison.

Blinking into the morning light, she closed her eyes and drifted over their time together, which had fallen into a simple rhythm. Mostly, she managed to kind of sidestep him, studying for most of her waking hours, though she knew he was always around. She'd taken to making her own little meals, even though he'd cooked dinner the night before, and it had smelled wonderful. She'd made a sandwich and drank a couple—maybe a few couples—glasses of wine.

She just couldn't spend that much time with him, because every time he was near…

He *affected* her.

There it was. The truth. The cold, hard truth she'd been trying to silence, but simply couldn't ignore anymore.

She sat up, the cool Egyptian cotton sliding over her sleep pants and tank top. She'd closed the translucent shades over the French doors and windows, so there was enough light to see around the room, but she couldn't see the outdoors. The whole villa seemed quiet, as it usually did.

Like it would be if she were alone. Which was all she'd wanted when she headed down here. And now? Did she want to be alone now?

Closing her eyes, she let the question fall around her heart. Of course she was dying for solitude. The intrusion of a bodyguard and violation of her privacy were nothing less than infuriating.

But every time she looked at him…

She bit her lip, thinking of his rough face, his huge muscles, his oversized, scarred, tattooed hand. His face was not handsome, his features not even close to conventionally attractive. Everything about him was rugged and harsh, nothing like the men she'd spent her life checking out.

They all seemed like pretty, delicate flowers compared to Alec. And she did find herself looking at him whenever he was near. Looking and…feeling.

But the slightest amount of conversation got ice from him. A little bit of eye contact, and he couldn't look away fast enough. And that was fine. Except, when she woke up in the middle of the night and wondered if he was awake…a few feet away…so close.

So close she could—

She threw the covers back and sat up at the thought. What the hell was wrong with her? Other than all those years of living in a loveless relationship and self-imposed celibacy had obviously gone on a little bit too long.

Just then, she heard a noise on the patio. She'd seen him out there every morning now, doing his yoga moves and martial arts kicks. She usually managed to look for just a moment, then turn away. Okay, a *long* moment.

It was quite a sight.

Stepping out of bed, she padded over the cool hardwood to the French doors, moving the sheer covering barely a centimeter.

He was in his gi and loose pants, his torso cut by a black belt that quietly advertised his competence in the sport. The pants were just short enough to reveal strong ankles and big, bare feet. The jacket pulled across his sizable shoulders, open enough to show the breadth of his chest, a blend of honed muscles, a dusting of hair, and the curved edge of a swirling tattoo.

His foot shot up, his leg parallel to the ground, then he spun in a one-eighty turn before withdrawing the kick. Instantly, that was followed by hand movements, sharp, snapping, furious, and fast. The next kick went as high as his head, straight up, then he sliced his leg down and whirled around, as graceful as a damn jaguar.

She could practically hear the air crackling with each smooth move and could only imagine the pain if one hit an actual target.

No, not pain. Anyone on the receiving end of those feet and hands would die…instantly.

He paused for a moment, letting his hands fall to his sides, his body completely motionless. His chest didn't even rise and fall with a breath. He closed his eyes, or at least cast them down, then folded to the ground, rolling on one hip, then the other, his legs twisting until he jumped back up in one move.

Then he did that again, on the other hip. And about five more times, supporting his whole bodyweight with just his arms. No wonder they were huge.

When he was finished, he stripped off the jacket and stood, bare-chested, in the sun.

Whoa, that was a glorious view. He turned so she could see only his back, her gaze following the lines of his shoulders, the curve of his back muscles painted with a swirl of ink. All of it narrowed into a trim waist. And that ass.

He might not be breathing heavily, but Kate could feel trapped air tighten her chest as she stared. Her heart rate kicked as high as his deadly foot, her hand clenched into a fist at her side. Her blood simmered, heating up sensitive nerves that made her tingle and tighten and tense with arousal.

Great. Now she was a regular Peeping Kate, getting turned on like some kind of creepy voyeur.

And then, he stripped off his pants in one smooth, sexy, satisfying yank and kick. And there he stood, buck naked in the sunshine, just about the most mouth-wateringly desirable specimen of man she'd ever seen. How could she possibly look away?

His legs were like tree trunks, his backside like something Michelangelo had carved out of marble.

Turn around, some evil voice whispered in her head. Him or her? Who was this devil talking to?

She *couldn't* turn around…but he did. And everything in Kate that made her a woman melted in a pool of craving.

Now *that* was a work of art. Before she had more than a second to stare at the nest of dark hair and the thick shaft that raised up out of it, he dove into the pool, barely making a splash.

And Kate finally stepped away from the window. Well, wobbled away.

Pressing her hands against inflamed cheeks, she swore under her breath, closing her eyes to get the image of his hard body out of her head. But it was there, burned forever, teasing and torturing and tempting her.

Oh, God, she *had* to get under control. She was stronger than this, better than this, bigger than this.

Speaking of big…

"Oh!" She fisted her hands. "Get a grip, Katherine Louise Kingston. Get a friggin' *grip*."

She wanted a grip. Of that.

She marched into the bathroom to drown her face in extra-cold water, burrowing into her soul for some sanity and sense.

Okay, so she was sexually attracted—what a flipping understatement that was—to the man who was supposed to be protecting her. And he clearly had zero interest in reciprocating that attraction; either he didn't feel it, or it was against his bodyguard rules.

But every once in a while, they had to speak to each other or brush by each other or acknowledge each other. And every time that happened, she had this sense that maybe…*maybe* he was feeling the same thing.

If so, he sure was good at hiding it.

She shot up from the last splash of cold water, staring at herself in the mirror. Wasn't it better this way? Why would she invite trouble by—

"Kate? You up yet?"

She startled at the question and the tap on her bedroom door. "Yeah."

"I'm making breakfast if you want eggs."

He'd tried to offer her food before, but she'd turned him down. And now she knew why. It wasn't that she hated the idea of him—well, she *did* hate the idea of a bodyguard. But the more time she spent with him, the more she started imagining things like…his hands on her breasts. His mouth on her—

"Kate? You okay?"

No, damn it. This wasn't okay. And she needed to man up, have breakfast with the guy, and crush these crazy sensations.

"Yes, I'm fine." She went to the door and opened it, hating herself for hoping he was still bare-ass naked. "I would like breakfast, thanks." She was only slightly disappointed to see him back in the baggy pants, a T-shirt clinging to some still-damp muscles. "Thanks."

"And tomato juice," he added. "It's good for a hangover."

"I don't have a hangover."

"You drank a bottle of white wine by yourself last night."

Because nobody would drink with her. She gave a casual shrug and walked by him. "Wine has no effect on me." *Your naked ass, however, made me downright woozy.* "I see your hair is wet. Were you swimming?"

She made sure he couldn't see her face as she continued toward the kitchen, straight to the coffeemaker.

"Poor man's shower," he said, coming in behind her.

"Excuse me?"

"Our accommodations have one shower."

Her jaw loosened. "Ew, you haven't had a shower in four days?"

"I'm clean. I make do."

Swimming naked. "You can use the shower anytime. Well, not..." *When I'm in there. Wait, hell yes, when I'm in there.* She blew out a breath at the direction of her thoughts, frustrated she didn't have better control.

He didn't seem to notice, though, pulling out a frying pan and setting it on the gas cooktop. "I'm afraid that's not a good idea."

Or maybe he *had* read her thoughts. Kate cleared her throat and, hopefully, her mind. "Why not?"

"I can't protect my principal while I'm in the shower."

"Principal? Is that a technical bodyguarding term?"

"That's what you call the person who is under protection."

"Under protection." She slammed the coffeemaker lid a little too hard. "I don't want to be under anything." *Or did she?*

He threw a look over his shoulder. "I don't want to take chances."

Is that why he was so cool to her? "Then what do bodyguards do when they have to shower?"

"Backup," he suggested.

"The ever-stalwart Poppy?"

He chuckled, cracking an egg. "Use what you got. Scrambled okay?"

"Fine. But, listen." She reached out and put a hand on his arm. And he jerked away so fast some of the egg spilled over the side of the bowl.

Wow, he really didn't want her touching him. The realization stung, especially in light of her thoughts of, well, touching. *One-sided, Kate. This attraction is one-sided and the result of a long, long dry spell in the sack.*

She moved away and took the coffee cup that had just brewed, careful not to spill the hot liquid on surprisingly shaky hands.

"Please use my shower," she finally said. "I swear I won't run away or open the door to any strangers." *Or join you.*

"I can't—"

"Alec." She didn't say any more because she wanted him to turn and meet her gaze. She wanted to make and hold eye contact with him. She wanted to force him to acknowledge her as more than just his...*principal.*

He did. And she nearly fell into the depths of the clear blue eyes that met hers.

"You need to shower," she said.

"Pool bath didn't work, huh?" He lifted an arm and pretended to sniff, which was somehow just as sexy as everything else he did that wasn't intended to be sexy but was anyway. "Sorry."

"I'm the one who should be sorry for keeping you out of a shower. Please feel free to take one after breakfast, and I'll..." She tried to think of somewhere that would feel perfectly safe, but he turned and looked at her during the pause, and suddenly nothing felt...safe. "I'll lock all the doors and windows and stay..."

"*I'll* lock all the doors and windows," he said. "And I'll leave the bathroom door open so I can hear you if you need me."

"Okay." She forced herself not to look at his lower half and remember how he'd looked by the pool. Hard. Stiff. *Huge.*

"What did you just say?" he asked.

Oh, God, had she said that out loud? She tried to cover with a sip of coffee.

"You said okay," he reminded her. "I don't think I've ever heard you agree to anything so easily." He gave a hint of a teasing smile, easing her nerves enough that she slipped onto the barstool to watch him cook.

"I admit I don't acquiesce easily."

His shoulders moved with a slight laugh. "Because why use one syllable when fifteen are available?"

"I like big words, so sue me."

"They do roll off your tongue."

She studied him from the back, analyzing the comment. "Does that bother you?" She didn't make him feel stupid, did she?

"I was raised by a..." He caught himself and stopped.

"By a what?"

"I have humble beginnings, Kate. Never got around to much higher education, and a lot of the time, the only thing I heard spoken was Russian."

He stirred the eggs in the pan with a wooden spoon, his left hand adjusting the gas flame to his liking, all of his movements in the kitchen as clean and spare as they had been out on the patio.

What would he be like as a lover?

Oh, Lord. She gulped some coffee as he turned to look at her again. "We're not supposed to do this, you know," he said.

Think about each other as lovers? *Yes, I know.*

"But..." She held his gaze as long as she could, but it was intense and did stupid things to her pulse, so she looked down. "Since we're alone in this villa, I think we can be totally honest with each other and swear on whatever it is you swear on that we will keep each other's secrets."

He'd returned to the eggs, dead silent and still except for the hand working the pan.

"You can tell me who you are, what you do, and why you're here," she continued.

"I can't."

She slapped the counter lightly as frustration rocked through her. "Why not?"

He removed the eggs from the heat, as calm as she was worked up. "Because having that information puts you in a dangerous situation, Kate. It's better if you don't know it."

"Puh-lease," she scoffed. "You don't really think someone is going to try to torture the truth out of me."

Every ounce of humor evaporated from his expression as his features turned hard, cold, and mean. "That is exactly what I think."

Her gaze dropped to his hand again, the one holding the

pan, the one marked with a Russian word. What kind of people would torture her to get to him? What kind of—

"Holy shit." She put her hand up to her mouth, but that didn't hold back the terrifying truth. "The Russian mob."

His whole body, every amazing muscle in it, froze. Without so much as a breath of response, he finished the scrambled eggs and put them on two plates, placing one in front of her with a fork and napkin from a drawer. Each move was spare, silent, and stiff with anger.

"Thanks." She spread the napkin on her lap while he got his own fork, waiting for him to sit next to her. But he made no move to come around the counter and join her. "Am I right?" she asked, pushing him like a reluctant witness in court, certain she was so, so right.

His jaw locked as he gave her a death stare. "Don't do this, Kate. Just...don't."

She lifted up her fork and imagined exactly what she'd do in court. Walk back to her notes. Take a minute to let the obvious answer, however unspoken, burn into the jury's collective conscience.

And try another line of questioning.

After she scooped some eggs, she angled her head and asked, "How long have you been teaching jiu-jitsu?"

He leaned against the counter, holding the plate in one hand, the fork in the other. As she hoped, he visibly relaxed when she changed the subject.

"I'm an MMA trainer, not a jiu-jitsu instructor," he said. "Though that's my strongest discipline. I know enough of all the martial arts to use techniques in training MMA fighters."

"MMA." She sipped her coffee, thinking about what she knew about martial arts. "That's more or less like a wrestling match, right? Only...more violent?"

A hint of a smile pulled. "Much more. And mixed martial

arts is more than wrestling, although wrestling is a big part of it."

Over the rim of her cup, she stole another long look at him, imagining him in some brief, tight, body-hugging shorts going after an opponent in a ring. She hated that kind of stuff, really had no stomach for it at all, but imagining him... Well, she didn't hate that at all.

"And they do this for fun?"

"Guys generally fight for money or titles or placement, if they're pros. MMA is a sport," he said, a thin note of defensiveness in his voice. "It's a legit athletic event with a commission and rules and championships." He defiantly filled his fork and shoved some eggs in his mouth.

"Don't you want to sit down?" she asked, still holding her first bite, uneaten.

"I'll stand."

In other words, I don't want to be that close to you. Kate finally took her bite, ignoring the punch of disappointment or shame or whatever made her feel wretched. And then she powered on.

"Do you fight like that? In a ring with an opponent?" The thought made her stomach tighten a little. He certainly looked like he'd been beaten up a few times.

"I don't compete, no. I have, but I really prefer to use my skills to train. After I got out of the Marines, I opened a school in Philly and..." He closed his eyes and shut himself up. "Man, you're good at that."

"At what?" But, of course, she knew.

"Getting people to tell you things they don't want to. No wonder you want to be a lawyer."

"Thanks."

Chewing another bite, he nodded. "Speaking of, guess you should hit the books soon, huh?"

Couldn't get her out of his sight fast enough, could he? "Thanks for breakfast," she said, slipping off the barstool and taking her plate. "Feel free to take a shower. I won't"— *drop by to watch*—"go anywhere."

"Or let anyone in."

"I promise I won't break a single rule of the ideal principal."

"All right. I'm going to trust you."

She smiled and put her dish in the sink. "Jeez, Alec, that's the nicest thing you ever said to me."

Chapter Ten

Two minutes. That was exactly how long Alec would let himself stay under the hot spray and soap his body. He scrubbed hard, wishing the tiny bar of soap was lye, and not just because he hadn't had a proper shower in days. It was almost like he wanted to scrub off the filth that clung to his life, the stuff that made a lady like her turn her lip up at every word he said and every move he made.

He squeezed his eyes shut and faced the water stream, but he could still see the disgust on her face at the topic of MMA. The light flush of revulsion in her cheeks when she forced herself to touch him, and take pity on him.

The general disdain for him that tinged every word she said.

And, of course, she zeroed right in on the real reason he was here. Guessed his name, fished out his story, and got him to tell more than he would to a person he considered a friend.

And every piece of him made her sick. He could tell by the way she shook a little when he came into her line of sight, how she stared at him when she thought he didn't notice.

Well, shit. In his whole life, he'd never bothered even

acknowledging the existence of a woman like Kate Kingston. After the first twenty-four hours with her, he knew exactly why. He couldn't even look at her for more than two seconds without seeing her recoil. He was ugly, scarred, and broken. She was beautiful, sensitive, and brilliant.

He twisted off the water and instantly heard the sound of...laughter? Was she on the phone again? He pushed open the glass door and heard her talking and...a man answering.

Son of a bitch!

He damn near knocked the door off its hinges, he threw it open so hard, barreling through the bedroom and into the hall, water still sluicing over his body. He charged into the living room to see her holding a huge bouquet of flowers, talking to—

"Uh, hello." Nino Rossi's bushy gray eyebrows lifted as his gaze dropped.

"You opened the door," Alec said to Kate, not caring that she was looking in the same direction, her face turning the color of the red roses in her hands.

"It was Nino."

"You opened the door," he repeated. "We had a..." A deal. A discussion. A *promise*. And she'd screwed him like a dirty opponent executing a finishing hold.

"It was *Nino*," she repeated. "I looked through the..." Her words strangled in her throat as she turned away, as if she couldn't stand to look at his naked body. "Thank you," she said to Nino. "You better go now."

Nino nodded once, shot a weird look at Alec, and backed out the door, closing it.

Kate stayed turned away. "You can get dressed now," she said, her voice strained.

He marched closer to her. "You opened the fucking door,

Kate," he said, hoping the third time it would sink in. "Do you understand now why I cannot confide in you?"

She whipped around, eyes blazing. "Don't ever talk to me that way!" she ordered.

He shook his head, not willing to apologize for his reaction. Instead, he moved an inch forward.

Her gaze dropped, as though she was horrified, but he had to make his point. "You swear to secrecy, you promise you can't be convinced to tell anyone anything, you use your...your talent to pull information out of me. And what's the first thing you do? Open the door after you told me you wouldn't."

"You're naked."

"I'm furious."

She slowly eased the flowers to the side and met his gaze. "I'm going to say this one last time. It was Nino. He's on our side. I didn't tell him anything. He was at the door and told me it was okay to open it."

"What if he'd been telling you that because some motherfucker was behind him with a gun?"

Her eyes flickered with the first real fear he'd seen yet.

"It *is* the mob, isn't it?"

He closed his eyes. "Kate."

"Just tell me."

Water trickled over him, his skin icy cold in the air conditioning and under the chill of her look. "Why do you need to know?" He gave his head a quick shake. "What difference does it make?"

"I want to know who you are," she whispered, the confession soft and surprising.

"I'll tell you who I am," he replied, taking the flowers because it looked like the heavy vase was making her arms quiver. "I'm the guy who has been given your life to protect." He looked for a place to put the flowers. He saw a table a few feet away and set them down, glancing at her and catching her stealing another look at his dick.

And her jaw loosened.

Shit. He was frightening fully clothed. Right now, he probably looked like a fucking caveman.

"And I'm the worst person for that task."

"Why would you say that?"

He looked past her at the door, reaching to snap the dead bolt, making her back up to avoid contact with him. "Never mind," he said, glancing down at his bare body. "And, well, sorry." He started to return to the bathroom, but a warm, slender, unexpected hand landed on his shoulder.

"Why are you sorry?" she whispered. "I broke the only promise I made to you."

He stood stone still, aware—crazy aware—of how close she was and how much it took for her to acknowledge that truth, making her as exposed as he was. And he sure as shit didn't mean the fact that he didn't have pants on.

He didn't answer, but couldn't bring himself to move away from her warm hand. Not quite yet. It was like that hot shower. It felt so damn good.

"Why would you say you're the worst person to protect me? Please tell me the truth."

The truth. She was always seeking it, and he had to hide it. All of it.

"Please tell me, Alec." She was so close, he could feel her breath on his shoulder.

"Let me go, Kate."

Instantly, her hand dropped, leaving his skin cold where it had been so warm.

"Maybe you'll tell me tonight," she said, her voice barely a whisper.

Not likely. "What's tonight?"

"The flowers that were delivered from the hotel came with an invitation to dine tonight as guests of the resort, at Junonia. I guess it's something they do for honeymooners."

Ah, yes. The cover. "We don't have to go."

"I don't think we have a choice," she said. "Nino said we were expected to be there. Gabe's orders."

Fuck Gabe. "Okay, but the only thing we're going to discuss at dinner is the life of Tilly and Benjamin. Not Kate and Alec."

"I can do that," she promised. "You have my word."

He walked away, swallowing the comment that he wanted to make. He'd had her word before his shower, too. He couldn't forget that, no matter how attracted he was to this woman, he couldn't really trust her. That could cost both of them their lives.

"Well, there go my hopes and dreams up in smoke. Nate Ivory really is getting married."

Robyn pulled herself out of the fog that seemed to surround her all the time now. Ever since she'd seen Cole—or had she?—she felt like she had her head in a jar and couldn't think straight. Blinking into the fluorescent lights of the doctor's office, she turned to the only person she considered a friend, a girl she'd worked with at the telemarketing place—until they fired Robin for taking too many sick days.

Selena, who'd dropped out of high school a year earlier, had big dreams of becoming an actress. As always, she was nose-first in her phone, scrolling through some social media site.

"What?" Robyn asked.

She angled her phone for Robyn to look. "I thought it was just a rumor, you know. But he just confirmed he's getting married to some bitch in Florida."

"Mmm." Robyn nodded, so totally not interested in the celebrities that Selena obsessed over. She closed her eyes and put her hand on her stomach. "Do you think they'll do an ultrasound? I have to know if it's a boy or a girl." And then, next time she saw Cole…

Selena didn't answer, making Robyn look to see if she was shooting glares of disapproval or back on the celebrity hunt.

Glares of disapproval.

"What?" Robyn asked. "Wouldn't you want to know?"

"You *know* what I'd have done the minute I missed my period." Selena made no bones about how she thought Robyn should have handled an unwanted pregnancy. Which was fine, that was Selena. Robyn was different.

"It's too late for that," she said under her breath. "Anyway, I want this baby. And what would Cole have said?"

"Maybe he wouldn't have ditched you."

Robyn closed her eyes as the comment hit its mark.

"And I know you think you saw him, but either you imagined it or he's up to no good with that Russian guy. Either way, I think you should forget about him."

She was probably right. Selena had the kind of street smarts Robyn admired and wished she had. Selena wouldn't have let herself get pregnant in the first place.

Whatever. She *was* pregnant, and there was nothing she could do about it except protect this little baby. "I just wish they'd call me back there already."

"She's not even that pretty," Selena said, elbowing

Robyn so she'd look. "I mean, the guy is so freaking hot, and he's a billionaire." She flicked her fingers to zoom in on the image.

"Mmm." It was all Robyn could muster.

"I guess she has nice eyes, but she has a *kid*."

"Oh, and someone wants to marry her. Imagine that."

"Sorry," Selena said. "But she did nail the hottest, richest guy in America. But, I'm telling you, she's not that pretty. How did some chick named Liza Lemanski get him? How?" She shoved her phone in Robyn's face. "It's like there's hope for all of us if she could get him. Look at her, Rob."

Robyn gave up and looked, seeing an attractive woman with pure joy in her eyes. What was it like to be that loved and happy? "She's pretty."

"Not really." Selena flicked at the screen some more, zeroing in on the lady's face, almost cutting out the crowd of gawkers around her. "She kind of looks like me, don't you think? I mean, I'm that pretty, right?"

No, and no. "Her eyes are really stunning."

"But she's not like J-Lo or something. She worked in the County Clerk's office, for fuck's sake."

"Shhh." Robyn put her hand on Selena's arm, glancing at the other, enormously pregnant, woman in the waiting room. This was a nice office, and she didn't want to get kicked out for swearing.

"I mean it!" Selena added in a hushed whisper.

"Just be quiet."

"Then look at her. I'm that hot, right?" Selena shook the phone a little, as if that could force Robyn to agree.

"Of course you are," Robyn said, studying the picture to see if she could find a flaw in the woman's face, because that would make Selena feel better and shut the hell up. "She's just…" The words faded as her gaze fell on something in the picture.

Not the woman's face, but the hand of a man in the crowd, curled around another woman's shoulder.

"Holy shit," she mumbled, grabbing the phone to pull it closer.

"I know, right? Not that pretty but—"

"Where was this taken?" Robyn sat up straight, squinting at the phone.

"I don't know. I follow the hashtag NaughtyNate on Insta. I see everything about him."

"Who posted it?"

Selena leaned in to look at the screen. "Somebody named CelebWhore6. Imagine that five other people wanted that handle before her." She tried to take the phone back. "What difference does it—"

Robyn whipped the phone away, hoarding it as she peered so hard at the image it danced before her.

The *letters*. The letters on his knuckles. бить

Her own knuckles shook a little as she tried to zoom out and see the face attached to that hand.

"Gimme the phone," Selena whined.

"Just a sec. Please." Her voice cracked with desperation as she took in the whole picture. Most of his face was covered by the head of the woman he was holding, and what she could see was just a baseball cap and shades.

Was that him? Was that Alec Petrov, the trainer?

"I thought you didn't care!" Selena gave Robyn's shoulder a good tap.

"Stop it! Wait! This is important." This was nine freaking thousand dollars' worth of important. Forget that, this was the ticket back into that house. Where Cole was!

The tattoo was so small. She'd never ever have seen it if

Selena hadn't zoomed in on the woman's face. No one would.

She started tapping madly, trying to read the comments and get more information.

"What are you doing?"

"How long ago was this picture taken?" she demanded. "And where?"

"How the fuck would I know?"

That got a vile look from the other pregnant lady, but Robyn was too worked up to apologize. "I have to know, Selena. I *have* to know."

A door opened, and a young, dark-haired nurse stood, holding a clipboard. "Robyn Bickler. You can come in now."

Now? She shoved the phone at Selena. "Can you find out where it is and when it was taken?"

"Why?"

"Miss Bickler?" The nurse's voice grew impatient.

"Please, don't ask. Just do this…for me."

"I'm already doing this for you." She gestured toward the waiting room.

"I'll pay you," Robyn exclaimed, desperate. "Please, Selena. I have to know."

"Are you going there to find Nate and steal him away?" she teased.

There was no room for humor. "Just dig through your social media stuff and find out where he is in that picture. If you can do it before my appointment is done, I'll give you"—how much could she spare?—"fifty bucks."

Selena's eyebrow lifted. "Deal."

Chapter Eleven

Casa Blanca Resort & Spa took their honeymooners seriously. The minute Alec and Kate arrived at Junonia, the elegant restaurant off the main lobby of the resort, they were whisked outdoors to an expansive deck built over the sand. There, a few private tables were spread far apart, each under a canopy, all flickering in candlelight.

The hostess seated them side by side on a cushion-covered bench, facing the moon-spangled water. Completely romantic. Fake romantic, but still. More romance than Kate had experienced in a long time.

Especially since Kate didn't feel fake at all, even all dressed up and on the arm of a man whose last name she didn't know. She felt a little dreamy. Or maybe her brain was just mush from studying torts all day.

"Chef Ian has prepared a special dinner just for you, our honeymoon special," the perky hostess said. "We're so happy you chose Casa Blanca for this unforgettable time in your lives."

As the woman held out two menus, she noticed Alec reaching for his with his left hand, his other hand under the table. Of course, that tattoo. Without thinking about it, Kate closed her hand over the one he was hiding, the gesture natural, she hoped, and protective.

"We're delighted to be here," she cooed, the lie rolling off her tongue.

Encouraged by the conversation, the young hostess's eyes lit up. "Where are you guys from?" she asked.

"We're from—"

"Chicago," Alec said quickly. They shared a look and a smile, but the hostess laughed out loud.

"Look at that, you're finishing each other's sentences already."

Because they didn't want to contradict each other. But he was right; their ID packets from Gabe had said they were both from the Chicago area.

"But we're in paradise now," Kate said brightly, hoping to deflect the next question.

Looking grateful for the save, Alec put his arm around her shoulders. "Anywhere is paradise with my wife," he added with maybe a little too much emphasis on *wife*.

"Awww," the girl said, angling her head to take in their affection. "I love the newlyweds. We do a lot of weddings here, did you know that?"

Kate let out a little sigh of frustration that only Alec could have heard.

"I'm sure you do, uh, Melissa," he said. "Now, could we get—"

"Nate Ivory is getting married here this spring!" she exclaimed. "He was just here the other day. Did you hear?"

"We saw him," Alec confirmed, then leaned forward and looked directly at the girl. "Can you bring us a bottle of champagne?"

God bless the man.

"Absolutely, Mr.—"

"As soon as you can." He threw a playful look at Kate. "She's been talking about it all day."

The hostess laughed, finally getting the hint that they wanted to be alone.

"Thanks," Kate whispered. "And that wasn't a lie. At least I've been thinking about a drink today."

"You earned it with all that studying," he said. "But don't get too soused and blow our cover," he teased.

"No worries." She leaned back, relaxing for a moment to drink in the absolute gorgeousness of the setting.

A quarter moon rested on its side like a drawing in a children's book, so big and beautiful it was hard to believe it wasn't painted in the sky. Around them, a slight breeze rustled the palm trees, the waves lapped over the sand, and music in the distance added to the magic of the moment.

Kate took in a deep, salt-tinged breath of tropical air and let it out on a sigh.

"That didn't sound too happy," Alec said softly.

She glanced at him, wondering if the comment was an invitation to open up or a reminder that she was an actress on a stage right now. "I'm just wondering…"

"About?"

"Everything," she admitted. "I'm wondering about you, about our fake past, about how long we could go in this confined situation and not share…anything." Or everything.

She swallowed that last thought, having already said too much.

"There's nothing so interesting about me," he said. "As far as our, uh, history, Gabe told us to make one up a while ago. And…" He clenched his jaw and looked straight ahead, as if looking at her for too long was impossible. "We'll go as long as we have to, and we'll share…nothing."

"Too late. I already know a lot about you."

"Against my will," he murmured, both of them barely whispering the conversation.

"I want to know why you think you're the worst person to protect me." The confession had haunted her all day, tearing her attention from the books and forcing her imagination into overdrive.

He threw her a look, then almost instantly averted his eyes, like he always did.

"Nuh-uh." She put a warning hand on his arm, pressing to make her point and feeling the muscle tighten under her touch. "You can avoid eye contact with me in the villa. But not out here, *honey*."

He barely reacted to the endearment, but he did steal another look and held her gaze. "It's not easy."

"Looking at me?" She couldn't help the note of disappointment that slipped into the question, hating herself for it, but starting to feel pretty damn dissed by this man.

He gave a quick, dry, sarcastic laugh. "If you think that, you should look in the mirror."

"Careful." She leaned into him, using the cover as an excuse to press her bare arm against the warmth of his arm and shoulder. "That was almost a compliment, Benjamin Carlson."

"I'm sure you don't lack for those."

Actually, she did. She lacked for a lot of things that men might offer, but since they came with such a heavy price tag, she'd managed to live without them.

A waiter approached the table, champagne in one hand, a bucket of ice in the other.

"Game time," she said under her breath.

"Let's sell this," he whispered, taking her hand and making a show of holding it on top of the table. His blue eyes narrowed slightly, as if he were mustering up whatever it would take to play this game.

"Tilly," he said, the name slipping off his tongue as though he used it daily. "There's no one I'd rather be with than you on this…this adventure."

Kate felt her jaw drop a little, the words hitting with the same force she imagined he landed a punch. He sounded sincere, even a little emotional. He was selling it, all right. If she hadn't known better, *she'd* have bought it.

And, worse, she'd have liked it.

"Thanks," she said. "You know I feel the same."

He cocked his head ever so slightly, a move that could have been interpreted as a question or a tease or an acknowledgment. They stared at each other for a few heartbeats, maybe more than a few, giving Kate a chance to openly study his every feature, that crooked nose and tough jaw, his soft lips parted just enough that she could see his teeth.

And his eyes. As blue as the sky that afternoon and crystal—

The champagne popped like a gunshot, and Kate let out a soft shriek, startled.

Alec gave her a squeeze. "You weren't expecting that."

She wasn't expecting *this*. She wasn't expecting to get lost in his eyes or drunk on the idea of his mouth…on her. She wasn't expecting to be so *attracted*.

"Here you go, Mrs. Carlson." The waiter handed her a crystal champagne flute, golden and bubbly in the candlelight, and Kate took it, cursing the slight unsteadiness in her hand.

At least she understood now. Understood the way her heart was always in high gear and her throat was bone dry and her stomach fluttered like butterflies had moved in. She *wanted* him.

But everything in his behavior told her that was absolutely not mutual.

The waiter took his time putting the bottle on ice, still smiling at them, no doubt taking notes to report back to the gossipy staff. She and Alec shared another look, and this time she could see the challenge in his eyes.

Let's put those rumors to bed, he seemed to say.

Alec tapped her glass with his. "To my bride, the most beautiful woman I've ever known."

Kate studied the two crystal rims, thinking of all the things that would impress the waiter, but right then, she wanted only to speak to Alec. Honestly. "To my husband," she whispered. "Who makes me lose control."

His eyes warmed. "And I know just how much you love that." They never unlocked their gazes as they put the glasses to their lips.

"And on that note, I will most certainly leave you lovebirds alone." The waiter made a slight bow and walked away, probably off to the kitchen to quell any talk of the Carlsons being unhappy.

Kate took another deep drink, nearly draining the glass to let the sweet liquid spark on her tongue. "Now you owe me some honesty."

He set down his own glass, barely having taken a sip. "I don't recall making any deals like that."

"Come on. Just a few questions that can't possibly incriminate you."

He huffed a soft breath. "Like what?"

"Have you ever been married?"

"Not until this week."

"No one serious?" She regarded him closely, using the excuse of the intimate interrogation to drink in each feature. Had she really thought him unattractive when she'd first met him? Those eyes were impossibly blue, and his mouth... Lord, his *mouth*. Perfect lips, just perfect.

"No one serious but you, Tilly." He added an edge to her name, likely to remind her why they were there and what they were *supposed* to be talking about. "You know it was love at first sight."

"And we're playing again." She sipped the champagne, surprised at how disappointed she was. "Okay, then, let's invent our romance. Where did it start?" she asked.

"Across the algebra classroom." He didn't miss a beat with that answer.

"High school?" She raised surprised brows. "You want it to be that long a courtship?"

"Well, there were all those years we didn't see each other when you left...Illinois to live in...China," he said.

She gave a soft chuckle at the sheer creativity of that one. "Oh, yes. The Beijing years. And you were..." She thought for a long time, still studying his face far too closely. "Working as..."

"I can't wait to hear this," he mumbled, averting his eyes.

"An actor."

He snorted. "An actor?"

"You got the chops. I just witnessed it." She shrugged. "So dream big for your fake life."

"Being married to you would be a big enough dream."

She froze mid-sip, frowning, not quite getting that comment. "What do you mean?"

"I think it's pretty obvious, Ka...Tilly."

She eyed him over her glass, not sure if he was angry or...squirming. "Not to me, it isn't."

"Look at me."

As if she needed an invitation. She'd all but devoured him with her eyes since they'd been seated.

114

"And then, as I said, look in the mirror."

"You don't think…we're…" What was he saying? "Complementary? Compatible? Sympatico?"

He looked up at the sky, fighting another laugh. "It's like you swallowed a thesaurus."

"Alec—" He fried her with a look, making her bite her lip and purposely put down the glass of champagne. "Come on. What do you mean it would be a big enough dream?"

"Not that I have ever given a crap about how many times my nose has been broken, or this scar that makes my one eye smaller than the other…" He tapped one of his eyebrows. "Or this." He patted the side of his jaw. "A punching bag that's been hit a hundred times. But…" He shook his head, words eluding him.

"You think you're not good-looking?" Well, she hadn't at first. But that sure didn't last long.

He chuckled as if the answer were obvious. "Just saying that we're in different leagues, which only makes this, uh, cover more difficult."

"I don't see you that way," she admitted.

He looked a little surprised, but the hostess breezed by and threw them a friendly smile, reminding Kate how out in the open they were, which was likely why Alec got a little closer.

"Let's get back to what we're supposed to be discussing," he said.

They should, but it was frustrating. She was much more interested in Real Alec, not Pretend Benjamin. Still, she nodded and picked up the champagne glass. "Where were we?"

"The Beijing years," he reminded her.

"Ah, yes. And while I was there, you were…" She gave him a questioning look. "If you bagged that acting career, what did you do?"

"I was on a fishing boat in the Bering Sea."

She laughed. "Well, that sounds *cold*. And did we talk during those years apart?"

"No," he said. "But I stalked you on Facebook and found you at our ten-year high school reunion."

That made her smile. "Sweet."

He tipped his chin toward her empty glass. "Can you be trusted with another?"

"I'll just drink yours since it's obvious you're not drinking."

"Not while I'm protecting you."

"No such constraints for me." She winked and picked up his glass, but she didn't drink. The first glass was just settling into her bloodstream, taking the edge off, leaving a nice, relaxing warmth. "But it would be easy, wouldn't it?" she mused.

"To drink all my champagne?"

She shook her head, looking out to the water. "To just make up a history and not have to have lived it."

"I guess. None of the good stuff, but then, none of the bad."

No bad marriages to bad men who made her feel bad about herself. "None of the bad," she agreed. How different would she be if she hadn't had Steven bearing down on her life for five years? If her father hadn't been so protective? If she'd—

"Hello!" A woman approached the table, reddish-blond curls cascading over her shoulders and a warm smile breaking across a lightly freckled face. "I understand you are the newlyweds staying in Caralluma."

Alec stood immediately, making it appear he was being courteous, but stiffly enough that Kate suspected he either didn't welcome or trust the intrusion.

"I'm Lacey Walker, the owner of Casa Blanca."

"Oh, my wife and I were just talking about how you met your husband while you were building this resort."

Lacey gave a musical laugh of acknowledgment.

"So it's true?" Kate asked, standing as well.

"All of it," Lacey said. "And, please, sit down. We don't want anything to interrupt the romance around here. I just wanted to say hello since we haven't seen much of you around."

"Well, we've been…"

"Relaxing in the villa," Alec finished for her.

Lacey laughed. "I'm sure of that. I do hope everything is good in that villa. You're our first guests there, since we recently added on to the resort."

"It's perfect," Kate assured her.

"We love to have newlyweds here," she said. "We tell everyone who comes to Barefoot Bay to kick off their shoes and fall in love. But I guess you've already done that."

"In high school," Alec said easily.

Lacey's brows shot up. "And you only now just got married?"

"We lost touch," Alec said.

"I was living in China," Kate added. "And Benjamin was working on a trawler in the Bering Sea."

They shared a look that Kate hoped appeared to be wistful, but was more like a silent, secret high five.

"Wow, and, if you don't mind me asking, how did you reconnect?" Lacey asked.

"High school reunion," they replied in perfect unison.

"Aww." Lacey put her hands together. "That's a perfect Barefoot Bay love story."

Except it was a total lie.

"I hope you have an absolutely fantastic vacation while you're here. We love the couples who come for an extended stay."

"Thank you so much," Kate said. "The whole place is amazing."

"Have you been to the spa?" Lacey asked.

Not for lack of wanting to, Kate thought. "Not yet. I haven't been able to, um, get away."

"Aw, you don't want to separate for that long." Before they could respond, Lacey tapped her fingertips in a silent clap. "Oh, I know what you need. A couples massage!"

Kate stared, not knowing how to respond to the idea of stripping down naked next to Alec while they were rubbed and oiled and...

"And, oh, tomorrow, Madame Valaina is here." She pulled out her phone and swiped the screen. "I'm going to schedule you for an hour with her. On the house."

"Wow, thanks," Kate said. "Is she an exceptional massage therapist?"

Lacey looked up from her phone, a twinkle in her golden-brown eyes. "You don't know who she is?"

"I do," Alec said, making both women look at him. He looked *horrified*.

But Lacey laughed. "I know, no one thinks they need her, but trust me on this. I'm adding years of marital bliss to your lives." She gave the phone a final tap. "You're all set. Be at cabana number three, right down at the beach, at two o'clock. A fifty-minute couples massage, followed by...well, he can tell you about it." Lacey gestured for them to sit down as she started to walk away. "Best wishes to both of you from Casa Blanca!"

She headed off to the next table as Alec sat very slowly and stared straight ahead.

"Who is Madame Valaina?" Kate asked. "She sounds like a fortune-teller."

"Not quite." He picked up her champagne and drained it.

"I thought you weren't drinking."

"I am now."

Chapter Twelve

By the time the waiter cleared the fancy after-dinner coffee that sat like lead in Alec's stomach, Kate seemed to have accepted their fate.

They had an appointment with a sex guru.

"What is her actual title again?" Kate asked as they headed toward a nearly deserted beach to return to their villa.

"You can read about her in the spa stuff that's in the villa," Alec said. "I think her business is called Vibes. Which stands for something like..." *Valaina's Intimacy Breathwork for Enhanced Satisfaction.* No way he was telling her that. "Something about breathing better."

When she read what this woman did—which was basically teach people how to have sex, though he hadn't been that blunt—she'd want him to cancel.

"So it's an acronym." She bent to slip off her sandals, and he took off his shoes, too. "Very Interesting Breathing for Every Soul?" she suggested.

He laughed, amused and a little surprised. "You just came up with that?"

"Or...Vascular Introduction to Breathing for Essential Success?"

Chuckling, his arm sort of ached to tuck her against him,

but no one was around, so he didn't. "Damn, you're smart, you know that?"

"You say that like you're not."

"I get by, but I'd love to have some of those nineteen-letter words to throw instead of a punch once in a while."

"You like words," she said, slowing her step like she'd just discovered something new about him that needed to be over-examined.

"They can be powerful."

"No kidding," she agreed. "Words like *shut up* and *go away* and *you're useless*. Very powerful, but not too difficult."

He didn't have to have any of those words spelled out for him to understand what she was telling him. The ex-husband, no doubt. "He hurt you," he said, almost under his breath.

"Oh, yeah." She didn't even try to play it down. "How about you? Who hurt you, Alec?"

"Who hasn't? Remember I've spent a lot of my adult life in a cage or ring, facing an opponent."

"I meant a woman."

"No woman's ever hurt me," he said quietly. "I told you I've never had a serious relationship."

"But you didn't tell me why not."

He shrugged. "I scare 'em off, I guess. You heard Gabe call me Conan."

"And you let that blowhard bother you?"

He laughed. "He's calling the shots, remember?"

"How could I forget?" She inched a little closer to him, practically sliding under his arm. Was that the moonlight? The champagne? Or did she really want to cozy up to him?

"Someone's coming," she whispered, looking past him.

Oh, that's what it was. An act.

He replied by putting his arm around her, pulling her

body into his, making it fit right against his side, managing not to smile when she slid her arm around his waist.

"Now we're undercover," he said.

A couple walked by, similarly arm in arm, but staring at each other, kissing, laughing, kissing some more.

"Not completely, I guess," she said.

"What does that mean?"

She looked up at him. "It was just an oblique comment," she said.

"Oblique?" He gave a dry laugh at the word. "The only oblique I know is this." He gave a squeeze to that very muscle along her side, making her jump and jerk away.

"Hey! What are you—"

He reeled her back in. "Then don't use words like oblique with your...husband," he finished, his voice feeling a little rough on the intimacy of that last word.

She shuddered slightly. "Oblique means sideways or kind of 'off to the side.'"

"Like the muscle," he said.

"Exactly." They fell in step again, heading toward the little wooden bridge. Neither one of them talked as they drank in the postcard view, the water still sparkling from the moon, lights under every palm tree giving the whole place the feel of paradise.

"I guess it's not the worst prison in the world," she finally said.

"You just have a shitty warden."

"You're my cellmate," she corrected. "The warden is"— her gaze slipped beyond him, peering into the night—"right there."

He turned to see a man emerging from the shadows near the end of the path by the resort. Even in the dim light, he recognized the lean, rugged physique of Gabe Rossi.

"Time for some more acting?" she asked.

For a second, they stood in an awkward embrace, looking at each other, both aware that in a few seconds, Gabe would likely see them. "It's time for…" God, he wanted to kiss her. Wanted to just pull her into him and press his mouth on hers. "This."

He closed his eyes, lowered his face, and pressed his mouth very lightly against hers. So lightly. Barely even there lightly.

But then he felt her hand travel up his arm and slide over his neck, her fingers gripping him tighter and tighter, her mouth pressing harder and harder, and then her lips parted with a quick breath, intensifying the contact.

Fire licked through him as the tip of her tongue flicked over his, and the softest, sweetest whimper escaped from her throat.

Finally, she eased away so slowly he could have sworn she didn't want to stop that kiss.

Her eyes were still closed, her lips still parted. And Alec's whole being slipped a little down a slope he shouldn't have even been near.

"Good acting," she whispered.

Not on his part. There was no acting involved, but he had to remember that's all it was for her.

What the *hell* was she thinking? Kate *wasn't* thinking, that was the problem. For such a smart girl, her hardest-working organ had essentially given up the fight to the ones way farther south.

"I like it." Gabe Rossi came right up to them, a sly grin on his handsome face. "I totally bought that kiss."

Because it was real. "We aim to please, boss," Kate said, sounding remarkably composed for how hard her heart was beating.

Next to her, Alec gave an uncomfortable laugh, and she caught him surreptitiously touching his lips, like he needed to check that they were still there. Like maybe he thought she ate them off. Five more seconds, and she might have.

"I'll say." Gabe inched closer. "I heard you have a couples massage and a session with the sex guru."

Kate's jaw dropped. "How—"

He cut her off. "Never ask how."

Kate took a second to really look at the man who currently controlled her life. Most women would think Gabe Rossi was too hot for words. Chiseled features, Wedgwood blue eyes with dark lashes, a couple of insane dimples, and a mouth that looked like it knew its way around naughty.

No doubt a man who could get many women to part with their panties. But she had no real desire to throw her arms around *him* and make a fool of herself in the middle of the resort property. The hulking beast next to her? Totally different story.

"Just remember while you're locked up with the sexologist, you can't give anyone a reason to suspect you're not who you say you are," Gabe said.

"Can't we just be a less-than-sickeningly-affectionate couple and still be married?" Alec challenged.

Sickeningly affectionate. Is that what he thought this was? Or maybe he was referring to that kiss. She had damn near shoved half her tongue down his throat and flattened herself against him like she was human cellophane. Was that affection *sickening*?

"No," Gabe said simply. "Because this is how it works when you're undercover." He got closer and pointed to the resort. "First of all, even when no one is around, you're *acting*."

"Oh, we are," Alec assured Gabe.

In other words, that kiss was a total act for him.

"Great," Gabe said. "And now, I'm *acting* like I'm telling you how to find the place where you check in for the couples massage."

"Cabana number three," Alec said.

Gabe closed his eyes quickly. "I know you know, but anyone seeing us talk would think I'm just a guy who works here who's giving you directions, while in reality we are talking about something else." Then he put his hands in his pockets and tipped his head as if he were about to ask them a question—where are you from, how are you enjoying your trip—but instead, he spoke through gritted teeth.

"For Christ's sake, put your fucking arm around her."

"Why?" Alec asked.

Gabe's eyes widened like he might explode, but Kate's heart just took a dip. Damn it, she *wanted* him to put his arm around her. She was damn near dying for it.

"*Why?*" Gabe repeated.

"I mean, if we're just standing here making it look like we're getting directions, I would think too much of…that…would be a different kind of red flag," Alec said.

"Dude." Gabe slowly lifted his hands. Elegant long fingers, blunt-tipped nails, tanned skin. Alec stared at the other man's fingers, too.

Without warning, Gabe's hands slid around Kate's neck and cupped her jaw. The touch was gentle and gave her a shiver.

"What the hell are you doing?" Alec asked, getting closer.

Kate just stared at Gabe, not sure what she was supposed

to do, other than feel super uncomfortable and wish that Alec would make him stop.

"What am I doing?" Gabe asked. "I could be making a move on your incredibly hot wife." He ran his thumbs along the side of her neck, leaving a surprising blossom of chill bumps over her skin. "Since her husband doesn't seem to be interested."

"Stop it," Alec ground out the words, moving another inch.

But Gabe just pulled her closer to his chest. "Or I could be about to break her neck."

Instantly, Alec knocked Gabe's hands away, nearly diving between them to scoop Gabe off the ground. In one heart-stopping move, Alec hoisted the other man over his shoulder with a grunt and took him to the ground, finishing with his knee centimeters from Gabe's chest.

Gabe looked up, fighting a smile. "Now that's what I'm talking about, motherfucker."

Instantly, Alec stepped off and held out a hand to help him up. "Sorry."

"Don't be." Gabe popped to his feet, brushing off and looking from side to side. It happened so fast, and it was dark and isolated enough, that no one had seen. "That's some sick shit, man. No wonder you don't carry. You don't need to."

Kate took a shuddering breath, drawing both men's attention. "You okay?" Alec asked, his touch sudden and genuine. "You're shaking," he said, squeezing her shoulder.

Yes, she was. But why? Was it fright at the unexpected display of violence or a thrill over just how *hot* it was to watch Alec take down another guy who was equally as strong and powerful, just to protect her. "Just surprised."

"Sorry," Alec said, wrapping an arm around her. "That scared you."

Normally, she would bristle at that kind of condescension. But he felt so strong and protective and...*good*. She tucked herself closer to his side, using the bizarre situation to steal the pleasure of this big, muscular body against hers.

On the other hand, Alec's victim was unfazed by the little demonstration. Gabe nodded his approval at their cozy posture.

"So here's why you don't take your hands, eyes, and mouth off her in public, Brutus," he said. "You get jealous, okay? You don't want any man from six to sixty checking out what belongs to *you*."

Kate waited for an expected ripple of distaste to tear through her, even disgust, at being called anyone's possession. But it didn't come. Instead, she actually pressed herself a little closer to him.

"Just like that," Gabe said, noticing it. "Not only will people stop wondering if you'll be divorced by Saturday, or start Googling your names to find out who you are, they'll leave you the hell alone. And the staff will stop speculating." He indicated the closeness of the two of them by flicking his hand from one to the other. "So more lip-locks and less ice. Can you do that?"

"Yes," Kate said. Maybe a little too quickly.

But Alec didn't answer, which was like a little kick in her teeth.

"Especially tomorrow afternoon," Gabe said. "My sources tell me the massage therapists at this joint are the biggest gossips on staff. Give 'em something to talk about, and I'll get off your case for a while."

"Something...like what?" Kate asked.

"Like what two madly in love honeymooners would do during a couples massage," Gabe said. "Act like you dig each other. Pet, coo, stare, play some tonsil hockey, whisper dirty words, call each other stupid nicknames, and, for God's sake, make sweet love with your eyes. Whatever it takes."

She could feel Alec tense up with every order, and on the last one, he actually prickled a bit. "We'll do our best," he said stiffly.

"Your best better be amazing," Gabe said.

Kate looked up at Alec, but his expression was dark and angry. Like the last thing he wanted to do was coo, pet, stare, and...*make sweet love.*

No, his expression was cold. No lust, no warmth, no affection. Just ice.

How could she forget how much she hated cold, emotionless men? Who cared if she was hot for him—he was everything in the world she wanted to avoid. She had to think of some way out of this situation before she did something she'd really regret.

Chapter Thirteen

Late the next morning, Alec counted to thirty, switched hands and balanced for another thirty drop lunges, wishing like hell he could close his eyes to test his balance.

Instead, he watched the villa, scanning every inch. It was damn near noon. Why wasn't she up yet?

He rolled to his ass for a series of glute bridges, centering himself while he stared at her bedroom doors. She rose by seven almost every day, drank her coffee, hit her books.

Was something wrong? She'd slept well, from what he could tell, her breathing steady, not as restless as she'd been most nights.

He switched legs and started firing, freezing mid-kick when the French doors opened, revealing Kate in nothing but tight black shorts like chicks wore for yoga, a top that could have maybe been a sports bra or just a really small tank top, hands on hips, hair pulled back in a tight ponytail.

"I was starting to worry about you," he admitted.

"Exactly." She took a few steps onto the patio. "Which is why you will like my brilliant idea." A half smile pulled at her mouth, reminding him of how good she'd tasted last night. "You're going to teach me self-defense." She spread her hands out as though she wanted to show him just how ready she was. "Then I won't need a bodyguard."

And have his hands all over her? What the hell did she think he was made of? "Bad idea," he said, turning to return to his series of kicks.

"Why?" she demanded.

"Because—"

"If you say 'because I said so,' you'll be the one who needs to defend himself."

He almost smiled at the threat, because she was so stinking cute. But he'd never tell her that and expect to live.

"Because...that's not what I do or teach," he said, firmly tugging his belt. "I'm almost done if you want to go get your coffee."

"And let me out of your sight?" she challenged.

"I can see into the kitchen."

"I would like to be out of your sight permanently."

He inched back at the announcement, not surprised she'd made it, but taken aback by the way it affected him. But why should it? From day one, all she wanted to do was get away from him. Why would that change? One pretend kiss wouldn't change that.

"Sorry. I'm a fact of your life." He shook out his arms and fired his foot straight out, keeping his leg parallel to the ground.

"I'm serious. I want to learn self-defense."

"Maybe they have a class at the spa. You can take it. I'll watch."

"Oh, sure, right after we study with the sex guru."

"It won't work, Kate. You can't learn enough to be on your own."

"Damn it!" She actually stomped her foot, and he expected her to charge toward her precious coffee, but she stayed right where she was, fury shooting from her eyes. "I hate to be dismissed. I hate to be ordered around. I hate that I can't be on my own. And I hate…" Her voice faded out.

"Me," he finished for her.

She sighed. "That's not what I was going to say."

"Yes, it was." He locked his hands behind his head and stretched his biceps, leaning from side to side.

"No." She stared at his arms. "That is not what I was thinking I hated."

"I don't believe you, and honestly, I don't blame you."

Her reaction was half laugh, half choke. "You don't get it, do you? You don't…"

He waited, but for once, her big-ass words didn't come.

"Just teach me a few moves to ward off the bad guys, Alec. Don't you think that would be a good thing?"

Good…for who? The basics of his sport required rolling on the floor, an arm, hand, and head between an opponent's legs. When he taught jiu-jitsu, there wasn't an inch of his student he didn't touch…and that went both ways.

"I don't think that would be a wise or safe idea." In fact, it would be a very, very dangerous idea. "If you don't know what you're doing, you can get really hurt. You'll break your own arm instead of someone else's." He moved away, turning his head so he didn't have to look at her expression, which he couldn't read anyway.

He whipped out his left leg, slicing the air and jumping to adjust his stance and do the other one. Just as he kicked out his right leg, she threw herself at it from the side, knocking him off-balance for one split second.

Without thinking, he wrapped an arm around her waist, used his leg to fold hers in half, and took her to the ground as gently as he could so he didn't crack her head or back on the bricks.

The whole thing took less than two seconds and was sloppy and slow.

He pinned her as if she were a rag doll, giant green eyes looking up at him with a flash of fear, then dancing with light.

She laughed—*laughed*!—in his face. "See? I need work."

"You need"—not to feel this good under him—"common sense. That was stupid, Kate. I could've hurt you."

She pushed harder, with enough force to tighten her stomach and thigh muscles against him. She wasn't strong, but she wasn't soft, either. "Look, I just want to know how to fend off a bad guy."

"You run and scream. I'll handle the fending."

"I don't want you...for that." She flinched as if she'd caught herself saying something she didn't want to. "I want you to teach me how to..." She hesitated, silent and still, except for her gaze, which dropped to his mouth.

Holy shit. He wanted to vault off her and let her go. He knew he should back away and brush her off. He had to do something to stop that crackling feeling, like there was a live wire tying them together.

But he didn't move.

"How to protect myself," she finished.

From him.

Very slowly, he pushed back, onto his knees, then up to a stand. She stayed right there on the ground, looking up at him. She was soft and sweet and beautiful and, God help him, she was *attracted* to him.

The possibility of it hit him like an illegal punch to the head, concussion worthy.

She lifted her hand for help, and he automatically reached for her, seeing his horribly, tattooed hand close over her slender, pale, flawless one. He stared at the mismatched pair, a slow sense of disbelief rolling over him.

Attracted to *him*. Was that even possible?

"Alec." She barely whispered his name, making no effort to rise to her feet, looking up at him like...like she wanted him to come back down.

And everything in his body—his brain, his heart, his gut and, oh, fuck, his dick—betrayed him by wanting to go right back there with her.

Which would make him only slightly higher on the food chain than a slug. He gave a stronger pull, and she lifted a little bit.

"I can't," he said.

She frowned. "Can't what? Lift me or teach me?"

Touch you.

He used enough force that she had no choice but to come to her feet, and he let go of her hand. "I *shouldn't* teach you," he said.

"What if I paid you in some way?"

He stared at her, not even sure there were any words to respond to that offer. She would *pay* him? For—

"I mean, I know it's your profession, so I don't expect you to teach me for nothing. So how about a *quid pro quo?* You know, an exchange of favors."

Holy Christ, he *knew* what that one meant. "What kind of favors?"

The palest shade of pink rose in her cheeks. "I could teach you something in return."

That sounded only slightly less indecent than some of the things that had gone through his mind when she was underneath him. "Like, what? How to read a contract?"

"I could teach you..." She bit her lower lip. "Don't take this the wrong way."

At this point, there really was no other way to take it. She

133

was offering sex. To him. And, God help him, he was going to—

"I could teach you words."

He nearly choked on the huge amount of his own stupidity he just swallowed. She wanted to teach him basic English, not sex. He must be imagining the attraction.

He was the one who woke up hard as rebar and sweating in the middle of the night dreaming of her. That didn't mean she—

"You seem to be interested in words," she added. "I'll give you vocabulary-enrichment lessons in exchange for basic self-defense." She added a sly smile and winked. "I'm a transcendent teacher, and you will be a meritorious student."

"No."

He saw the reaction in her eyes, fury, frustration, and a lot of old hurts welling up. And he knew why. Kate Kingston did not like to have someone make decisions for her.

Well, too bad. This decision was made.

"I don't want to cross that barrier," he added, as if that would soften the blow.

It didn't, at least not by the look on her face. She pivoted and went back into her room, slamming the door behind her.

Chapter Fourteen

Gabe checked his phone for the tenth time that hour. Mal's call would be brief, monitored, and likely unsatisfying, but the fact that Gabe had been able to arrange it at all gave him hope that Drummand hadn't been lying. Or Drummand was setting up Gabe in hopes that he'd say something that would land him in the same federal prison camp in Pennsylvania where Malcolm Harris currently resided.

Still, if anyone could help him, it was Mal.

His door burst open like a shot, revealing his grandfather wearing a scowl and holding a serving pan of some sort, two oven mitts covering his giant hands.

"She stole my recipe."

Gabe yanked himself from his thoughts, a fiery resentment shooting through him. "You're fucking kidding me, right?"

"I wish I were!" He lumbered into the room and set the steaming hot pan on the edge of Gabe's desk. He lifted the corner of tin foil to reveal something that looked and smelled like the very lasagna Gabe had been raised on. "Of course, she screwed up the sauce, but still. You don't steal people's recipes and *change* them with…with…oh my

God, Gabriel, I think she put *scotch bonnet peppers* in this!"

Gabe stared at him, utterly speechless and digging for the humor in the situation, which usually deflected his grandfather when he went batshit crazy.

Nino dropped into the chair and ripped off the mitts, throwing them on the desk in a dramatic display of disgust. "I tell you true, she's sitting on my last nerve."

"Getting," Gabe corrected, knowing, at that moment, exactly how that expression got invented in the first place. Someone was definitely getting on his.

"She took it into housekeeping!" he exclaimed. "With a little handwritten note that she'd made it for the staff from her *mother's secret recipe*." Nino made a mocking face with dramatic air quotes. "First of all, I assume her mother is from that island, and she's no *Napolitana*. Who's going to believe her mother made lasagna?"

Gabe shoved into the depths of his very soul for some molecule of caring, but no. He didn't care a fat fuck about food, and only the shreds of love for his grandfather kept him from howling. Instead, he looked at his phone and checked the time. Mal should have called by now.

"What should I do?" Nino asked.

"Stuff it up her ass? Those scotch bonnets would burn like a moth—"

"Gabriel! I'm serious! Family recipes are like state secrets, and you don't mess with them."

State secrets—exactly why Mal was in prison, he thought with one more demanding look at his phone. "Listen, Gramps, you gotta work this out with her. It's food, it's a recipe, it's—"

"You took it!" Poppy came lumbering in, her big brown eyes shooting sparks at Nino.

"Of course I took it," Nino said. "It's not yours."

"Oh, really? You see that orange baking dish? It is mine."
The strength of her Jamaican accent directly correlated with
how pissed off she was, and right now, Gabe could barely
understand her.

"You might have *made* it," Nino said, standing up. "But
you didn't *invent* it."

"You didn't invent lasagna!" Poppy fired back.

"Shut the goddamn hell up, both of you."

They whipped around in unison, and Gabe shut his eyes
when he realized those few words were going to cost him a
lot.

Gabe reached into his pocket, opened his wallet, and
grabbed two twenties, stuffing them into the jar. "I'm
covered for this because some doozies are about to roll out
of my mouth one letter at a time until you"—he pointed to
Nino—"and you"—his finger moved to Poppy—"get this
shit"—he flipped his finger down at the lasagna—"under
control."

"It's not shit," Nino said softly.

"Then stop fighting like a couple of whiny-ass babies and
work it the hell out."

They both blinked and stared at him.

"But she—"

Gabe glared at his grandfather, shutting him up.

"I didn't—" When he flattened Poppy with the same
look, she had the good grace to sigh and hold up her hands.
"Sorry to bring you into this, Mr. Gabriel."

Nino crossed his arms and breathed in and out so hard his
nostrils quivered. "At least you could have the decency to
admit you stole my recipe."

"I didn't realize recipes were *secret*."

"You've never heard the expression 'secret recipe'?"
Nino asked, his voice full of sarcasm, which was rich for a

man who butchered idioms with the same gusto he attacked a raw chicken. "You stole it from my recipe file."

"You left it on the counter in your kitchen."

"You shouldn't have been in my kitchen."

"I'm the housekeeper."

"We don't need—"

"Stop!" Gabe's shout brought them both to silence. After a beat, he dropped down in his chair. "I need you two to get along."

They said nothing.

"Or one of you is going to be out of a job."

"Well, it won't be me," Nino said. "Blood is better than water."

"Thicker," Gabe said. "And so are you."

"And I don't technically work for you, Mr. Gabriel, so you can't fire me," Poppy chimed in. "I am on Miss Mandy's payroll in housekeeping."

Gabe let out a sigh. "I might have to leave Barefoot Bay for a day or two." That is, if Mal ever called and gave him anything to go on. "And I don't want to come back to one of you charged for murder...or dead." He gave them both hard looks. "Work it out, okay? Share the recipes and the food love." Although he suspected this wasn't at all about food. A clash of cultures, personalities, and two people who both worked for one man. Two people he needed very much.

"I'll try," Poppy said.

Nino nodded, his scowl firmly in place.

"Now get this lasagna out of here and go eat it together."

"What?" Nino looked like Gabe had suggested they go down to the local fleabag and bang for days.

"Without arguing," Gabe added.

But Poppy was already using the oven mitts to pick up

the goods. "I think I'll just take this over to our newlyweds and leave it in their fridge for dinner."

"I saw them last night," Gabe said. "Making out on the beach."

Poppy nearly dropped the lasagna on the desk. "You must mean someone else, Mr. Gabriel."

Gabe laughed. "No, I mean them. I talked to them." He rubbed the back of his head. "Fucker flipped me right on my ass. Sorry," he said to Poppy. "I should still be covered with the jar, though."

She reprimanded him with a look, then shook her head. "Well, I was just over there to clean, and you could cut the tension in that villa with one of Nino's overpriced, fancy knives."

Nino moaned. "They are not—"

"Well, they weren't tense last night," Gabe said. "They were pretty cozy. And headed for a couples massage and an hour with the sex doctor, my sources tell me."

"Madame Valaina?" Poppy asked. "That's not good."

"Why not?" Gabe asked.

"Mr. Gabriel, they aren't really married," she said, so serious he almost laughed.

"I know, Poppy. I set up the cover."

"Well, they can't...you know."

"I'm sure they won't." Although, after the way they kissed last night, Gabe actually wasn't sure of any such thing.

"But, I don't—" Her argument was cut off by the buzz of Gabe's phone.

"Thank Christ," he mumbled, reaching for it.

"Mr. Gabriel! My Lord and Savior costs ten dollars!" She pointed at the jar, and Gabe just glared at her.

"I paid it with my arbitration skills. Now take the food, make nice, and get out."

Thankfully, they obeyed, and Gabe picked up the phone and heard the sound of his old friend's hello. "Is it true?" he asked Mal.

"It is. I'm getting out, but, you know, they'll keep an eye on me."

More than one. So he couldn't get into Cuba, either. But once he was out, they could talk freely, and Mal might know something. He hadn't worked for the CIA or consulted for them, like Gabe, but he had a spy's good instincts, and he knew shit. God, Mal knew shit.

And, best of all, they both still hated the same people: the ones who put him in prison on trumped-up charges. Sergeant Malcolm Harris hadn't done anything wrong. On the contrary, he'd done everything right. But he and Gabe both had paid the price for being good guys. They both lost something. Mal lost a couple of years in prison and his reputation. And Gabe lost...

Well, that was the point of everything, right? To find what he lost. And to get her back.

"Good to hear your voice, Mal," Gabe said. "I'm always thinking about the good old days." He hoped that vague statement—and the fact that they both knew those days in Gitmo were anything but good—would clue him in.

"Guess we left a few open doors behind us, though." Mal's voice was low, always cool, always husky. It matched his dark looks, his inky eyes, and hardened features.

"As long as they're open, dawg, and something decent is on the other side."

Mal was quiet for a long time. "Bet you'd like to know."

Yes, Mal, I would. "Some things we might never know."

"Then you need to get better information."

Gabe's heart kicked up as he gripped the phone tighter.

Yes, Malcolm I need better information. A direction. A town. A name. Hope and a plan. Mostly hope.

His need for all those things was what had sent him to this sandy little hellhole that was closer to another sandy little hellhole where he couldn't go.

"Then you should hit the news."

There was something on the news? Plenty of current events and buzz about the changing status of Cuba, and Gabe had watched everything. Every single stream of video content had been combed and culled, but none of it gave him what he wanted. "I watch a lot of it," he said.

"Try listening instead."

Oh, yeah, the big guy had some impressive covert convo skills, because that was real information.

"Anything in particular you think I'd like?"

"Well, here in the country club, we don't exactly get satellite radio," he said, just enough emphasis on the last word for Gabe to know it was important.

Radio. Radio. And it hit him. Radio Martí, the American-based broadcaster of news to Cuba. "So, anyway, dude, when you get out, what are you going to do?"

He snorted. "Well, I sure as shit am never talking to a *reporter* again." There was that subtle inflection, which might have been a dig at the bastard who ratted him out and landed him in jail, or it could be a clue. "But, you know, I'll see my friends. Have a nice cold Amber Bock."

And there was that emphasis again. He scribbled the words *Amber Bock* on a pad.

"Where are you?" Mal asked.

"Here and there," Gabe said, having no intention of telling their invisible audience anything else.

"Some things never change," Mal mused.

"You have, but then prison does that to a man."

141

Mal laughed. "I haven't changed," he said coolly. "I'm still your biggest fan, Rossi."

"God knows I could use one."

"Hey, I gotta go. I'll see you on the flip side, Angel Gabriel."

Something twisted at the sad note in Mal's voice. He'd gone down, way down, for doing the most honorable thing. Gabe would never forget that. "When you're out, man, call me."

"You bet."

Gabe ended the call and stared at the paper in front of him, considering what he had. Radio Martí was basically a federally funded broadcaster that distributed news to Cuba, to the consternation of the Castro regime. Plus the word *reporter*, maybe, and the name of a beer. He'd had worse clues to find things. And he never wanted to find anyone more than he wanted to find her.

Kate came out of her room in a long, strapless, yellow dress, with a bikini top tie visible around her neck. She looked like she'd walked out of a magazine advertising summer clothes and beach living. All pretty and bright and warm. Except for the look in her eyes, which was sharp and cold. Still pissed, Alec guessed.

He glanced down at his own choice of board shorts and a T-shirt, totally clueless about what one wore to a couples massage at an exclusive resort. Rough and painful Russian massages after a fight were done bare-ass naked.

He swallowed at the possibility that they might also be done that way at beachfront resorts and how he'd handle that as a bodyguard. And what if her massage therapist was a man? How would he handle that?

"Ready?" she asked.

"To lay down and have my body slathered in oil and slapped by a masseuse?"

She gave him a look he couldn't quite read.

"What?" he asked. "Is it *lie* down?" He was going for a joke, but her green eyes didn't spark with laughter.

"Yes, and it's…massage therapist. No one says masseuse anymore."

He knew that, but really wanted to break her ice. "Got it. I'll keep my mouth shut so I don't embarrass you." And his eyes, so he didn't embarrass himself by springing a boner at the sight of Kate half-naked on a bed next to him.

"You don't embarrass me. Tick me off, but not embarrass."

"I got that, too."

She breezed by him to the door, but he caught up to her, grabbed his ball cap and sunglasses from the table, and walked her out into the sunshine.

He slapped on the hat and glasses and put his arm around Kate's bare shoulders, almost sucking in a breath at how smooth and feminine her skin felt under his hand. Of course, she tensed under his touch.

"It's show time," he reminded her, leaning close enough to whisper the words and get a whiff of her clean hair.

"I know." But she still felt stiff as he tried to make them look like a couple.

"Work with me here, Tilly."

She looked up at him, no sunglasses to cover the storm brewing in her eyes.

Just then, a couple came out of the front door of the next villa, laughing and talking, stopping while the man wiped some sunscreen off of the woman's nose and finished the job with a kiss.

Kate turned away and walked a little faster, making him speed up to keep hold of her.

"We should be behaving a little more like that," he said, knowing that anyone who watched them with even casual interest would see they had zero connection.

"And cross *barriers*?" she asked, slapping some serious attitude on the last word.

And making him remember his final words during their conversation on the patio this morning. "Out here there are no barriers."

She nodded. "I'm cognizant of the situation."

He stifled a laugh. "Whatever that means."

"I'd love to teach you, but, you know. *Barriers*."

He slowed his step as they reached the beach, adding a little pressure with his arm so she didn't just shoot forward without him. "What exactly is wrong with you?" he asked.

She let her head fall back to really put all she had into an eye roll, which anyone could see was rich with sarcasm—including the two women in bathing suits who walked past them just that second.

"Hey, if it's that important to school me in your great big words, knock yourself out," he whispered after they'd passed. "But let's not fight in public. Any one of these people could be one of those 'eyes and ears' Gabe warned us he had."

She didn't reply, but kept up her quick steps even when they were on the sand, headed toward the row of draped cabanas along the shore. This time, he snagged her with a stronger hand and stopped her. "You need to chill," he warned her.

"I'd love to chill," she shot back. "I came here to chill. I didn't come here to...to..."

Another couple came closer, holding hands and umbrella drinks. They smiled at Kate and Alec, and he nodded, pulling her close, as if they'd just stopped to confess true love. He put his hands on her cheeks, her face feeling small and delicate against his fingers.

"Seriously," he said between gritted teeth, "I don't know about you, but I don't have any other option but this place. Let's play by the rules and make it work."

She shuddered slightly, her jaw quivering. "I just wish you didn't…"

"What?" he asked, half-terrified and half-dying of curiosity at what she might say.

She shook her head, biting her lip.

He kept his hands on her face because it made it impossible for her to turn away. And because it felt so good to hold her. "You wish I didn't what?"

"Dislike me so much," she said on a whisper.

He couldn't have heard that right. His hands loosened and fell away from her face. "You're kidding, right?"

"You don't have to lie," she said. "It's so obvious you look for the closest hole to hide in when you have to look at me. I don't know if it's because you're stuck here with me, or you think I'm some kind of prima donna, or you just can't stand redheads, or you feel like you're cheating on someone, or what." Her voice rose with every word, making him pull her closer, wondering if he should just kiss her to shut her up before the lady in the orange dress and massive sunhat coming their way heard her.

"Listen to me," he said, reaching for her shoulders to pull her in. "Just listen. We'll talk about it later, okay?"

"No, we won't," she insisted, managing to wrest from his hands. Twenty feet behind them, the giant orange sunhat was powering closer.

"Yes, we will. Come here." He reached for her hand, but she jerked away.

"I'm sorry, I know I'm acting stupid, and I feel stupid, but all I wanted from you was—"

"Stop," he ordered, now able to make out the features of the woman who was about to witness all this. She had dark eyes and red lips and was riveted on their little drama on the sand.

"—a simple lesson! How hard would it be to teach me—"

"Tilly, honey," he said firmly. "I really do want to, I promise."

She closed her mouth, staring at him, obviously not sure what he was talking about.

"You're right, it's a great idea."

"You'll do it?" Kate drew back. "You're not lying?"

He gave her the warmest, most husbandly smile he had just as Orange Hat was next to them, making no effort to hide the fact that she was eavesdropping.

"I would never lie to you," he assured her.

Orange Hat hadn't moved, still taking it all in. Finally, Alec turned to her. "Can I help you?" he asked coolly.

She lifted a carefully drawn brow. "You appear to have your hands full, young man. And the couples massages are right there in cabana three," she added with a quick smile. "And it's not good that she thinks you might be lying."

Alec fought the urge to let his jaw open in shock and give the orange busybody a piece of his mind. Instead, he just nodded, using Kate's own moment of being off guard to wrap his arm around her and lead her across the sand.

"Let's go, baby," he said sweetly. "This should be fun."

Chapter Fifteen

"Hello there!" A young woman stepped out from the linen-enclosed cabana and waved Kate and Alec closer. "You're Tilly and Ben, right? What's taking you two so long out here? Hailey and I were starting to think we heard an argument."

"My wife thinks she can teach me a thing or two," Alec said quickly.

The therapist's eyebrows raised. "Is that so?"

Damn it. Kate *had* to get in this game. She shook off the last argument and jumped into her role. "And my husband has never had a couples massage, so I was trying to explain what to expect."

"Expect the unexpected," the woman said, making a grand gesture toward the opening of the cabana. "Expect to relax and fall even more in love than when you walked in here."

They shared a look that would have been funny except...it wasn't.

The cabana was cool, thanks to what looked like a special sun-blocking material on the top and privacy drapes all around. Inside, it was filled with brightly colored pillows, a table with cold drinks and fruit, and two white-draped massage tables not two feet apart. New Age music played from tiny speakers, and the scents of spices wafted through the air.

"I'm Brenna, and I'll be massaging Mrs. Carlson."

"And I'm Hailey." From behind a curtain in the back, another woman appeared, dressed similarly in clean white scrubs. "Unless you prefer a male therapist, Mr. Carlson."

"No, I'm...fine." But he didn't sound very fine.

"And, of course, there's Madame Valaina." Brenna swooped in and directed them to the massage tables. "She'll be joining you after we've finished." She added a sympathetic smile. "You two sounded like you could use an hour of Vibes."

Kate didn't dare look at Alec to get an *I told you so* warning.

"It's not unusual," Hailey added. "After the stress of the wedding, and all. Madame Valaina is just what you need."

"What exactly does she do?" Kate asked. The description in the resort brochure had been brief and left plenty to the imagination. And, of course, Kate's had gone wild.

"Vibes," Brenna said, laughing. "Really good vibes."

"Valaina's Intimacy Breathwork for Enhanced Satisfaction is what she calls it," the other woman said. "She's one of the foremost breathing experts in the country."

"Breathing," Kate and Alec said in near unison, both sounding relieved.

"Is that all?" Kate asked.

"We know how to breathe," Alec said.

"Not like this," Brenna said with a wink. "She specializes in intimacy, ecstasy, and, of course, Tantra."

Tantra.

"You've heard of Tantric sex, of course."

They both just stared at Brenna, silent, making her laugh.

"Trust me," she said. "You will love her. And each other even more."

"We really don't need...that," Alec added. "Thanks, but a quick rubdown is all we want. Just the basics. In fact, I can wait while—"

"Dude!" Brenna gave him an easy punch. "You're here to have fun and chill with the love of your life." She turned to Kate, who was trying to balance her reaction to the breathing coach and her disappointment that, of course, Alec wanted nothing that would require them to get closer than five feet to each other unless Gabe might be looking.

"Typical man," Hailey said with a laugh. "They all think they know how to breathe and have sex, but after an hour with Madame Valaina, you will realize just how wrong you've been doing it. And by it, I mean *it*."

Kate's mouth went completely dry.

"Why don't we leave you two to get undressed?" Brenna asked.

And then Kate's legs went a little weak.

"Anything you like," Hailey said. "Down to suits or nothing at all. Though"—she turned to Kate—"I do recommend at least taking your top off. We'll be right outside, and all you need to do is reach out of the drape and drop the yellow flag that's there. We'll know you're comfortable."

Alec looked like *nothing* could make him comfortable.

Brenna gave him one more compassionate smile. "You'll love it, trust me."

"That's what I'm afraid of," he murmured as they left and closed the front drape, but Kate caught the comment.

"What are you afraid of?" she asked.

He met the question with a direct gaze, taking a few seconds before he replied. "Not much," he admitted. "I face killers in the cage and fighters in the ring. I marched around

Baghdad on patrol and picked up a few IEDs with my bare hands."

"But you're afraid of me," she said, suddenly realizing what had been eluding her.

"I'm afraid of…" He closed his eyes. "Yeah, let's go with you."

There was more to it, much more, but she wasn't going to find out here in this cabana with two massage therapists waiting for them to strip. And the way he looked at her, the little bit of vulnerability that darkened his eyes, was not only so out of place on such a big man, it was endearing beyond description.

"Let's make a deal, then."

He laughed. "Always the dealmaker, aren't you?"

She smiled. "A good lawyer can compromise." She took a step closer and lowered her voice. "Let's play the game they expect us to play. How hard can it be?"

His eyebrow twitched, and he nearly smiled. "How hard?"

Then she realized what he meant, shooting a blast of heat through her. "Oh, I get it. A double entendre."

The corner of his mouth lifted. "It only gets worse when you use those big words, Smarty-Pants."

She bit back a laugh, still heated from the thought of what he'd meant. "So instead of us being all weird and uncomfortable around them and making them jump to a million wrong conclusions, which would only incur the wrath of Gabe Rossi, let's just…"

"Get our fakeness on and our clothes off?"

She nodded.

"Okay."

For a long second, they stared at each other, neither one moving.

"I guess I could make this easy and turn around," he said, a thin note of resignation in his voice. He pivoted slowly. "Go ahead and get on your massage table and cover up, and when you're ready, I'll take my T-shirt off and let them know we're ready. That ought to satisfy them."

Kate stayed right where she was, pulling down her strapless sundress and untying the bikini top before climbing onto the massage table and pulling the sheet over her bottom.

"Okay," she whispered, lying flat.

Slowly, he turned, and even more slowly, his gaze drifted over her prone body. Staring at her, he grabbed the neck of his T-shirt and yanked it over his head, revealing his hard, hot, muscular body.

As he walked by her to go to the drape and drop the notification flag, he put a light hand on her head.

"Now all we have to do is relax."

She snorted, because they both knew that was impossible.

Alec pretended to sleep, or at least be in a Zen state, but the little massage therapist hadn't even come close to untying his knots. Kate, on the other hand, drifted off fairly quickly, allowing him to stare at her through nearly closed eyes and watch her body be oiled, rubbed, pressed, and caressed.

And through an act of God and the world's most incredible willpower, he did not sprout an erection against his massage table. But for fifty minutes, he didn't turn his head—if the massage therapist thought that was weird, then too fucking bad—but used the time to do what he'd done for days: watch Kate.

But something was different now. He couldn't put his finger on it, or maybe he didn't want to, because she let some kind of wall down that really was better, safer, saner, and easier left up.

The sheet was pulled down to her waist, giving him a view of her bare back, her arms at her sides, denying him a chance to see even a glimpse of her breasts. But he could imagine—and did, way too often. As always, his gaze shifted back to her face, making him think about what it had been like to hold her cheeks in his hands out in the sun and how much he'd wanted to kiss her to quiet her. And just kiss her again.

Her eyes popped open, and she caught him. But he didn't look away. For what seemed like an eternity, they stared at each other, playing the game, of course. They looked across the small space that separated them like lovers would, unblinking, unsmiling, all the walls down.

A very, very dangerous place for Alec Petrov to go.

"And we're done," Hailey whispered, keeping the mood calming in the cool cabana. She pulled up his sheet at the same time the other woman completely covered Kate. "Rest for a few minutes, have some coconut water and fruit. Madame Valaina will be right in."

"I'm already here."

Alec lifted his head and squinted into the light pouring into the open cabana, the sun nearly blinding him. No, wait. That wasn't the sun.

It was a big orange hat.

Swearing under his breath, he turned to Kate and watched her come to the realization that the woman who'd witnessed and commented on their argument on the sand was their own personal sex guru.

They shared a long look, and Kate bit her lower lip, her eyes lighting with a laugh.

"All right, ladies, scoot." Orangie dragged the curtain across the front, closing off the view. "Let me have my darlings all alone."

The two massage therapists scurried away, offering hasty good-byes and thank-yous and disappearing off to the beach.

"Hello, Mathilda and Benjamin!" The new arrival swooped in like a tangerine hurricane, swooshing through the little area to place herself right between their heads, blocking any chance for Alec and Kate to silently communicate.

"Well, well, well." She looked from one to the other, flinging off her hat and tossing it to the floor, shaking out a mass of thick black curls. "I guess I have my breathwork cut out for me today."

Alec turned enough to lift his head and get a good look at her. "We know how to breathe."

A black eyebrow angled north. "And you know how to fuss, fight, and fume, too. You're quite good at silencing her in the middle of a sentence, and she's clearly holding in a lot of frustration where you're concerned."

Alec felt his jaw drop and saw Kate's sheet rustle as she turned and sat up. "I don't think you know what—"

"Oh, I know what," she shot back.

"Speaking of cutting her off in the middle of a sentence," Alec said, pushing up, too. The madame pressed him right back down with one sharp nail.

"I'm allowed. But you're her husband, and after today, you will never interrupt her again, even with a kiss, as you were considering earlier." She dragged that pointy talon over his shoulder. "Do you know why these beds have been placed only eighteen inches apart? Because during a couples massage, most pairs tend to hold hands and look lovingly into each other's eyes."

And they'd done neither during their massage.

"But we will fix that," the woman said. "We will fix...*you*." She pressed on Alec's back, her fingers even stronger than the massage therapist's, pushing him right back into the table.

He didn't know if *you* meant just him or included Kate, but he suspected he was the one who needed fixing. But right now? Right here? Half-naked and already pretending to be something he wasn't?

Alec's stomach tightened as he braced for whatever was ahead.

Valaina put one hand on Alec's head and the other, he assumed by her posture, on Kate's, still standing in the small space between their massage tables. "As you may know, I am Madame Valaina Bonaparte. No relation to the famous one, I'm sorry to say. For the next hour, I am one hundred percent in charge of you. You cannot argue with me or each other, you cannot leave, you cannot say no to anything I request, and you cannot—this is of paramount importance—you cannot be dishonest."

They were so screwed.

"In return, I am giving a gift, a wedding gift in your case, that will last a lifetime." She fluttered her fingers on his back. "I am giving you the gift of tenderness, which I assure you will be what you will need in the fifty or sixty years ahead."

Tenderness. Jesus H. He did not *do* tenderness. He didn't even know what it was.

"I feel you tensing, Benjamin. I feel you resisting, and do you want to know how? Your breathing stopped," she announced before he could answer the question. "We will correct that."

"Great," he mumbled.

"We'll work on a lot of things today, starting here." She tapped his head. "I want you both to think right now. Close your eyes and think all the way back to the day you met. The first time you made eye contact."

Less than a week ago.

"I understand that was in high school." She let out a little laugh. "Yes, news travels fast, but I would have known that rumor was true just by the slight hitch in your breathing, Mathilda."

"Tilly," Alec said. "My, um, wife goes by Tilly."

"What do *you* call her?" she asked.

Kate. "A lot of things," he said.

"What is your secret pet name that only you use when you are alone or making love or taking a shower together?"

They were both silent, then Valaina hooted. "My guess based on the way you both silently gasped? You shared that shower this morning."

"We did not," Kate said.

"I can sense when you gasp," Valaina replied. "I'm a *breathwork* expert. Alec, your pet name?"

"I don't—"

"Smarty-Pants," Kate said. "He calls me Smarty-Pants."

He stole a look up at the woman to see if she was buying that, and also to try to catch Kate's eye to thank her for the save. But the wall of orange still separated them, and Madame Valaina gave a knowing nod.

"Of course he does," she said. "And what do you call him? Big Guy? Superman? The Beast?"

He heard Kate choke a soft laugh. "I like that."

Because it was accurate, he thought.

"Woo hoo! Smarty-Pants and the Beast." Valaina chuckled at her own wit. "I'm loving this already."

Glad somebody was.

155

She took a slight step forward and moved her hand to his back. "Let's talk about what's in here."

"Lungs for breathing?" Alec guessed.

"Heart for loving." She tapped his back. "Think about the very first time you said the words *I love you* to each other. Remember?"

More like *I hate you*. Though Kate had never said that, he imagined she'd thought it.

"Who said it first?" Valaina asked, breaking a long silence.

Still they didn't answer—both certain they'd contradict the other, no doubt.

"Tilly, was it Benjamin?"

He heard her sigh. "No, it was me."

His heart dropped a little, and he had no doubt the madame felt it, too. Why would Kate say that? And who in their right mind would believe it?

"All right, then, lower parts." Suddenly, the woman's hand was on his ass, but she'd moved enough that Alec could see Kate's face. She was flushed, her eyes bright, a lock of auburn hair slipping over her eye. She held his gaze, but neither one of them even smiled. They were both too scared to get yelled at.

"I want you to remember…"

Sex, Alec imagined, bracing for the order.

"The very first time one of you had an orgasm. Who was first?"

Alec looked right at Kate, waiting to get the sign of how they should answer. She closed her eyes. "Me again."

Valaina nodded. "I'm happy to hear he's a giver."

She finally opened her eyes, and Alec's breath caught in his throat as their eyes met.

"And now your feet." Valaina was at the other end of the

massage tables now, her hands over their sheets, on their feet. "Who will walk away?"

Alec frowned. "Not following the question."

She squeezed his heel. "Of the two of you, who is the most likely to walk away and end this marriage?"

After a beat, or ten, of his heart, Alec opened his mouth to answer.

"Not me."

But it was Kate's voice he heard, saying the same words. They'd said it in perfect unison.

"Wonderful!" Valaina clapped. "There's hope for you two, after all. Now, sit up. It's time for deep breathing and some eye-to-eye, mouth-to-mouth, heart-to-heart, and body-to-body intimacy. Or what I call...*bliss*."

Chapter Sixteen

Kate glanced around for where she'd left her bathing suit top. On a pillow, a good six feet away, and about two inches from Madame Valaina's foot.

Alec was already standing, still wearing the dark blue trunks that hung so low on his hips that she could see the indents under his abs, perfectly cut and pointing to...what was underneath those shorts.

Bliss.

She looked up and realized he'd caught her staring. "My top," she mouthed.

"Oh, absolutely not." Valaina scooped up the bathing suit top with her toe and kicked it across the cabana. "I insist this is done while wearing as few clothes as possible to maximize your skin-to-skin contact."

"Madame—"

"I have what you need." She cut off Alec's protest and produced a long piece of persimmon chiffon from a bag, flinging it across the space so it floated like red wind. "This will drape you."

Not very effectively, Kate thought, as she fingered what looked like a sheer curtain panel.

Alec was next to her in a second, taking the fabric to wrap it around her, turning his head.

"You don't want to see your wife's breasts?" Madame Valaina asked.

Oh, *God.*

Alec speared the woman with a look. "Pretty much nothing I want more. But not with an audience."

"Thanks," Kate whispered, wrapping the material like a shawl around her bare shoulders. She had a bikini bottom on—a small bikini bottom—and at that point, all she could do was pray to whatever gods this sex guru followed that Alec could stay dressed during...bliss.

"Benjamin, sit on this pillow, please, and cross your legs." Valaina indicated an oversized tufted pillow on the floor, and he followed the orders.

Valaina nodded to her. "Now you, Tilly."

"Where?" she asked. All of the other pillows had been removed.

"On his lap," she said. "Straddling him. You know, as if you're making love in a chair. Surely you've made love in a..." She looked from one to the other, closing her eyes and shaking her head slowly.

Had she figured out the truth? Kate didn't move, waiting for the accusation and verdict: *You two are complete fakes!*

"Excuse me while I walk into this wall between you two," she said dryly. "You may say it's because you aren't comfortable with another person in this room, but I heard you bickering on the beach. Moreover, I saw the unnatural stiffness between you, and I can smell the tension in this tent. And I don't mean of the sexual variety."

They stole another look at each other, as if they could silently agree not to let her know she was right.

"Let go of whatever it is keeping you two apart," the woman said, flicking her hands toward Alec on the floor. "Sit on his lap, Tilly." Her voice softened, taking the sting out of the order. "And, for heaven's sake, wrap your legs around your husband."

Kate let out a slow breath and walked across the hard-packed sand of the cabana floor, clinging to her flimsy wrap to cover her bare breasts. Alec stared straight ahead, his jaw clenched, his arms at his sides.

He looked like a man being sent to a torture chamber.

"Why?" Kate whispered, not even realizing the word slipped out.

"It's the only way to do this exercise," Valaina replied. "And, dear girl"—she put a hand on Kate's shoulder—"I'm rarely wrong about these things, but my impression is that Smarty-Pants has something to teach her Beast."

Did she? Well, it certainly wasn't *vocabulary*.

Kate lowered herself to his lap. She hesitated a split second, then she heard Alec's breath catch as she found a place for her bottom, right on his hard, unforgiving thighs. Slowly, she curled her legs around his hips, and in this position, she was ever so slightly taller than Alec, her mouth at about his eye level.

She inched back—

"Oh no," Valaina said, settling on a pillow she'd tossed to the floor a few feet away. Kate noticed that Alec surreptitiously glanced at his right hand, currently out of the other woman's sight. Kate would have to remember to cover his tattoo. She'd have to remember to cover a lot of things, like her boobs, her thoughts, and her response to being sealed against a man this...hot.

"Let your chest touch his, and your mouth to his ear."

She leaned forward, letting the thin material come

between her and his bare chest, her lips at his left ear, his mouth in the vicinity of her throat.

And both of them left their hands clumsily at their sides.

"Okay," Kate said, giving a little laugh. It was awkward, but it was also...warm. And not just because the sun beat down on the cabana roof.

Ha managed to make his whole body perfectly still—except for his wildly beating heart. Nice to know there were some things he couldn't control.

"Benjamin." Valaina's voice had grown much softer, the edgy demand replaced by something that sounded more like a yoga instructor. "Put your hands on your wife's shoulders."

Slowly, he lifted his hands and set them lightly over the fabric, carefully angling his right hand so Madame Valaina couldn't get a good look at his tattoo.

"What do you feel?" the woman asked.

"Muscles and bone. Slender shoulders, but strong."

"Oh, gods and goddesses," the woman exclaimed. "We do have work to do." They both looked at her, their cheeks brushing as they turned. "What do you feel in *here*?" She tapped her chest. "When you touch your wife, what do you feel?"

Nothing. Kate waited for the word. Or worse.

Slowly, he turned back and repositioned them so their opposite cheeks touched.

"I feel...awestruck."

A splash of something nice and satisfying rushed through her. "Awestruck?" she whispered.

"I know, big word for me."

And so...sweet. Kate's mouth lifted in an unexpected smile.

"All right, it's Tilly's turn. Hands on his shoulders."

Alec released her and settled his hands on her waist so

161

Kate could close her fingers over his massive shoulders. Speaking of being awestruck. She was, at the size, strength, and powerful masculinity of the man.

"Tilly?" Valaina prodded. "What do you feel in your heart when you hold your husband's shoulders?"

"Protected." The word slipped out, and she felt Alec's cheek move as if he'd smiled, but she was pressed too close to see.

"Good, good, that's good. Now, I want you to touch each other's chests."

Neither one of them moved.

"Benjamin, please touch your wife's breasts and tell me what you see when you imagine her heart."

He didn't move, unless she counted the twitch of muscles that were pressed against her crotch. Oh. Maybe there were more things he didn't control.

Kate fought a smile...and the urge to rock her hips and torture them both.

"Please," Valaina urged.

On a slow exhale, he lifted his hands and placed them over the rise of her breasts, over the red fabric. Kate looked down at his hands and sucked in a soft breath, her heart slamming against his touch.

She stared at his beat-up fingers, huge and masculine and tattooed.

"Under." She barely breathed the word. "Under the cloth." To hide the tattoo...and let him put his hand on her skin.

He carefully lifted the sheer fabric to hide his marks. His hand seared against the most delicate and sensitive flesh, her eyes shuttering as she resisted a moan and sigh of pleasure.

"Yes, yes," Valaina said. "This is the moment you slowly take in all you can. Breathe. Through your nose, Benjamin.

Not just air. Breathe in Tilly. Breathe in the scent and flavor of your wife."

He had to feel Kate's body shaking and hear her own ragged breath. The fragrance of the room had changed from sweet spices to something more...human. The scent of desire.

In her belly, lower, heat coiled and nerves tingled, and oh, God, everything was melting inside her...but doing just the opposite in his, right where the hottest part of their bodies met.

Surely this lady would stop the madness soon.

But Valaina was relentless. "How do you imagine her heart, Benjamin?" she asked. "What is it about that heart that made you fall for her?"

He hasn't fallen. They barely knew each other. But that didn't stop Kate's bathing suit crotch from growing damp from the natural female response to the pressure of his hard-on.

She heard Alec try to swallow, looking down at his hands instead of up at her eyes. He stared at them for a long time. "Bruised. Battered. Broken."

Her heart? Yes, her heart was all those things. "How do you—"

He looked up, silencing her question. "My hands, I mean." His eyes were dark and pained. "Are not good enough for your heart."

The admission slammed at her chest, making her draw back, not sure she'd heard right.

But Valaina did just the opposite, practically crawling off her pillow like a tigress moving in for the kill. "And we find the first brick in your wall, Benjamin. You breathed it right out of the way."

They simply stared at each other, his hands on her chest,

163

hers on her lap, clutching the edge of the material so his tattoo remained covered.

"But she loves your hands, right, Tilly?"

Slowly, Kate nodded.

"When do you love them most?" Valaina urged. "When he uses them to make love?"

What would be the most honest answer? The one that would be real to him—and to Valaina. And to Kate. She might love if he used his hands to make love to her—no *might* about it. But he hadn't.

Yet.

She took in a slow, deep breath as that thought landed on her.

They hadn't made love *yet*. She couldn't let Madame Valaina know that, and she couldn't deny the fact that something deep inside of her wanted to make love to him. Her chest rose and fell as she tried to cope with that reality.

"That's right, Tilly. Use your breathing, but not so shallow. Deep and slow. Inhale your man. Smother yourself in his aroma. And tell me—"

"I love when he uses his hands to protect me."

His eyes flashed when she said it, appreciating the compliment, as much as anything could be appreciated in this situation.

"How does it make you feel?" Valaina urged.

"Less vulnerable," she answered honestly. The truth of that was as warm and welcome as his hands. Considering that she was furious that a man was taking away her power and control, the fact that he made her feel less vulnerable meant he was doing his job, and doing it quite well.

Valaina crawled closer, her face only a few feet from theirs. "Benjamin, you must tell your wife exactly why you do not feel your hands are not good enough for her. And,

Tilly, you must tell your husband why you feel vulnerable."

But they just stared at each other.

"Try to share your breathing," she said, but it was like the woman wasn't even in the room, her voice barely a whisper in the distance. Kate kept her attention on Alec, memorizing every angle of his face, the slash of his sharp cheekbones, the crooked slant of his nose, the scar above his right eye. How had he gotten that? And how could she keep from touching it?

She couldn't. As if mesmerized, she lifted her hand and brushed the split in his eyebrow. His only reaction was to add pressure to her breasts, making her nipples bud under his palms.

"Put your lips close, but don't touch."

Kate dipped down to close the tiny space between their mouths.

"Don't kiss," Valaina ordered in that raspy whisper. "Breathe. Tilly, breathe him in. Benjamin, breathe her out. And again."

The tip of his tongue flicked against Kate's lower lip, making everything in her twist and squeeze.

"In and out," Valaina whispered.

They breathed, their lips sparking when they accidentally touched.

"And do not forget my questions."

The questions. Kate could barely remember them. Why did he not feel worthy of her? Why did he make her feel helpless?

"Now prepare the answer in your head. Prepare. Know what you're going to say." Her voice seemed so distant, lost in the hum and pulse in Kate's head, the thrum of hot blood rushing through her body, the buzz in her brain that screamed *kiss!*

"Tell her about your hands, Benjamin." She was quieter still.

Kiss!

"Tell him why you feel weak, Tilly." Her voice was almost impossible to hear.

Kiss.

"And I'll be back in one hour."

The swooshing sound of her disappearing behind the drapes was drowned out by the moan that escaped Alec's throat as he finally, finally closed the space and smothered Kate with his kiss.

Alec opened his mouth and tasted her, curling his tongue against hers and angling his head to get what he wanted. *More.*

"She's gone," Kate whispered into the kiss.

His blood surged with need. Finally able to really use his hands, he caressed her soft, sloping breasts, thumbing the hard buds of her nipples, battling the urge to break the kiss so he could suckle and lick every inch of her skin.

"She's gone." The words pulled him out of his haze, making him aware of the strangled breath trapped in his chest, and that his dick was fully engorged and throbbing against the sex-dampened crotch of her bathing suit.

Finally, slowly, achingly, he broke the kiss and opened his eyes. But Kate's were still closed as she tilted her head back, offering him direct access to her throat.

"She's gone," she whispered one more time.

In other words, *Don't stop*. Had he read that right? "Kate."

"Tilly," she corrected, looking at him from under thick lashes. "We could be under observation. From Gabe. From her, making sure we're doing our homework."

"Then maybe we should go back to the villa and do it."

Her eyes flashed.

"Homework, I mean."

She sat straight, staring at him, sliding her hands around his neck, her fingers warm and strong and demanding. "Please."

A slow smile pulled at his mouth.

"Why are you smiling?"

"Because I love it when you use simple, one-syllable words I understand."

"Please," she repeated, kissing the word into his mouth.

She didn't have to say it a third time.

They kissed with pent-up fury. She was as desperate as he was to let their tongues battle it out and turn the mouth-on-mouth contact into mouth-on-throat and mouth-on-breastbone and, as he leaned her backward, mouth-on-nipple, which was hot and sweet and perfect.

It was an act, right? For the invisible audience or secret cameras or whatever? He clung to that excuse and her body, laying her back on the pillow. She kept her legs wrapped around him, pulling him against her, palming his back and arms and shoulders, and rocking her hips so his cock slammed right between her legs.

"Oh my God," she whispered. "That feels so good."

She *wanted* him. She wanted him to touch her and rub her. She arched her back, adding pressure, letting his dick slide over her mound, making him almost howl with pleasure.

One tiny piece of bathing suit out of the way, and he could be all the way inside her.

He pushed up, shocked by the thought. "Is this what you want?" he asked.

"I don't know what I want," she admitted on a torn breath, spreading her hands over his back and dragging them up and down. "Except…" She bit her lip and looked up at him. "Can we pretend a little longer?"

"Yeah."

The bright red sheer thing had fallen to the side, revealing her breasts wet from his mouth, her nipples like sweet raspberries. "We should pretend a little longer," he whispered.

He dragged his hands over her stomach and between her breasts, touching her nipple—and freezing. Suddenly, the ugliness of his fingers against the beauty of her skin stopped all that nice rush of pleasure.

"What?" Kate asked.

She sat up enough to follow his gaze. Instantly, he tried to move his hand, but she snagged it and squeezed it, keeping his hand pressed to her velvety skin.

"No one is here to see your tattoo."

He shook his head, feeling the shame, the familiar, hot, hated shame rise up through him.

"I have no right—"

"I've given you the right," she said, pressing his hand harder. "Touch me."

He didn't jerk his hand away, but he didn't fondle her, either.

"I like it," she whispered, rocking her hips as if that could emphasize that she was telling the truth. "A lot."

Very, very slowly, he stroked her breast. "My hands are—"

"Sexy," she finished.

He bit back a smile, his heart doing stupid things at that.

"No, my hands are…" Meant for killing and hurting, maiming and fighting. Not tenderness.

"Masculine."

He laughed. "My hands are—"

"About to make me come." She lifted her hips again, pressing hard against his painful erection. "If you will just…keep…touching me."

He obeyed the order and lowered his head to add a kiss, wanting her tongue against his again, his cock enormous now, rolling against her wet suit, firing raw pleasure into his balls. The rhythm grew natural, their breathing impossible, and the kiss only stopped when she lost control and clutched his back and sank her teeth into his shoulder and fell apart with a long, sweet, exquisite-sounding orgasm.

He fought not to do the same, knowing on every level that that wasn't what should happen. But it wasn't easy. She rocked a few more times and trembled with an aftershock and pulled him even closer to her, burying her face in his shoulder and neck.

When she got her breath, she turned her head to look at him, saying nothing.

He wanted to kiss her lips, and cheek, and throat. And all of her. But he didn't, deciding it was much better to make light of what just happened.

"I bet we get an A on our homework," he said.

She frowned. "She didn't tell us to make out. She told us to share secrets."

"Don't you think we shared enough for one day?"

A flicker of hurt danced over her expression, so fast he almost missed it. "Of course." She pushed him back, snagging the corner of her flimsy cover-up and pulling it over her breasts, giving him a harsh look.

"What?" he asked, propping up to look at her. "Not enough control for you?"

She bristled at the question, arching upward enough to put her mouth against his ear. "Listen to me," she hissed out on a breath only he could hear. "I'm flat on my back in a beach cabana, half-naked and fully satisfied. We were one thrust away from copulation, and I wasn't saying no. It doesn't *get* any more vulnerable than that." She eased him off her, rolling away. "Get up, Beast. Party's over."

He didn't argue. They were halfway down the beach before he realized she'd brought the see-through red sheet and was letting it fly in the breeze like a red-hot wake.

Chapter Seventeen

There was no way she'd sleep. Not even a chance. Robyn eyed the two beers in the back of her refrigerator, so tempted—just to make herself sleepy. Otherwise, she'd be up all night, pacing, worrying, anticipating the trip to Vlitnik's tomorrow and the possibility of seeing Cole.

After Selena helped her figure out where that photo had been taken, and when, she'd called and left a message and, next thing she knew, she got a call from some lady who said Mr. Vlitnik would see her at nine tomorrow morning.

She was surprised he wanted to wait, but whatever. It gave her ten more hours to be prepared.

She poured a large glass of milk and picked up the baby-name book she'd found for a dollar at a garage sale, turning to the boys' names.

Rubbing her belly, she thought about the little baby boy she already loved. Flipping to the C's, she scanned the names. Not Cole, of course, but maybe Cade for a boy. Or Cameron—

The front door lock snapped, making her gasp. Did someone just unlock her door? The complex of cheap apartments in Flatbush, New York, wasn't crime-ridden, but it wasn't the safest place in the world, either.

The knob turned, and she stifled a scream, staring at the chain that would prevent anyone from fully opening the door. She hoped.

Silent, her heart hammering, she backed into the sofa, dividing her gaze between the door and the cell phone she'd left on the kitchen counter. Could she—

"Robyn? Robyn, are you home?"

"Cole!" She flew off the sofa and ran to the door, her hand shaking too hard to undo the chain. Of course he still had a key. She stuck her face through the tiny opening to make sure she wasn't dreaming this time.

There he was, his golden eyes as warm as ever, a gray hoodie over his short blond hair, his nose…

"What happened to you?"

"Just open the door!"

She got the chain halfway across and then stopped, thinking about the only boy who mattered more than Cole— the one she was carrying inside. She glanced down at the oversized sweatshirt and leggings she wore. At a glance, he'd never notice. But if he looked closely—

"Robyn, come on. This is important!"

Should she tell him? Could she *not*?

She closed her eyes and said the closest thing she knew to a prayer. "God help me," she whispered. "And little…Cade." Then she slid the chain across and had to jump back when the door practically slammed her in the face.

"Cole!" She covered her mouth to keep from squealing with happiness. "Where have you—"

"Where is Petrov?" he demanded.

She took a step back. "What?"

"Alec Petrov, my old trainer. I know you know where he is."

She stabbed her fingers into her hair, inching away,

emotions swirling so hard she couldn't think. "How do you know that?"

"Because you're going to see Vlitnik tomorrow. And you can't, Robyn. You can't go there. He'll never keep his end of the deal."

She swallowed and fought for air, staring at the boy—no, he was a man now—she thought she loved. The guy she left Philadelphia to live with, until he disappeared.

The father of her baby.

"How do you know that?" she asked.

"I got friends who know him really good."

Her brain finally started working again. "Where have you been? Why did you just disappear?"

"You know..." He shrugged.

"No, I don't know. You just vanished, Cole. You never called or came here or—"

"Forget it, okay?" He was tense and nervous and looking around, like he was searching for something.

Searching for whatever she knew about Alec Petrov.

"Is that why I saw you at Vlitnik's house?" she asked. "'Cause you have friends who know him?"

"Yeah, and you can't tell him where Alec is, Robyn," he said. "They're going to kill him."

She gasped. "Wha—why?"

"Don't know." He shrugged, as if killing someone were no big deal, and she hugged herself against unwanted chills.

"But he knows that I know where Alec is," she said, suddenly wondering if that knowledge put *her* in danger. Real danger. Like, *getting killed* danger.

She wanted so badly to rub her belly, but a sixth sense she didn't understand kept her from drawing his attention there.

"Just make something up to tell him," Cole said. "But tell

me the truth." He flipped down his hood to reveal more cuts and bruises on his face than she'd ever seen on him.

Cole had been fighting MMA for a long time, as a hobby and a way to make extra cash, and he was good. He rarely got hit that hard. "What happened to your face?"

Another shrug. "Usual shit. Listen, you have to tell me where he is."

She did? What if *he* told Vlitnik and got the reward? "Cole, I really need money."

He snorted. "So do I."

"I *gotta* have the money."

He eyed her hard. "Believe me, he's given you all you're ever going to get. A grand for next to nothing?"

"How do you know about that?"

"I told you, I got friends. Fighters. Guys who work for him."

A chill ran up Robyn's spine. Was Cole telling her everything? Was it really just his fighter friends who worked for Vlitnik, or was he working for that monster, too? The thought made her stomach drop, but she couldn't help but wonder why Cole, after being MIA for five months, suddenly showed up, seeming to care more about what she knew than how she was.

"But I have to find Alec," he said. "So tell me where he is."

"Why?"

He rubbed his fingers together in the universal gesture for cash. "Alec will pay me not to tell Vlitnik. It's called blackmail, Robyn, and it's not a sucky way to make money."

She stared up at him, hating the sinking feeling in her chest. She'd loved him. She still did…didn't she? She didn't love this shifty, lying side of him, though. "Blackmailing someone is illegal."

He looked like he was fighting a laugh. "It's the only way I can…" He tipped his head and softened his expression. Then he reached up and slid his hand under her hair, curling his fingers around her neck. "Hey, Robyn's Egg. C'mere." He pulled her closer, but the move didn't work, and neither did the old nickname.

Robyn's egg was fertilized now. And not only did she suddenly not trust the man in front of her, the child in her belly was worth ten of him.

"I missed the shit out of you, baby."

Right. She stayed stiff. "Why do you want to find Alec so bad?"

"Money, honey," he said, inching closer. "Petrov owned his own MMA studio. He's got cash and plenty of it. He'll pay thousands to someone who's inside the operation and can tell him Vlitnik's every move."

He certainly had enough money to stay at a ritzy resort in Florida.

She shook her head, inching away. "I'm not gonna do that, Cole. I'm"—*pregnant*—"hurt," she admitted. "You broke my heart."

He nodded, dropping his hand. "That's cool. I get it. But we're friends, right? After all that, we're friends?"

That's cool? We're friends? Oh, *hell* no. "Sure."

"Then you gotta tell me where he is." When she didn't answer, he said, "Listen, I'll pay you, 'cause I know Alec and he will pay good money for this information. A shit-ton of money. Definitely more than that dick Vlitnik."

She couldn't speak because her brain was whirring with one question: *What's the best thing to do for my baby?*

And some small voice whispered: *Don't say a word.* So she didn't, just shaking her head instead.

"Robyn, if you don't fucking tell me…" He lowered his

head, his eyes narrowing the way they did before he damn near took someone's head off. What was she thinking? He could kill her right now.

She had to tell him something. But what? If she made something up, she'd have to have proof. And the only proof she had was a screenshot of an Instagram picture and some printouts from Web sites that Selena sent her about a resort in Florida where Alec Petrov *might* be.

"Robyn, come on," he insisted.

"He's back in Philadelphia." The lie just slid right off her tongue like a pat of butter.

"How do you know?"

"I saw him. I talked to him. I went to see my brother a few days ago because, you know, he's—"

He shook his head like the last thing on earth he wanted to hear about was her brother. "You saw him? At the studio where he trains?"

He sounded like he was baiting her. Hadn't he just said Alec *owned* a studio? As in...he didn't anymore? She couldn't fall into his trap.

"Oh, no," she said, her brain ticking through possibilities. "No, no. I saw him at the"—where the hell would she have been?—"doctor. I went to the doctor. My doctor in Philadelphia."

She had no doctor in Philadelphia, and if Cole had been a caring, loving, attention-paying boyfriend, he'd know that. And he'd ask why she'd gone to see a doctor.

"What was he doing at the doctor?"

But he wasn't a caring boyfriend. He was shit on a stick, and she was a freaking idiot for not realizing that sooner. "Getting his head stitched, I guess." More lies. Easy lies. "He was all bandaged up." Because he could be, as a fighter.

"Did you talk to him?"

"Yeah, yeah. He asked about you." Oh, the shit she could fling to protect her baby. Motherhood was an amazing thing, considering five months ago she couldn't have told a lie if her life depended on it. But now a life did depend on it.

Cade's life. No, not Cade. She'd never name her child after this asshole, not even the first letter of his name.

"Robyn!" he insisted. "What did he say?"

"Just that he was, um, freelancing. Working out of a studio in South Philly, across town. A place called..." Holy crap. She snapped her fingers like she was trying to remember what Alec said. "Cade's. Cade's Gym. He said he'd be there for a while and told me to tell you to come in and see him if you go back to Philly."

He looked hard at her, searching her face from eye to eye, clearly judging the whopper she'd just told him. "Okay," he said. But she couldn't tell from the frown on his face if he believed her or not.

"Cole, you will pay me, right?"

His scowl deepened. "I don't remember a place called Cade's."

"He said it's new," she said. "You go there. You'll find him."

"And you're not going to see Vlitnik tomorrow?"

She shook her head, finally honest. "I don't want to go. I want you to find Alec and get money. What should I do, though? Vlitnik thinks I'm going to tell him."

"Yeah, just call that number and tell him you were wrong." He stepped back to the door, doing one more visual sweep of the counter tops, his gaze falling on the *People* magazine opened to a picture of the future Mr. and Mrs. Nathaniel Ivory at the posh resort where they'd be married soon.

Robyn literally felt her heart stop.

"God, Robyn, you shouldn't waste your money on that shit," he mumbled.

"Yeah, I know."

He went to the door and stepped out, obviously dying to get out as fast as he could.

"Cole?"

He turned and looked at her. "What?"

Guilt pressed down on her chest. *I'm carrying your baby.* She should tell him. She was supposed to tell him. This baby was half his. Not telling him was so, so wrong. Maybe—

"What, Robyn? I gotta go." Impatience made his voice sharp.

No, he'd have no love or concern for a baby. It was always about looking out for number one with Cole. "You sure they'll leave me alone?" she asked.

"Probably."

Probably not. But if he didn't work for them, then how would he know? "'Kay. Bye."

She closed the door and quietly locked it, grateful now that she wasn't sleepy. She could start the drive by midnight and be in Florida in, what, eighteen or twenty hours?

If Alec Petrov was paying anyone, it would be her. After all, she'd just saved his ass. And she had a feeling that if she didn't show tomorrow, Vlitnik—and maybe Cole—would be back for hers.

She had to get out, fast.

Chapter Eighteen

t wasn't enough. And, holy hell, that terrified Kate because…what *would* be enough?

As if she didn't know.

She closed her eyes, but the view she'd been staring at stayed burned in reverse behind her eyelids, the crescent moon black instead of a slice of white, a star or planet burning bright right next to it. Those celestial beings shed very little light, but Kate had been out on the dark patio long enough to have her night vision and still be able to see the sands and water of Barefoot Bay.

She'd cautiously avoided Alec all afternoon and evening, studying in her room—well, trying to study. Each of them ate, alone and separately, a delicious and spicy lasagna Poppy had left in the fridge. It wasn't a truce or anger or even an uncomfortable silence that kept Kate from her bodyguard.

It was the fact that she wanted more of him and too much time with him and, well, it was so tacky to beg. But she might beg for more. More of his mouth and hands. More of his hard body. More of his…

And not just that, she thought with a little splash of adrenaline. She wanted more of what was on the inside. She wanted to know what made him tick. Why did he seem so strong and commanding one minute and so vulnerable the next? Why was he scared of touching her, yet his fingers had been beyond capable of bringing her right to orgasm on his lap?

She just wanted—

"I don't suppose you'd want to take a walk."

She turned from the blackness of the night sky to see Alec's powerful silhouette in the open doors, lit by a single light in the living area. He wore a T-shirt and shorts that came just below his knees. He must have changed and even sneaked one of his pool baths while she was hiding out, because he seemed fresh and clean and...hot.

After her shower, she'd changed into a thin linen skirt that skimmed her ankles and a loose sleeveless top, skipping a bra she barely needed anyway. But maybe she should put one on before walking barefoot in the moonlight with him.

Or maybe not.

"I'd love to," she said, surprised at how huskily her voice came out.

He reached out a hand, silent.

And, God help her, she walked to him, took his hand, and let him lead her to the door. As he opened it, he brushed her bare shoulder with his knuckle, making her shiver involuntarily.

"It is a little cooler when the sun goes down," he said. "You need a sweater or something?"

Something like a *bra*. "I'm okay." Her gaze moved to the entry table where she'd dropped the sheer red fabric she'd taken from the massage cabana. "This will work," she said, grabbing it as a wrap.

"Your Superwoman cape," he teased.

"It did the job," she agreed, then caught the inadvertent

double entendre. "I mean, of covering your hands in front of Madame What's-Her-Name."

"My hands…" His voice drifted off, the thought unfinished, or kept intentionally silent, as they walked side by side to the path and followed it toward the first bridge to the beach.

If his silence was intentional, it wasn't because anyone was around. Late on a weeknight, Casa Blanca was dim and quiet, its well-attended residents and efficient staff tucked away or out of sight. The beach was deserted, too, with all the umbrellas and cabanas removed and no wedding or outdoor event to fill the sand with tiki torches or the air with live music.

Tonight, everything was still. Except for Kate's heart, which had pretty much pounded at double time since their session with the "breathwork" specialist.

"What about your hands?" she asked after a minute.

"You know."

She laughed softly. "If I knew, I wouldn't have asked."

"I hate them," he said simply. "Always have, always will."

"I guess the obvious question is why, but"—she held up her hand to keep him from interrupting her—"I know you better than to expect anything but a monosyllabic response."

He gave her a side-eye. "You and your words."

"See? You and your words. All one syllable," she said.

"My favorite kind."

"What is your last name? Is it one syllable?"

He chuckled at the not-so-sly trick question. "Carlson." He didn't miss a beat as they put their bare feet on the sand and sank in a little. "Just like yours, Tilly."

She elbowed him. "Come on."

"Come on?" He chuckled and put a hand on her back. "That's the best you have, counselor? *Come on?*"

"I'll rephrase." She thought for a moment. "Mr. Carlson, can you tell the jury where your parents came from? Please don't make me remind you that you're under oath."

He laughed again. "I am, am I?"

"Answer the question."

"St. Petersburg."

"Have you ever been there?"

"No, never. Never been to Russia. Have no interest in going." There was just enough vehemence in his voice to tell her this wasn't a casual decision.

"No relatives there? No other...what was the family name again?"

He just laughed.

"All right, I give. No more interrogation. Can we just have a conversation? I want to know more about you. Anything. Nothing incriminating, just anything."

She heard him sigh in resignation. "Like what?"

"Like..." Given the open door, she wasn't sure exactly how to go through. She grabbed the first thing that came to mind. "When did you start learning the martial arts?"

He hesitated and shook his head. "I'm really not supposed to tell you anything, Kate."

"And you're not supposed to call me Kate," she fired back. "Look, Alec, we're in such close quarters. I don't want to be strangers."

"The sky is not close," he said, looking up at the stars. "The gulf is at low tide. The sand stretches for a mile or two. Don't interrogate me out here in this piece of paradise."

She swallowed, the poetry of his words sweet in her ears, and the honesty in his plea hard to ignore. Maybe later, he seemed to say. "Okay," she said quietly.

He put his arm around her, gentle and warm. "You're so much nicer when you agree with me."

"Typical man," she muttered, but the comment lacked her usual bitterness.

"No, I'm not," he said.

She looked up at him, breathing in the salty air that clung to him, taking in his rugged features in the moonlight. "No, you're not," she agreed. "A typical man would have never let today's, uh, activities end when we got back to the villa."

He stopped walking, staring at her. "Is that what you want?"

Her insides tilted, and she almost swayed on the beach. She wanted more, that's what she'd been thinking all day. But...not sex. Well, not *just* sex.

"What I want is for you to tell me something about you. Something I don't guess or drag out of you one syllable at a time. Tell me your last name. Or something about your life. Or...why you hate your hands. Tell me *something*."

He looked at her for a long time, searching her face as though he was really considering her request, making her hold her breath for the answer.

But he didn't say a word, silently continuing their walk toward the hard-packed sand left from the tide that was far, far out now. They walked along the sand to the water's edge, the low, frothy waves threatening to submerge their feet with each ebb and flow, but running out of steam before they did.

A full five minutes passed as they walked in complete silence, the only sound the splash of water and the light breeze in her ears. He dropped his arm, and Kate pulled her sheer makeshift wrap around her shoulders, letting it float behind her like wings.

Maybe she'd asked for too much. Sex would have been simpler. Even a kiss would—

"They're ugly. They're marked. They're scarred. And they were really only made to do one thing well, and that is to inflict pain."

It took a second for her to realize he was talking about his hands. And another for her to come up with ten reasons he was wrong. That wasn't pain his hands inflicted on her today.

But gut instinct told her not to interrupt.

"I was born with these giant paws." He held out his left hand, fully open to demonstrate how huge it was. Huge. His fingers would easily extend an inch and a half past hers. "My dad was a butcher, and I had to help him, so I got my first knife scar before I was six." He pointed to a nearly invisible scar on his index finger, and she tucked away another tiny piece of information about him. Dad was a butcher.

"These hands have bad memories," he said.

"Tell me one."

He thought for a few seconds, then, "My dad was holding my hand when he died," he said, his voice gruff.

"Oh." She touched his shoulder in sympathy. "That's sad."

"It was, but he wasn't that young. He was almost twenty years older than my mother, but still, it hurt."

And she knew exactly how much it hurt. Her mother died while in a coma—a coma Kate had caused. She would have loved to hold her mother's hand and say good-bye. And *I'm sorry*.

"Then there was this tattoo, which I got at thirteen."

The new tidbit pulled her from a dark memory. "Wow, that's young."

"Against my will."

She stopped walking, remembering how he and Gabe had both referred to it as a mark. "You were forced to get a tattoo that says... How do you pronounce it?"

"Like *oo-bah*," he said.

"Kill," she recalled.

"Actually, it's more like a demand that you should kill, or at least that would be the closest translation in English. Like saying, 'You will do that,' as opposed to 'Do that.' Does that make sense?"

"It's the imperative tense."

He smiled. "You would know that."

But what she didn't know—and wanted to—was why someone would force him to be marked or demand that he kill. She wasn't going to hold her breath for that confession.

He fisted his hand and turned his knuckles to face him, like he was going to punch his own nose. "This is an order, in more ways than one."

Or maybe he *would* tell her. She took a step so she was face-to-face with him, his fist between them. "Who made you get that?"

He slammed shut, his body tensing, his jaw clenched, his mouth a straight, tight line of silence.

"Why won't you tell me?"

"Because you're safer if you don't know." He scanned the darkness and put his arm around her. "Kate, remember, I made a promise to guard you in any and every way. That means not sharing more, no matter how badly you want to know. Or how much…"

"How much what?"

"How much I want you to know."

The admission silenced her, even satisfied her briefly, as he walked them far from the ambient lights of the resort to a group of graceful palm trees that formed a protected, shadowy, secret place on the beach.

She took the sheer wrap off and let it fall like a filmy

185

blanket on the sand. "Sit on my Superwoman cape," she invited.

He did, taking her hand to pull her down next to him so they could look out at the moon slice over the water. He stared straight ahead, his legs up, his elbows propped on his knees, deep in thoughts that Kate yearned to know. She reached over and touched his joined fists.

"For what it's worth, I don't think your hands are ugly."

He snorted a laugh.

"They were...lovely today."

He drew in a slow breath, not answering.

"Another thing you don't want to talk about?" she asked.

Even in the darkness, she could see his smile was wry and sweet at the same time. "It's awkward."

"That you made me lose control? If it isn't awkward for me, the lover of control, why would it be for you?" She leaned into him a little. "I have to be honest. It was amazing." Almost scary, it was so perfect.

He shook his head slightly, the infinitesimal move crushing her spirit. But then, the experience had been pretty one-sided.

"It wasn't amazing for you, I guess," she said.

"That's not why...yes, it was..." He worked to find a word, slowly turning toward her, then placing his hand—his so-not-ugly hand—on her cheek. "No woman has ever said that to me."

Said what? "It was amazing?"

"Not like that. Not like it was real."

How could that be? "I have to believe that, even without some tutoring from Madame V, you know your way around the bedroom." And a woman's body.

"I'm not much of a lover, Kate. I'm a..." He stroked her chin with his thumb, dragging the blunt fingertip lower, leaving a wake of chills on her skin. Finally, he settled his thumb in the hollow of her throat, where he could surely feel her pulse race. "I'm more of a fighter," he finished.

Without thinking, she reached up and closed her hands around his powerful neck, spreading her fingers, easing his face even closer to hers.

How could she expect him to bare his soul if she wouldn't do the same?

"I think you would be an incredible lover," she whispered. "Kind and thorough and tender."

He looked at her for a long time, unable to hide the wonder in his eyes. "What do they call it when a prisoner falls for their captor? I bet you know that, Smarty-Pants."

"Stockholm syndrome," she answered with a smile. "And you're wrong. That's not what's going on."

"Then what is?" he challenged. "Because I don't believe for one minute you're attracted to some guy who was raised in Little Russia by a butcher, not when that guy has a face that's been hit more than it's been kissed, a shitty vocabulary, and an even shittier future."

She stared at him. "That's not how I see you."

He didn't answer, obviously waiting for more.

"When I see you, I see a strong, protective, intelligent man with a quietly wry sense of humor and a lot of pain in his past." She touched his cheek. "I see a man with his soul shining through gorgeous blue eyes and a smile that gives me butterflies when it's aimed at me." She dragged her hand down his arm and closed her fingers around his hand. "And when I look at your 'giant paws,' I see a man's hands that could probably make me come with one tender touch."

She saw him swallow and try to breathe. "Show me how to do that now," he said gruffly, circling his thumb over her knuckle. "Show me how to be tender with you. I want to, Kate. I want to so much."

She had to fight for air, the words punched so hard. Every inch of her responded to the request, her body getting warm and soft and ready for him. "You are tender," she assured him.

"You make me that way." He closed the space between them, putting his lips over hers. "You make me want to be better."

A tiny whimper of helplessness escaped her throat, her head hammering as blood rushed. "Kiss me," she said. "Easy and slow and sweet."

He did exactly as he was told. So easy, so slow, and so damn sweet. His lips molded to hers, parted just enough that she could taste the tip of his tongue. He deepened the kiss, covering half her face with a hand that felt anything but tentative.

Feathering more kisses on her jaw and throat, he eased her onto her back. Hovering over her, he looked up and around, scanning the empty beach and silent night.

"We're alone," she assured him.

He still looked, narrowing his eyes, then returned his gaze to her. "Teach me more," he said.

She wet her lips, looking up at him with a heady sense of power she'd never really experienced before. Who was the captive here? Who had control? Who cared? She'd never felt like this—completely under a man's spell, yet utterly free. She hadn't even known a woman could feel like this.

He came closer, adding some of his weight on her legs, the first press of a mighty erection branding heat on her hip and thigh.

"Lift up my top," she said, mentally congratulating herself for skipping that bra.

Slowly, he dragged the cotton over her chest, the night air giving her flesh a chill, and his intense gaze making her nipples harden, already tingling for his touch.

"Everything," she whispered, closing her eyes in anticipation. "Touch everything."

He let out a sigh and covered one of her breasts with his massive hand, the calluses rough and sexy against her skin, the heat of his fingers making her hips rock automatically.

With a low groan, he dipped his head closer.

"Yes," she breathed. "Your mouth." He suckled her and licked, thumbing the other nipple and sending lightning bolts of pleasure through her body.

His hand slid lower, over her stomach, making the outside burn and the inside flip like she was free-falling. Lifting his head, he looked into her eyes, an expectant expression on his face.

"Keep going," she whispered, holding his gaze as she bunched the linen of her loose skirt and started pulling it higher up her thighs. "Here."

His eyes half-closed as if the word hit him hard, his head falling to follow his hands on her stomach. More kisses, more tongue on her skin. And then he helped her with the skirt, pushing the fabric up to expose the tops of her thighs and a white thong, already damp and sticking to her.

On a rough breath, he inched his body lower, flattening his hand against the inside of her thigh, searing her. He looked up, waiting for her next instruction.

"Touch me there, Alec. Touch me."

He placed his thumb over her mound, on top of her panties, never taking his gaze from hers as he made a slow, crazy slow, circle. She fought the need to cry out and lift her hips toward him, a plea for more caught in her throat.

Instead, she bit her lip and nodded her permission, and he

took it, sliding the silk aside enough to touch skin. Then he lowered his gaze and stared at her, at his hand on her, as he rubbed her most tender spot and slowly, slowly slid his finger inside her.

"Oh," she moaned at the touch, losing the battle to not rock her hips. "Right there, right...*there*. Just...like *that*." She wanted his mouth on her, but his hand, his rough and scarred and masculine hand, was so magical, she stopped instructing so she could simply revel in his touch.

"I have you, Kate," he whispered. "I have you."

Yes, you do. The twisting agony and pleasure of an orgasm started low in her belly, making her squeeze his shoulders and grind her body against his hand. He slipped in and out, two fingers, thick and delightful, his thumb never stopping its pressure.

He kissed her stomach and bare breasts, licking as he continued the pleasure between her legs, his hard-on pressed mercilessly against her thigh.

"Come, Kate," he ordered, kissing his way back to her mouth, owning every inch of her. "Come," he said again, against her lips.

And she did, furiously, helplessly, reckless and shameless and lost.

He moaned with her, as if her pleasure was his, as if their wrecked breathing was the result of a mutual orgasm. As if he was just as lost as she was.

After a moment, he looked at her, smoothing her skirt back down and then her top. His eyes were intense and dark, his mouth wet from their kisses, his chest heaving as he struggled with each breath.

"Petrov," he whispered.

She frowned at him, trying to understand the word. A Russian expression? A term of endearment?

"My name is Alexander Petrov."

And her heart skipped and slid around in her chest. "Thank you, Alexander Petrov, for trusting me."

"Thank you, Katherine Kingston, for teaching me."

He lowered his head to kiss her, but suddenly jerked away.

"What is—"

Alec cut off her question with a quick shake of his head and light finger to her lips, sitting up silently, peering around, getting to his feet in one smooth, predatory move. His shoulders hunched forward, his hands fisted, he stopped breathing and slowly, slowly turned.

Was someone there? Someone watching?

Kate froze, too, except for the rush of blinding fear that shot through her.

The man who wanted to hurt her…or the one who wanted to kill him? Was he here? A thousand chills prickled skin that had, seconds earlier, been warm and sated. She didn't move, didn't even sit up as cold fingers of fear closed around her heart.

Alec looked into the darkness, toward the beach, all around them.

"Should I—"

The crack of a branch snapped his attention, and Alec exploded into action, scooping her up like she was no more than a puppy and running across the beach so fast the wind screamed in her ears.

"Hey!" a voice called.

Kate gripped him hard, letting him hold her aloft, letting him have control as he tore over the bridge and to the path.

"Stop!" The voice was male, and insistent. Alec never even hesitated, didn't slip or slow one inch until he reached the villa, unlocked the door, and practically threw her inside.

"Al—"

"Shut up!" He slammed the door in her face, and instantly, she heard footsteps running toward him, up the path.

She reached for the security bar, her hands shaking as she tried to lock herself in, but then she stopped. That would lock him out.

"What the fuck are you doing?" That was Alec, his voice so low and furious, sending another explosion of adrenaline cascading through Kate.

"I was out for a jog when I heard you guys fooling around."

Moving closer to the door, Kate tried to place the voice. It wasn't Gabe and certainly not Nino.

"You could have identified yourself."

Alec knew this guy?

"Why should I? Your reflexes were good, I'll give you that. But you shouldn't have been out there messing around in the first place."

Kate stood still, her hand still on the cool bar, her ear pressed to the door.

"I knew what I was doing."

"Yeah, it looked that way." The comment was sarcastic and not threatening. Not threatening at all. "Consider it a test and you passed, but not with flying colors. Oh, and speaking of flying colors. You left this behind."

She heard Alec grunt on a strained breath, then a set of footsteps disappearing. She waited a few seconds, then slowly opened the security bar, inching away from the door.

The handle unlatched, and the door pushed open. Emotions she couldn't quite read darkened every feature, and his chest still rose and fell from a run that had winded even his mighty lungs.

"It was Luke McBain," he said. "Head of security."

She blinked at him, almost dizzy from the rush of relief.

"And he was right," Alec said. "That was stupid. This…" He made a vague gesture from him to her.

Please don't say it's stupid, Alec. Please don't say—

"I'm stupid for letting it happen," he said.

For letting her in, he meant. "You're anything but."

"Go to sleep, Kate. I can stay out here tonight. I won't sleep anyway."

Disappointment drained from her head to her heart and left the rest of her cold. Way too cold to…*beg*.

"Okay." She walked away, and so did he, his footsteps as heavy as bricks as Alec Petrov stacked them one-by-one, rebuilding the wall around him.

Chapter Nineteen

A noise near the front door pulled Alec out of a restless sleep on the sofa in the living room, where he'd chosen to sleep that night. Her room was too small and close, and neither one of them could have avoided the dangerous temptation.

He listened to the sound, imagining what—or who—was making it. It was barely dawn, he guessed from the thin light outside, so too early for housekeeping, even the ever-efficient Poppy.

But someone was out there. He walked barefoot to the front entry, soundless and ready, throwing a look to make sure Kate's bedroom door was still closed.

With his ear to the door, he heard a grunt. A breath. A man.

The peephole revealed nothing, so he listened again. Another grunt. Someone was definitely out there, purposely staying out of sight.

He gave his hands a shake, balanced his body, and prepared to stop, maim, kill, or just give some shit if this was some kind of fucking security test.

He yanked the door open and vaulted outside.

And damn near tripped over Gabe Rossi on the ground doing one-armed pushups.

"What the hell?"

Gabe switched arms with one smooth move and started pumping, his muscles bulging through a thin white T-shirt. "Heard you got busted on the beach last night."

"What the hell are you doing?"

"Multitasking. I was in a rush this morning, so I didn't get my workout in. What the hell were you doing on the beach last night?"

"Acting like newlyweds, which, last time I checked, were your instructions."

He stopped after about twenty, then popped to his feet to give Alec a hard look. "Not at midnight on the beach, horizontal with your tongue down her throat."

Alec narrowed his eyes. "What's your point?"

He wiped his brow with his forearm and looked beyond Alec into the villa. "My point is that this is not a game. It's not a vacation. It's not even a chance to get lucky or laid. I came to tell you Vlitnik is on the move."

"What?" His growing frustration at what Gabe was implying—even though it was a little too close to the truth—disappeared, replaced by a different sensation. Something that teetered between hate and fear. "How do you know that?"

"I talked to your buddy, Gregg."

"Why didn't he talk to me?"

"You were busy playing hide the kielbasa."

"Shut up." Alec pulled the door behind him almost closed, in case Kate heard them talking and came out. "What do you mean he's on the move? Here?"

"No one knows where, so Gregg raised a red flag."

"He's not coming here," Alec said. "And if he did, he's hard to miss."

Gabe nodded and came closer. "There's more."

There always was with Dmitri Vlitnik. "Tell me."

195

"Someone in his operation said they had a lead on you, a solid lead."

What the hell? "Who?"

"You know a chick named Robyn Bickler?"

He searched his memory and came up blank. "Never heard of her."

"Well, she's apparently heard of you. Told Vlitnik she knows where you are, then disappeared the next day, before she gave him the information, at least that's what Gregg's guy thinks. So he's after her. If he's after her, he could be led to you."

How could anyone know where he was? "I swear to God I haven't told a soul where I am."

"Did Kate?"

"She talked to a friend on the phone and said she was in Florida, but that's all. I heard the whole conversation."

"Does she know your name yet?"

The question strangled him like a guillotine choke, stealing his air.

Gabe just shut his eyes, disgusted. "I thought that might be tough. S'okay. I'll get you out of here soon. I'm close to finding you a final name and home."

"What about Kate?"

"What about her?"

He stared at Gabe. "She can't be here alone. What about the person who sent threats to her father? Are they any closer to finding out who that is?" His voice rose in a harsh demand.

"Nothing concrete, but her father's house was broken into a few days ago."

"What? I thought he had security."

"He wasn't home, and it looks like a routine Beacon Hill theft, silver stolen, no notes left."

"Did he have information in the house about where she is?" Alec asked.

"No, but my cousin's investigating along with the FBI. And her dad doesn't want her to know about it."

"She'll hate that."

Gabe shrugged. "Not my problem. Dad's the client, and he wants her in the dark, out of sight, and *safe.*"

"And you think I should leave? How is that keeping her safe?" Alec demanded.

"We'll take care of her."

They'd take care of her? "The staff thinks she's my wife."

"Apparently, so do you."

Alec bristled at the accusation.

"Look," Gabe said. "We've got this covered. When you go, the Mrs. stays for an extended vacation because you had to travel on business. Luke can find her a bodyguard, and he'll—"

"Not a fucking chance while I breathe. *I'm* her bodyguard. I'm not leaving her until her problem is solved and whoever is making threats is behind bars or"—*dead*—"taken care of."

Gabe cracked his knuckles. "Your dedication is commendable. But if her father finds out you've been naked wrestling with his little girl, shit could hit the fan. I told him she'd be protected down here."

"She is protected."

"I don't mean by a condom."

Alec gave him a dark look. "Thanks for letting me know. I don't let her out of my sight." Except last night when he knew he wasn't strong enough to sleep ten feet away from her and not—

"She's out of your sight now." He leaned in closer. "Dude, can't say I can blame you for taking advantage of the proximity—"

He had Gabe's T-shirt collar in his fist before the man could think about finishing his thought. "I'm not taking advantage of anyone or anything."

Gabe didn't move, staring him down. "My other piece of unsolicited advice was going to be don't get emotionally involved, but I see it's too late for that."

He opened his hand and let the T-shirt loose. "Thanks for the tip. Keep me posted."

"I will. But I'll be on the road for a day or two, so don't fuck up. I'm trusting you, and I expect you to put her safety before your dick."

"I am," Alec said. That was exactly why he hadn't slept in her room last night. "Anyway, if I make another mistake, I'm sure your spies will let you know."

Gabe grinned. "I'm sure they will."

Alec stepped away, into the house, pissed off that he could hear that cocky son of a bitch laughing as he left.

He stood for a moment after closing the door, centering himself, thinking about what he needed to do if Vlitnik or one of his animals or *anyone* came near Kate. He'd kill. He'd kill hard. But what if he had to go? What if Gabe sent him away to some island in the middle of the Pacific? He'd agreed to go anywhere to escape Vlitnik.

But that was before Kate.

Taking a slow breath, he walked to her room and didn't even bother to knock, opening the door to find her sitting on the bed in nothing but a tank top, underwear, and a dreamy smile. She startled at the sight of him, then her face softened.

He forced his to do the opposite. "Get dressed, Kate. We're doing soft targets today."

Her eyes widened, and instantly, he recognized the look of desire in her eyes. "That sounds...fun."

"Self-defense lessons," he said. "That's what you wanted, right?"

Her mouth twitched in a smile. "Right."

"Get ready. Now."

He left before she could bitch about how much she hated to be told what to do. Before she could ask any questions or make demands. Before she could coax one more piece of dangerous information out of him. And before he gave in and got right in that bed with her.

"Okay, one more time," Alec demanded. "What are the eight soft targets?"

He stood in front of Kate on the patio, bare-chested, the morning sun pouring over the sinewy cuts of his chest and biceps, highlighting every angle and bulge and bead of sweat. She tried to concentrate on the question...soft targets.

There was nothing soft about him. Including the glare slicing her in half.

"Kate? Remember the poem."

She rolled her eyes, the singsong melody still in her head. *Stab the eyes, twist the ears, slam his mouth right up his nose. Then grab the throat, kick the groin, bend the fingers, and stomp the toes.* "I don't need a freaking nursery rhyme to remember stuff, Alec. I know where a person's weak spots are."

"You will panic and forget."

"I hate the way you say that, like an attack is inexorable."

It was his turn to roll his eyes. "Speak English."

"Okay." She got in his face. "I. Want. My. Coffee. Is that English enough for you?"

He put his hands up. "You'll get it when you learn all eight techniques. First, what's your objective again?"

"To inflict pain."

"And get away," he reminded her. "Not pain for pain's sake, pain so you can escape. Remember that."

Something was bubbling under his surface, that was for sure. "Escape to coffee?" she teased, trying to lighten his mood.

"If you can."

It was all the motivator she needed. "Great. Hurry, then."

"Okay, now try to stab my eye out."

She blinked at him. "Just poke it out?"

"Try."

"Of course you'll overpower me and flip me down on the ground and flatten me and…" Actually, that didn't sound so bad. She shot her hand up with no intention of actually hitting his eye, and he snagged her arm and whipped her around and had her in a choke hold before she could take a breath.

"I told you," she said, wiggling out when he released her.

"Try the ears next. I'm coming at you…" He took a step closer. "Reach up to get my ears."

She did, and he easily elbowed her hands away from his head.

"Well, shit, how can I do anything if you keep stopping me?"

"Find another soft target," he demanded.

She scanned his body again, zeroing in on his throat. "Okay."

He had her shoulder and jerked her around before she could get within five inches of his throat. In a flash, he had her immobilized with his arms banded around her, with her back to his front, shockingly vulnerable.

"What's the rest of the poem?" he demanded. "Think, Kate."

She couldn't think. Her ass was against his crotch, his arms were thick and strong, and he smelled...good. How could she—

"Can you grab my throat?"

She couldn't possibly raise either hand higher than her chest. "No."

"What's the easiest soft target open to you?"

She lifted her foot to stomp his, but he deftly moved and she missed.

"The groin," he reminded her. "You can step to the left and use your right hand to punch, grab, twist, and pull. I can't stop you without letting go of you."

"Is that why you're so insistent we do this now? A groin grab?" As she asked the question, she inched to the side and lowered her hand, landing right on the bulge in his pants. And stroking once.

"No!" He whisked her off the ground and flipped her to the other side of him, spinning around, his eyes sparking. "That's the last thing you do, Kate."

It was the *only* thing she wanted to do. She stared at him, the rejection stinging. "Why are you doing this?"

"For your protection."

"You told me the other day it could be worse, not better, for me."

"And you're proving my point, Kate." He shook his hands out, something she'd noticed he did a lot when he was mad or frustrated. "Listen, I'm serious now."

Yep, something was definitely different and weird. Was it because they'd fooled around on the beach? Because Luke McBain had essentially "caught" them? "Why now? Why not before?"

He shook his head. "Just pay attention and let's work on—"

"What changed?" she demanded, knowing instantly from the tiny spark in his eyes that something had for sure. And it wasn't good. "Did you see someone? Find something out?"

"No, I just want you to be safe if...if I'm not here."

Her heart dropped a little. No, a lot. Too much, in fact, to be a normal reaction to him leaving. "Why would you not be here?"

"I'm going to have to leave eventually. And you might...stay."

She could feel the blood draining from her face, hating that her body betrayed her emotions like that. "That'll be interesting to explain to the staffers who think we're newlyweds."

He rocked back on his heels. "I guess they'll tell them you're hanging out while I travel on business or something."

"You *have* talked to someone!"

His eyes flickered, and she silently thanked that moot-court mentor who'd taught her to look for the shuttered-eyes tell. "Let's just keep doing this, Kate. You need to know at least three foolproof ways to escape an attacker. Also, how to get out of duct tape, a locked trunk, or a moving vehicle."

"When are you leaving?" she asked, hating the way the question almost strangled her. Good God, what was wrong with her? A few days ago she'd have killed to have been rid of him. And now...

Maybe it *was* Stockholm syndrome.

"Eventually," he said.

"But so am I," she replied. "I'm sure Gabe could time it so that happened around the same time."

He lifted a shoulder. "Let's talk about setting your feet.

That's part of your problem, you know. You're off-balance."

"You do that to me." She met his gaze while she made the admission. "And it scares me."

He shook his hands at his sides, then became like a statue. "What should scare you is—"

"We're going to sleep together. You know we are."

He let out a breath. "That."

"It doesn't scare me," she announced. "But I have to know more about you before I do. The inside stuff. The real you. I can't sleep with you until I do."

He looked like he was having a hard time swallowing, let alone coming up with a good answer. "That's good," he finally said.

"What do you mean?"

"You shouldn't sleep with someone you don't know. So that's good." Not only did he sound unconvinced, the way he said it pissed her off.

"How is that good?" she pressed.

"It's smart."

"But you would sleep with me even if you didn't know anything about me."

"I wouldn't..." At her notched eyebrow, he dipped his head. "I shouldn't."

"But you would. I guess you're a guy, and a fuck's a fuck, even if—"

"Stop it." He ground out the words and got right in her face, grabbing her arm for emphasis. "I'm not telling you more about myself for your own protection, the same reason I'm doing everything. Watching over you, ready to kill for you, making sure you stay safe."

She stared up at him, her pulse pounding, the air crackling, his eyes narrowing as if...he wanted to kiss her. And she took the opportunity of his intense concentration to grab one of his fingers and bend it in the wrong direction, forcing him to release her.

He barely flinched at what she knew had to hurt. "Awesome, Kate. You were listening."

"Where the finger goes, the hand has to follow," she said, echoing one of the first things he'd taught her. "And I earned coffee." Before he could even think about stopping her, she shot toward the kitchen and pounced on the coffeemaker, staring at the machine as it brewed, her back to the patio and Alec.

"Do you think I'm taking advantage of you?"

The question startled her, along with his quiet entrance. Then she thought about what he was asking and laughed softly. "I think we can be honest about who's driving the sex situation here. Like I said, you make me lose my balance." She gave a dry laugh. "In fact, you make me lose a lot of things, like my common sense and sanity and my hard-won belief that I need to be completely alone to be safe and that I will never, ever, ever, ever depend on a man for anything, because I hate how they control me..." Pausing for a much-needed breath, she finished, "All that stuff, just poof." She snapped her fingers. "Gone at the sight of a big man who would...kill for me."

He'd stayed still through the whole speech and finally lifted one hand and placed it on her cheek, the touch so incredibly light and gentle and tender that her legs almost buckled.

"What did he do to you to make you that angry?"

"He...he..." She nuzzled her cheek against his palm, like a kitten desperate for affection. "He never touched me like this." She closed her eyes, not wanting to see the pity in his.

"Then he's an idiot."

She smiled. "Sadly, he's anything but. He's a shrewd, conniving bastard." She put her hand over his, stroking it and pressing it harder to her cheek. "Your hands..." She sighed again. "So different...from his."

"Did he hurt you, Kate?"

"He never hit me, if that's what you mean. But, you know, he made decisions for me, he suffocated me, and he oppressed me, and, God, he put me down. And before you ask why I allowed that to happen, just understand that of the five years I was married, four and change were spent knowing I had to extricate myself from the situation, which was no mean feat with that man."

He stroked her chin and jaw, studying her. "How'd you finally manage to do that?"

"My dad helped a lot, once he finally realized Steven was not all he'd dreamed for a son-in-law. He pushed things through the court system when Steven did everything to delay our divorce and protract the legalities. It just took Dad a long time to see through Steven. Everybody falls for his charm," she said. "But when you get to know him..." She shuddered. "He is so full of hate. I didn't see that, though. I was completely fooled."

She looked up and blinked, a tear she hadn't realized she'd shed dribbling down her cheek until it was brushed away by a large, but incredibly *tender*, thumb.

"As soon as we were married, the real Steven emerged." The words rushed out, like they'd been pent up for too long. "He overpowered me mentally and emotionally. He made every choice for me, held every purse string, issued every order, and maintained complete control. I was forced to do everything."

His eyes widened in horror.

"Not that," she added. "Never that." And another dry

laugh. "He hated..." God, this was hard, but she had to tell him. She didn't know why, but she had to let it out.

"Tell me, Kate."

"He hated sex," she finally admitted. "The times we were together, it was perfunctory, dark, quick, more to shut me up than anything. He was like an asexual man who got off on money and power, but really didn't care about anything emotional or...physical. And I guess it was another way to control me, because I wanted a normal, healthy, sexual relationship with my husband."

She closed her hands over his arms, needing his strength right then, his solid, masculine power that propped her up. "I guess that's why I seem so hard up."

"You aren't hard up. You're..." He stroked her face again, two hands now, clasping her cheeks like she was precious, but he didn't finish his sentence.

"Lonely? Horny? Starved for affection? Go ahead, I can take it."

He just smiled. "You're the word lady. I was going for something more like...*worthy*. Yeah." He nodded. "You're worthy of so much better than being controlled and ignored."

With a long, pained sigh, she slipped her arms around him and let herself be pulled into his chest. An achy comfort warmed her, making her feel completely safe and secure.

"Come on, Smarty-Pants. Get your coffee, and then I'm going to teach you some foolproof escape methods, and we still have more soft targets to master."

But her softest target was the one in her chest and, right that minute, it felt like Alec Petrov was moving toward ownership of it.

There was no foolproof escape for that, was there?

Chapter Twenty

Gabe had his cover set up flawlessly, as he always did going into a situation like this. It had taken some research, a few trips to the Casa Blanca administrative offices to flirt with the pretty brunette in sales, and hours of combing through the Radio and TV Martí Web site for English transcripts. Now, he was ready.

Nailing an appointment with someone at the Miami-based broadcasting network was almost as difficult as slipping into Cuba itself; security was serious. But that wasn't Gabe's concern. He had an appointment, a bulletproof ID package, and a goal for his meeting. He just wasn't sure he had the right person.

Amber Martinez was a low-level administrative assistant in the IT department of the news conglomerate, not a high-profile reporter who might have real information for him. But Gabe had worked hundreds of informants in his day, and he knew they lurked in the most unexpected places.

And he couldn't go barging in demanding to meet her. This took finesse, and finesse was Gabe's middle fucking name.

Actually, today his name was William James Bishkoff, executive public relations director for Casa Blanca Resort &

Spa, seeking promotional coverage for his hotel property.

The Miami sun kicked his ass as Gabe crossed the parking lot, but he kept the uncomfortable suit jacket buttoned and his tie tight. The dress shoes squeezed feet that had been bare more than anything for the past few weeks, and his face still stung from the morning's razor. But Bill Bishkoff would never go to a meeting with a client unshaven or underdressed.

He sailed through the metal detector, showed his ID to the front desk, and waited for his contact from the features department to greet him in the lobby. As he waited, he watched the monitors that lined the wall, all of the major news stations running silent with Spanish subtitles, the last monitor on TV Martí, blaring its audio in Spanish.

It took him back. Back to—

"Mr. Bishkoff?" A young man, fresh out of college at best, hustled toward him and held out his hand. "Welcome to Martí. I'm John Ramirez, an intern in features."

An intern? So, not even out of college. Should make things easy. "John, thanks for taking the time to see me."

"I'm sorry the features editor is in a meeting this morning, but if you have a press kit or something, I'll take it in and we can get back to you."

Not a chance he'd be put off that easily. "I do, but it's all on my tablet, and I'd like to walk you through it. Do you have five minutes?"

The intern gave a fake smile. "Could you e-mail it to me? We get a lot of information for features, which"—he gestured toward the serious newsman spewing angry Spanish on the TV—"as you can see, aren't the highest priority around here. But of course we'll look at your material. For a resort, right? We'll consider it for our new travel segment."

"I would imagine that part of your news is heating up

right now. Soon enough, the last barricade will be down, and tourists will be going both ways to and from Cuba."

"That's happening," he agreed. "Which will be great."

"And when they do, we want the Cuban vacationers to find their way to our resort."

He nodded, clearly not interested in the pitch, probably hungry for lunch and pissed that his boss couldn't be bothered to meet the resort PR person hawking American sunshine and villas that only about one percent of Cubans could afford—if and when the country opened up.

Gabe got that. "Listen, why don't we download my presentation onto a flash drive and you can be on your way?"

John's youthful features lit up at the way out of an actual meeting. "Go ahead and do that."

"Okay, hang on for a sec." Gabe started patting his pockets, then reached inside his jacket, swearing softly. "Have you ever been to any of the little islands off the Gulf Coast, John?" he asked, feigning frustration as he looked for a jump drive he knew he didn't have. At least, not one he'd use…yet.

"Just Sanibel, but I stay local," he said.

"The resort is something," Gabe said, moving to his laptop case and looking in every crook and cranny. "I could set you up with a full comp weekend for you and a friend. You have a girlfriend?" He rechecked every pocket.

"Uh, yeah, I do."

"Would you like to take her to a villa on the beach, all expenses paid?"

"Are you trying to bribe me?"

Gabe laughed heartily. "Dude, you have a lot to learn about how PR works. That's what we do. It's called a press comp. I'll arrange one in your name, if you could just"—he gave up the search—"let me borrow a jump drive?"

"Sure," he said, eyeing Gabe. "You could really do that? I'm only an intern, you know."

"And I bet you make plenty of decisions about which products and places actually get a coveted spot on that new travel segment."

He gave a modest shrug. "Some. We're probably going to start taking advertising, and that's what I'd really like to do."

They'd take advertising because federal funds for the station would go bone dry when Cuba opened up to American travel and TV. "You can count on my company for that." Which would probably help his little résumé. "Where can I get that jump drive? Or do you want me to wait?"

"No, no. Come with me to IT. If there's one thing we have, it's flash drives."

"That's how a lot of your news gets delivered, right? Since the Cuban government jams your transmissions so much?" He hoped against hope that Amber Martinez was indeed who Mal meant when he'd mentioned Amber Bock beer in their conversation. Otherwise, this was just another lap in the wild-goose chase he'd been on for a long time.

But he'd never stop until he found that goose.

"Usually, yes," John replied.

"How do you get the flash drives into Cuba?" Gabe asked as they went through a set of steel doors.

John gave him a look and chuckled. "If I told you that, I'd have to kill you."

Gabe almost laughed out loud at the cliché that he used himself—and meant—so often. "But all that's going to change soon, right?"

"From what I understand, it's a slow process, and the people who work here are really dedicated to getting news from the free world to their families and countrymen." His little speech sounded canned, like he'd heard his boss say it a thousand times.

"I already know there's an underground group of volunteers who distribute the flash drives," Gabe said.

"That's no secret," John said, stopping at the last door in the hall. "But who they are is. This is IT. They should have a drive we can borrow."

Gabe would have to work smart and fast. "Great," he said, scanning the office cubicles inside, the fluorescent lights off, but each individual area lit by computer screens. The hum of conversation and the general buzz of business hovered over the cubes as they walked past a few.

"Hey, can I borrow an empty flash drive?" John asked the first person they came upon who wasn't on the phone or wearing headphones.

He gave a shake of his head. "None empty. Talk to Joella or Amber."

Amber. Bingo. Gabe stayed close on John's heels, acting like he was just so flat-out fascinated by the tech department, but his brain was whirring with possibilities. Amber had some connection…he hoped.

"What up, Johnny?" A young woman stood in a tiny, messy cubicle, her spiky dark hair reminding Gabe of a twenty-five-year-old version of his cousin Vivi back in her skater-girl days.

"I need a clean flash drive, Amber."

This was his target. "Hi, Amber. I'm Bill." He slid just a little in front of John and gave his deadliest smile. "The flash-drive borrower."

She did a little double take, as if she'd been ready to dismiss him, then changed her mind. "Hi, Bill The Flash-Drive Borrower. What's your deal?"

211

Gabe kept his smile. "I'm giving away free weekends in paradise. You want one?"

She lifted a dark brow, playful and pretty. "Really?"

"He's in PR with a resort over near Naples."

"Which one? My granny lives there."

"It's on Mimosa Key, you know it?"

She nodded. "It's pretty there." She gave Gabe an alluring smile. "Are you really giving away free trips?"

"Press comp packages," John said. "So don't try and flirt your way into my freebie, Martinez."

She laughed and put her hands on her hips. "I can try."

"And you can succeed," Gabe assured her. "Especially if you let me sit in here for a few minutes and download my presentation."

"Oh, hell, for a trip to a resort, you can give *me* the presentation," she said.

John rolled his eyes. "Give him an empty flash drive."

Gabe pulled out his phone and pretended to be checking messages while he took the guest chair in her cubicle, clicking on one of his favorite apps to send a text. Surreptitiously, he aimed his phone directly at John's pocket while Amber unlocked a file cabinet.

As Gabe took out his laptop, John's phone beeped twice. He read the text and sighed. "I need to sign for a package in the lobby," he said. "I'll be right back, Mr. Bit...Bishk..."

Gabe laughed. "It's just Bill, and I've taken enough of your time. I'll make the copy of this presentation and leave it at the front desk for you. Do you have a card?"

"Sure." He brought out his wallet and gave Gabe a card. Gabe handed him one back, complete with the Casa Blanca logo in the corner and a number that rang only at Nino's desk.

"If you like the presentation, call me and I'll arrange your trip."

John shook his hand, considerably warmer than when Gabe first arrived. "Great, thanks."

After he was gone, Amber handed him a tiny thumb-sized drive from a small pile on her desk. "You can show me the presentation," she said. "I'd like to see this place."

"Sure." The longer he talked the better, and if that failed, all he needed was for her to leave for two minutes, maybe three. Her cube was situated privately enough, and the position of her computer would work for him.

He loaded up the canned Casa Blanca PowerPoint, glancing up to catch her looking at him. Hard. Interested.

He gave a slow smile. "How long have you worked here, Amber?"

"Since I got out of college about three years ago."

Why would Malcolm Harris have her name? "You a tech guru?" he asked.

"Not really. I'm in what you'd call distribution."

The first point on the chain of smuggling flash drives full of news and information into Cuba. But a PR guy at a hotel wouldn't likely know that, so he just nodded. "Have you always been in this department?"

"I interned here, like Johnny, when I went to UM."

"Good school," he said, giving her an impressed nod.

She shrugged. "I was born and raised in Miami, so I'd really love to move somewhere else."

She had zero trace of an accent, but few young Cuban-Americans did. And based on her looks, name, and choice of jobs, he was certain of her descent. "Parents or grandparents move here?"

"My grandparents brought my mom over on the Mariel Boatlift in 1980. She was ten and had to leave two brothers who are still there."

He gave her a look. "Is she going to be reunited with them when the diplomatic knots get untied?"

"She hopes they'll come here, but nobody really knows what's happening yet. Still too soon to get hopeful."

He looked up from his computer screen, studying her, guessing her weakness and soft heart. "That's why you work here, then."

Amber laughed. "It sure isn't for the money. Like, I couldn't ever afford to stay in a resort like that." She pointed to his laptop monitor showing a stunning shot of the endless white sand and turquoise water of Barefoot Bay. "Holy crap. I'd love to go there."

"I'm trying to get it featured in one of Radio and TV Martí's travel segments, so when Cubans come to America, they'll visit us."

She gave him a screwed-up face, then shook her head, her expression a blend of amusement and disdain. "You know that Cuba is a poor country," she said, as if speaking to a five-year-old.

"I know."

"And that very few Cubans actually get our news," she added. "And they aren't, you know, *resort* goers."

He knew that, of course. Every job, every undercover operation he'd ever been involved in, had some thin ice, and he was skating over it right now with this "advertising" shit. Of course, no resort in the free world would spend time and money promoting to poverty-stricken Cubans who weren't even sure how the new world order would shake out for them.

But it had gotten him this far, and now a good old-fashioned sob story would do the rest.

"Amber." He leaned closer and held her gaze. "My boss is Cuban, second generation, just like you. And Hector is trying to find his cousin, who he's lost touch with for ten years. Hector's cousin—Jorge Salazar—you don't know him, do you?"

She gave a sympathetic smile. "There are about ten thousand Jorge Salazars in Cuba, Bill."

Which was why he picked the name. "Anyway, my boss is hoping that this footage will reach his cousin somehow, so he will know he has a place to go in the United States."

"If the whole deal goes through with these two governments, your boss's cousin will be able to come to the US openly and easily. How would Jorge know the footage is for him, and why would Hector go to this trouble?"

Because he didn't exist. "Hector's cousin has been in some trouble with the law," he lied easily. "Leaving Cuba, no matter what the legalities are for average citizens, won't be easy for Jorge."

She sighed and looked at the screen again. "I'm sorry to tell you this, but even under those circumstances, we're not likely to use your stuff for a fluff piece on a travel segment."

"I know, but I was hoping…could you help?" He put his hand out and placed it over hers. "This is a desperate, broken family."

"Cuba is full of desperate, broken families," she said. "Which is why I do what I do."

"Distribution? How does that help families?"

"I'm the liaison with the volunteers on the ground who distribute our flash drives. The broadcast signals are blocked almost entirely by the Castro regime, but these things"—she picked up one of the flash drives on her desk—"these are like little gold nuggets we hand out to the country."

Gabe studied the device, thinking. What would the

connection be? Why would Malcolm send him here? Gabe wasn't sure, but he trusted his friend and his instincts. "How do you find the volunteers?"

"Well, they're activists who want to be involved."

Activists. That sounded about right. "And how do you reach them?" he asked, pressing because he sensed this lead was going somewhere.

"I have a list."

A list he now wanted so badly his mouth was watering.

He gave her hand a squeeze and slid his strategy to what would work with her, and it wasn't talking about lists of activists. "It's about the families, isn't it?" he asked. "The broken families who want to be reunited."

"It always is with Cubans." She gave a smile. "And I'll see if I can help you. I'll try to convince the guys up in features to do something."

"That would be great. And I've taken enough of your time. Let me finish saving this, and I'll be on my way." He stuck the drive into the laptop and secretly slipped his hand into his suit pocket, touching his phone. It rang immediately, and he took it out and looked at the screen. "Speak of the devil. It's Hector."

"Tell him you're having success," she said. "It will give him hope. That's all we all want, anyway."

Damn right.

"I'll be right back." She stood and gave him a smile, and he blessed her good manners as she gave him privacy.

While he carried a soft one-sided conversation with no one, he reached into his other pocket and pulled out the far more memory-heavy flash drive he'd been carrying all along, slipped it into a USB port on her computer, touched the mouse, slid it over to the C drive, and hit copy. His gut told him there was no way they'd keep something so sensitive in the cloud, and he didn't have time to go searching for one, anyway.

In less than fifteen seconds, a green light flashed, and he ended his call with his imaginary friend.

Then he copied the standard Casa Blanca Resort & Spa sales pitch onto the drive she'd given him, closed his laptop, and stood as Amber came around the corner.

"Do you have any more information than the name Jorge Salazar?" she asked. "I might be able to help your boss in a somewhat more efficient way than what you're doing."

Two words. Two words was all he had to say. *One woman's name.*

But he couldn't take the chance. No one could be trusted. Amber might be one of the good guys, but that was no guarantee she could be trusted. He had most of her computer in his pocket, and that was better than giving away the name of someone he…someone who mattered so much.

"Sorry, that's all I have," he said.

"Well, call me if you get more." She pressed a business card into his hand. "Or your boss, he can call, too. And you don't even have to give me a free weekend at the hotel."

"Okay, thank you. Thank you so much." He shook her hand and left the way he came in, dropping one flash drive at the front desk, as promised, but walking out with information he hoped would get him closer to the one thing he wanted most.

Chapter Twenty-One

B y midday, Alec and Kate were both damp with sweat as the sun blared down on the patio, the hours of sparring and teaching, laughing and fighting—and, holy shit, so much touching—had taken their toll.

And he couldn't remember the last time he'd had so much fun.

"Okay," she said, wiping her brow, her chest rising and falling with the need for more air. "This time I *am* getting away from you."

"You haven't yet," he reminded her with a sly smile.

"I came close, though. Even with your damn duct tape." She pointed to the roll they'd used half of teaching her how to break it.

"One more time," he said.

"All right."

"You know what to do, Kate."

Her gaze dropped for a second to his crotch. She hadn't yet even tried to knee, punch, or grab him there, and she should. Not that he wanted his dick on the receiving end of her surprisingly strong knee, but it was definitely the most effective technique he'd taught her, and he wanted to be sure she could get the job done.

"Let's do a real-life situation." He pointed to the table where she usually worked. "Sit and study."

She rolled her eyes and let out a grunt. "Don't remind me of what I haven't done yet today."

"You fully escape one attack, and you're free."

She shook her head, a trickle of sweat meandering over her temple, sticking to a lock of hair that had fallen out of her ponytail. "But I'm not free," she said on a sigh. "How long do I have to stay in prison because some lunatic might hurt me?"

"I know the feeling," he said.

She stepped closer, squinting up in the sunshine. "Do you? Who's after you, Alec? Why can't you just stop them?"

His chest and gut squeezed with how badly he wanted to tell her. How much he wanted to hold her sweet face in his hands and stroke her pale skin and tell her all his dark secrets. Then he wanted to lay her down and bury himself and his sorrows in her body.

"Wow," she whispered. "I don't know what you're thinking, but I'd love to play poker with you."

He touched his own face, wondering how it had betrayed him.

"What were you thinking just then?" she asked.

"You don't want to know."

She gave a dry laugh. "I'm pretty sure that's at the root of all our problems, Alec. I *do* want to know." She reached a hand up to his face. "I really want to know, and you really want to tell me."

He took a breath and almost confessed. Everything. Almost. Instead, he snagged her arm and pulled her forward, purposely rough, getting a wide-eyed gasp in response. He flipped her around to pull her back against him, instantly feeling her find her balance.

Good, good.

She lifted a foot and tried to hammer his toes, but he jumped out of the way. She managed to get the very tip of his thumb and pull, but he was just strong enough to escape her shaky grip.

"Come on, Kate," he urged near her ear, half attacker, half encourager, the way he egged on all his students. "Leopard's punch, thumb gouge, trachea twist. Do something!"

He locked his grip and used his calf to buckle one of her knees, enough to knock her off-balance, but she kept her footing and jabbed her elbow into his stomach.

"Not a soft target," he reminded her as her arm might as well have hit a concrete wall when he flexed his abs. "Find it, Kate." He jerked her body a little to juice up her adrenaline. "Find the vulnerable spot."

"Damn it!" she exclaimed, making every effort to whip out of his grasp.

"Soft target!" he reminded her. "Wiggling gets you nothing!"

He lifted her a few inches off the ground, just to show her how light she was, how small and, shit, perfect in his arms.

She flailed for a second, then caught herself, turning just enough to land the heel of her hand under his nose

"Yes!" he grunted, throwing his head back at the punch of pain, but not letting go.

And, wham, her fist came down on his cock like a brick, nailing him hard, and instantly, he let go while she scampered away, hooting for a second with her victory. Then she stopped and put her hands over her mouth.

"Oh my God, are you okay?"

He bit his lower lip hard enough to almost draw blood, agony shooting from his dick to his brain and back again like lightning bolts. "I've had worse," he ground out, his jaw clenched.

She came closer to him, still covering her mouth. "I'm sorry."

"Don't be," he ordered, blinking as the first white-hot wave subsided. "You did what I taught you to do."

"Is it broken?"

He bit back a half laugh, half moan of misery and shook his head.

"Are you—" She reached out her hand, and he didn't even give it a second of thought, grabbing her again and pulling her into him, twisting her around, and damn near flipping her over.

"Never come back!" he ordered. "He's just a mad bear now, and you're really putting yourself at risk."

She froze, on only one foot, completely off-balance, a little shocked. Then she sucked in a breath and gave a merciless kick at his knee and another jab with her elbow at his mouth, and burst out of his arms, throwing herself free, ending up one foot from the side of the pool.

"Take that!" she barked at him, her eyes glowing with success.

"Kate!" He stood frozen, pain and pleasure colliding. "That was awesome!" He pointed at her, then drew his hand back before she schooled him by bending another one of his fingers.

She made two fists of victory and danced like a happy little boxer. "I beat you, Alec Petrov." She grinned at him. "Now what do I get?"

Kissed. Touched. Sucked. Licked. *Possessed.*

He took a step closer, silent and intent on doing all those things and more. "Kate," he whispered, not surprised his tortured voice came out gruff.

She stared back at him, her feet braced, her arms taut.

221

Even her shoulders were squared and ready for a fight.

"You're the best student I ever had."

A slow smile pulled on her lips as he came a step closer.

"And the best looking."

She tipped her head at the compliment.

"And definitely the smartest." He was barely a foot from her now, their gazes locked, her chest rising and falling with strained breaths that pushed her dampened breasts against the tank top she wore.

"So I'm sorry to tell you this," he said softly, finally closing the space and putting both hands on her shoulders. "But you have to pay for that."

Her eyes widened, no fear but plenty of anticipation. "Really?"

"Really." He gave a solid shove, and she gasped and started to scream, but hit the water with a huge splash before it came out. By the time she sputtered up for air, he was in the pool with her, ready for her retaliation. She came up fighting and splashing and laughing and so damn beautiful, he could have cried.

He let her dunk him, then pulled them both up and gave in to everything he was feeling, covering her mouth with a kiss that made them both wobbly as they stood in four feet of water. She leaned into him, dragging her hands over his body as he did the same to her, so damn happy to touch her like this. No threat, no test, not a single bit of doubt that this was what they both wanted and needed.

She murmured his name and clutched him tighter, pressing against him as they explored wet clothes and sweet flesh and a whole different kind of soft targets. He closed his hand over her breast, and she swayed a little, kissing him while she stroked his back and ass and then where his erection somehow grew despite her earlier assault.

"Alec," she murmured into his neck.

"Kate." Blood slammed in his head.

"Kate!"

Her hand closed over his dick.

"Katherine Louise Kingston!"

And they nearly exploded apart from each other, whipping around to see an older man with white hair and a murderous look in his green eyes.

"Dad." Kate whispered the word, biting back a shocked and self-conscious whimper. "What are you doing here?"

"I think a better question is what are *you* doing?"

Alec never really wanted to die more than he did right at that moment.

Chapter Twenty-Two

Despite the sun, despite the thick robe wrapped around her, despite the fact that she still burned from one of her more embarrassing moments, a chill shot through Kate as she processed what her father had been trying to tell her since his unexpected arrival.

"So this guy *targeted* my friend Laurie to get to me?"

Dad nodded and shifted in his seat under the patio umbrella, glancing to the villa, where Alec had disappeared after one of the most awkward introductions ever. To his credit, Alec had been completely cool and didn't even take Nino's head off for bringing Kate's father into the villa without so much as a whisper of warning.

Well, how would Nino have known they'd be carrying out their undercover roles so…completely?

Dad's arrival didn't really faze Kate, but his news that they'd apprehended a man they believed might have been leaving the notes did. Everything in her world just shifted…again.

"And you know this guy, this Mike Wesley?" Kate asked. "I don't think I've ever met him, but I remember the name from when I interned at Steven's firm."

"He was a prosecuting attorney on a case I had a few

months ago, and things did not go in his favor. He's made public statements about how much he hates me. And, like I told you, they found three more notes to me in his condo."

"Is he in jail? Out on bond? What?"

"He's still being held and questioned, and I don't think he'll be out on bond anytime soon since we know how ineffective a restraining order can be. He'll be charged with criminal harassment."

She thought about that, knowing the penalty could be light. "And Laurie." She blew out a breath, thinking of the situation this had put her friend in. "Have you talked to her? She knows this?"

"I did, right before I left to come down here. She can't reach you and hoped you'd call her."

She shrugged. "I haven't thought to call her again. I can't believe he totally hit on her and asked her out just so he could get to me." Another chill made her shudder. "What a jerk."

Dad nodded slowly, searching her face. "You seem to be doing okay."

She bit her lip at the sideways comment. "You caught me at a slightly inopportune time."

Dad lifted one gray brow. He'd never been very comfortable with the subject of boys or men in Kate's life, except he'd, at one time, been very comfortable with Steven Jessup. Maybe because getting Kate married was a way for him to stop worrying about her.

"Don't blame him," she said quietly, glancing toward the villa. "I've been, um, rather aggressive."

Dad shifted again, clearly uncomfortable. "I know you've had to play a...role to stay safe."

"And we both know what you witnessed was not role-playing."

He cleared his throat and took a drink of the cold water she'd brought him. "You're a grown woman, Kate. I just hope you're being careful and protecting yourself."

"He's a bodyguard, Dad. I'm covered."

"Just be careful." He might have meant her heart, or he might have meant birth control, but both would be equally difficult for her father to discuss. Instead of pressing, she took her own drink of water.

"His chance of survival is nearly zero."

She choked as the water caught in her throat. "What?" she croaked.

"He's wanted by the Russian mob."

She finally cleared her windpipe and took a much-needed breath. "I've surmised as much."

"This man who's after him doesn't give up."

Oh, God, poor Alec. "He's getting a new name, and I suppose he'll be moving out of the country."

"Which will be fine for a while, but from what I know, which isn't much, they'll find him and kill him."

Her heart quite literally skipped a beat, maybe two. "Why are they after him?"

Dad lifted a shoulder. "I honestly don't know. Don't you?"

"He won't tell me." And yet there she was, about to strip down and give it all to him. And he wouldn't even tell her why he was hiding.

Dad leaned forward and put a hand over hers in a rare show of affection. "You've been hurt a lot, Katie." The use of the childhood nickname tweaked her heart. "Don't make the same mistake again."

"Alec is hardly cut from the same cloth as Steven," she said sharply. "And you were the one who practically threw me at Steven."

He winced. "I think about that every time I talk to him at the courthouse."

"He *talks* to you? Outside of a courtroom?" Revulsion rolled through her.

"Once in a while, and I have to be civil to him, but…"

"You don't have to be civil to him out of court, Dad. The marriage is over, and I'm moving on, and you should, too."

"Of course I have," he said. "Speaking of moving…" He flattened his palms on his legs as if he were going to get up. "How long will it take you to pack?"

She inched back. "What?"

"You might as well be on my flight back to Boston. You're safe to come home now, and I'd feel better if…"

As his voice trailed off, she realized she was shaking her head.

"I can't," she said, all of the reasons why rising up from her heart. Many reasons, crazy reasons, complicated reasons. One reason: Alec. "You can't make me leave."

He frowned at her. "I'm not making you, honey, but as I recall, you were the one who balked at getting out of town in the first place."

"But that was before"—*I fell so hard*—"we knew who it was. And we do now, so…"

"So now you can come home, and until this Wesley character is permanently behind bars, you can stay with me."

"I'm safer here," she said, pushing back her chair, tamping down the low-grade panic at the thought of leaving Alec. Except…

His chance of survival is nearly zero.

"He needs me as his cover."

Dad closed his eyes, obviously knowing who "he" was. "Mr. Rossi can arrange another cover for him, Kate, but you—"

"No." She stood up, an old fury ricocheting through her. "Dad, you can't sweep in here and tell me what to do. You can't."

"I'm trying to protect you."

Always, always, trying to protect her. "I *am* protected. I have a bodyguard."

"Who was stripping you naked in the pool when I walked in unannounced."

She shook off the admonishment. "If you're trying to imply he can't do his job, you were let in by one of two people with a key who know the code and can get to me."

"I'm implying nothing. I'm saying that it's time you come home, Katie. For your own good."

Oh, those words. Those flipping *words*.

For your own good.

An old, familiar thrumming started at the base of her head. Dad telling her what to do…for her own good.

She stared at him, mustering up what she needed to fight this fight, and suddenly she was aware that Alec had stepped onto the patio and was standing a few feet behind her. For one second, she was ready to rebel, knowing they were going to gang up on her, just like Dad and Steven used to, and force her to—

"Kate is perfectly safe here." He took a few steps closer, dressed and dried, the composure that she'd seen slip when he met her father firmly back in place.

"With all due respect, you're saying that because you need her here," Dad said. "She's your cover. But I think she should come home now."

"She's free to leave, but the decision is hers." Alec turned to her and gave her an expectant look. "I'll respect whatever decision you make."

And, really, that was all she'd ever wanted from a man. "I'm staying," she said quietly.

She was pregnant. Just about as far along as Robyn, too, so there was an instant connection. Plus, the lady interviewing Robyn was so pretty, with perfect nails and flawless skin. Not anything like Robyn would imagine a maid at a resort to be. Well, she owned the housekeeping service, so that must be why Mandy Nicholas had her shit so together.

"You seem a little nervous, Robyn," she said, leaning forward and crossing her arms.

"Well, I've never been a maid before, so I'm worried you won't give me the job."

She searched Robyn's face like she was looking for more than just a decent résumé. "I'd never been a housekeeper before when I started, either." She smiled, with green eyes that lit with a warmth that seemed real. Of course, that gave Robyn a twinge of guilt. She had no other way to get into this la-di-da resort to find Alec Petrov, but the idea of applying for a job as a maid seemed like something a super-smart girl would do.

"I'm kind of desperate, Mrs. Nicholas," she admitted, her confidence in just how super-smart she was growing less every day of this trip.

"Call me Mandy, and, honey, I know all about being desperate."

Robyn couldn't help letting her gaze slide over the pricey maternity clothes and a diamond ring the size of a small country. *Desperate, my ass.*

Mandy angled her head as if she could read Robyn's mind. "But working at Casa Blanca as a maid changed my life." She absently touched the ring, and some color rose to her cheeks. "I met my husband here."

"I'm not trying to meet a man," Robyn said, unless finding Alec Petrov counted. "I just need a job, and I don't have any references. But I'm a hard worker, and I'll start today."

The lady nodded as if she'd been battling with herself and one side had just won. "You need to get fitted for a uniform and set up for training." She stood and gestured for Robyn to do the same. "Let's go see who's available to get you started."

Robyn exhaled with relief. The trip down here had been long, and she'd slept in her car, wondering if she was even doing the right thing.

Mandy put her hand on Robyn's shoulder, a warm and comforting touch that made her ache for more and question just what the hell she was doing here trying to find Alec. Could he help her? He might not even be here. But this lady was offering a job, and this island was nice and far, far away from Cole. Maybe she could stay and have her baby here. Would she make a friend? Someone to help her take care of the baby? Maybe...

"Honey, it's gonna be okay."

Robyn looked up at her, blinking back tears she'd had no idea had filled her eyes.

The woman crouched down to get face-to-face with her. "Life deals you some lousy hands sometimes," she said. "You're doing the right thing by taking a job, no matter how lowly it might seem, and taking control of your life. Every step you take is one step closer to being completely self-reliant. For you *and* your baby."

She sucked in a light breath. "How do you know?"

"You're too thin for that to be anything but a baby bump."

And she thought she'd been doing such a good job of hiding it. Another thing she wasn't smart about. "And that's okay with you?"

The woman smiled, making her even prettier. God, what would it have been like to have a mother like this, rather than a drug addict who didn't care if Robyn lived or died? "Yes, it's okay. I want to help you," she said. "And I promise we have plenty to do that doesn't involve you breathing in cleaning solvents or lifting too much, but you can work."

Gratitude filled her, enough that Robyn felt a little unsteady as she got to her feet. As if sensing that, Mandy kept her hand on Robyn's back and guided her into a small office area where two other ladies worked on computers at desks.

"Is there a senior housekeeper not on duty at the moment?" Mandy asked one of the women.

"I just saw Poppy go into the break room," she said. "I think she's done with her morning villas. She can't get to Bay Laurel and Rockrose until after checkout time."

"Fantastic," Mandy said, leading Robyn toward another part of the building. The place felt like it had once been a house, tucked away from the main resort with a few others just like it, but now it was clearly being used as a busy office.

In a kitchen area, a large black woman in a pink uniform was at the microwave, pressing buttons. The whole room smelled delicious.

"Poppy, I want to introduce you to Robyn Bickler, our newest hire."

The woman turned and burst into the sweetest smile.

"Welcome! We could use a new face around here." Her gaze dropped to Robyn's stomach, and her eyebrows shot up. "Or two."

Wow, she really was showing. Robyn smiled at her. "I can work hard," she assured the woman.

"Of course you can! If Miss Mandy wants you, I want you."

"Can you get her fitted for a uniform and maybe take her on your afternoon rounds, Poppy?"

"I would love to." She gestured for Robyn to come closer. "Don't be afraid, child."

Robyn said good-bye to Mandy, resisting the urge to be totally pathetic and hug the woman who'd just given her something that felt like more than a job or even an in to the resort. That lady had just given her a new lease on life.

Maybe she should just forget Alec Petrov and take this nice ride.

She followed Poppy into what looked like it might have once been a walk-in closet, but the only thing hanging in it were brightly colored maid's uniforms, all different shades of pastel.

"Where are you from, Robyn?" Poppy asked.

"Up North."

That got her a quick look of disbelief. "The North Pole? Canada? New York? Atlanta? There's a lot of places north of Mimosa Key."

"New York." It was big enough that she could say that, and it was always better to keep lies straight.

"Mmmm." Poppy wasn't buying it, but thankfully she let it go and shifted her attention to Robyn's body. "I have a few with stretchy bottoms and loose tops."

Robyn touched her stomach, knowing it could only get bigger. "That'll work." And she inhaled the incredible smell that had drifted from the kitchen to the closet. "Wow, what is that?" She sniffed loudly. "It's making me hungry."

"Child, mud would probably make you hungry, but what you're smelling is my—"

"She did it again!" A man's voice echoed from the kitchen, followed by what sounded like the slamming of the microwave.

"My *pollo caribe*," Poppy finished, leaning close to whisper, "Which is *my* version of what *he* thinks is his—"

"Why do you mess with perfection?" a man hollered.

"Because my perfection is better!" Poppy called out, and one second later, a man's footsteps pounded. "Oh, here he comes," Poppy said under her breath. "Nino Rossi, who thinks he's the only person on God's green earth who can cook and if you don't do it his way, you're not doing it at all."

Robyn turned to the door to see a little old grandpa who had to be near eighty lumbering into the closet, a furry frown crinkling up his face even more than age had.

"Lemon chicken is not spicy," he announced.

"*Pollo caribe* is not lemon chicken," she replied.

"But that's my recipe."

"Not anymore. I fixed it up with a little jerk seasoning, ol' mon."

Big brown eyes grew wide at the Jamaican-sounding expression.

"And is this any way to act in front of a new staff member?" Poppy chided. "Nino Rossi is an assistant to one of our senior security executives," she explained. "And this is Robyn Bickler, a brand new housekeeper."

"Hi," Robyn said shyly, getting a quick nod from a man who was way more intent on yelling at Poppy than greeting the new kid. "Listen, you have to…" His frown deepened, and he glanced back at Robyn, studying her for a moment. "What did you say your name was?"

"Robyn," she replied.

"Bickler?" he asked pointedly, making her suddenly warm and uncomfortable, mostly by the way he was staring at her.

"Yes," she said. He certainly couldn't know her, right? "Why?"

"Because..." He searched her face again. Like he recognized her, but that was impossible. "I knew a Bickler once."

He had? "It's...not that common." Could he know someone in her family? Her dad? No, this old man didn't hang out with guys like her father, and there weren't that many Bicklers running around.

"Nino, why are you staring at the poor child like that?"

Yeah, why *was* he staring at her?

"Robyn Bickler?" he asked again, and this time a slow heat rolled through her as another possibility hit her. Vlitnik! He could have people anywhere. Hell, he could have already infiltrated this place looking for Alec, just like she had.

Why the hell had she used her real name? Because she was an idiot, like her mother always said.

She barely nodded, and the old man backed out the door quickly, without even saying good-bye.

"Well, that's some kind of magic you work there," Poppy said with a laugh, turning back to the uniforms. "When he gets on a rant, ain't nothin' can stop him. Okay, now, this one should fit."

She should get out of here. This was stupid and crazy. She probably walked right into a hornet's nest of Vlitnik's people. *Dumb!*

"Actually, I'm not going to take the job," she said, backing away just like the man had.

"What?" Poppy barked at her. "Don't let him scare you off! He's actually quite sweet when he's not—"

"No, I can't. I have to go." She darted out the door and zipped through the little office, ignoring the surprised stares of the two ladies at their desks. "Bye," she said lamely, looking at Mandy's closed door and wishing so hard she could run into that lady's arms for help. But there was no help for her. "Sorry," she whispered, yanking open the front door and rushing out into the sunshine.

She practically tripped over the stone walkway trying to get to her car, the rest of the world whizzing by. Now that she was on Vlitnik's radar, she'd never, ever be safe again.

"Robyn Bickler?"

She froze at the man's voice behind her. A low, strong, serious voice that sent chills up her spine. Very, very slowly, she turned and met the eyes of a man who looked intense enough to kill her.

She couldn't even speak.

"You're not going anywhere until we talk."

She put her hand on her belly and felt her knees give way.

Chapter Twenty-Three

Alec sat on the love seat in Kate's room and listened to the shower run for well over fifteen minutes. It reminded him of her first day here, when she was hiding from him. Was she hiding from him now?

He knew the bathroom door wasn't locked and that she was, most likely, in the shower, naked and fully accessible to him. Her desire to sleep with him was clear and strong.

But it couldn't be casual or meaningless, not now, not with Kate. She wanted inside his head, and, damn it, he wanted to let her there. The first time he ever wanted anyone to know his truth. And, like her, he didn't want to roll around and…and…

Yeah, he did. He wanted to more than anything. But sometime in the last few days, his desires had gone way past simple, easy sex. He had to tell her. Everything. And then she wouldn't want him anymore, and he wouldn't blame her.

But he wasn't going to tell her afterward. That wouldn't be fair. She needed to know before they got in this bed. Which, by the way things were going, wasn't going to be tonight. It would be soon. It would be now.

The shower water stopped, and he sat a little straighter, expecting her to step into the bedroom, but only hearing her humming. She sounded happy and free. Free from her worries, free to leave if she wanted to, but she didn't want to. Which meant—

The door popped open, and she sucked in a quick breath at the sight of him, involuntarily tightening the white towel wrapped around her body. Soaking wet hair curled over her bare shoulders, and the flush on her face from the hot water deepened.

"I didn't know you were there," she said.

He gnawed on his lip, staring at her for a good twenty seconds. Good God, she was gorgeous. No doubt, the prettiest woman he'd ever—

"Do you think I made the wrong decision to stay?" she asked.

"You tell me...after I tell you."

She frowned, sliding a lock of wet hair over her shoulder. "Tell me what?"

"Everything."

A smile tipped the corners of her lips. "'Bout time, Petrov."

He grimaced at her light tone, because she didn't know. She really didn't have any way of knowing, so he had to forgive her efforts to take the lid off this pressure cooker.

He stood and crossed the room, somehow needing to be closer to her when he made his confession. "You know I'm hiding from people. From one man in particular. A man who essentially owns me."

A shadow darkened her eyes, the look of a person who got it. Of course, she'd been "owned," too. Only in a different way. Hoping for sympathy he didn't deserve, he took a breath.

"I was promised to him as a kid, bought and paid for. He technically owns me, at least in his world."

She narrowed her eyes, confusion making them a deeper green than usual. "So this *is* a Russian mob thing?"

It was a Dmitri Vlitnik thing. "Yes."

"Was your father in the mob?" she asked, more tentative than when she normally grilled him like a lawyer. Probably because she didn't want to know the answer. But, oh, honey, it was so much worse than that.

"He was not," he said, dropping onto the edge of the bed, but she stayed standing. That was good. She'd probably want to run after he finished. "But he paid into the system to protect his business and his family."

She sat down next to him. "Why don't you start at the very beginning, Alec?"

He puffed out a breath of raw resignation. After a second, he took her hand and closed it in his, her fingers lost in the mass of his. For a long time, he stared at their joined hands, his gaze locked on the letters were nothing but a constant reminder of what he was.

Okay, the beginning.

"When my father was diagnosed with terminal cancer, only he really understood the risk of leaving us alone," he finally said. "My mother could run the business, and I was a decent enough butcher to help her. But she didn't know about the payments and likely wouldn't be able to afford them and stay in business. Plus, she was...defenseless." He closed his eyes at the thought, just remembering how his father had worried. "I was a big kid, but I couldn't protect her if someone wanted to...if he wanted to..."

"Who?"

He shouldn't tell her the name. She shouldn't know. "The man at the head of all this is...was..." He shook his head. "All of his guys were thugs who couldn't be trusted, but he, in particular, seemed to be interested in my mother." Just saying it made him sick. "So I guess my father was worried about more than just the business."

Kate nodded, getting his drift. "What did your father do?" she asked, stroking his hand with her thumb, sliding over the letters like she could erase them. And she could. That was why he was doing this, because she *could* erase his pain. She probably wouldn't; she'd probably run like hell. But she could be the one to heal him.

"Get it all out, Alec."

With encouragement like that, she *could* heal him.

"This guy was in the process of building an empire in Brighton Beach," he said. "And emperors need armies, and armies need foot soldiers. My dad promised him that if they left the business alone and, more important, left my mother alone, then they could have me as an enforcer once I was old enough."

She blinked at him. "As a hit man?"

"Exactly. Using these." He splayed his hands in front of himself, letting go of hers.

"He could just give you away like that?"

"I guess, because he did. There was probably a drink, a blood oath, and promises to Mother Russia." He closed his eyes, not even close to forgiving his father for the decision, even though he understood why he'd made it.

"So how have you managed to avoid this life imprisonment?" she asked.

"What makes you think I have?"

She studied his face for a moment. "Besides gut instinct and my sense of people? You're not running from them because you're sick of the life. My guess is you're running from them because you don't want that life."

"Yes, that's right." And the fact that she had that much faith in him was like balm on his wound. Didn't take away all the pain, but it helped.

"Which makes you good," she assured him. "Bone-deep and genuinely good."

He couldn't help looking hard at her crystalline green eyes, seeing his reflection in them, or at least seeing that she perceived him to be a different man than he'd spent most of his life believing he was. That was more intoxicating than her brain and body, more attractive than her personality and fire. That was magic to him.

"You *are* good," she whispered, as if she read his mind and saw the lingering doubts that hung in every corner of his conscience.

He put his finger over her lips as if he could seal that thought there, forever. *You are good.* She looked at him for a long time, then kissed his finger lightly.

"What happened, Alec?"

He turned away, the lovely sight of her replaced with…a different girl. Barely seventeen. Pretty, innocent, scared out of her mind.

Oh, fuck. Now he was there. In that warehouse. On that night. With that girl.

Bile rose up and made his stomach turn.

"Alec?"

He'd never told the story. Not in its entirety, since the only person who'd ever discussed it with him was Gregg, who knew enough of the details that he didn't have to pull them out of Alec.

"They tried to break me in early. Not a month after my dad died." No surprise, his voice came out husky. "It didn't go well."

She sat silent, waiting. And he tried to dig for his inner calm, for the Zen he could muster before a fight, for the wall he put around his conscience and the world. None of his tricks would cooperate as he realized his hand was trembling.

240

"There was a girl, a teenage girl a couple of years older than I was." He swallowed. *Anna.* He never knew her last name, but he remembered her name was Anna. "Her father wasn't cooperating with the *Mafiya*, and they wanted to make a point. Actually, they wanted *me* to make a point to prove my worth." They being Vlitnik, the heartless bastard.

"Oh." It was more a groan than a word, a syllable of fear about what she was going to hear.

He turned to her. "You asked, counselor."

She nodded, her face pale.

He gave himself a second to get composure that wasn't really there for the taking, but he tried anyway. "I didn't want to...hurt her. I didn't want to hit her." But he'd watched one of Vlitnik's enforcers rough her up so badly that Alec had peed his pants.

And Vlitnik had howled with laughter.

He closed his eyes. "But then they made me hurt her."

"Alec, stop—"

"No," he said, not caring that his voice cracked. "I won't stop. You have to know what I am."

"You were a kid, and they forced you—"

"Don't make excuses for me! There are no fucking excuses. I did it. I hit her. With this." He bunched his fist and turned it so the dark letters were in front of their faces.

бить

"How did they force you?"

His heart lurched when she asked the question. Her faith in him was strong. "They didn't have a gun on me or a knife or anything. But if I didn't do what they told me to do, Vlitnik said the deal with my dad was off and my mother was fair game."

"That's the guy's name?"

Son of a bitch, he'd said it. No taking it back now. "Yes.

And he always had a thing for my mother." Revulsion rolled through him. "He made it perfectly clear what he'd do to her if I didn't do what he said. He'd take her. Rape her. *Own* her." He sobbed out the last words.

She swore softly, reaching for him, but he jerked out of her touch, shame burning.

"So I thought it was better that he owned *me*," he said. "And as his slave, I had to do what I was told. And I was told to…beat that girl."

He could still hear her high-pitched screams. Then her pleas. Then helpless, pitiful sobs. It all came back to him. The jolt of his fist slamming her tender stomach. The blood and snot and tears on her face.

He looked straight ahead, seeing that young girl's disgust and knowing that, right then, Kate was no doubt looking at him the same way. As she should.

He was the worst scum of a human being.

After a moment, he continued. "That night, after they…took her away…Vlitnik had me branded. Tattooed my hand right there in that warehouse with these letters that sit on my knuckles as a daily reminder of my worth and my purpose. To kill."

"Did she die?" she gasped.

He shook his head. "No." He wiped his eye, the tear stinging. "And I was so careful not to hit her somewhere that would scar." He had to swallow a sob on the last word, her pretty face still clear in his head. He'd never forget it. Or how he'd vomited when they dragged her away, and again when they jabbed his hand with needles full of ink and marked him as one of them.

"And he got away with this?" Kate's question was cold and surprisingly unemotional, and then he remembered she was studying to be a lawyer.

"He didn't do anything, Kate." He finally looked at her. "That's how he works. That's how he manages to avoid the law. He never gets *his* hands dirty."

"He's still guilty."

"No shit."

"Was there an investigation? Did her family press charges? Did she identify you?"

He snorted a laugh at the naïve questions. "You don't understand the power of the *Mafiya*. No, there wasn't an investigation. Her father coughed up the cash and sent her somewhere to heal up. But I did get a visit from Grigori Nyekovic, and that changed my life."

"Who is he?"

A guardian angel. "Gregg's a Russian businessman who's always, always on the good side. He was a fixture in Brighton, a guy who'd swoop in and give money instead of taking it, or build something that the community needed but couldn't afford, and sometimes, he'd take kids under his wing to get them out of trouble and away from the mob." He didn't tell her that Gregg worked as one of the FBI's top informants, using his insiders to get anything they could to bring as many members of the Russian mob to justice as possible.

"He helped you?"

That was an understatement. "He had someone convince Vlitnik I was too much of a wimp to do the job at that age and that I needed to toughen up. And I did, but not so I could help the mob. Gregg paid for me to take martial arts classes, and I almost immediately found my purpose. Jiu-jitsu in particular, but all martial arts in general, gave me the grounding I didn't have."

He took another chance at looking at her, bracing for her to be backing away, planning her escape, but her eyes looked soft and sweet and, oh, God, sympathetic.

"Jiu-jitsu isn't really about fighting," he told her. "It's about balance and power and control."

She gave a shaky smile. "I'd probably love it."

"You would," he agreed.

She inched closer, clearly not done with his confession. "So how did he treat your mom? And you?" she asked.

"He left us alone after that. I took my martial arts classes. I worked in the butcher shop. I kept my nose clean and graduated from high school, all the while thinking it was over. I wasn't made of what they wanted, so I was safe." And then, tragedy. "Until my mom died when I was in my first year at Queens College."

"They got her," Kate said on a gasp.

"No, she contracted a freakishly rare disease you can get from handling raw animal meat, called brucellosis. She had no idea she had it, an infection got too far, and she died in a couple of days."

"Oh, God. I'm sorry."

He closed his eyes and nodded. "She was a good lady," he said. "And when she died, Vlitnik came calling."

"So he wasn't done with you."

"On the contrary. By then I was big, strong, and could kill anyone I wanted to. Except, obviously, I didn't want to."

"What did you do?"

Turned to Gregg, of course. "I dropped out of school, enlisted in the Marines, and got my ass over to Iraq as fast as possible, because it was clear to me I'd rather be on the receiving end of an insurgent's bullet than do anything for that lunatic."

He took a minute to rub the original tattoo. He'd gotten many more since then, but had never covered the first one. It reminded him of what he didn't want to be.

"The war in Iraq was really heating up back then with a

244

second surge, so I kept re-upping for more tours and ended up doing three until I got injured and had to come home."

She let out a sigh, because it was pretty obvious Alec Petrov couldn't catch a break.

"And wait till you hear what happened," he said with a dry laugh. "Nothing heroic like I saved lives by picking up an IED. No, I fucking got hit in the head by a cement brick on patrol." He tapped his skull. "I had a concussion, obviously, and actually couldn't remember a lot of shit for a long time. They sent me back home, and Gregg put me up in Philly with a friend of his. He helped me get on my feet, literally, and lent me the capital to start a training studio, where I could use my skills but not really fight." He turned to her. "I had a few years and really had my shit together, until Vlitnik found me, and that's why I'm here. End of *The Alec Petrov Story*."

She reached for his hand, and this time, he let her hold it. "But the beginning of someone else's story."

"If Gabe Rossi can really do what he says, yeah."

"How do you feel about that? About starting over as someone new?"

He gave a sharp laugh. "The past never goes away, regardless of the name on my passport or where I live or what I do. I still wake up and see her face. I still avoid anything that remotely stinks of a relationship. I still—"

"Why?" Her question cut into his speech, silencing him. "Don't you think a healthy relationship with a woman would help you?"

He considered all the ways to answer that, but settled on the one she deserved to hear: the truth. "I'm not worthy of a relationship with a woman, Kate. I gave up the right the first time I took a swing at that girl. I wasn't exaggerating when I say I hate my hands and, sometimes, the man they're connected to. I don't deserve the kind of...of affection you're talking about. The kind you were offering before."

She made a slow circle with her fingertip over the letters, the knuckles, the bumps and bruises and scars. For a long, long time, she said nothing, sitting silently next to him on the bed, staring at the skin he'd spent the better part of his life trying to hide. Finally, she lifted his hand to her mouth and kissed the knuckles, looking up at him with eyes so deep and sincere, he could actually feel himself falling into her.

Very slowly, barely breathing, she placed that hand over her beating heart and lay back on the bed, the invitation, the certainty, and the forgiveness in her eyes the most beautiful thing he'd ever seen.

Chapter Twenty-Four

Kate pulled Alec into a kiss, squeezing her eyes shut as if she could squeeze out everything but the pleasure of his hard and heavy body on hers. She'd gotten what she'd wanted...mostly. She'd wanted to see inside his soul and understand all that darkness, and he'd shown her.

And now she wanted to take it away.

His mouth trailed fiery kisses over her throat and chest, her towel falling open to give him complete access to her naked body.

"Kate," he murmured in between frantic, anxious kisses on her breasts, cupping them both and lifting them to his mouth. Slowly, he lifted his head, the pain on his face so real and raw. "Are you sure?"

She stroked his cheek. "Never been more sure of anything, Alec."

"I don't deserve you."

"I'm doing my damnedest to prove you're wrong about that." She pulled him against her, intensifying every kiss and touch. Heat pooled inside her, driving her to slide her hand into his pants, hungry and desperate to touch him the way he was touching her.

He hissed noisily when her fist closed around his thick

erection, his kiss on her shoulder turning into a gentle bite.

"You're beautiful," she whispered, getting a soft laugh in response. "You are," she insisted.

She stroked the length of him with one hand, pushing him to his back with the other. "I think you're beautiful and tender and worthy, Alexander Petrov. And hot. Did I mention really"—she kissed his mouth—"really hot?"

He just looked at her, a smile pulling, like maybe, just maybe, he was starting to believe her.

She straddled him, naked now that the towel had fallen, her damp hair tickling her shoulders. She unsnapped his jeans, delighted that there was nothing else to remove to get to him.

Lowering the zipper tooth by tooth, she finally dragged her gaze from the size and shape of his hard-on to his face. His gaze was on her, his jaw slack, his chest rising and falling, his big, bad, bruiser hands relaxed for once at his sides as he let her have complete control.

"Hot," she repeated as she spread the denim to reveal all of him. She trailed a finger over the head, circling the droplet just to watch him shudder with pleasure. "And sweet."

He smiled with the next breath. "Kind of short words for you, Smarty-Pants."

"All the blood is gone from my brain." She cupped his balls, and he grunted.

"I know the feeling."

She scooted lower and dragged his jeans over his hips, his hard-on closer as he lifted up to help her. As she lowered her head, he answered with a moan, reaching for her, threading his fingers into her hair, guiding her mouth toward him. "Please," he murmured.

He didn't have to ask twice. She took him between her lips, loving the taste of him, the salty, manly taste. And the way he moaned, helpless and happy. And how he moved, in and out of her mouth, taking his pleasure, gripping her head, surrendering to her.

"Kate..." He mumbled more, incoherent, the sound of his words lost as her blood pumped with the need to do this right. To give him exquisite pleasure. To show him just how worthy he was—

"Kate!" He pulled out of her mouth, too fast, and she jerked her head up. "Someone's here."

Then she heard a sharp rap on the villa door, impatient and loud.

She just grunted and closed her eyes, the frustration like physical pain. "No."

"Mr. Benjamin! It's an emergency! Mr. Benjamin!"

Poppy. Really. Now?

"Please! Mr. Gabriel says this is really an emergency!" The words were muffled by the door and distance, but the message was loud and clear.

Alec sat up, his bodyguard face replacing the lost lover she'd nearly consumed.

"I don't want to stop," Kate moaned.

He stifled a smile and stroked her hair. "Neither do I," he said, easing her back, rolling off the bed, and zipping up on his way out. "Wait here."

Kate let out a noisy sigh and fell on the bed, a thread of worry curling around her heart at the idea of an emergency. She might be safe from threats, but was he?

She closed her eyes to listen to the conversation, really only able to pick up bits and pieces, enough to get that Gabe needed to see Alec right this minute.

Would she have to go? No, the threat to her was gone now, and she did not want to deal with smartass Gabe Rossi when she—

"I'm going to the security office," Alec said as he marched purposefully back into the room. And, being a foolish and confused woman, she actually felt disappointed for getting what she wanted. "Poppy will stay here with you."

"No, she won't," she said, pushing off the bed. She didn't want to deal with smartass Gabe, but she *really* didn't want to deal with Poppy scrutinizing and passing judgment. "Can I just stay here alone?"

"Poppy told me your dad's still here," he said, adjusting his jeans. "He's staying at the resort one more day. You could go to him or…leave. I wouldn't blame you at all," he added quickly.

Leave? Why would she do that? "What's going on? What's the emergency?"

"There's someone here from Brighton Beach."

She shook her head, the information not computing. "Your friend Gregg?"

"Someone who is looking for me on behalf of Dmitri Vlitnik."

A slow panic seized her. "And you're just going to talk to him? What if it's a trap?"

"Not a trap. There's a pregnant teenager in Gabe's office, crying out a story I need to hear." He stuck his wallet in his back pocket and looked at her. "If I come back and you're gone, I understand. If I come back and you're here, we're…it's…I'm…you're…"

"I'm yours," she whispered.

He just looked at her, speechless. Then he leaned over, touched her cheek, and kissed her forehead.

"I'll be here when you get back," she promised. "You can post Poppy outside if it makes you feel better."

She stayed still after he left, long enough for the air

conditioner to chill her body and her heart to settle down to a normal rate, surprised at how out of sorts it felt to know she was alone in the villa.

Yet, that's what she'd wanted from day one. That's how she'd wanted to live life, all alone and independent and autonomous.

Except now...she didn't want to be away from him. And whatever he was facing, shouldn't she be with him now? Weren't they a team?

Dressing quickly, she grabbed her bag and opened the door to find Poppy standing just outside, her features screwed up in a miserable expression.

"Are you okay?" Kate asked as she stepped out to inspect her more closely.

"I gotta go." She tapped her belly. "Bad."

"You should have knocked, Poppy." Kate held the door wide for her. "Go in and use the bathroom."

"Mr. Benjamin said you wanted to be alone."

"Not if you have to use the bathroom. Go ahead. I was just going to go over to the security offices."

Poppy pressed a hand to her belly and widened her eyes.

"Go!" Kate nudged her inside. "Please."

Poppy blew past Kate into the house, moving so fast that Kate had to step out of the doorway to let her by. As she did, the door closed behind Poppy. Kate reached to grab the knob, but it latched before she could prevent that, leaving her locked out.

"Poppy!" she called, but obviously the woman was likely around the corner and into the powder room by now. Kate turned and glanced up and down the path that ran in front of Caralluma, seeing nothing but sunshine and palm trees in her slice of paradise. No one to help her, but no one to hurt her, either.

On a sigh, she stepped away from the house, onto the path, looking again for any sign of life. There was none, so she slipped her bag off her shoulder, digging for the phone to call—

A large hand slammed over her mouth and nose from behind. "Mathilda Carlson."

The voice, male and low and threatening, blew into her ear, sending a billion chills of raw panic through her.

"That's a good one," he snorted in her ear.

Wait...*what*? She jerked to get free, adrenaline making a freefall through her system, blanking her mind.

"Let's go!" He jerked her hard, toward the back of the villa.

Think, Kate, think. Soft targets, eyes, ears, nose...

The knock against her head was so hard that, for a split second, she literally saw white spots like stars and felt as though her brain joggled loose. And then her vision blurred, her power evaporated, and a black cloud started to descend over her eyes.

Her legs folded, but he caught her before she hit the ground, leaning over her long enough for her to see his face and know, deep down in whatever consciousness she had left, that his could be the last face she ever saw.

Chapter Twenty-Five

The minute he laid eyes on the waif named for a bird, Alec's low-grade hatred for what Vlitnik had put him through came bubbling back to the surface. For a few blissful minutes, Kate had turned that constant boil to only a simmer of self-loathing with a different kind of flame, but one look at this girl's tear-stained face and frightened eyes, and it all came back.

She'd already confessed a hell of a lot, if not everything, and it was obvious she was terrified.

"So let me get this straight," Gabe said, resting his backside on his desk and crossing his arms as he looked down at Robyn. "You saw his tattoo on Instagram"—he shot a disgusted look at Alec—"and recognized him as a trainer you once knew and decided to drive more than a thousand miles to find him."

She nodded, eyes wide.

"Why would you do that?" Gabe asked.

"I thought he might know where my boyfriend is."

"Is that the only reason?" Gabe demanded.

She nodded. "I need to find him, and Cole—you remember Cole Morrow, right?" At Alec's nod, she looked encouraged. "Cole told me he'd do anything to train with you again, so I saw the picture and recognized your tattoo and thought maybe he'd come down here to find you. Wasn't that smart?"

"Oh, it was effing brilliant," Gabe said. "Like what are you doing getting a job as a maid when you're obviously a Mensa candidate?"

She swallowed visibly. "I don't know what that means."

"Gabe," Alec said, spearing him with a look, "she's been through enough."

He barely sighed. "Okay, but let's just review how smart she is. First, she finds a picture of your tattoo on some social media site that's no bigger than a speck on a gnat's ass. *Or so she says.*"

"My friend showed me that picture. It's there on Insta. You can see it."

"And," Gabe continued, straightening so he could look down at her, "she is able to find this rather secluded resort, drive herself here, and get a job as a maid. *Or so she says.*"

"The name of the resort was in *People* magazine!" she said. "And, hello, GPS."

"And you haven't told a living soul that you're here. Not your mother or sister or best friend or anyone?"

"No." She shook her head hard. "I swear I didn't. I just got in the car and took off, because I have to find Cole." She touched her protruding belly with shaking fingers, the move hitting Alec somewhere primal and protective.

"Are you absolutely positive you didn't tell anyone?" he asked, far more gently than Gabe, and he knew why. The story he'd just told Kate was fresh in his mind, and this girl was just a few years older than the one he'd just talked about, but her fear was as tangible as Anna's had been that horrible night.

"I swear." She held up her right hand and gave him a look of desperate honesty. "I haven't told anyone."

Gabe fired another look at Alec. "This is a fine mess now. We have to..." He shook his head. "We have to keep her here."

"Why?" She shot up from her chair. "You can't do that to me! I'm not under arrest for anything."

She was right, Alec thought. But she could also be a direct link to Vlitnik, whether she admitted it or not.

"Just stay for a while," Alec said to her. "We'll make sure you're safe."

She eyed him as though she wanted to trust him, but couldn't. "I just need some money," she finally said. "And I swear I won't tell anyone you're here."

Gabe snorted and picked up his phone. "Nino, can you take Miss Bickler for a few minutes?"

Nino couldn't protect her if Vlitnik or any of his goons showed up. "She can stay with me," Alec said quickly. "With us," he amended, because deep in his soul, he knew Kate wasn't going anywhere. Not yet, anyway.

"I don't need to stay with anyone," Robyn said. "You can't keep me here."

"Do you think you're safe if you leave?" Alec demanded.

"Why wouldn't I be?" She lifted her delicate chin in defiance. "I didn't tell anyone I was here. I'm perfectly safe, and if you want to help me, just give me some gas money and I'm out."

The door opened, and Nino came in, gesturing for her. "Come on."

She looked from one man to the next, rage darkening her skin, fear in her brown eyes. "You can't just muscle me around! This isn't a police station, and I didn't do anything but apply for a job!"

"Go with him," Gabe said.

"No."

"Please, Robyn," Alec added.

She crossed her arms defiantly.

"I have cheese ravioli and garlic bread with your name on it," Nino said.

Her shoulders caved along with her determination. "Fine. But I'm not staying for good," she said as she walked out, following Nino and her stomach.

When the door shut, Alec braced for the wrath of Gabe Rossi.

"Fuck," he murmured, dropping back into his chair and tapping an open laptop, but the computer screen stayed blank.

"She's scared and pregnant," Alec said, taking the seat Robyn had vacated.

"And lying," Gabe said, his gaze on the screen as he hit the return key repeatedly.

"What do we do?" Alec asked, ready to take Gabe's shit about how dumb it was his tattoo was visible in a photo on Instagram. Because it was dumb.

But Gabe seemed torn between the problem at hand and something on his computer screen. "How can this motherhumper be *encrypted*?" he growled at the laptop, then pushed it away to focus on Alec. "You're going to have to leave, that much is obvious. Cover is blown to kingdom come."

"As long as I'm here, I'll babysit Robyn." He'd never throw her out to Vlitnik's wolves.

"We can't keep her against her will," Gabe said.

"Nino can ply her with food."

Gabe gave a mirthless smile, stealing a glance at his computer again. "This kind of shit happens, you know. You were doing what I told you to do, acting like a married couple at the resort. It's just dumb luck you were caught in the picture of some celebrity billionaire."

He appreciated being let off the hook, but Alec was still mad at himself. "At least Kate's safe now."

"Not completely. I just got a text from my cousin. They let that Wesley guy out on bail last night. Bastard must have some kind of friends in high places."

Shit. He stood, wanting to end this bullshit and get back to Kate immediately. What if she'd left?

"Don't worry, Poppy's got her," Gabe said.

"She wouldn't let Poppy in the villa," Alec told him.

"Well, Poppy won't let her leave. But get back to her, and I'll come up with something. I'll see if I can get you two somewhere safe—somewhere else safe—until this blows over."

Get you two. How would she feel about that? Alec knew how he felt about it. Damn good. "And this new girl?"

He returned to his computer. "We'll figure it out."

Alec took a step closer. "Gabe? Anything else I can do?"

Gabe managed a smile. "Unless you have some hacking skills I don't know about and can break through encrypted software, then no."

"Sorry."

Gabe shrugged. "Fortunately, my little sister does." He picked up his cell phone and nodded to the door. "Go stay with Kate. Take your new ward. Stay out of sight for a day or two, and I'll get all three of you somewhere, but I can't promise paradise this time."

"That's cool." Alec opened the door and practically walked right into Poppy, breathless and glistening with a sheen of sweat. "Where's Kate?" he demanded.

Her eyes popped and her jaw loosened. "Here?" she said, sounding both hopeful and terrified at the same time.

Alec glanced behind her, but he already knew that if Kate were in this building, she'd be next to him. "You left her?"

She put her hand to her mouth. "I had an emergency and used the bathroom and I thought she came here. She said she was coming over—"

He whipped around to look at Gabe. "Lock this resort down!" Alec ordered, shooting to the door. "Close down the whole damn island if you have to."

"Get McBain in here," Gabe hollered to the McBain Security staff in the office. "Start a search and call the Mimosa Key sheriff to close off the causeway. She's not getting off this island."

But Alec barely heard the order, because he was already running back to the villa. He'd know if she left him...or someone had taken her.

And if that was the case...someone was going to die. And it wasn't going to be Kate Kingston. Not on his life.

Chapter Twenty-Six

The dream drifted away like fog on a warm morning, leaving behind a pounding, thumping ache in Kate's head that sent fiery shots of pain with each throb of her pulse.

Pain. God, it thrummed through her. Everything hurt so bad. Kate tried to open her eyes, but they weren't cooperating. Neither were her hands and feet. She couldn't move. Nothing would—

"My reservation is in the name of Michael Wesley. Can you confirm that?"

The voice punched through the fog, low and powerful and so damn familiar. Not just the voice, but the tone. She knew that voice.

"I'll give you the credit card number right now. Are you listening?"

Michael Wesley. The man her dad had said was questioned about the threats. The one dating Laurie to get to her. A stranger. But that *voice.* That voice did not belong to a stranger. Something pulled at her memory. His face as she was falling...his face. But she couldn't focus on anything with the sledgehammer of agony echoing in her head.

She listened to him recite a string of numbers, digging

into her memory for how she knew that inflection, that timbre, but everything was...

"Thank you. I'll be arriving in about"—he sighed heavily—"sometime after midnight."

That voice made her stomach tighten and her pulse race. It made her whole body rebel. That voice was...oh, God. Oh, *God*.

Steven.

She heard an old familiar sigh of profound discontent and involuntarily shuddered, but something deep inside kept Kate from opening her eyes.

Steven had her. *Steven.* How was this possible? She didn't know, but she knew the voice of her ex-husband. And now she knew the fear of being trapped...really trapped. Like *bound and gagged* trapped.

If you've been drugged or knocked out, never let them know when you're awake.

That voice, the one in her head, was so much more pleasant and comforting than the one she'd just heard. Alec.

"Kate? Are you awake?" The demand was loud and close, so close she could feel his breath on her face. But she didn't budge. Her eyelids didn't even flutter. No, she would never let him know she was awake.

"You better sleep, you little bitch. Because I'll kill you here if I have to, though it wouldn't be very neat." She sensed him moving away, hearing shoes hit hardwood as he walked. "Of course, I've had worse evidence to deal with in a case, and I didn't even get to plant it all myself. That poor schmuck Wesley will never get away with this, and I'll be rid of both a pesky ex-wife and that little prick who thinks he can make me look like a fool in court."

She heard water running, far enough away to give her the courage to open her eyes to slits and figure out where she was. A bed. A dark room. That looked so much like hers. She was in another Casa Blanca villa.

The knowledge that she was still on the property buoyed her and, for a split second, numbed her pain. Alec couldn't be far away.

In fact, this was one of the new villas, she'd bet. Steven couldn't have gotten her much farther than that, but he could have easily gotten her here through the connected back areas without being seen, if he'd rented the villa next to theirs.

Would Alec come back and think she'd lied to Poppy? That she'd run? Was his guilt that massive that he didn't trust her to stay?

And yet she was *right next door*.

She had to think, but the slamming headache made that nearly impossible. Pain shot from the base of her neck, down her spine and arms to her…her bound hands.

Shit. Her wrists were stuck together, and her bare feet, too, bound with what felt like iron bands but also felt eerily familiar. Duct tape.

She could break duct tape! Except…she tried to lift her hands, a thud of disappointment hitting hard as she realized her arms were immobilized, likely taped to her waist with more duct tape. So much for the trick that Alec had taught her. And the same tape squeezed her lips and cheeks, making it impossible to scream, even if she'd thought that could save her.

Which she didn't. She would have to outsmart him to find a way out of this, and knowing Steven Jessup, that wouldn't be easy. A criminal defense attorney orchestrating a murder? Yeah, it would be very difficult to outsmart him.

She fought the urge to moan at the pain in her head, refusing to give him any edge, or any reason to hurt her again. Instead, she lay perfectly still, modulating her breathing, trying like hell to use a brain that felt flat and numb and...she couldn't think of another word. Her, Kate Kingston, queen of big words.

He'd probably given her a *concussion*, the son of a bitch. But he'd give her more than that if she moved.

A loud knocking yanked her from stillness, making her jerk.

"Go the fuck away," Steven murmured, his voice telling her he couldn't be more than five feet from her.

The knocking just got louder. "Resort security! Please open the door or we will enter."

It took everything and more not to react, not to jump for joy and raise her bound hands in victory. Hell, *yes*, they were good. But she had to stay perfectly still.

"Goddammit." Footsteps accompanied his curse, but Steven didn't go far. He was in the vestibule, as best she could tell, and if this villa was anything like hers, he could see her *and* the front door from there.

"Please don't come in," he called.

"We need to speak with every guest."

"There's no need to speak to me."

Oh, yes, there was. *Storm the place, Alec.* It didn't sound like him, but her instincts told her he couldn't be far. He'd found her missing, he'd called in the cavalry, he wouldn't let her die.

She let her body sink deeper into a fake sleep, hoping that it would be enough to get Steven to go to the door. Maybe if she could have a minute alone, she could figure out how he'd taped her. Maybe figure out a way to free her arms so she could get it off her mouth and scream bloody murder.

She heard him move, but couldn't be sure which direction without turning her head and looking. She couldn't take the chance Steven would see her move.

"We'd like to talk to every guest, immediately," the man on the other side of the door said. "We have a missing-person alert on the property and would like to show you her picture."

"Slide it under the door. I'm just out of the shower."

"We'd like to talk to you, Mr. Johnson."

Johnson, my ass. Still, Steven didn't move, no doubt spinning through the legalities of what resort security was allowed to do. Get a warrant for any guest who wouldn't cooperate, but they couldn't enter. Not legally or without probable cause.

"I need a few minutes," Steven said. "Please come back later."

"We'll wait."

Steven didn't answer, but she could hear him move swiftly, returning to the bed to give her a hard shake. Testing her. She had no idea what he'd hit her with, but it hadn't been hard enough to knock her out for so long. He must know that.

But the only thing that moved on her body was her heart, and she wouldn't be surprised if he saw it pounding against her chest.

Fear was an amazing thing. Fear and determination to live. Her mouth didn't even twitch, and her eyes stayed still.

He scooped her up, sliding his hands under her knees and back, grunting with the effort to lift her off the bed. Steven had never been much for working out, she thought, so she prayed he didn't drop her and force her to "wake up."

Her feet banged the doorjamb of the bathroom as she knew exactly where he was taking her. He put her in the soaker tub, not caring when her head tapped against the marble. She flinched and moaned, but made it sound like she was still asleep.

He shook her again. "Don't die in here, Kate. That will completely fuck up the TOD and ruin everything."

Time of Death. Oh, *God*.

Don't move, Kate. Don't breathe. Don't fling your bound hands up and try to smash his face in, because you'll lose.

It wasn't Steven's voice she heard in her head, or even her own; it was Alec's. Walking her through everything she needed to do. And right now, she needed to play nearly dead, if not all the way dead.

She heard Steven's shoe scuff, the door close, a latch click.

She had to be absolutely certain he was out in the hall and talking to security, and not trying to fool her.

She waited a few seconds and sneaked a peek. The tub, the floor, the toilet. She was alone. As quietly as she could, she pushed herself up, trying not to fall backward and make a thump. Her hands were bound with tape, but, like she thought, he'd wrapped the tape around her waist so she couldn't lift her arms and split the tape like Alec had taught her. Her ankles and calves were taped securely with what had to be ten feet of duct tape.

Damn it!

From the other side of the door, she heard men's voices, but couldn't make out the words. Should she throw herself at the door and hope they heard? Or would her ex-husband be able to explain it away, all silky, smooth Steven-style?

She managed to get her feet over the side of the tub, then lift her body using only the power of her abs. Which weren't very powerful, but got the job done. She got her legs over the marble ledge and thrust herself up, enough to tumble to the ground.

Noisily.

Biting back a moan of indescribable head pain, she made

her way to the door, turning around to open it with her hands. The knob didn't budge. He couldn't have locked it from the outside.

But something was jamming the mechanism.

Damn it! She searched the room for something, anything, to rub the tape against to cut it. She shook now, fully aware that if that door opened and Steven walked in, he'd kill her.

What the hell was wrong with him? She'd known he was a control freak, a narcissist, and an asshole, but a *killer*?

Apparently, yes.

She couldn't think about that. Instead, she forced herself to a wobbly stand and scanned the room again, zeroing in on the shower door latch. One tiny sliver of chrome with an edge that was about the right height to cut the tape in the back. Then she'd have to either try to split the tape that bound her wrists or rip it off her mouth and scream.

She hopped to the shower, managed to maneuver enough to open the door, and turned, getting up on her tiptoes to line up the chrome strip with the tape around her waist.

Rising and falling, rubbing and praying, she worked frantically to saw through the few layers of tape. But it stayed firm and secure. She stopped long enough to listen to the distant voices, imagining the scene.

Someone from McBain Security at the door, Steven using his glib tongue and snake-charmer appeal to keep them out there. Taking a flyer with a picture of her, nodding seriously, promising to report it if he saw her.

She dug into her memory of a hotel lawsuit she'd studied in school. Security couldn't enter the premises...unless hotel management had reason to believe the occupant was engaged in something illegal.

If she screamed, they would believe just that. If she could get this damn tape off!

She pushed harder against the door and managed only to slam it closed, forcing her to turn around and start the whole process again. Sweat rolled down her back as each breath was a battle and her heart rate soared.

Come on, come on.

Finally, she heard the slightest crack of the tape, and that just made her move up and down more furiously. Please rip, please rip, please—

She heard the tear, slow and sweet, like music to her ears, instantly yanking her hands up once they weren't secured at her hips. Should she scream or try to get her hands free?

If they heard her—the door slammed outside.

Shit! They left?

She hoisted her hands high over her head, smashed her elbows together, and took a breath. Then she swung her arms ferociously, spreading her elbows at her hips, and instantly heard the *frrriiiip* of the tape tearing open.

At precisely the same second that the bathroom door flew open, smacked her in the face, and knocked her onto her ass.

"Oh, Kate. What the hell are you trying to do? Outwit me?" Steven just chuckled, like he always did when he had the upper hand. And, damn it, he *always* had the upper hand.

Chapter Twenty-Seven

Alec had to hand it to security head Luke McBain, and everyone in his employ, including Gabe Rossi. They moved like a well-oiled machine in a crisis, but the machine didn't produce what Alec wanted: Kate.

She had to be somewhere on this island, most likely still at the resort, because he hadn't been away from her that long. But, as Luke had just reminded them, the first fifteen minutes to an hour of any disappearance were the most critical.

Each minute that passed, Alec had a harder time reining in his need to run, howl, punch, and kill someone. Kate was gone, and nothing in him would allow him to believe she'd left on her own. If she had, wouldn't she have gone to her father? That poor guy was almost as miserable as Alec.

"The sheriff's office has closed off the causeway and is starting to search the island, but right now, we're handling this property," Luke said, standing in the middle of McBain Security, surrounded by anxious faces. Alec had done one mission with French Foreign Legionnaires, and those guys were badass and serious. Right now, Luke's training was showing. "Now I want to hear about every room and villa we didn't get into."

A woman Alec didn't recognize came to the front with a piece of paper, naming the flowery villas like Rockrose, Saffron, and African Daisy, giving occupants' names and reports of who let security in. "Obviously, Caralluma is empty." That was Alec's villa. "So is Blue Casbah. The south villa, Sea Heath, is where a Mr. Robert Johnson is staying. He declined entry."

"He's alone?" Luke asked.

"He's checked in under one name."

One pretty damn common name, Alec thought.

"Who talked to him?" Luke asked.

"I did." Another one of Luke's security professionals came forward, a brawny guy named Miles, whom Alec had met only once. "Lots of legal double-talk, but he wouldn't let me in without probable cause for...something."

"Fucking lawyers," Gabe growled. "Everything's a damn fight."

"Oh, you should have heard this blowhard," Miles said. "Sounded like the reincarnation of JFK or something."

A few people chuckled, but Alec turned to him. "A Boston accent?" he demanded.

"Thick. That made deciphering his legal mumbo jumbo even tougher."

Alec whipped around to share a look with Gabe, who was no doubt thinking exactly what he was. A lawyer? From Boston? Without another word, Alec shot out of the bungalow, vaguely aware that at least one other person was behind him. But he didn't wait.

"Get a golf cart," Gabe called.

But Alec ignored him, trusting his legs and speed far more than machinery. He tore up the side of the farmette, ducking tree branches with every long stride, raw determination fueling his steps.

Was it that Wesley character? Someone else? Didn't matter. It was too close to home, too personal. Which was the worst-case scenario. He tore through the resort, praying he wasn't too late.

"I saw a man leave." Steven loomed over her. "You were supposed to be alone." He braced his body over Kate and grabbed one of the arms she'd just worked so damn hard to free.

What did he mean, she was *supposed* to be alone? How did he even know—

"I thought the whole idea was that you were alone." He dropped to pin her upper arms to the floor with his knees, his crotch in her face as he essentially crucified her to the merciless marble. "Kate!"

He almost spit his frustration, sounding so like the Steven she knew: *Of course it's your fault my plan is falling apart, Kate. You fuck up everything.*

She looked up at him from the bathroom floor, fighting a nauseous mix of fear and regret and frustration. She had to think. Had to think of everything Alec had taught her.

Steven Jessup was *not* going to win this one. She would escape and run, exactly as Alec had taught her to do. Except he hadn't taught her what to do when her ankles were bound and her mouth was taped shut. Her hands were free, but how long would they stay that way?

"It's time to leave, Kate." He looked up to the bathroom counter, probably for a weapon, while Kate rooted around her brain for a weapon of her own.

Stab the eyes, twist the ears, slam his mouth right up his nose. Then grab the throat, kick the groin, bend the fingers, and stomp the toes.

Alec's soft-target song echoed in her head, but she wasn't able to follow any of the instructions in this position, with her arms under the weight of Steven's body and—*oomph.*

He sat down hard, his ass on her chest. She looked up at him, trying to communicate, moaning noises that he might think were words…words he had to hear. Maybe he'd take the tape off her mouth.

Instead, he just looked down at her as if she disgusted him. "Did you really think you'd beat me at life, Kate?"

She ignored the question—not that she could answer it, anyway. Nobody beat Steven Jessup at anything, and she'd never understood what drove that competitive insecurity, beyond being the second child of a demanding father.

Didn't matter. Psychology wasn't going to get her out of this. She continued spinning through every possible scenario, like Alec had taught her. Look for weapons anywhere. The toilet was hard, the shower was glass, and she had her knees. If she could knee him hard enough in the back, it might put him off-balance.

"Surely you knew I wasn't going to let you win," he continued. "I wasn't going to let you divorce me and make me a laughingstock. You're going to die, and that prick Mike Wesley's going to be charged for your murder, which will ruin his career no matter how that trial comes out. Although if I do this right, he'll get life at least. And you'll get what you deserve." He grinned, so pleased with himself.

What the hell was the matter with him? Maybe she did need to use psychology to outsmart him.

"I really would like to get this over with," he said, reaching down to close his hands around her throat. "And while the pleasure of killing you right now is irresistible, I wouldn't get away with it."

He wasn't going to get away with it anyway, didn't he see that? It gave her some sense of security, knowing he was too smart to do something that would leave evidence. Not if he was trying to pin this on some other lawyer.

His fingers tightened around her throat, and she automatically jerked, throwing her knees up to slam him in the back, but he was far enough forward that the move did nothing but make him grunt...and squeeze her throat harder.

"I'd like to kill you right now," he said, the statement weirdly, freakishly calm. "But I've been planning this for too long. All those notes and setting up Wesley. Convincing him to get in line and hit on your friend. Working your dad's new assistant to find out where he sent you. It took time and planning, and so will the rest."

Of course he could get access to Dad's assistant. He was the former son-in-law, practically family. He could charm anyone, especially a woman.

"Although, if I kill you now, I could get you out of here when it's dark, especially if there's no blood. No clues. No evidence. The evidence has to be up in North Carolina where Wesley and Laurie are going on a little trip together to a cabin that just happened to become available for them." He pressed harder, making her choke into the unforgiving tape. "But that would screw up the autopsy report."

So he couldn't kill her now. He relaxed his hands, and she could breathe through her nose, then he jerked to his feet and yanked her up, suddenly twisting her around and getting both her arms behind her.

Stab the eyes, twist the ears, slam his mouth right up his nose.

271

She couldn't, damn it!

Then grab the throat, kick the groin, bend the fingers, and stomp the toes.

Except her hands were immobilized, and her ankles taped.

He pulled her out of the bathroom like that, practically dragging her, yanking her arms backward so hard she thought her shoulders would pop out of their sockets. He threw her on the bed and turned away long enough to reach for the roll of duct tape.

It was all she needed. She flung herself sideways, thrusting her legs over the side of the bed. He lunged at her, and she instantly stabbed her extended finger at his eye. He jerked away just in time to avoid it, but the move gave her access to his ear, which she grabbed and twisted like it was a water faucet.

"Fuck!" he screamed, throwing his whole weight at her, but as he came down, she let go of his ear, turned her hand, and plowed the pad of her thumb right at the tender spot between his lips and nose.

He yowled and jerked backward, giving her enough time to get to her feet and hop toward the door. Almost immediately, he grabbed her from behind and pulled her to the ground, but she wiggled away and kept crawling, sliding, fighting her way toward the bedroom door.

He lunged after her, falling onto her back and smashing her face into the hardwood floor. "I *am* going to kill you now!" he growled at her. "You bitch! You thought you could beat me. Nobody beats me. Nobody." He twisted her head to the side, shooting excruciating pain down her back, so hard she was sure he was going to break her neck.

He lifted her head and slammed it against the floor again, making her brain explode with pain. Suddenly realizing her right hand was free, she reached around to fight him off, grabbing his thigh, then higher, finding his balls and squeezing with every ounce of strength she had.

He yelped and jumped up to escape the pain, giving her a chance to shoot forward, reach up to the door—

"Kate!"

Alec! She heard his voice and heard banging on the front door, hammering like his foot would surely break it down. *Hurry, Alec!*

But Steven leaped on her, rolling her away from the bedroom door. She managed to flip around and take one more stab at his eye, her fingers straight and stiff and unyielding, jabbing right into the soft side of his eye.

"Fuck! Damn it!" He covered his eye and moaned just as she heard the front door explode open with a crack.

"Kate!"

She pushed herself to her knees, determined—so damn determined—to escape. Twisting the doorknob, she pulled it open and threw herself into the hallway just as Alec came running toward her.

He fell to his knees next to her, but Kate shook her head and pointed behind her, where Steven lay on the floor, writhing in pain.

Behind Alec, at least four more men came barreling into the villa, led by Gabe Rossi. "Nice work, Benjamin."

"I didn't do a thing." Holding her with one arm, Alec gingerly worked the duct tape on her mouth, concern darkening his expression as he searched her face. "Oh, God, I'm sorry. I'm sorry." His voice cracked as the tape pulled and pinched and finally, finally came off.

"Alec!" She reached up and seized him in an embrace, adrenaline and relief and gratitude surging through her. "He wanted to kill me," she rasped, her voice trembling like her whole body was. She'd come so close to dying. So close. "He wanted to…"

"Shhh." He pressed her into his chest, his clutch as desperate as hers.

"I was so scared."

He squeezed harder. "I'm so sorry I left you."

"No, no. I shouldn't have…" She let out a sob, all hope for control gone now. "I thought I was going to die."

"No, you're too strong for that." He stroked her hair.

"Hey, don't touch me!" Steven screamed from the bedroom. "That bitch poked my fucking eye! She ripped my balls off!"

Alec couldn't help smiling. "See what I mean? Nice work, Smarty-Pants."

"Had a great teacher." Great teacher. Great man. Great lover. Great…everything.

Holding him with desperate, vibrating arms, she closed her eyes and ignored the chaos and Steven's yelling and Gabe's swearing. It all disappeared as she clung to Alec like he was her lifeline and her happiness and her whole world.

"Alec, you have to go." Gabe's voice cut through everything else. "You can't stay here."

Alec released her gently, looking up at the man looming over them. "I can't leave her."

"This place is going to be crawling with cops in a matter of minutes. I have to get you out of here, now." He gave Kate a sympathetic look. "You're safe now."

"She is not," Alec insisted. "She's coming with me."

"No can do." Gabe gestured for Alec to move it. "She has to talk to law enforcement and tell them she's been at this resort hiding from her crazy ex, under protection. You we cannot explain."

"I'm her bodyguard," he ground out.

"She just got a new one." Gabe waved another man over. "Miles, get over here and meet your new principal."

Alec didn't budge. "It's not that simple, Gabe."

"Fine." Gabe stepped back and crossed his arms, fury darkening his handsome features. "You stay with her, talk to the cops, get your name plastered all over this, and then you can watch when Vlitnik hunts her down and makes her his personal punching bag. Is that what you want?"

A whole new kind of fear rolled over Kate.

And Alec looked like he felt the same thing. Silent, he inched away from Kate, gently letting go of her.

She reached up to him. "Alec—"

"He's right, Kate. This is why I shouldn't have told you anything."

"No shit," Gabe added, along with another push. "Let's move it. The Carlsons just got a divorce."

One of the security professionals came up behind Kate. "I've got her, Gabe. You two can go."

Outside, a siren blared. With one more look of sheer agony, Alec took off with Gabe, disappearing into the sunshine pouring over the back patio.

Chapter Twenty-Eight

Gabe still had a shot at keeping Alec safe and under the radar, but he'd have to move him to a new location, possibly a new country, very soon. Until he could do that, he'd sent Alec down to a safe house on the south part of the island with Nino, put Robyn to work as a housekeeper under Poppy's care, and started trying to figure out exactly how Steven Jessup had found Kate.

After being examined by a doctor and pronounced concussion free, Kate interviewed with law enforcement, and her reason for staying at the resort under a false name made perfect sense. With her loony-tune ex caught dead to rights, the sheriff wouldn't have to question the staff. But Gabe still needed to find out how the security breach had occurred up in Boston.

He suspected it stemmed from the judge, but he had to be sure it wasn't through his cousin's security firm. That link to his organization down here had to be airtight or this operation would fall apart.

He personally escorted Kate to her father's room.

"Judge Kingston," Gabe said after they arrived and the older man had had a chance to confirm his daughter was in one piece. "You were to tell no one where Kate was going or why."

"I didn't," he said. "No one, not even my admin knew."

"She had to, Dad," Kate said. "Steven said he worked your new assistant."

"And likely got something out of her, but…the only place I had information about where you were was in my chambers."

"And he got in there?" Gabe asked. "How?"

The older man sighed and looked sheepishly at Kate. "I…forgave him."

"What?" She choked the word. "Dad, I know you have to acknowledge him in the courtroom or if you see him in the courthouse, but"—she fell into a chair and stared at him—"you forgave him?"

"Not completely." His eyes, much the same shade of jade as his daughter's, filled. "He made me believe he still cared about you, and I thought maybe it would be better for you."

"*Dad*. Seriously?"

He shook his head. "I'm sorry, Katie."

"You told him where I was?"

"No, no. But, thinking back, there was one time we were talking in my chambers and I had to leave for a moment. He must have rifled my files."

Gabe stood, not needing to be here for the rest of this father-daughter chat. Kate was going to ream her old man a new one, and it sounded like he deserved it. But Daddy was the client, so at least the error was on him and not Gabe. "I have my answers now. I'm out."

Kate stood immediately. "Not without me. I need to see Alec."

"Not happening."

Her jaw dropped, and color slipped from her cheeks. "What do you mean?" Her eyes widened in panic. "Please tell me he's not already gone. Please tell me you haven't sent him somewhere with a new name." Her voice cracked, and she put her hand on her chest. "Please."

"Listen, it would be better if you—"

"Don't tell me what would be better!" She practically launched herself at him, her eyes wild. "If one more goddamn man tries to tell me what he wants from me, what I should do, or what would be *better* for me, I will kill someone. And I know how."

The judge stood. "Mr. Rossi, I insist you help my daughter. Don't keep her from this man. She's been pushed around by too many people."

Gabe huffed a breath, considering all the implications. He could risk it. After all, he'd stuck the two of them in a villa and let them have at it. He should have guessed that something more than a casual friendship could boil up. And by the look in this woman's eyes, it was way more than that.

"All right, I can take you to him tonight," he said. "When it's dark. But now, I'm going back to my office, and you and your dad are going to stay in this room, and no one is going to leave. I promise I'll come and get you as soon as it's dark."

She nodded and sat back down in the chair. "Okay. Dad and I need to have a long talk anyway."

Gabe left and made it halfway across the lobby before his cell vibrated again, this time with a call from his younger sister, who had what he hoped was a solution to a different problem.

"I got nothing," Chessie said instead of hello when he answered.

"Nothing?" He pinched the bridge of his nose, slowing his step on the marble to listen to his little sister, his only hope of hacking into the encrypted files he'd stolen from Radio and TV Martí in Miami. "Hey, I thought I was talking to my sister. She can find anyone."

She snorted at her family's motto for her. "Not from what you e-mailed me," Chessie said. "As I suspected, I might do better with source material. Can you send me something physical?"

And risk losing what might be highly sensitive, world-shifting material? "No, but I have the physical files on a drive."

"Send it to me."

"Not a chance, Chess. Come on down. Tell Vivi you need a vacation, and get your ass to Florida. Plan on staying for a while. I could really use you down here."

He heard his sister sigh. "I can't—"

"It's that d-bag Matt, isn't it?" he asked, driven by instinct and his profound knowledge of what made Chessie tick.

"I gave him the ultimatum."

"And that always goes over so well with men."

"He's thinking about it."

"Thinking about *what*?" Gabe shot back, his intense dislike for his sister's on-again-off-again boyfriend firing through him. "What an incredible catch you are? How lucky he would be to lick the bottom of your overpriced stiletto? What it's going to feel like when I kick the ever-loving fuck out of his empty head?"

She made a noise that might have been a laugh...or might have been a sob. "He's not sure, is all."

"Then why do you want him, Chessie?"

"Do you have any idea what it's like to be a single, thirty-year-old woman who wants a child?"

"Obviously not. But I know what it's like to be a thirtysomething guy, so I'm here to tell you that chicks with your brains and looks are not found on every street corner."

"Pffft. You're my brother. You have to say that."

279

It was true, but she was too tender to hear it right now. "Then just take a long weekend and come down here to help me. I have to read what's in those files."

"I did crack a little of it," she said. "I thought you were done with Cuba."

He swallowed hard. "Just curious about some people left behind," he said.

"But after what happened at Gitmo, aren't you, like, never allowed in the country again?"

He wasn't going to put her in the position of knowing any more classified information than she already did. "Chessie," he said softly. "Come down here and help me find someone, please. You can find anyone, remember?"

She huffed out a breath. "I'm going to see Matt one more time. Then we'll see."

Taking that as a yes, he hung up and headed back to his office.

"Six months?" The big Jamaican woman's question pulled Robyn from thoughts that hummed along much like the golf cart she rode in on the way to a villa called Rockrose. "You're tiny for six months. You need to eat."

Robyn looked over at her, stilling the hand that, yeah, was always rubbing her belly. "I do my best." She took a deep breath, and that turned into a hiccup.

"A boy with a lot of hair," Poppy said as she turned the cart into an opening between tall bushes that hid another one of the expensive-looking vacation homes on the beach. "That's the third time you've had the hiccups in the last two hours."

"And that means it's a boy?"

"That means it has hair and a lot of it. Does your baby daddy have thick hair?"

She sighed and looked away, closing her hand over the rail in front of the passenger seat to keep from rubbing her belly, a habit she found impossible to break.

"I have thick hair," she said, gesturing toward the ponytail Poppy had made her wear.

"So you ain't sayin', or you don't know?"

She bit her lip. "I know." Poppy hadn't been in the room when Alec and the other guy interrogated her, so she might think Robyn was just a slut. "His name's Cole Morrow. He was my boyfriend."

"Was?"

She shrugged.

"Are you keeping this child or giving it up for adoption?"

"I'm keeping him." No foster homes, no adoptive parents, no miserable messes for her little boy. Robyn had grown up with a mostly missing drunk for a dad and mother more interested in getting high than anything else. Her child would be loved beyond reason.

"Fine, fine, that's good." But Poppy didn't sound all that sure if it was good or not as she brought the cart to a stop and climbed out. Then she stood like some kind of warrior woman, hands on hips, fire in her eyes. "And I'll help you."

The offer was so sincere and unexpected and sweet that Robyn drew back. No one ever wanted to help her. Not really, not for no reason.

Poppy walked to the back of the cart, shaking her head. "All that hullabaloo today, and I never went down to the laundry and picked up my fresh towels. We can't finish this last villa without a new set."

"Why would you help me?" Robyn asked as she met the other woman at the back of the golf cart.

Poppy's giant brown eyes flashed and then softened. "'Cause it's the right thing to do. You need help, and the good Lord landed you in my lap, so I suppose He's telling me to get to work on you."

Robyn stood there, the heat blasting her, making a trickle of sweat roll from under her bra over her expanding belly. "I don't believe in God," she finally said, turning to the cart to grab the rags and mop, since Poppy wouldn't let her even touch the buckets full of cleaning solutions.

"All the more reason He sent you to me."

She snorted softly. "Trust me, Poppy, I'm not on God's radar."

"Well, you're on mine, child, so don't you be worrying about nothing now."

She hiccupped in response, fighting a smile. "It doesn't mean he has hair," she told Poppy. "I hiccup when I'm tired."

Poppy eyed her, then put a gentle hand on Robyn's shoulder. "Can you drive the golf cart?" When she nodded, Poppy continued, "Go down to the resort building. You know where that is? In the way back, on the far side away from the beach, is the laundry loading dock. The towel truck is due in any minute, so you get a stack of fresh towels—I love 'em right off the truck—and put them on the cart, and come right back here. Will you do that for me?"

"Sure." She walked by Poppy to get behind the wheel.

"An' child?"

Robyn turned to her.

"Don't you be talking to anyone about anything, you understand? Towels and back here. Can I trust you?"

Who would she talk to? Where would she go? For the

moment, she was here, in this swanky resort with people who wanted to help her and asked for nothing in return. "I won't, Poppy," she promised. "You can trust me."

A few minutes later, Robyn was rolling down the wide path that curved through the resort property, the deep blue water on her right, jungle-thick trees on her left, and sun bouncing off the palm fronds, making her feel like she was living in a postcard.

"The scenery certainly doesn't suck, little dude." She patted her belly and let out a noisy hiccup. Maybe he would have a lot of hair, she mused. Curly blond hair and light brown eyes like Cole's.

The thought of her baby daddy, as Poppy had called him, made her heart drop hard into her stomach. She didn't miss him, but driving down here, guilt had gnawed at her gut. A man had a right to know when he had made a baby.

But everyone else could tell when they looked at her now, so hadn't Cole noticed she was fatter when he was at her apartment? Wouldn't he ask? Wouldn't he *want* to know if his girlfriend was going to have a baby?

Coming around the side of the building, she squinted into the afternoon sun to remember where she was supposed to go, when suddenly a large van pulled up to a loading dock in the back, the words Gulf Coast Industrial Laundry painted on the side.

The towel truck. She'd get a stack fresh and clean for Poppy and make her happy. Her heart swelled for a moment as she thought about the wonderful Jamaican woman who loved God and wanted to help Robyn. She was like a guardian angel.

Poppy would know what she should do, Robyn decided as she waited for the truck to park, climbing out of the cart so she could get the freshest of fresh towels. She'd tell

Poppy about how guilty she felt and see if she had to call Cole and tell him the truth.

Was that best for the baby? What would help *him* the most in life? Those questions were the only ones that she asked herself, and had helped her make every decision she'd made since she'd realized she was pregnant. Maybe they hadn't been the smartest decisions—like coming to Florida to find Alec. But that decision seemed to be working out okay in the end.

The driver was sitting in the front seat, on the phone, so Robyn went around to the back to wait for him near the loading dock when suddenly she felt someone come up behind her.

"Hey, Robyn's Egg."

What? She spun around and squinted into the late afternoon sun, because she really, truly wasn't sure if she was imagining that Cole Morrow was standing two inches from her face. Fear and shock froze her. "Wha...what are you doing here?"

"I followed you here."

He'd *followed* her? "Why?"

"You think I'd just let you leave me, Rob?" He reached around her and flipped open the back of the van. "Quick, hide in here."

"What? Why?" She barely got the word out before he pushed her in and climbed after her, shoving her deeper into a mass of soft, fluffy towels, pulling the door closed behind him. "Cole, what's going on?"

"You have to hide." Cole was strong, a fighter with solid muscles and he easily got control of her, burying them both in a mountain of white, the overwhelming smell of laundry detergent suddenly making her feel sick.

"What are you do—"

He slammed his hand over her mouth. "Shut the fuck up," he said. "Or I'll hurt you."

She tried to scream, but it was muffled under his hand, his fighter's body easily holding her down. She couldn't breathe. She couldn't *breathe*. She tried to squirm and flail, but his grip got tighter, then his knee was on her stomach.

No, not there. Don't hurt me there. The baby! But she couldn't scream any of that, because he'd smothered her mouth with his hand.

"How the hell did this open up?" A man's voice made it through the barrier of white towels that hid them, then the doors slammed hard, and the back of the van went black.

Cole didn't loosen his grip for a few seconds, but he finally did, moving the knee that terrified her so much.

"You're coming with me," he said in a gruff voice, his hand still over her mouth.

She shook her head, hard. "No."

"Oh, yes, you are. You're coming with me, Robyn Bickler, or I swear to God I'll cut that baby out and drive this truck over it."

The last meal she'd eaten rose in her mouth, a familiar feeling of nausea that she knew couldn't be stopped. He jerked away and disappeared through a small opening to the front of the van, and suddenly it started to move, barreling out of the resort at a fairly high speed.

Robyn threw up in some towels and wept.

Chapter Twenty -Nine

Alec sat at a kitchen table in a house he'd never been in before, looking at an unfamiliar backyard and wondering where the hell he'd be tomorrow.

This was his life now. Was this what he'd signed up to do? Hide and run and land in strange places with strange people?

Not that the old man who worked a pizza dough on the kitchen island was strange—he was just one in a sea of people who would come and go and come and go. Mostly go.

A dark pain squeezed his gut. In the turmoil of the moment, when Gabe whisked him out of the scene, he'd barely been able to say good-bye to Kate.

"I'm not going to see her again, am I?" he asked, not really expecting an answer from Nino, but desperate for someone, even this old man, to give him good news.

"You might if Gabriel pulls a rabbit out of his hat." He flipped the large circle of dough in the air with expert ease. "And, let me tell you, he not only pulls rabbits out of hats, he'll probably find a pig, a dog, and a gerbil in there, too." He gave a yellowed grin. "My Gabriel is amazing like that." He patted the pie and sprinkled it with flour. "Thick crust?"

"Don't you understand?" Alec demanded. "I can't just...disappear."

Nino looked up from his pizza crust, peering over his glasses, his dark eyes fierce. "Correct me if I'm wrong, but that's what my grandson is being paid to do for you, right? Hide you so some lunatic mobster doesn't try to..." He used two fingers to slice across his neck. "What's the Russian equivalent of 'swim with the fishes'?"

He shook his head, doubting this guy had ever had many brushes with the Mafia his country made famous. And if he had, he still wouldn't know what brutal was. Vlitnik's *Bratva* made *La Cosa Nostra* look like child's play.

"Gabriel will get you to another place, another continent, with a new name and a new job. You won't have to look over your shoulder anymore."

He would as long as Vlitnik was alive. It was so *personal* with that bastard. He probably didn't even want Alec to work for him anymore. No, he *definitely* didn't want Alec to work for him now. He wanted to punish Alec for...something. What?

"Don't you want that?" Nino asked, producing some kind of heavenly smelling red sauce from God knew where to spread on the pie. "To live in some pretty town in Australia or South America, near the beach, in the sunshine? Safe from this guy who's after you?"

For a second, his head cleared, and he regarded the other man. "No," he said simply. "That's not what I want."

"Then you want to die?" Nino challenged.

"No, I want to be a trainer, to live in peace in my home country, the United States of America, the place where I was born, the country I fought for. I want to live with the name I've had my whole life and pass that name on to another generation." His voice rose with passion, but he didn't care.

He didn't care about the sting in his eyes or the way Nino was staring at him or the crack of his heart with every word.

"I want to live openly and free. And I want—"

"Special delivery." Gabe's voice came from the front room.

"Better not be pizza, Gabriel. I won't eat that cardboard from Tropical Pizza." He inched a little closer over the counter to whisper, "Who names a pizzeria 'Tropical' anyway? It wasn't invented in the tropics."

"Not pizza," Gabe said as his footsteps came closer to the back kitchen. "A secret guest."

At the sight of Kate, Alec almost knocked his chair over as he stood. He opened his mouth to speak, but nothing came out. Not a single sound. He just had the overwhelming urge to sweep her into his arms and squeeze and kiss and touch every inch of her to make sure she was real.

"Hey," she whispered, giving him the impression that maybe she was holding back, too.

"You're bruised," he finally said, coming closer to see the bluish-purple discoloration left by that dickhead under her cheek.

"But free." She touched her cheek. "More or less."

"No more or less about it," Gabe told them, spinning a kitchen chair around and dropping in it backward. "Don't forget the basil, old man."

Nino flattened him with a look. "We're working under less-than-ideal conditions, Gabriel. You see a garden in this backyard?"

"No basil?"

Nino flipped his hand like he could smack Gabe. "I'm *improvising*."

Alec ignored the family argument to concentrate on Kate,

and what Gabe had just said. "Is she really free?" he asked.

Gabe eyed one, then the other. "From her ex-husband, yeah. He tried to bury the cops in legalese, but they have all the evidence they need to keep him behind bars without bail for a while."

Kate crossed her arms, hanging back in the doorway, her gaze on Alec. "I thought you left," she said softly, just quiet and scared enough to break Alec's heart.

"Tomorrow, right, Gabriel?" Nino asked as he slid his pizza into a ready oven. "Where is he off to tomorrow?"

Gabe let out a sigh, closing his eyes. "I pulled out a favor and got a temporary place in Costa Rica. I can keep you there for at least six months, then I think I can set up something permanent Down Under. Hope you like kangaroos, mate."

Color drained from Kate's face, leaving her bruise the color of an eggplant and her eyes wide. "Australia." It wasn't a question. More of a whisper of disbelief.

"It might as well be the moon," Alec murmured, turning away.

For a long moment, neither one of them spoke, everything fading away as Alec looked back at Kate and thought one word.

Tomorrow.

The tension broke when Gabe's cell rang, and he stood to pull it out of his pocket and answer, walking out of the room and speaking in low tones.

Nino wiped his hands on a cloth with a sigh. "They have good food in Costa Rica," he finally said.

Kate smiled, a soft, sweet expression that made Alec reach out his hand to her. *You could come with me.* Could she read that request in his eyes? Would she even consider it?

"Son of a bitch." Gabe marched back in, seemingly unaware of the dynamics in the room. "Robyn left."

Alec whipped around. "Where'd she go?"

"If I knew, I'd be on her ass. Poppy's a basket case, Nino. She's convinced it's her fault."

"Well, she was supposed to watch the girl." Nino slammed his rag on the table.

"She wasn't under lock and key, and we have no reason to believe she's in touch with Vlitnik, but we need to find her," Gabe said. "One of the hotel vendors had his truck stolen, so maybe she changed her mind and made a break."

"Why wouldn't she just take her car?" Alec asked.

Gabe shrugged. "She left it in the main lot, and Luke's searching it. Nino, you need to calm Poppy down, and by *calm her down*, I don't mean get into a food fight." Then, to Alec and Kate, "You're both safest here. This house is completely off the radar, and no one knows I use it as a safe house except Nino. No one will find you here. We'll look for her and keep you posted."

Nino checked the pizza. "When you smell it, it's ready. *Mangia*."

"Chain lock and dead bolt," Gabe called from the front room. "Nino, you drive. I'm leaving that purple GTO in the driveway. Here are the keys, in case of an emergency, which I would rather there not be." He flipped them to Alec. "Put a scratch on it, and I'll kill you with my bare hands and enjoy every minute."

Alec followed him and the security instructions, returning to the kitchen to find that Kate hadn't moved.

"So, you're free," he said, taking a step closer.

She lifted her chin defiantly. "I'm free of some things," she said. "Free of my ex, who was more of a nut job than I even knew, and there are no more threats on my life." She lifted her hand and set it on his shoulder, like a silent invitation to dance. "And I unloaded some guilt this afternoon with my father."

"Really?"

She nodded. "I think the trauma of what Steven tried to do was a wakeup call, and, honestly, it helped my dad and me talk about some things that have been on our minds for years."

"You mean from when your mother died."

"Yes, and when he turned taking care of me into an obsession." She gave a wry smile and dragged her hand down his arm, lingering on his bicep. "I officially gave him his walking papers as super-protective dad today."

He touched her face, lightly skimming his thumb over the bruise. "So you really are a free woman. A free, strong, resourceful, smart, gorgeous woman. With a mean eye-gouge."

Her smile was slow but didn't quite reach her eyes. "I'm not free of you."

"Me?" He snorted and slipped his hand into her thick mahogany-colored hair. "You will be tomorrow."

She looked up at him and met his eyes, a world of hurt and uncertainty and...something else making those green eyes darken to the color of priceless emeralds.

"I kind of hate tomorrow," she whispered, leaning closer. "I'm not done with you, Petrov."

He lowered his head, touching her forehead with his lips. "You have gigantic words yet to teach me."

She closed her fingers around his hand, then placed his palm over her heart. "And little words. Like *now* and *yes* and *please* and *now* and...*now*. Did I mention *now*?"

Now was good. But tomorrow? "Kate." He barely breathed the word. "You know what's going to happen, don't you?"

"I hope we're about to have wild, hot monkey sex." She broke away from him, walked to the oven, and flipped the switch to off. "Followed by cold pizza because you are not going to leave me, move to another country under a new name, and become nothing but a great memory without...without..."

He grabbed her arm and pulled her closer. "I'm not going to..." He kissed her hard, burying the rest of the sentence. But he *was* going to leave, so he shouldn't say those words. "I'm not going to be nothing but a great memory."

But maybe he was, so right now, he just wanted to use his hands and body and mouth and heart for exactly what they were meant for...loving Kate.

Chapter Thirty

The closest bedroom still seemed like a mile away right then, with need gnawing at Alec's whole body. He couldn't take his hands or mouth off Kate, kissing her down the hall to a bedroom he vaguely remembered seeing when he'd arrived.

They stopped halfway to strip off some clothes, her top and his shirt, and then he pushed her into the wall so he could touch what that exposed. He unsnapped her bra and let it flutter to the floor, and she worked on his pants, both of them moaning, groaning, fighting as each breath grew more ragged.

No, not fighting. Nothing about this was like fighting. He was using his hands to appreciate her and excite her and thrill them both. It was working.

They finally made it to an unlit room that smelled vaguely of powdery perfume and floor polish, falling onto a bed that barely fit them both.

It was like his hands had become unlocked, along with his head and all the crap that had been holding him back. A dam broke somewhere in his chest, and everything he ever knew about inflicting pain disappeared as he used his hands and body to delight and please both of them.

She arched and bowed, laughed and whimpered, and whispered his name so that it sounded like sex on her lips.

His hands were everywhere, on her breasts, opening her jeans, sliding over her backside. And so were hers, rubbing appreciatively over every muscle, grasping at his zipper, reaching to stroke him.

Suddenly, the gears shifted. He wasn't just taking pleasure or giving it, he was immersed in her touch. He thrust into her palm, a sweet, sweet agony that fired from the tip of him to his balls and back to his brain. Nothing had ever felt so good, ever. So hot and achy and *good*.

On his back, he let her kneel up, straddling him, her jeans unbuttoned and unzipped, open to a V that led right to the very place he longed to invade.

She paused for a minute, getting her breath, gathering her thick auburn hair to lift it off her shoulders to cool down. Looking down at him, she crooked her head.

"Why is this man smiling?"

"That's a stupid question, Smarty-Pants."

"No, you're, like, grinning."

"I'm, *like*, so turned on I'm going to explode." He tried to pull her down and shut her up, but she was having none of it.

"You look happy."

"I am." He gave up the effort and just caressed her stomach and breasts. His eyes had adjusted, and he could see the shape of her in the shadows, the hard pebbles of her nipples, the indent of her waist. He traced his finger over one breast, circling and making her drop her head back with a grunt.

He dragged that finger down, seeing the way his hand looked against her. Seeing it…differently. Watching chills blossom in his wake, feeling her hips rock in response.

He reached the zipper and traveled lower, one finger over creamy, tight skin, over the mound. Lower.

"You're *really* smiling now."

"I'm *really* happy now." He dipped his finger lower to touch the wet folds of his woman. His woman. *His.*

She'd hate that, but...that's how he felt. Like she belonged to him in the most fundamental way.

He'd ruin everything if he told her that. "I've never..." *Felt like this.*

"Touched me? You did it the other night on the beach. I liked it. I loved it." She lifted herself so she could push the jeans farther down. "I *really* loved it."

He stroked the tender center, making her hiss. "I've never..." *Wanted to make love.* He'd wanted to get off, to get laid, to get a much-needed release. "I've never thought I could make you feel like this," he finished.

She lowered herself, letting her hair tickle his cheeks and giving his finger even more access to her body. "You do, Alec. Now stop talking and get inside me."

He rolled her over and helped her get rid of the jeans completely, stripping his own off with surprisingly shaky hands. He stroked the skin between her breasts, letting his cock rub against her for a preview of what was about to happen.

Fire licked through his balls, up his back, into his chest. This was too real, too much. Too good.

And he was leaving tomorrow.

"What?" she asked, lifting her head.

"I didn't say anything." He cupped her behind and lifted it.

"You sounded frustrated. Disappointed. You don't have a condom?" There was a slight rise of panic in her voice that, for some reason, he adored.

"I have one." He rooted on the floor for his jeans to get the wallet from his back pocket. "Nino took my ID and credit cards, but left the important stuff."

"I wonder if he thought you'd need one."

He grinned around the packet between his teeth. "Nino's a pretty smart old guy."

Her eyes popped as the foil ripped. "Do you think Gabe set this up and planned, you know, us?"

He pulled out the rubber disk and slid it over his shaft, loving that she reached to help him. "If he did, he shouldn't send me to fucking Costa Rica tomorrow." The words came out gruff, mostly because he didn't want to talk. Not about that. Not about anything.

But she lifted her hands and cupped his face as he got into position on top of her, forcing their gazes on each other. "We'll work it out tomorrow. Let's just…"

"Yeah. Let's." The words got lost in the next breath, a gasp of pleasure as he slid into her.

He kissed her forehead and her cheek, then pressed his lips against her ear as he eased in with a ridiculous amount of control, considering how his body was screaming to plunge all the way.

She was so hot and tight, a perfect pocket, warm and wet, whispering his name between each strangled breath. He kissed her ear and held her so close she was almost as inside of him as he was in her.

They belonged together. The thought slammed his head with as much shock as her body slammed his other head. They belonged together, no matter what. Was that possible? Would she…

"Kate," he murmured, his mouth barely working as ecstasy took over. "Come with me, baby. Come with me."

"Not yet." She bit the words.

And somewhere in the fog of his sexed-up brain, he realized she'd taken that the wrong way, and this was no time to tell her. He gave in and thrust all the way, calling out as the pleasure whipped through him.

She dug her fingers into his shoulders, and he just squeezed his eyes closed because everything was hazy and hot and unfocused as she rocked with him.

He found a rhythm that felt like heaven, all the way in and out and in again, pushing her closer and closer to the edge, forgetting everything.

Only one thought with each stroke. One thought. She was his. In and out, harder and faster, more and more. She was his. She was *his*.

This beautiful, brilliant woman who didn't want to belong to anyone. She...was...his.

He rose higher, as deep into her as he could be, heat bouncing between them, the sounds and scent of sex filling the room, and the hole in his heart—the one he didn't even realize he had until he met this woman—closed and even disappeared while he claimed her the only way he knew how.

"Kate, I can't stop. I can't stop. I can't..." With a hard spasm, he surrendered to his orgasm, stunned by the perfection of it. Every nerve exploded, unraveling into a dead spin of pleasure as he released everything he had into her and she lost all control against him.

"Come with me," he murmured again, hoping she'd understand what he meant this time.

"I just did," she moaned.

No, she didn't understand. And, honestly, neither did he.

An hour later, Kate stared at the ceiling, listening to

crickets outside and the easy rhythm of Alec's breathing. But he wasn't asleep. She realized that she'd slept with him fifteen feet away for enough nights to know.

"What's wrong?" she finally asked, rolling over to look at his profile.

"Nothing."

"You're lying."

He turned and met her face-to-face. "How would you know?"

"Your breathing. I know when you're sleeping. I know when you're…troubled." She stroked his face, traveling the masculine lines that she once thought were beastly. Now they were beautiful. "Tell me."

A smile pulled at his lips. "You have to know everything, don't you?"

"No. Yeah. Only about you."

"Well, you do now. You know my past and secrets and real name." He closed his eyes as her finger trailed over his face and chest, slipping under the covers to continue south.

"I know your soft targets."

"Mmm. Keep doing that, and that target won't be soft for long."

"That a challenge, Petrov?" she teased.

He didn't answer, still studying her face, his expression so serious it was almost stern. "I asked you to do something when we were making love."

She frowned a little, trying to remember all that he'd said. Most of it had been the desperate murmurings of a lover. All of it, right? But from the look on his face, she was forgetting something.

"I asked you to come with me."

"And I told you I did." She gave him a playful squeeze. "Couldn't you tell?"

"That's not what I meant."

It wasn't? Had she done something wrong? Disappointed him in bed? Was he...oh. *Oh.* Oh, God. "You mean tomorrow? To Costa Rica?"

He nodded, and a million emotions clashed in her chest like fireworks. He wanted her to be with him, and he wanted her to move and hide and run with him. Could she live a life like that? "No," she mumbled. She couldn't. There had to be another way. There had to be some solution for him to live a normal life and for her to live it with him. Because that's what she wanted. Costa Rica and Australia? "No," she said again.

"Shit." He rolled off the bed, and she realized how he'd misinterpreted that.

"Alec, no. Don't leave. I just meant—"

"My phone's ringing."

She scrambled to the side of the bed. "Ignore it. This is important. Please."

"It could be Gabe." He marched down the hall, the sound of a man wounded in every way.

Damn it. *Damn it all.* She pushed off the bed, hitting the floor as she heard him say, "Hey, Gregg."

His mentor and friend. Ignoring the fact that she was as naked as he, she followed the sound of his voice, stepping over the evidence of their lust littering the hallway.

Come with me.

Could she?

Better question: Could she *not*?

"He has her? Are you sure?" His voice cracked with fear, the same way it had cracked when he'd told her about the teenage girl. Of course. Vlitnik had Robyn.

"Where is he?" Alec asked.

In the silence that followed the question, Kate tiptoed closer, already knowing where this call would go.

"Okay, tell him I will."

He will *what*? Except, she already knew.

"Hey, he's dangling the bait, Gregg. I'm just taking it."

She swallowed hard. He was going to Vlitnik to save that girl. No doubt he was the ransom itself.

"Sorry, but I don't have anything to lose," he barked into the phone.

Not now. Now that he thought she'd just refused his offer.

"What do I give up if that SOB kills me? Some fake life on the run, always missing out on real life? Sorry, but that girl has a baby on the way and a life and a future. She can have mine to save hers."

How could she have even doubted that she'd follow this man to the ends of the earth? He was so worth it.

"Production Park. Naples. Domestic Drive. Last warehouse. Got it."

So, so worth it.

"Then I have to come up with a way to explain how I know where he is," Alec said. "I'll tell him I put a tracker on Robyn. I won't blow your guy's cover. You get him to video that fat fuck trying to kill me. That ought to fly nice with the FBI."

She heard the truth in his voice. He'd die or Vlitnik would, but this life had to come to an end before another fake one started.

"Thanks, Gregg," Alec said, lowering his voice to make his point. "You've always been there for me, man, and if this helps you bring in Vlitnik, then maybe I've come close to paying you back."

But what if he died trying?

Kate took a deep breath, stepping out of the shadows as Alec hung up. "I'm going with you."

"Like hell you are."

"Alec, I'm going with you."

"Don't even—"

"I mean to wherever you're going. Costa Rica. Australia. Wherever. I want to come with you."

He let out a soft grunt. "You didn't seem to love the idea five minutes ago."

"I don't. But I'm pretty sure I could love you. I might already." She wrapped her arms around him. "You're going to save Robyn, aren't you?"

"I have to."

"Yeah, I already love you."

"I know how that feels." He pressed his lips to her head. "One more good-bye, Kate. Let me do this."

She inched back. "Come back to me."

"I will, but if you tell Gabe where I went, it's a deal breaker. The only way to stop him is to catch him in the act."

"Of killing you?"

"I have a helluva reason not to let that happen now." He tipped her chin up and looked at her. "You belong with me. Not *to* me, but *with* me."

She waited for the revolt possessive words like that always caused, but for some reason, there was none. She kissed him lightly. "Yes, I do."

Chapter Thirty-One

If she died, her baby died.

The words had echoed in Robyn's head since she'd been dragged from the laundry truck—by a son of a bitch she once thought she loved—and tied up, taped shut, and thrown in a corner of some dark, giant metal box that stank like fish and was hotter than hell.

If she died, her baby died.

So Robyn had to do whatever it took to stay alive. The problem was, she had no idea what that was.

Her hands ached to rub her hard belly, especially when her baby kicked, but they were tied behind her, the rope Cole had tied her in burning her wrists every time she moved.

Cole. She couldn't believe what he'd turned out to be. A thug. A mobster. A heartless yes-man who worked for that horrible Dmitri Vlitnik. She hadn't seen the fat bastard yet, but she put it all together easy enough.

But what happened next?

Not knowing was the hardest part.

She tried to adjust her position, the hard concrete painful on her backside. Someone would be in here soon, and she had a feeling she knew what they wanted from her: Alec Petrov. Would she tell them?

Only if that would save her, and her baby. Or she could play dumb, and then maybe they wouldn't hurt her or her baby. Or maybe she should just tell them where Alec was, and they'd let her go.

Yeah, and maybe angels would drop from heaven and take her home. Except she didn't believe in angels and couldn't remember ever feeling like somewhere was home.

A low-pitched rumble and a splash of bright light told her the big garage door was opening and a car was pulling in. From where she was, she couldn't see the car or who was in it.

What if it was someone who'd come to save her?

No, Robyn, no one is going to save you. No one even knew she was here. Poppy probably figured she'd bolted, and they'd left it at that. And that Gabe guy was just so pissed, he probably didn't care if she died. And Alec? Well, she'd blown everything for him, so he certainly wasn't going to save her. The lump in her throat grew, and a sob she couldn't swallow threatened. She was so alone. Just Robyn and this—

"Where is she?"

Vlitnik. Her heart dropped, and her stomach rolled and not in the *feeling the baby* way she'd come to love. No, this was more like, *I'm going to die now.*

And so would her baby.

Heavy footsteps pounded on the concrete floor, but the exchange of conversation was too low to hear. The only light went off almost immediately, making everything so, so dark. Words and snippets floated to her, mostly Vlitnik's low voice and occasionally Cole's despicable voice.

Alec Petrov.

Pussy.

Bait.

Reel that fucker in for good.

The last few words grew louder, closer, and were punctuated by footsteps.

"We meet again, Miss Bickler."

She blinked up at Dmitri Vlitnik's obese figure looming over her.

"Take the tape off. No one can hear her."

Cole leaned down, avoiding her gaze, and ripped the tape off her mouth so hard he had to have taken skin with it. She bit back a cry, not wanting either one of them to see how weak and scared she was. So weak and scared. And pregnant.

And so not the street-smart runaway she liked to imagine herself as being.

"Chair!" Vlitnik barked to Cole, who ran to do his bidding like a pathetic lackey.

God, she hoped her baby didn't take after him.

Cole hustled back with a folding chair, placing it behind Dmitri and stepping back as though allowing the king to sit.

"Not for me, you dumbass. For her. Put her on the chair and untie her hands and feet."

Cole looked suitably shamed, tearing at the tape and pushing her into the seat, untying her as he'd been told.

"Don't hurt her," Vlitnik said, the words and tone surprising her, and giving her hope. "Or *your* baby."

Cole choked. "We don't know it's—"

Vlitnik pushed him so hard, he almost fell over. "Fuck you, Daddy. We know whose it is." He speared Cole with a harsher look. "Go watch the door." As Cole walked away, Vlitnik turned to Robyn. "You missed our appointment."

All she could manage was a nod.

"And I had to send this nitwit all the way down the East

Coast to find out what I need to know." He leaned closer. "Where the hell is Alec Petrov?"

Her knowledge, that information, was her only bargaining chip. She couldn't waste it. "I...I don't know for sure." She rubbed her bruised and chafed wrists, a lump of fear growing in her throat. Why did he have Cole untie her? What was Vlitnik going to do to her now?

He was strong, and ruthless.

So the only decent weapon she had was information, and she needed to use it wisely.

Cole disappeared, and a few seconds later, the garage door opened. The sound echoed over the metal walls, and there was enough light to see that, oh, God, Vlitnik had a gun in his hand.

Then he came very close to Robyn, leaning all the way over her, sour breath on her face. "Where is he?"

She looked up at him. "Let me go, and I'll tell you."

"Don't be stupid, girl. I can't do that."

Then what was going to happen to her?

He bent over in front of her chair, holding the gun to her head. "Where is he?"

If she told him, she'd be dead, she knew that. And if she didn't...she'd still be dead. Either way, she was—

The gun clicked, and she sucked in a breath and nearly fainted.

"Oh, that one was empty." He chuckled softly. "Let's try the next one. You know this game, right, little girl? It's named after my country."

Russian roulette.

"There's one bullet. Six chambers. Well, five now. Where is he?"

Okay, she should tell him. But then he'd kill her anyway, right? But if there was any chance, then—

Click.

Blood whirred through her brain, pounding and screaming. If she died, the baby died. What was the best thing for her child?

"Where is he?"

"He's..." She stole a glance at the gun. "He's..." He pressed the trigger harder. One in four chances that she'd be dead on her next breath. "He's..."

Click.

"I'm right here. Put the gun down and let her go, Vlitnik. You have no reason to hurt her."

Blood rushed so hard from Robyn's head, she fell over, out before she hit the floor.

Alec lunged forward to try to grab the fallen girl, but Vlitnik was closer, instantly on her, the gun pointed directly at her belly. "I knew you couldn't resist the bait."

Is that why it had been so easy to take down the kid? Vlitnik wanted Alec in here and put weak sauce on guard. Alec had left Cole flat out on the driveway, but he wouldn't stay out for very long.

And neither did Robyn, who moaned, waking up.

"Let her go," Alec repeated. "You don't need her anymore."

She came to quickly, giving a soft whimper.

"Oh, no. We're going to have some fun with her, Alec." Vlitnik gave her a kick in the side. "Just like old times."

Alec breathed slowly, memories threatening to swamp him, but this time he had training. He knew how to be still and forget. He knew how to ready his body for an attack. He knew how to fight to kill.

And he would kill or be killed tonight.

Vlitnik lowered his girth so all two-fifty of him was smashing Robyn's belly, his gun at her head. She cried out, and Alec vaulted to push him off and—

Click.

The hammer fell on another empty chamber. And Robyn shrieked louder.

"What do you want from me?" Alec demanded, not willing to take the fifty-fifty risk that was left in this sick game.

Vlitnik let out a long, slow sigh, rich with some meaning only he understood. "I want to know what you're made of, *Aleksandr.*"

"I think you know that already, or I would have been working for you for the last ten years."

He couldn't move fast or take any chances. The next shot could end Robyn's life, and she knew it by the way she was sobbing. If it was empty, Vlitnik would just fire again and that chamber *wouldn't* be empty. So he had to talk this through, but he had to get that fat bastard off the poor pregnant girl.

He held up his hands in surrender. "I'm not armed, I'm not here to fight. I'm here for you. What do you want?"

"I told you." Blessedly, the position was uncomfortable enough for him that he pushed up, but didn't move the gun away from Robyn's tear-stained face. "What are you made of?"

"I'm not a killer, no matter how hard you try to turn me into one."

He moved the gun down, pointing it at Robyn's chest now. "Some people are born that way. I guess I thought you would be, too."

As much as Alec didn't care about the asshole's chatter, something…wasn't right about that last sentence.

"You thought I would be…what?"

"More like me," he said. A slow, ugly tremble of a smile pulled at his face. "But you're a carbon copy of Daria."

Daria. His mother. *What was he saying*? The possibility rocked him, nearly stealing his breath with the shock, just as footsteps scuffed behind Vlitnik.

"He's alone," Cole said. "I made sure."

"Well done, Cole," Vlitnik said calmly.

So Cole *hadn't* put up a fight. He might not even have been knocked out. His job was to make sure Alec arrived without backup.

"And you're just in time," Vlitnik added. "For our science experiment."

Cole walked past Alec without sparing him a glance.

Vlitnik stood up, more confident now that he wasn't alone with Alec, not that Alec couldn't take Cole down—for real—in five seconds. But by the time he did that, Vlitnik's bullet would be in Robyn's head.

"Cool," Cole said, cocky with his position of power. "What's the experiment?"

"Who has balls?"

Cole snorted and grabbed his crotch like a preteen showing off on the playground. "Steel 'nads, my man."

"Good. Then give your girlfriend a punch in the belly."

Cole stood stone still, his swagger fading. "But she's…"

"Knocked up," Vlitnik said. "You want to work for me? You want to show your teacher here what it takes to work for me? Fucking punch her, you shit bag!"

Robyn rolled up a little, looking from Vlitnik to Cole. "No, please, the baby. Your baby."

"Have him punch me, asshole," Alec said, moving closer

308

to position himself to take down Cole if he so much as made a fist.

"I don't want him to punch you. I want to see if he has what it takes to work for me."

Cole choked indignantly. "I don't need to beat up some defenseless chick, man. That's sick."

"Sick!" Vlitnik turned, wild-eyed. "You think I'm sick?"

Alec moved the second Vlitnik turned, throwing his full weight at the man, nearly toppling him, and sending the gun flying.

"Hey!" Cole jumped them, attempting to wrap his legs around Alec and get back precious control, but Alec easily threw him off.

"Go!" Alec screamed at Robyn. "Run!"

Cole moved again, fighting for good arm and hip position, desperately trying and almost getting Alec down. Alec threw a jab at his face and an elbow strike at his chest, vaguely aware that Robyn was running...in the wrong direction.

Cole glanced long enough at Robyn for Alec to hook his arm and pull it backward, a move he recalled Cole never saw coming in training. It worked, forcing Cole to writhe in pain long enough for Alec to give his attention to Vlitnik.

He was fat and weak, and Alec threw himself at the man, shoving him to the ground, threading one of his legs through Alec's to almost break his knee, earning a yelp of misery.

Alec couldn't see where Robyn had gone behind him, and wouldn't think of letting up on Vlitnik, but he sensed Cole scurrying across the room.

"Gimme the gun, baby."

Alec jerked into another move, sliding his arm under Vlitnik's head to execute a perfect guillotine choke. Enough pressure and the bastard would die in his arms. He whimpered like the wuss he was.

Alec couldn't turn to watch the drama behind him, but kept his gaze locked on the man he'd spent most of his life hating.

"Don't, Cole. I'll shoot you."

"She won't shoot him," Vlitnik said to Alec through clenched teeth. "He's the father of her baby. Same way your mother didn't stick a butcher knife in me when she had the chance."

The words slid through Alec like hot oil, burning with the truth. The ugly, ugly truth.

"You thought you were Sergei's son?" Vlitnik choked the words when Alec froze. "That old bag of nothing? Your mother was smart, though. She'd do anything to protect him from the brotherhood. *Anything*." The meaning layered into the last word was unmistakable.

Hate and fury and vengeance rocked him, making Alec push harder, cracking Vlitnik's neck. "No way," Alec ground out. "No fucking way."

Vlitnik managed a sneer. "Sergei couldn't even make a baby. You really think that impotent old man signed some oath to give you to me when he was dying? He knew you couldn't possibly be his. And he knew I could just come and take what belonged to me anytime. And you belonged to me. You always have and you always will."

He hated hearing his parents' names on this beast's lips. Hated everything he was saying. "You bastard!" He twisted Vlitnik's thick head harder as fiery hate and venom shot through him. "You fucking bastard!"

"No, son, that's what you are."

Rage blinded him, the desire to kill licking like flames through every cell in his body. It would be so easy. So *easy*. So satisfying and easy.

Because being a killer was in his blood, as he now knew without a doubt.

"Just give it to me, Robyn," Cole pleaded to the still-sobbing girl.

"Why do you work for him, Cole?" she demanded. "Why would you give him your life? For money? To be like him?"

Alec blocked out the conversation, his brain completely focused on not killing the son of a bitch. One more ounce of pressure, and this man…his *biological father*…would be dead.

No one would ever have to know the truth.

"Robyn, just—"

They scuffled, she screamed, and the gun went off, no empty chamber this time.

Cole howled, loud and hard enough for Alec to know who'd been shot.

"Run, Robyn!" Alec hollered, and the sound of her footsteps confirmed she took the command.

"Kill me," Vlitnik ground out, looking to the side so he could catch Alec's eyes. "Show me what you're made of, my son."

He pushed a little harder, enough to hear the tendons crack, but not his neck. Breaking his neck would be so simple.

Cole's moaning in the background faded away as Alec stared down at Vlitnik. It all made sense now. He wasn't worthy of life, because it had been given to him by a ruthless, narcissistic beast who deserved to die.

"Come on. You can do it," Vlitnik coaxed. "Live up to your name and brand, Aleksandr Vlitnik. Be worthy of being my son. Kill or be killed."

Be worthy. Be worthy. Be worthy of something…better than this.

He loosened his grip. "I'd rather die." Pushing up, he swallowed, not even willing to spit on the man who gave him life. Instead, he stood, turned, and walked away, offering his back for the killer to put a knife or bullet in it.

Suddenly, everything lit up. The garage door opened, the place flooded with light, and men in tactical gear poured into the warehouse, screaming orders for everyone to drop their weapons and get down.

Alec ignored them and just kept walking, his head pounding with the fact that would haunt him for the rest of his life.

"Hey!" a man called out to him. "Get down or get shot."

Alec turned toward the voice, fearless as three men closed in on him, guns drawn.

"Don't shoot him." Gabe Rossi came running through the open garage door. "He's one of us."

Was he? He gave a flat look to Gabe.

"That's it?" Gabe said. "The fucking cavalry shows up, and you stare at me and say nothing?"

"How'd you find me? Gregg?"

"Your *wife*," he said. "Don't be pissed at her. She'd have come here alone to save you, but we thought this was a better idea."

His *wife*. That was something she'd never be.

He managed a shrug and walked past Gabe, staring straight ahead, barely seeing the flashing lights, the military-style precision of the SWAT team attack, or the two women hugging on the street.

Robyn and...Kate. For a second, his heart soared, then it slammed down to the ground with the realization of who, and what, he was.

He walked right past her and kept going, knowing that even though Vlitnik could no longer hunt him or hurt him, Alec Petrov would never be free of the man, and he would never, ever be worthy of Kate Kingston.

Chapter Thirty-Two

Everything was so quiet. Freakishly, wickedly quiet, as it had been every morning—and afternoon and evening—in the villa where Kate had spent the last week. No maid fussing around, pretending to clean but really eavesdropping. No old grandpa dropping by to be sure she had food.

And no Alec Petrov, bodyguard, trainer, lover. *Ex*-lover.

All that waited for Kate was a mountain of legal books, hours of studying, and gallons of sunshine. Not the man she longed for.

Alec had disappeared sometime in the middle of the night after Dmitri Vlitnik had been taken down. They hadn't even talked, though Gabe had done his best to be a go-between, delivering cryptic messages, none of them telling her where Alec was or when he'd be back. Or if.

Vlitnik was behind bars, and his mob was either with him or running scared. Maybe Alec felt he still had to hide, but Gabe wouldn't confirm or deny anything. He just said he was gone, and Kate assumed she was supposed to carry on with her life like the time in Barefoot Bay hadn't changed it irrevocably.

Come with me, Kate.

She sat on the sofa, twirling the wedding ring she'd gotten so used to wearing. Had he taken his off? Did he remember the soap trick?

"Oh, stop torturing yourself," she murmured, pushing up to stand and do something other than moon over a man who wasn't coming back.

But *what* changed? she asked herself for the four millionth time in a week. Was that a plea from a man humming with an orgasm? Or was he sincere? Because if he was…

A soft tap on the villa door pulled her from her reverie and, of course, shot a blast of hope through her. He'd come back. After all, wasn't that the reason she'd put off leaving the resort? On the slim-to-none chance that—

"Kate? It's Gabe."

She put down her cup and let out a soft sigh of disappointment, heading to the front door. Maybe he had news from Alec. Maybe he'd come to tell her Alec wanted to see her. Maybe he knew exactly where Alec was and she could go there.

She opened the door to meet his now-familiar blue gaze, darker than the one she longed to see.

"I got bad news," he said, coming in without being announced.

Her heart squeezed. "Alec? Is he okay?"

"Hell if I know. He's checked out, and I haven't heard a word. Gregg paid his bill, Alec helped the FBI seal up the case on Vlitnik, and now he's gone. And, I'm afraid, you will have to be soon, too."

She tried to process all that but had gotten stuck on *he's checked out*. Checked out of Kate's life.

"I have access to only a few places at this resort," Gabe said. "One of them being this villa, and I've got more business at hand."

She gestured him into the living room. "So you're kicking me out."

"'Fraid so." He grinned, a sly, crooked, attractive smile that probably made women swoon, but Kate was immune to Gabe's charm. She'd fallen in love with another man, who'd...*checked out.*

"I guess I should go back to Boston."

"There's a lot of media coverage there about Steven."

Which she'd been using as her excuse to stay. "I'd rather be somewhere else."

He shrugged. "Wish I could tell you where he went, Kate. But then I'd have to—"

"Kill me?" she finished with a smile.

"I'd have to go on the lam myself, because that beast you like so much would break me."

So Alec had ordered Gabe to stay quiet. That hurt even more.

"Hey," Gabe said, tipping her chin up when she looked down to the floor. "You might not have all the facts."

She took a wary step back, something in the way he spoke making her legs weak. "Why don't you tell me?"

"I shouldn't, but I'm going to. He doesn't know I know, and he sure as shit won't know *you* know, but I think I have a clue about why our boy disappeared that night."

"Why?" She felt her fingers clench, her imagination flying.

"Vlitnik's his biological father."

"What?" She took another step backward and let herself fall into the sofa the backs of her knees hit.

"He confessed in prison. Said he told Alec that night. He used Daria Petrov as a lover, and she let him to protect her husband."

"Oh my God, he must be devastated." And think even

316

less of himself. "He must be so lonely," she murmured. "And broken. And wrecked."

"Oh, he's strong," Gabe said.

In other words, *he doesn't need you*. She pushed up and crossed her arms. She needed to be strong, too. "I'll check out this afternoon. I really don't know how to thank you for letting me hide out here."

"Tomorrow's fine," he said. "Even the next day. My sister is coming down in a few days to help me out with a project, and I'm putting her up here. But by the end of the week, I'll need the place."

She reached out and gave him a hug. "Thank you, Gabe. I appreciate all you and your people have done."

"Housekeeping!" a woman called as the door unlatched.

"There's one of my people now," he said.

"That's not Poppy." She frowned and looked around Gabe's shoulder to see Robyn Bickler in a yellow maid's uniform.

"Robyn's going to work for us here for a while, until the baby's born. They need her for the investigation, and I've offered to keep her here."

The young woman smiled, already blossoming at the resort where she'd obviously been adopted. "I'll start on the bedroom, Ms. Kingston."

The staff knew her real identity, now, and that her "honeymoon" had been an act to protect herself from a crazy ex-husband. As Gabe walked to the door, she glanced down at the ring that she'd become so used to seeing on her hand. "Oh, Gabe. Do you want me to take this over to your office, or do you want it back? You might need it for another pretend marriage," she added.

"I probably won't be doing another one of those for a while, but yeah, I'll take it, thanks."

She slipped the ring off her finger and instantly felt empty and sad.

After giving it to Gabe along with one more hug, she wandered into the bedroom where Robyn was making the bed.

"How are you feeling?" Kate asked.

"Never better. I'm staying with Poppy until the baby's born," she said brightly. "There's nothing that woman loves like an orphan, and she decided I am one. And Little A won't be."

"Little A?"

"Something for Alec, since he saved my life."

Funny, he saved mine, too.

"Anyway, I'm so happy."

"I'm thrilled for you," Kate said, meaning it.

Someone around here ought to be happy, because Kate Kingston certainly wasn't.

Little Odessa hummed with life, colorful and vibrant, the Russian influence touching every corner of the heart of Brighton Beach, from the street signs to the Cyrillic letters on storefronts. Though a number of other cultures had squeezed into the landscape, along with plenty of tourists, Alec still felt the same vibe he'd known as a kid.

The neighborhood was just this side of dangerous and edgy, but those hard edges were softened by many good memories.

One stared him right in the face, on a street corner he'd crossed a thousand times or more. Petrov's Meat Market had long closed, become a café, then a cigar shop, and now, a vacancy.

The owner wanted an astronomical sum to buy less than a thousand square feet, and Alec leaned against a lamppost across the street, trying to figure out how he could raise that sum and open an MMA studio there.

"It won't last long on this market."

Alec turned at the sound of a man's voice, familiar, warm, and welcome. "Hey." He reached out his arm and gave a quick hug to his mentor and friend, getting a hard pat on the back in return.

"Sorry I'm late," Gregg said. "Someone needed to shop." He turned and gestured toward a teenage girl with hair as blond and shiny as her father's, half her face covered by a cell phone as she texted with the intensity of most kids her age.

"You're going to walk into a pole, Kristina," Gregg called.

"Not a Pole. A Russian." She looked up, grinning with pleasure at her joke. That grin only grew wider when she saw Alec. "Hey there." She reached out and gave him knuckles. "What up?"

"Hi, Kristina." He tapped her hand, marveling at how fast the little girl was growing up. And how nicely. Gregg's daughter was clearly going to be a classic Slavic beauty, with dramatic cheekbones and smoky eyes, her silky hair tumbling haphazardly nearly to her waist.

"Dad, can I run over there to that boutique?" She pointed across the street. "They sell those amazing scarves."

"Stay here with me, Kristyusha." Gregg's Russian accent, heard distinctly in the use of his daughter's pet name, seemed to get more pronounced in Brighton Beach, where the native language was heard and seen almost as much as English.

"But Raquel loves those scarves, Dad. You could bring one home to her."

He sighed, the sound of a dad giving in. "Go, but that one store only. And keep your face out of that phone. We'll be in that building looking around. Come straight there the minute you're done."

She rewarded him with a quick kiss on the cheek. As she walked away, both men watched her cross the busy street, and Gregg shook his head.

"I want to put her in a bubble and protect her from the world," he said. "And yet, I want her to have every experience."

"I'd probably do the first one, if I were a dad."

Gregg laughed. "Fortunately, I married the world's smartest woman, and she and Kristina are like that." He held up two entwined fingers.

"She's certainly safe with Raquel," Alec mused. "Nothing like having a bodyguard for a mother."

Gregg nodded. "That's how I met her, as you know. She was Kristina's bodyguard and that got...interesting." A smile pulled across features as finely chiseled as his daughter's.

"Has it stayed interesting after all these years?"

Gregg drew back, considering the question and, more likely, the source. "Are you looking for romantic advice from me, Alec?"

He quickly shook his head. "No, no. But I wouldn't mind some real-estate guidance." He gestured toward the corner shop. "I'm serious about buying this place. And you know I'll need a loan."

"Let's go look at it," Gregg agreed readily. "I think the idea of an MMA training studio here is brilliant. And having it in the same building where your parents had their business? Interesting choice."

Alec shot him a look. "It's what I want," he said. A way

to erase the past and ghosts that haunted the building, and start something new.

Gregg put his hand on Alec's back. "You do realize you can go wherever you want now, Alec, live however you like? You are completely free of the shadow of Dmitri Vlitnik. They have him for life, he's singing like an opera star, and they're bringing in his entire *Bratva*. All because you had the self-control not to kill him even though you had the chance."

That may be so. But he'd still carry the bastard's DNA in every cell for the rest of his life. "This is my home," he said simply.

Gregg didn't answer as they waited for a car to pass and then strode to the other side of the street. The front door opened from inside, and the well-dressed real-estate rep smiled at the two men. "And you've brought your second opinion," he said.

Alec made quick introductions, and then the Realtor stepped away. "Take your time and look around again. I'll be right on the street."

Appreciating the privacy for the second tour of a space Alec could navigate with his eyes closed, he led Gregg deeper into the empty unit. But it wasn't empty to him.

It was full of memories, the thump and bustle of meat being delivered in the back, his father's soft-spoken voice giving orders, his mother's easy laugh, a line of customers calling out orders, the smell of beef and wax paper and the powdered sugar tea cakes they always gave away with every purchase. She was a strong woman, despite the hand life had dealt her. Maybe because of it. She'd done what she had to do to protect her husband and his business.

And his father hadn't signed away a son, after all. So he could be forgiven, too.

"You could mirror that wall and build a cushion-flex floor, maybe a cage over there for practice?"

Gregg's ideas faded in and out of Alec's attention as he let his mind drift back, picking up snippets of conversation, shared looks, and secret communication between his parents. They'd loved each other, very much. Whatever happened with Vlitnik had to have ended when he was born, thank God.

"You could actually run small, private classes simultaneously in those two back rooms," Gregg continued. "Or use one for weight training."

And how did this truth change his life? Could he rise above the shame that his biological father had left in his gut? He'd been asking himself that question nonstop since he left Florida.

"Of course, you'll need a private office."

The truth had already cost him the woman he loved.

Gregg got in his face and snapped his fingers, making Alec jerk. "What's the problem?"

Life without Kate. That was the problem. "I have to be worthy of her. I was almost there. So close, then wham."

Gregg inched back, his eyes darkening under the shadow of a frown. "You don't mean…"

"I do. Kate Kingston."

"Your pretend wife."

Alec took a pained breath, not sure how to explain it to his mentor.

"And you don't want it to be pretend?" Gregg crossed his arms. "What's stopping you?"

The very blood in my veins. "I have a dark past."

Gregg gave him a *get real* look. "And a great future, right here, with a new business that is going to boom. She's a lawyer, right? You know what this town needs? A badass

322

prosecutor. From what I've heard, she'd be great at that."

She would. So great.

Kate would take the New York bar exam in a heartbeat; he knew that about her. "She knows why I'm staying away."

"Why?" Gregg demanded.

"Because she's perfect, and I'm not worthy of perfect."

Gregg slid his hands into his pockets and his blue eyes turned to icy blades aimed at Alec. "You know I don't agree with that. You cut me with comments like that, my friend. I've protected you for years, and why do you think? Because you're worthy."

"Sadly, it's not you I want to marry."

A smile flicked at the corner of his lips. "Marry." It wasn't a question. He turned and looked around the space again, as if seeing it again. "Would it help if I asked you to be my eyes and ears here in Brighton Beach? I need someone on the ground who can help me feed information to the FBI. Vlitnik's *Bratva* might be dead and his men scurrying away like rats in the sunlight, but another one will emerge."

"Of course I will. I planned on it."

Gregg shrugged. "Then you even have a worthy cause. You're worthy of her."

Alec just stared at him. "She said I was, too, but she doesn't know—"

"So tell her."

"I can't. It's more complicated than you know."

"I know exactly how complicated it is, Alec." He leaned in to whisper, "I know *everything*, and let me tell you, that doesn't change who you *are*."

Alec stared at him, waiting for something, anything to tell him it wasn't true.

"And it sucks—"

"You have no idea."

"—that you think you can't rise above the sins of your dirty DNA and set a new example, create a new history, and have as positive an impact on this town as he had negative. Because if you truly think that, then you're right, you're *not* worthy of her. Or me."

Alec swallowed hard. "I hadn't thought of it that way."

"Yes, you have. That's the reason we're here, buying this property. That's the reason you're more than willing to risk your business, or even more, to share information. Because, if you were so ashamed or miserable about this, you'd take the ticket to Costa Rica and hide."

Alec didn't answer, letting Gregg's words echo through the empty space.

"You don't give yourself enough credit," Gregg said softly. "And that's going to cost you a woman."

"Hey, Dad!" Kristina popped in through the front doors, carrying a bag and wearing a bright pink scarf around her neck. "Got one for Raquel, too."

Gregg reached out and put an arm around his daughter, giving her a squeeze. Alec watched the exchange, his heart twisting so hard he had to look away.

While they talked about her purchases, Alec walked over to the window, the one his mother decorated with white lace curtains, where she kept a table with two chairs so patrons waiting for their order could sit and eat Daria Petrov's free cookies.

She'd done what she had to do, and so had her father. They were victims of the system, a system he had to fight. But he didn't want to fight it alone. He didn't want to live another day alone, frankly.

Gregg surprised him by putting a hand on Alec's back. "You should make an offer on this place," he said.

He looked at his friend, not caring that the man who'd brought him through some of the worst times of his life could see tears in Alec's eyes. "I can't do that on my own."

"I told you, I'm good for the loan, Alec."

"That's not what I mean." He smiled, already feeling less hollow. "I have to talk to…my wife."

Gregg laughed, nodding toward Alec's hand. "And I thought you still had that ring on because it was stuck on your supersized finger."

"It's not stuck," he said with a smile. "I just didn't want to take it off." *Ever*.

Chapter Thirty-Three

Kate packed up the last of her books and clothes, leaving out something to travel in later, and stepped into a beach cover-up over panties. It was all she needed for her last treat at Casa Blanca, the much-needed massage the spa had called and offered as a complimentary going-away present.

A consolation present, more like.

She grabbed the key and stepped out into a blast of sunshine, taking a minute to let it warm her, then padding barefoot to cabana number two.

At least it wasn't the same one where she'd lost her control and mind and heart to Alec Petrov.

Still no word from him. She'd finally stopped waiting. Or she would, soon.

She hadn't quite reached the cabana when she saw the woman in a giant orange hat step out of it and wave to her. "Oh, hello. So good to see you again!"

Kate mustered a smile, despite a heavy heart. Madame Valaina wasn't around here every day, so she probably hadn't heard the truth about the honeymooners in Caralluma. But Kate didn't feel like telling her story.

But Madame Valaina came closer, sliding her sunglasses

down to inspect Kate with her usual scrutiny. "You miss him."

So maybe she had heard. "So bad it's a miracle I'm not rolled up into the fetal position weeping."

That made Madame V grin. "I could tell it was intense between you two. He couldn't take a decent breath when he looked at you."

Well, he was taking them now. "That's how I feel today," she admitted.

The woman put a gentle hand on Kate's shoulder. "Then you better go inside and feel better."

A massage was not the answer, but Kate smiled and headed to the cabana, pulling back the drapes to blink into the dimness of the small area. Her gaze went straight to the single massage table with fresh sheets folded down, but no therapist in sight.

"Hello?" she called, knowing there was a private space closed off in the back behind another curtain, but no one answered. "Hailey?"

After a second, she slipped out of her cover-up and climbed onto the table to slide into the envelope of the sheet, leaving her barely covered backside out. No need for modesty this time around.

Although she hadn't been modest with Alec. She'd been honest. Real. Out there. Vulnerable. And now she was—

A large, heavy hand landed on her back. "Oh!" She started to sit up and turn, not expecting a male massage therapist. But the hand was strong and held her immobile, the man it belonged to standing so she couldn't see him.

"What do you call these?" A finger flicked at the lace trim of her thong. "Smartypants?"

Alec.

She gasped in surprise and left her mouth open to say

something…but nothing came out. Not a word, big, small, or otherwise. He'd left her speechless.

"Whatever you call them…they're perfect." He punctuated that by placing his hand on her exposed buttocks, caressing and, of course, sending a million sparks through her body and chills up her spine. "Just like you."

She tried to push up. "Al—"

"Shhh." He pressed her back to the table. "You just breathe. I'll do the work. Madame Valaina gave me some tips."

Without speaking, he slowly rubbed his thumbs in two circles over her spine, making her feel boneless and loose. And confused. And thrilled.

Mostly thrilled.

"You're really tense," he said, adding pressure to muscles bunched under her neck. "Like you've been in a lot of pain."

"Broken heart," she muttered.

She heard his soft, soft moan of sorrow, enough of an apology that she accepted it instantly.

"I can fix that," he whispered. "I can use my hands"—he splayed them wide on her back, easily covering the width of it—"to do good things. Many good things. Like this."

Very gently, he helped her turn over on the bed. She closed her eyes as she did, not quite ready for the impact of Alec.

She heard him hiss in a breath and met his gaze, which was as hot as a gas flame, and just as blue. She gasped, too, just at the sheer joy of seeing him again.

She started to sit up, but he placed his hands on her shoulders and kept her on her back, looming over her, teasing her with how close he was and how much she wanted to hold him.

He splayed his fingers against her skin, dropping his gaze

to look at them. "I never realized that my hands could be good, until I used them to touch you."

She made a little sound in her throat, biting her lip, glancing down to see his dark, marked hands juxtaposed against her pale skin.

"And I never knew that I could be worthy of anything, until you made me want to be worthy of you."

"Alec, you—"

He put his finger over her lips to quiet her, clearly bent on getting his speech out. "And, Kate, I never knew that I was capable of love, until I fell in love with you."

She tried to swallow, but couldn't. Tried to blink back the tears, but couldn't do that, either. Instead, she just closed her hand over his and squeezed, nodding.

Slowly, he lifted her up so she could sit and face him. He reached underneath the table and pulled out a swath of red chiffon, exactly like the one she'd kept and packed in her bag.

"She must give these to all her favorites," he said, draping it around her shoulders. He leaned closer, their faces nearly touching now. "Damn, I've missed you."

She felt the brand of his lips on her forehead and finally found her voice. "Where have you been?"

He kissed her again, then inched back to look at her. "I went home," he said. "To Brighton Beach, to face some things."

She didn't answer, suspecting she already knew what he'd faced. Would he tell her? He had to. If he didn't, then she wouldn't know if she could trust anything he said. "Things like what?" she asked.

He leveled his gaze on her. "Like the fact that my biological father is a killer and a monster."

She closed her eyes and imagined how that must have felt. "Oh, Alec."

"Gregg met me there," he said. "And helped talk sense into me."

"What does sense sound like?" she asked.

He kissed her eyes and cheek, brushed her lips. "Like the sound of your name."

She sighed into a light kiss.

"I came back for you, Kate," he whispered. "I need you in my life. I want you by my side. I cannot live another day without you."

Each confession tumbled over her heart, healing the cracks he'd left there.

He leaned away and gave her a funny look. "But I know how you feel about…men."

"Not all men."

"And your independence?"

"Feels like another word for lonely these days."

She could see hope lighting his eyes to a new shade of blue. "And marriage?"

Marriage. She took a slow breath, letting that word, that word that once had terrified and infuriated her, fall back into the realm of what was possible.

She inched closer to him to make her point. "It would be…impossible—"

He closed his eyes with a grunt, as if she'd punched him.

"—not to dream about that with you."

"Really?" The joy and hope and certainty on his face were so beautiful, she closed her hands over his cheeks just to feel it all.

"Really."

"I dream about it, too," he admitted. "And that's what I want. Kate, you'll…wait. Wait. I have to do this right." He inched back and got down on one knee, making a laugh and tears bubble up at the same time.

"Alec, you don't—"

"Katherine Louise Kingston." He closed his eyes to compose himself, and she tried to crystallize the moment in her memory, her heart slamming against her chest, her breath caught in her throat. She sat half-naked on a massage table in a cabana on the beach, wrapped in red chiffon and real love.

It was perfect.

He reached into his pocket and pulled out a small black bag, one she immediately recognized. Opening it, he dropped the ring she'd so recently returned to Gabe into his palm.

"I know this fits, Kate. I know *we* fit. Please say you'll spend the rest of your life letting me show you what a partner can be. What a husband can be. Please say yes, Kate. One little word, one single syllable."

"Why use one syllable when four will do? Absolutely."

Laughing, he stood and pulled her off the table and into his arms to kiss her. "I love you, Kate. I love you so much."

As they broke the kiss, she took his hands and lifted both of them to her mouth. First, she kissed his tattooed knuckles. "I love you, too." She kissed the wedding band he still wore on his left hand. "My wonderful, sexy, tender, worthy husband."

As they kissed, the red drape fell to the floor in a soft sigh, like the sound of pure contentment.

Epilogue

"What have you got?"

"A headache from you asking me what I got." Chessie looked up from her laptop, her eyes tapered in warning.

"I thought you can find anyone."

She glared at Gabe. "The magic doesn't happen in five minutes, dear brother."

"You've been at this for over an hour, Chess," Gabe said. "How long can it take to break a code?"

She sighed, adjusting her horn rims. "It's a tricky one, and a lot of the keywords are in Spanish. You can come in, it's your office."

He stepped inside, closing the door so Poppy or Nino didn't come barging in. At the moment, they had no clients for the undercover operation, giving Gabe a chance to concentrate on what was the most important. Cracking his knuckles, he paced the length of the office, while his sister returned her attention to the computer, gnawing her lower lip like she always did when she was trying to break code.

"I know this is stating the obvious, Gabe, but it *would* help considerably if you'd actually tell me who I'm looking for."

He shook his head. "Don't need to know. Get me the whole list, Chess. Every name and their status. I'll take it from there."

"Not all of them have a status or address. Like, there are a few thousand e-mails on here, and I did crack them, but they're just cryptic e-mail addresses, like Rojo1 and CasaL2. Do you want those?"

"I want actual names, but I'll take the e-mails if that's all you have."

"Okay." She clicked quickly. "I made a database and forwarded it to you."

"Thanks." He crossed the room and grabbed his laptop, trolling through the supersized spreadsheet Chessie had sent him. "Shit, that's a lot of names."

"Think how simple it would be if you would tell me her freaking name, Gabriel Rossi. And don't try to tell me you're not looking for a *she*, because you would not go to this much trouble for another dude."

He didn't answer, studying the addresses. "These aren't in alphabetical order."

"Sucks to suck."

Huffing, he started scrolling, easily skimming the sea of meaningless handles, looking for a word or a clue that would strike him.

"So you haven't asked about Matt," Chessie said.

"Because I want you to work, not moon over your ex."

"What makes you think he's my ex?"

"The fact that you're here. You wouldn't have left if you thought there was still a chance with him. He's a dumbass dickhead cocksucking moron with webbed feet, Chess."

"No, his feet are fine."

He smiled. "You'll meet another guy."

"I don't want another guy."

Gabe didn't answer as he reached a group of e-mail addresses that used English words, forcing him to look harder for something that felt right. No luck. "They all say they don't want another guy, Chess," he murmured. "Then they meet me." He grinned at her.

She rolled her eyes.

"Seriously, you should stick around here," he said, back on his campaign to get her to stay. "Lots of hot guys for you to hook up with."

"First of all, I don't want to hook up. Second, this place is crawling with newlyweds and nearly deads."

"Not true. Luke's hiring bodyguards, and there's a whole baseball team coming in. You like athletes. And look at what a matchmaker I turned out to be with Alec and Kate."

She gave him a dreamy look. "They're so in love, Gabe. Is she really going to live in Brighton Beach with him?"

"Yeah, she's all fired up. No law firm for her. Now she wants to be a prosecutor and take those Russian bad boys to task. And Alec's going to step into Gregg's shoes and mentor the younger ones." He gave a smug grin. "I totally knew that was going to happen."

"You're totally full of shit."

"The fact that you know that makes me love you even more, Chess." He abandoned his spreadsheet for a full-court press. He *wanted* her here. "Luke is really hiring. Maybe he needs a tech specialist."

She snorted. "Vivi would have a cow instead of a baby." Then she slammed her hand over her mouth. "Shit, I wasn't supposed to say that."

He blinked at her. "Wait...*what*? They did it? Lang is actually not shooting blanks? I'll be damned."

"No, but I will be for telling you. She's not even two

months along yet." Chessie grinned, but there was a definite sadness in her eyes. "I'm so jelly."

"Your time will come."

"Yeah, right."

"Chessie. You're a female version of me." He gestured toward his face. "Impeccable bones, killer dimples, and eyes the color of heaven. The only baby blues in the whole Rossi clan."

"Yeah, Mom had a lover," she joked, calling up one of their favorite theories as to why they looked a little different than the other Rossi kids.

"I think it was Bud the lawn guy."

Chessie giggled. "Or that handyman, Timmy. She was always flirting with him."

He laughed and gestured toward the computer. "You know, we'd have fun if you were here, Chess. Plus, you could keep Nino and his Jamaican nemesis in line."

"I can't leave with Vivi pregnant."

"Just for a few months? Before she takes maternity leave?" He leaned forward. "You are always doing stuff for someone else in our family. What do *you* want?"

"A family to do stuff for," she said. "Of my own," she added.

"Like a husband, two-point-five, and a picket fence?" That was what his super-brained little sister wanted?

"You make it sound horrible."

"It just doesn't seem like that fits with your love of souped-up cars and supercomputers."

She shook her head. "I want Mom and Dad's life, Gabe."

"All those kids, a couple of Italian orphans, and Nino?" He drew back. "I can't see that."

"I mean I want the love they have. The permanence. The stability." She sighed. "I just can't find the right guy."

"This from the girl who can find anyone."

She gave a wistful smile and looked back at her monitor. "Oh, yes, I can," she said, a smug smile breaking. "And I just did."

"What?" Gabe shot up and came around the desk, leaving his spreadsheet to break his sister's cardinal rule of no spying over the shoulder when she was hacking.

"I got the list of couriers. I've been trying to get into this for an hour."

A little zing shot through him. "Those are the volunteers on the ground who distribute the news throughout Cuba." The *activists* the young woman at Radio and TV Martí had told him about.

Chessie hit a few more keys and waited while nothing happened on the screen. "You *do* know that our relations with Cuba are just about normalized now. There is essentially no need for subterfuge."

"There is always a need for subterfuge in my life."

The screen flashed, then darkened, then flashed again. Suddenly, it was filled with names, a long list, each with an address and phone number. Gabe's heart rate kicked up, and he hoped against hope that this was the lead he needed.

He *had* to find her. He had to.

"And, lookee here, it's alphabetical." Chessie scrolled, still in the C's and D's. "Tell me when to stop."

W. "Go way down."

"Past H, I, and J?"

"Way."

"Past Q, R, and S?"

His chest was so tight, he couldn't catch even a shallow breath. It made sense that she'd be a volunteer, an activist, and a courier.

"U, V, W—"

"Stop." He pushed closer, taking over the touch pad to slow down the slide, reading every single name. *Viteri. Vivas. Vives. Ybarra.*

"Where're the W's?" he demanded.

"Spanish surnames don't start with W, do they?"

Her name's not Spanish.

Frustration and desperation clashed like symbols in his chest as he swore mightily, flipping his finger angrily over the touch pad so the list scrolled full speed to the very end, stopping on *Zubizarreta.*

"*Damn* it." He rocked back on his heels, the familiar sensation of bone-deep disappointment rolling through him.

Chessie didn't respond, probably being too sensitive to his pain or not wanting to get barked at in his wrath. Instead, she scrolled some more as he fought the sting in the back of his eyes.

Son of a bitch, he wasn't going to let his sister see how much this mattered. There had to be another way. When Mal got out—

"Gabe."

"It's okay, Chess. Keep digging around those files, but it's okay."

"No, I just want to—"

"I don't care!" Anger fired through his veins because, shit, he *did* care. He'd never cared about anything in his life so much.

"Gabe." She put her hand on his arm, a gentle touch that just made him madder because—

"There are more names."

He stared at her, his flash of fury subsiding.

"One starts with W. Winter. Isadora Winter. Is that who you're looking for?"

He froze completely, almost unable to believe what he'd

just heard. Had he wanted it so bad, he *imagined* Chessie saying that name? Very slowly, he crouched back down, vaguely aware that he was shaking. All this time. *All these years*. All the nights of wondering and hoping and, yes, damn it, praying.

He'd found Issie.

"Where?" His voice scraped out of his throat, barely audible, the words dancing before him on the screen.

"Right here." She pointed to the name, one of five in a group.

Isadora Winter.

Holy, holy *shit*. He was only somewhat aware that he'd gripped his sister's hand as he leaned forward and stared at the name of the only woman—

"Gabe." Chessie's voice was so, so soft, barely a whisper.

"That's her," he said, desperately wanting to share his joy with someone. He looked up at Chessie. "That's her."

"I'm sorry," she said, laying her hand on his shoulder.

"What? Why? You found her, Chessie. You really *can* find anyone! You found the woman I—"

"Gabe." Why were Chessie's eyes filled with tears?

An ice-cold fear slithered up his spine and into his veins, turning him numb. In slow motion, he looked back at the screen, taking a second to find her name and slide his gaze across to the right to—

Deceased.

He blinked, checked again.

No, oh, God, no. Not possible. It had been only five years. Five years since…

No, she can't be dead.

He inched back, denial blinding him until he looked one more time and double-checked the line.

Isadora Winter ………….. Deceased

338

"Is that who—"

He cut Chessie off by standing and slamming the computer closed. "We're done here."

Done. Done. *Deceased.*

He left the room, walked out into the night air, and tried to breathe. To think. To accept the fucking unacceptable.

He'd never see her again. Never. No chance of good-bye. No chance of an explanation. No chance of exactly the kind of love his sister had been mooning for.

Forever.

He leaned against the rough trunk of a queen palm, sliding down to the ground with a thud.

Now what would he live for? His hope was gone.

"Gabe?" Chessie's voice cut through the night and his pain.

"Not now, Chess." His voice broke.

"Gabe, listen to me."

"Not now, damn it!"

He heard his sister's footsteps and knew she'd want to comfort him when all he wanted to do was howl in pain and swear in tongues that hadn't even been invented yet. *Nothing* could comfort him. Nothing, ever.

"She left behind a four-year-old son."

"What?"

"He's still living in Cuba, her son."

Issie had a son? A four-year-old?

"His name is Gabriel."

He opened his mouth, but nothing came out. Not a sound. But Chessie dropped to her knees. "I'll help you, Gabe. I'll do whatever we have to do. I know you can't go to Cuba, but I can. We'll find him. I promise. We'll find your son. Aunt Chessie can find anyone."

He just reached out and wrapped his arms around his sister, and they both cried.

Enjoy your trip to Barefoot Bay? There are more love stories set on this island! Don't miss a single one.

The Barefoot Billionaires
Secrets on the Sand
Seduction on the Sand
Scandal on the Sand

The Barefoot Bay Quartet
Barefoot in the Sand
Barefoot in the Rain
Barefoot in the Sun
Barefoot by the Sea

The Barefoot Bay Brides
Barefoot in White
Barefoot in Lace
Barefoot in Pearls

Don't miss the next Barefoot Bay Undercover romantic adventure, Barefoot with a Stranger...*coming soon!*

Sneak Peek

Barefoot with a Stranger

Barefoot Bay Undercover #2

No way. There was no way in heaven or hell she was going to sit in this airport for three hours. Chessie glared at the departures screen, willing the numbers to change with a miraculous digital flash.

But there were no miracles for Francesca Rossi today.

Hers was one of many flights delayed, and the line at the gate desk, along with the grumbles of unhappy travelers, told her getting on another flight was probably unlikely this late in the evening under rain-drenched skies.

All right. She could handle three hours in Atlanta on what was supposed to be a forty-eight-minute layover. But could her older brother handle one more delay?

Scanning the gate area, she couldn't find a single empty seat, and a glance at the neighboring gates suggested the scheduling problems were widespread and included much more popular flights than her commuter to southwest Florida. Even though it was evening, the concourse behind her bustled with impatient people rolling their bags, and the airport restaurant teemed with captive customers. Leaning against the nearest wall, Chessie pulled out her phone and tapped the screen to text Gabe, instructing him not to send their grandfather to pick her up until takeoff was guaranteed.

Her brother wouldn't like it, of course. Gabe was chewing nails in his desperation to accomplish "the plan."

The *plan*. No fancy covert titles, like Operation BabyLift or Munchkin Mission for this one. Finding a child that Gabe hadn't even known he had until a few weeks ago was too serious and too real for cutesy code names, especially since only Chessie knew the truth. And not even all the truth, because life with her ex-spook brother meant nearly everyone was on a "need-to-know basis."

And the only thing Chessie knew for sure, so far, was that Gabe had devised a plan for her to find the kid. She wouldn't know what it was until she got back to the island off the west coast of Florida, where he was currently running his latest covert op.

Her phone buzzed with his reply. *Delayed? WTF? Get your ass on another flight!*

Like she could do anything about this. She typed back a sisterly "shut your pie hole" and peered over the gate crowd again, all of whom looked generally pissed to be stuck. Out of the corner of her eye, she caught sight of a woman getting up and freeing a seat near the back. Shouldering her handbag and grateful she'd checked her suitcase, Chessie headed straight to the vacant seat, weaving past a few travelers with determination. But she was two feet away when a middle-aged man beat her to it, practically throwing his backside into the chair to make sure he got it before she did.

She stopped her momentum with a soft grunt, a little stunned at his audacity. The man whipped out an iPad and ignored her, leaving Chessie feeling awkward as a few people stared at her. She glanced around on the off chance she could slide into an open seat.

But there were still no miracles for her today.

Her gaze landed on the man in the chair directly across from the one she'd almost snagged, meeting dark eyes that glinted with a mix of dismay and humor. Instantly, he stood.

"Here, take mine."

"Oh, no, I…" Damn, he was big. Not just tall, but solid and broad. "That's not necessary."

"I insist."

She started to reply, but had to take a good look at his face, which was pretty much a straight-up dime. A rugged blend of chiseled and rough, a strong nose, soft lips, and a cleft in his chin that was downright lickable. "I…I…can't."

At least five people watched the exchange—but not the tacky seat-stealer.

"Please, take my seat. It would be rude for me to let you stand there." He put the slightest emphasis on rude, more of a deep rumble from that impressive chest, and at least four of the people watching shifted their attention to the really rude guy. Who didn't look up from a riveting game of Words With Friends.

"I can stand, really," Chessie said, gesturing to the seat. "Please, you had it first."

"That doesn't make it mine when a lady is involved."

Chessie laughed lightly, aware that her heart tripped a little when she noticed a silver thread or two at the temples of his thick, dark hair. "I'm young and strong," she assured him. And so was he, despite the bit of frosting, which only made him hotter.

"I see that." He let those smoky brown eyes drop over her, sending a mix of chills and heat to every inch he eyed.

Easy, girl. You're nursing a heartbreak, remember? At

343

least that was the excuse she gave for leaving Boston indefinitely on this secret assignment.

"Yeah, well…" Clearly, Tall Dark And Handsome had sucked the pithy right out of her. "Please." She tried again to refuse his offer of the seat. "This is getting uncomfortable."

"It sure is." The seat-stealer spoke without looking up from his iPad. "Do us all a favor and go flirt in the bar."

The man standing in front of Chessie flinched ever so slightly, his eyes flickering to the right but not actually shooting the yahoo a proper dirty look. Instead, he gave Chessie a slow smile that took him straight to an eleven. And a half.

For one, two, maybe the span of three insane heartbeats, they looked at each other, and at least one X in every double-X chromosome climbed out of their breakup funk to momentarily consider what else was out there.

He checked her out for a few seconds, his gaze practically feasting on her face, then the faintest shrug gave her the impression he'd lost some kind of inner battle.

He nodded toward the concourse. "Can I buy you a drink?"

Chessie opened her mouth to say no. But that would be ill-mannered and stupid and, jeez, three hours was a long time. And she was officially single now. *And* Gabe didn't say she couldn't talk to anyone, just not share why she was on her way to Florida. *Aaand*, holy *God*, he was hot.

"Sure, thanks."

The man leaned over to grab a duffle bag, then turned and got right in the seat-stealer's face. "I owe you one, dickhead," he whispered.

As they walked away, the woman next to the seat-stealer gave a loud, slow clap, and at least three others joined her.

344

What do you know? Maybe there was a little miracle today for Chessie after all.

Mal knew they'd be watching him from the minute he walked out of Allenwood federal prison and started his journey. But he honestly didn't think they'd be so damn *obvious* about it, throwing a tag team at him, using the worn-out cliché of a sexy woman being mistreated by a smartass stranger.

Or maybe they thought Malcolm Harris had lost any ability to shake a tail during his forty-two-month knuckle-rapping.

Mal had taken two different cars, a train, and a bus to get to Atlanta, and now he just wanted to fly to his final destination, for God's sake. But he mustn't have been clever or deceptive enough, because the babe and her buddy nailed him like a wanted poster on a tree.

Mal hung back as the hostess led them to a table, taking the opportunity to check out the woman they'd sent to soften him up.

Well, nothing about him would be *soft* around this woman. She had that thick, inky black hair that he'd always liked, though sloppily braided and hanging down to the middle of her back. It wasn't her hair that got his attention, though. Her ass was perfection, round and high and youthful in faded jeans, swaying with a sexy beat brought on by boots with just enough heel to tap a drumbeat on his stretched-to-the-limits libido.

They'd chosen wisely.

When they sat down, she ordered an Amstel Light but

said no to a frosty mug. Beer from the bottle. Okay, that was hot.

Of course, he was a man six days out of federal prison, and she was the first female he'd talked to in three and a half years who wasn't washing his con clothes or shoveling chow onto a plate. So, she could have ordered piss in a bucket and he'd have probably sprung a boner.

"Thanks for the rescue," she said after the waitress left, crossing her arms to settle her elbows on the table and lean in enough to treat him to a glimpse of cleavage. He appreciated the effort, though it wasn't necessary. "I think we shamed him effectively."

Yeah, sweet thing. Like you two didn't plan that since you followed my ass to the gate.

"He should be ashamed," Mal agreed. And so should Mal if he thought this was legit.

He'd noticed this woman on the tram, then spotted her again in a bookstore. Hartsfield was a big airport, and a double sighting of anyone was unusual, but when she just missed the empty seat five feet from his face and looked right at him for help? They might as well have put it on the loudspeaker.

Attention, Malcolm Harris. You are currently under surveillance.

And now he was going to let her believe he was duped by her ruse, and awestruck by her baby blues, which got even babier and bluer when she pushed her black-rimmed glasses to rest on top of her head.

Except, if she needed glasses, why not keep them on?

Mal inched just a little bit closer to inspect all the pretty she was showing him. And be sure her mic could pick up whatever he was saying, so his half-truths would have all her colleagues scratching their heads instead of their balls.

"What's your name?" he asked.

She actually took a little breath before answering, as if she had to think about it. Field rookie, no doubt. "Chessie."

"Jessie?" Couldn't even pronounce her fake name?

She shook her head. "No, Chessie. Short for Francesca."

Wasn't like them to use unusual names. "You don't look like a Francesca."

"No kidding." Her smile was quick and seemed real, softening her features and putting a nice warmth in her eyes. "That's my mother. Frannie. And you?"

Why lie? She knew damn well what his name was, along with his Social, his empty bank accounts, his stellar prison record. Shit, his whole miserable life was probably downloaded in her phone and filed under W for *Whistle-blower*.

"I'm Mal." He added a sly smile and extended his hand over the table. "Pleasure to meet you, Francesca."

"Mal?" She slid silken and slender fingers into his grip and lifted one perfectly shaped dark brow. "Then we're even in the weird-name department."

As if you didn't know. "Malcolm," he explained. "Not so weird."

"Traveling on business?" she asked, letting go of his hand after an extra second of contact.

Oh, yeah, let's get right down to what the hell their man was doing crisscrossing the country and headed south. *Spill the beans, Harris. You're good at that. Classified beans, please, and then you'll be headed home to Allenwood, cell block fourteen.*

"More or less," he replied. "You?"

"Um, family. I'm going to see my brother down in Florida."

Pretty smooth. Only the slightest hitch in her voice. He

nodded as the waitress arrived and placed two beers on paper cocktail napkins. When she stepped away, Chessie lifted her bottle. "To chivalry. Long may it live in the heart of a perfect stranger."

He tapped her amber bottle with his bright green Heineken. "I'm not perfect." *As you well know.*

She held extended eye contact over the bottle. "Pretty close," she whispered with the hint of a smile, and damn it, his body instantly betrayed his head with a low, deep, primal stir. No surprise there. He hadn't gotten laid in so long, his balls had fallen into a temporary state of dormancy.

He took a long pull on the beer, still locked on her mesmerizing eyes, knowing he had a challenge in his own gaze. Part of him wanted her to know he was not ignorant of her ploy, and part of him—that formerly dormant part— wanted to see just how far she'd go to impress her bosses.

"Um, you're staring," she said softly.

He leaned closer. "Um, you're gorgeous." And that was no lie. With the little bit of beer moisture, her lips looked luscious, and when she looked down, long lashes lay dark and thick against olive-toned skin. She brushed an escaped lock of ebony hair off her cheek, just the right blend of self-conscious and flirtatious.

Man, those pricks had pulled out all the stops today.

"Thanks." She glanced up, all wide-eyed and womanly. "I haven't felt very gorgeous lately."

And now we get the made-up sob story, meant to get him to open up and share. He knew the deal. He'd stood guard in the room when lesser men than he were brought to their knees and made to vomit state secrets.

All right, darling. Game on. "You haven't felt gorgeous?" He snorted softly. "Are all the mirrors broken in…where are you from?"

"New England," she said, sounding obviously vague. Maybe they hadn't worked out her cover that thoroughly.

"Something you're not telling me, Chessie?"

A slow burn started down by the pretty cleavage, the blush working its way up to her cheeks. Whoa, she *was* a rookie. Suddenly, inexplicably sympathetic, he reached for her left hand to save her from herself. "Because I don't flirt with married women."

Her ring finger was bare—he'd already noted that—but she gave his hand a squeeze. "Not married. And so nice to meet a solid citizen."

"Define solid," he teased, still holding her hand because it felt so damn good to touch a woman, even if she was the enemy.

"I'd define it as a guy who offered his seat, bought me a drink, and doesn't flirt with married women." Slipping out of his touch, she searched his face, no doubt comparing the real thing to pictures in her file. "Are *you* married?" she asked, her voice just the right amount of tentative and hopeful.

"I'm completely free." Out of prison and on his own. And, man, they were going to do anything they could to change that. Including entrapment, it seemed.

They stared at each other for a few seconds, and this time she didn't look away. "And you're from Texas," she said. At his raised eyebrows, she laughed. "Very subtle, but I hear…Houston?"

You should know, honey. "Dallas. And San Antonio. And…" Where the hell had they lived after that? Some trailer park in some dump. No doubt she knew all the details about his sorry childhood. "Yeah, around Texas."

"What do you do, Mal?"

Time. He did lots and lots of time, and if it was up to her, he'd do more. He stalled with a long, slow sip of beer. "I'm between jobs now, Chessie."

"Ahh." She gave a knowing nod.

"What about you?" he asked.

"I'm in, uh, well, I guess you'd call it computer research."

He almost laughed out loud. Is that what the kids were calling it today? "You must be smart," he said, adding a smile for the sheer pleasure of getting one back.

"Well, I work for my family, so I get away with a lot."

Family. How sweet. He gulped some beer.

"Will you be looking for work in Florida?" she asked.

This was getting tiresome. Not looking at this pretty woman—he actually could do that for hours. But the volley of lies was wearing him down. He wasn't going to lose her now, that much was certain. She'd end up next to him on the flight, then follow him after they landed. He'd be *wearing* her. So what should he do?

His dick, his poor, lonely, unloved, semierect-twenty-three-hours-a-day dick, answered for him. What should he do? *Her.*

He leaned much closer and ran a light finger over her knuckles. "I'm boring, Francesca. Let's talk about you."

She let her gaze drop to where he touched her hand. "No one calls me Francesca."

'Cause it's not your name. "It suits you. It's a graceful name, with depth and class. It's sexy."

"You're good, Mal." She frowned and eyed him playfully. "But 'mal' usually means 'bad.'"

"I'm a walking paradox, huh?"

She answered with a soft, sexy laugh. If he didn't know better—and he did—this woman was as turned on as he was. By the wordplay? Or his touch? Or the electricity that had been zinging over this bar table for the past twenty minutes, complicating the whole deal for both of them?

Maybe she just got hot and bothered thinking that she was winning her game.

Didn't matter; it all worked in his favor.

"Chessie." He closed his hand over hers. "Why don't you tell me who made you feel like you weren't beautiful, and I'll find the jerk and make him eat my fist."

"God, you really do work this knight-in-shining-armor thing."

"I'm serious. Who was this bonehead who let a girl as pretty and sweet as you slip through his hands?"

Emotion, raw and tangible, sparked in her eyes as she looked across the table at him, pulling off awestruck that he'd even asked. Nice touch from the acting coach.

"Matt."

Frowning, he drew back. "Excuse me?"

"His name was, well, *is* Matt. He was my boyfriend for the past year. And two months. And ten days." She gave a self-deprecating eye roll. "Pathetic, right?"

He searched her face for a tell, but couldn't find one. No color rising, no averted glance, and her hand was utterly still under his. She was damn good.

"He's the one who's pathetic," he said, dying to hear the tale she'd spin. There might even be some truth in it, if he knew anything about these guys. And, sadly, he knew too much about these guys. "What happened?"

She took a drink and looked back across the concourse at their gate, a frown deepening. "Oh, shoot. We have trouble."

He followed her gaze, wondering if her buddy had blown their cover. But as he watched the flock of people milling about and caught a glimpse of the departure board, he knew exactly what trouble they had.

"The flight's canceled," she said, standing up. "Son of a…"

"Come on, let's go see what the deal is." He threw money on the table and grabbed his bag, following her out to the gate.

But he knew what the deal was. They'd canceled the flight to see what he'd do next. Yes, damn it, they had *that* much power.

"There are no more flights tonight," a man said, sounding disgusted as he walked by.

"I have to find an airport hotel," another woman said into her phone. "I am not sleeping in the terminal."

Chessie looked up at him, her eyes wide, as if this news actually surprised her.

He put his hand on her shoulder. How far would she take this little manhunt? "A hotel sounds good, Francesca."

He felt her shudder under his touch, all the answer he needed.

He'd be gone before she woke up, and then she'd realize she was the one who got screwed. Maybe a few times, if he had anything to say about it.

Books Set in Barefoot Bay

The Barefoot Bay Billionaires
Secrets on the Sand
Seduction on the Sand
Scandal on the Sand

The Barefoot Bay Brides
Barefoot in White
Barefoot in Lace
Barefoot in Pearls

Barefoot Bay Undercover
Barefoot Bound (prequel)
Barefoot with a Bodyguard
Barefoot with a Stranger
Barefoot with a Bad Boy (Gabe's book!)

The Original Barefoot Bay Quartet
Barefoot in the Sand
Barefoot in the Rain
Barefoot in the Sun
Barefoot by the Sea

About the Author

Roxanne St. Claire is a *New York Times* and *USA Today* bestselling author of more than forty novels of suspense and romance, including many popular series and stand-alone books. Her entire backlist, including excerpts and buy links, can be found at www.roxannestclaire.com.

In addition to being a six-time nominee and one-time winner of the prestigious Romance Writers of America RITA Award, Roxanne's novels have won the National Reader's Choice Award for best romantic suspense three times and the Borders Top Pick in Romance, as well as the Daphne du Maurier Award, the HOLT Medallion, the Maggie, Booksellers Best, Book Buyers Best, the Award of Excellence, and many others. Her books have been translated into dozens of languages and are routinely included as a Doubleday/Rhapsody Book Club Selection of the Month.

Roxanne lives in Florida with her family and can be reached via her website, www.roxannestclaire.com, her Facebook Reader page, www.facebook.com/roxannestclaire, and Twitter at www.twitter.com/roxannestclaire.

CPSIA information can be obtained at www.ICGtesting.com
Printed in the USA
LVOW10s0248160715

446355LV00011B/914/P

9 780990 860730